"JUST WHAT ARE YOU HERE FOR, ANYWAY?"

As he spoke Brian gripped Midge's shoulders and swung her around to face him. His pulse beat seemed to become a part of her, a surging force that swept through her like a tide, and his quicksilver eyes blazed with a mixture of anger and something even more turbulent....

"Damn it," he went on, his voice ragged, "I won't have you spying on me!"

"You flatter yourself," Midge retorted hotly. But he cut her off with a scorching kiss, setting into motion a cascading rush of desire. Pressed tight against him, Midge was thoroughly, tremendously aware of every rugged contour of his body.

Then Brian thrust her from him so abruptly that she struggled for balance. "That," he said bitterly, "was the very last thing I intended to do...."

MEG HUDSON

Is also the author of
SUPERROMANCE #9

SWEET DAWN OF DESIRE

The man's sarcastic carping was driving Joy
crazy! She didn't care if he was a famous
British spy—she had feelings even if he
didn't!

When she was assigned to edit James
Duncan MacCaithness's memoirs, New York
editor Joy Carrington had been both
delighted and nervous. Now she was ready
to call it quits even before they started.

But something made her stay. And every day
she fell more deeply in love with the most
complex man, the most dangerous man,
she'd ever met....

LOVE'S SOUND IN SILENCE

MEG HUDSON

A SUPERROMANCE FROM
WORLDWIDE

TORONTO · NEW YORK · LOS ANGELES · LONDON

To Henry and Tessie Kress, who introduced
me to Coxsackie in the first place.

———————————◆━◆━◆———————————

Published October 1982

First printing August 1982

ISBN 0-373-70036-9

The historical and other details involving Coxsackie, the Catskills and the Hudson River Valley in this story are based on fact; but there is no *Hudson River Valley Voice*, and the persons and situations described in the book are purely fictitious.

CHAPTER ONE

THERE WERE NO CLOUDS, either real or metaphorical, to spoil the afternoon. San Francisco, an eternal temptress of a city, lay below Midge, the Golden Gate Bridge a slender red ribbon to the left, the Oakland Bay Bridge a flexible platinum bracelet to the right. From this vantage point Alcatraz Island did not seem far offshore, yet she knew that in years past, when Alcatraz had been a notorious prison, few escaping convicts had survived the swim across to the mainland, for the currents ran swift and were extremely dangerous.

Beyond both bridges the contoured hills were a study in shades of browns and tans, making it seem to her as if this were late autumn instead of only September; yet the color scheme, which might have been drab elsewhere, was exactly right here. It enhanced the rich lapis of the Golden Gate's famous water and deepened the gentian blue sky.

The hills, the water, the sky, the architecturally fantastic buildings marching down the steep streets beyond the floor-to-ceiling glass window through which Midge was peering—all combined to create a canvas that was eye-boggling. She sighed deeply, thoroughly contented yet somehow distrusting this contentment, for it was a long time since she'd felt so relaxed.

She had succumbed totally to San Francisco, unable to resist its versatile charms. It was an endlessly fascinating city with its many ethnic districts, marvelous international restaurants, chic shops and boutiques; with the enchanting flower stands blooming on its street corners, the clang of cable-car bells, the excitement of Grant Avenue and Fisherman's Wharf as well as The Cannery and Ghiradelli Square, the beautifully groomed women, the shimmering golden onion-shaped domes of the Russian Orthodox Cathedral on Geary Boulevard and so many, many other entrancing things, people and places. Its marvelous cosmopolitan quality definitely was a mood enhancer, putting her in a holiday frame of mind; which was surprising in view of the fact that she'd come West with a damaged, if not broken, heart.

San Francisco had woven precisely the magic curative spell Midge had needed, no doubt about it, and she intended to enjoy her final hours here to the hilt. There would be plenty of time tomorrow on the plane going back to New York to think about her future, questionable commodity that it was. For the moment it was more than enough to be sitting with her best friend by a window in this cocktail lounge high atop the Bank of America building, feasting on the view she would forever find incredible.

The waiter had brought them frozen daiquiris that looked like delectable mounds of luscious pink sherbet piled high in glasses, but Midge had become so entranced with the scenery that she had yet to sample hers. Becky Vandervelt Ross, on the other hand, had promptly sipped and savored, and now she said accusingly, "You haven't heard a word I've

said! If you like it so much out here, why don't you
stay?''

Midge forced her eyes away from the window and
focused on Becky, who was as blond and pretty as
ever, though a bit plumper than she had been the last
time they'd met. Becky obviously was thriving on
marriage and motherhood, and this was to be envied.

She answered a little sadly, ''I wish I *could* stay.
Three does make a crowd, though.''

''You wouldn't have to live with your father and
your stepmother,'' Becky pointed out. ''You'd have
no trouble getting a job—Tim could help you with
that—and you could easily find a studio apartment
for yourself.''

''True,'' Midge agreed, ''but I still think if I were
living here dad and Lila would feel at least somewhat
responsible for me, and I don't want that. They
deserve a longer honeymoon!'' She smiled. ''No,''
she went on, ''it's time to go back. They've both been
great and it's wonderful to see them together.
They're so much in love! I don't want anything to
spoil that. Dad is happier than he has been in years.
Mother was sick for so long before she died. . . .''

Becky sighed. ''I don't know which way is harder,'' she confessed. ''We had it all at once, when our
parents were killed in the plane crash. We were ten,
old enough to remember yet really too young to cope
with that kind of grief.''

We. For a moment Midge was startled; she actually had forgotten that Becky was a twin. And this, she
realized now, was because Becky had not mentioned
her brother, though they'd been together now twice.

Sunday afternoon the Rosses had given a barbecue
for Midge at their delightful Spanish-style home in

Menlo Park. It had been a fun occasion: she had
been captivated at once by the two Ross children,
four-year-old Timmy and two-year-old Brenda. It
also had been a time of reunion with Tim Ross. He
and Midge once worked together in the same New
York advertising agency; in fact it was she who had
introduced him to Becky.

Today she and Becky had met for an hour or so of
shopping and browsing before coming to the cocktail
lounge, and she supposed there really had been no
reason for Becky to mention her brother. For that
matter, Brian had always been a figure in absentia
where she was concerned. Their paths had somehow
never crossed in earlier years when the two girls were
in school together, nor later in New York. Thus there
was an unreality about Brian Vandervelt to her. In
her mind he was more of a photograph than a person, she thought whimsically, and was reminded of a
picture of him in his midshipman's uniform she used
to see on Becky's dresser. In it he had looked exceedingly correct, blond, devastatingly handsome;
but with an air of aloofness that had a chill about it,
totally unlike his sister. He must be long out of the
Naval Academy at Annapolis by now and doubtless
was married with children of his own.

Becky had been toying with her drink, and now she
said solemnly, "Sometimes I think Brian adjusted
better than I did when we lost our parents. He
seemed to, anyway. I suppose it was just as hard for
him, but he didn't show it as much as I did."

"Perhaps he felt he had to be strong for your
sake."

"I suppose," Becky conceded. "Brian and I are
fraternal twins, of course, so we don't have that

mystical bond between us that they say identical twins often have. But we did have a very special relationship, and that's why it was so hard when we were sent off to different boarding schools."

Becky's usually sparkling eyes had become clouded, and Midge reminded her gently, "You know, you can't blame your aunt and uncle for having sent you both away to school. You've told me yourself that they were middle-aged when you and Brian went to live with them. They'd never had any children of their own; it must have been downright traumatic for them suddenly to have two active kids on their hands."

"Yes, I suppose it was," Becky agreed. "I think Aunt Maude could have managed, though. It was Uncle Horace who was not about to let anything or anyone upset his routine." She paused. "You knew he died?"

"Yes," Midge admitted. "It was on television and in all the papers. I meant to write you. I'm sorry—"

"There's no need for you to be," Becky said bluntly. "I suppose it's awful of me, but I felt no grief about it, no grief at all. Oh, I *am* sorry for Aunt Maude. I can't imagine how she goes on living in that horrible old house." She smiled ruefully, confessing, "I have such mixed feelings about the place. As a child sometimes I loved it, sometimes I hated it. Brian and I *did* have wonderful times there during vacations. It's a miracle, when I think of it, that Uncle Horace didn't send us to summer camps. Maybe he felt we needed his influence at least part of the time. Regardless, the summers almost made up for everything else. There are beautiful grounds around the old place, gardens and apple orchards that slope all the way down to the Hudson River. We used to climb down the hill back of the house to a little beach and go swimming. Once Uncle Horace found out, and I thought he was going to beat us both, he was so angry.''

"Why?"

"He seemed to think it was terribly unhealthy to swim in the river, and maybe he was right. As I understand it, it's just now that the Hudson is beginning to become unpolluted again, after a great deal of work. Anyway...our fun times were despite Uncle Horace, not because of him.''

Midge smiled. "Well," she said, "*some* good came out of it all. If you hadn't gone to Pine Haven Junior College you might never have met me!''

"True," Becky agreed enthusiastically. "And if you hadn't managed to get a job writing copy for Anderson-Brent Associates I might never have met Tim." She shivered. "That sounds too close for comfort. I don't like to think meeting Tim was just a matter of chance....''

"Maybe there's such a thing as fate," Midge teased.

"I more than half believe in it," Becky said solemnly. "Remember, you're talking to someone who was brought up in the Hudson River valley. We're still loaded with superstitions and legends, like the story of Rip Van Winkle.''

Becky was indeed a product of the Hudson River valley. The Vandervelts, Midge knew, dated back to the days of the Dutch patroons along the river, as did the Roosevelts and so many other prominent families. Midge had seen pictures of the Vandervelt mansion, a huge architectural monstrosity that, Becky assured her, was even worse on the inside than it was on the outside. Still, Becky had never talked very much about her family, and Midge had learned more about the Vandervelts from the late Horace Vandervelt's obituary in the *Times* than she ever had from her friend. The *Times* had delved deeply into the family history, detailing the long amassing of a fortune that had been increased significantly by Horace himself.

As owner and publisher of the *Hudson River Valley Voice*, a weekly newspaper printed in the river town of Coxsackie, about twenty miles south of Albany, Horace Vandervelt had certainly been a figure of local authority. But the *Times* had made it clear that his influence had gone well beyond the town, spreading past Greene County, the river valley and even the Catskill Mountains to become a considerable force in the state. Until she read his obituary, Midge had not realized what a powerful man Horace Vandervelt had been or how extremely wealthy.

Now it occurred to her that Becky must have inherited at least a part of that wealth. If so, it surely had not changed the Ross life-style, at least on the surface.

Becky finished her daiquiri and motioned to a waiter to bring refills. Then she forced a smile. "Enough for the moment about the Vandervelts. We were talking about you. You're sure you want to go back to New York?"

Midge was looking out the window again, and she answered wistfully, "*Want* isn't the right word. I *must*. I left too many loose ends behind me, including an apartment. Jennifer Lund, the girl I'm sharing it with, is a photographer, and she's in France on a magazine assignment. She probably won't be back till after Christmas, which will give me plenty of time to be by myself and sort things out...."

"Then it's really all over with John?"

"It's really all over with John," was Midge's firm reply.

"Well," Becky observed judiciously, "I never did think he was right for you. For one thing, he was so much older—"

"Only six years," Midge said. "He's thirty-two."

"Really? I would have thought he'd be closer to forty by now! Even though we used to have good times double-dating before Tim and I were married, John always seemed so...well, so world-weary, I guess you'd say, and I always had the feeling the agency came first with him."

"It did and it does," Midge admitted. "It's now Anderson-Brent-Pemberton Associates. They're expanding into larger offices, and I have to admit John fits the popular image of the Madison Avenue man more than ever. The real John was lost somewhere along the road to success , and I can't imagine him ever surfacing again. It took me quite a while to see that. It is," she finished slowly, "a painful thing to dissect an idol."

"It must also have been a painful thing to leave your job," Becky said with quick sympathy. "Tim says you were the best copywriter they ever had."

"Tim's prejudiced because I'm a friend of yours," Midge said, smiling. "It was hard to give up my job," she went on slowly, "but I knew it would be impossible to keep work and John separate."

"What are you going to do now?"

"I don't know. I want to think about things for a while and try to get some real sense of direction. Then perhaps I'll find another agency job, or maybe I'll try something else."

"So," Becky said, "for the moment you're free?"

There was something about the way she said it that made Midge look up swiftly, and she was startled to catch an expression in Becky's blue eyes she had never expected to see.

Fear.

Although Becky had pounced on her second daiquiri, devouring the cherry that garnished it as enthusiastically as she'd demolished the first one, Midge suddenly realized that all this exuberance was a superficial thing. Beneath the surface there was something she should have been aware of before now. Even Sunday, at Menlo Park, Becky had been *too* bubbly; she had chattered too much, laughed too much. Now Midge could see her behavior for what it was: a form of camouflage.

"Becky," she said, both puzzled and concerned, "something's the matter. What is it?"

For a second Becky shut her eyes tightly. Then she swallowed hard. "Brian," she admitted, and her voice was husky as she spoke his name. "That's really why I asked you to meet me here this afternoon for a farewell drink. I wanted the two of us to have a chance to talk alone."

"Where *is* Brian?" Midge asked. "Is he stationed near here?"

"No," Becky said, and swallowed again. "You see, he never was graduated from Annapolis. Something happened to him. Something terrible, I'm afraid."

She stretched an imploring hand across the table. "I'd give anything in the world to find out what it is, but with Timmy and Brenda as young as they are I've had no opportunity to...to investigate for myself." Her eyes were pleading. "I know it's a tremendous favor to ask," she said, "but since you're at loose ends for the moment, is there a chance you could do it for me?"

Midge frowned. "What could *I* possibly do?" she demanded, moved by Becky's touching misery and yet determined not to become involved in something she was not ready for. It was freedom she was seeking at the moment, the chance to explore new horizons. She remembered Brian Vandervelt's photograph, his cool blond aloofness, and she knew instinctively that he would not be one to welcome an "investigator" into his affairs, even an emissary of his twin sister!

She said slowly, "Becky, what makes you think something terrible has happened to Brian? Where is he now, for that matter? And how could *I* possibly find out anything about him for you? I've never even met him, remember?"

"That's all to the good," Becky responded hastily. "I know this is a lot to ask," she said again, sighing. "That's why I wanted to be sure you were going back East and that you've given up your job for once and for all." She hesitated. "Brian is in Coxsackie. Will you go there for me?"

"Go to Coxsackie? Becky, how could I possibly do such a thing? Oh, naturally I could *go* to Coxsackie; that's simple enough. But what could I do once I got there?"

"See Brian."

"What good would that do?"

"I know something's wrong," Becky said tersely. "I mean, I know something's wrong with *Brian*, and I've tried to find out what it is, believe me, but my brother is a...a very private person. He's not about to confide in me, I know that now, and whatever has happened to him certainly isn't obvious from his letters. But if you met him, if you talked to him, I'm sure you'd find out what it is."

"I'm not sure about that at all!" Midge countered. "What do you *think* has happened to him?"

"I don't know," Becky said flatly. "That's what's so dreadful. I've wondered and wondered, and I still have no idea. All this time...."

"All *what* time?"

Becky sighed. "I'd better start at the beginning."

"Yes," Midge agreed dryly, "that's usually a good idea."

Becky flushed slightly, but she said with a determination that made Midge think of her stalwart Hudson River Dutch patroon heritage, "I can't blame you for feeling I'm being ridiculous, but I'm not, believe me. This goes back more than four years, and certainly I would have come to my senses by now if I were merely imagining things. Actually, it goes back to four years ago this past April, to be precise. Brian was in his last year at the Naval Academy—he was scheduled to graduate that June—and I was *very* pregnant with Timmy. We'd only been here in the San Francisco area six months; Tim had transferred to Castillo-Jones Associates just before Thanksgiving the previous year, remember? We were moving into our present house. I had my hands full.

"Brian evidently was on leave at the time when— the accident—happened, but he didn't go home; to

Uncle Horace's, that is. As I understand it, he went off with a girl. I realize there's nothing so unusual about that, but it happens he was engaged. In fact he was going to be married, during June week at Annapolis, and this girl was not his fiancée.

"She and Brian went to a beach resort down on the Chesapeake Bay where her family had a cottage. I don't know all the details, only that there was a space heater in the place and it exploded. She was killed."

"What happened to Brian?" Midge interrupted.

"I don't know," Becky said simply. "That's the strange part of it. I haven't been able to find out that *anything* serious happened to him, yet he didn't graduate."

"You mean. . . Annapolis kicked him out?"

"No, evidently he resigned. Afterward for a while he just dropped out of touch. I tried again and again to reach him by phone, but I never managed to connect with him. Timmy was born about then and there was just no way I could leave here and go back East. I had to rely completely upon Uncle Horace and Aunt Maude for information."

"Well, what did they have to say?"

"Uncle Horace was always the spokesman for both of them. He wrote that Brian had been through a bad experience but that he was all right. Then after a while Brian wrote me himself—but his letters were so empty somehow."

"Are you sure he really did write them?"

Becky nodded. "Yes. He has a certain style, and also his handwriting is distinctive. I'm sure he wrote them. In fact I still get a letter from him occasionally, and every now and then either I call him up or he calls here. But we have nothing much to say to each other, just platitudes. I've asked him to come visit a thousand times, and he promises he will but never does. He never suggests that we come East, though we could take a vacation there now that the children are older if we planned well in advance. And...I don't know...Brian's my own twin brother, but he's always been able to build a sort of wall around himself when he wanted to, and that's the way it is now. I know I'd feel like an intruder if I simply went back without an invitation.''

"You say he's in Coxsackie?"

"Yes. A few months after the accident he went to work for Uncle Horace on the *Valley Voice*. I couldn't believe it!"

"Why?"

"Brian wasn't that fond of Uncle Horace, Midge. I can't imagine him going to work for him. Also, though he was always pretty good at writing and did some reporting summers when he was in prep school, I didn't think he had any real interest in journalism.''

"Well," Midge suggested, "maybe he developed an interest in the newspaper business but didn't mention it. I wouldn't say the two of you have communicated all that much since you were younger." She hesitated. "Becky," she asked then, "what is it, really, that you're so worried about? Do you think Brian was injured in the explosion but for some perverse reason of his own doesn't want you to know about it?"

"That's the first thing I *did* think. I was sure he had been blinded or crippled. But he wasn't."

"How do you know?"

"I have a subscription to the *Voice*," Becky explained. She shook her head despairingly. "Uncle

Horace died almost two years ago, just about the time I was due with Brenda. I couldn't get back East then, either. Shortly afterward Brian took over as editor and publisher.''

"You mean he inherited the paper?''

"Not exactly. Uncle Horace's will is terribly complicated—I'll tell you about *that* in a minute. What I want to say first is that when Brian took over the job there were pictures of him, and he looked as great as ever. Then, just the other day, there was a full-length picture of him presenting a trophy at a sports award dinner. Believe me, I looked over every inch of it, and physically there's nothing wrong with him. Naturally I've wondered if it might be something mental. But if his mind were affected he could hardly be running a newspaper, could he?''

"I shouldn't think so,'' Midge admitted.

"Still,'' Becky said, "there's something; there has to be. Brian just hasn't been Brian these past four years.'' She sighed. "I confess I don't have the courage to go simply to Coxsackie myself and face him. As I've already told you, I think I'd be made to feel anything but welcome right now. So I keep telling myself that Tim and the children need me here, and of course they do. But the truth is I'm actually afraid to go, and yet worrying about Brian is getting me down...too far down, Midge.''

"Becky, really, I think you're imagining things,'' Midge said. "Very possibly Brian had a bad reaction when the girl he was with was killed; it must have been a terrible shock to him. But time does heal. It may be a tragic memory at this point, nothing more, even though at the time it caused him to give up his naval career. He may have adjusted to an entirely new life very well.''

"Perhaps,'' Becky conceded, "but I'll never have any peace of mind until I know! If you could possibly drive up to Coxsackie some weekend and see him for yourself, I'd be more grateful than I can ever tell you.''

"What makes you think he'd agree to see me?'' Midge demanded.

"You could call on Aunt Maude,'' Becky said quickly. "She's a sweet person, even though I've been able to get nothing about Brian out of her at all. I'm sure she'd arrange a meeting between you and Brian; and whatever his faults, he certainly wouldn't be rude to a friend of mine.''

"I don't know,'' Midge said doubtfully. "The mere thought of facing your Aunt Maude gives me qualms, to say nothing of facing Brian under the circumstances....''

She flinched from the look on Becky's face. It was so entreating that it was going to take an infusion of steel to resist it, she thought wryly.

"Let's backtrack for a moment,'' she hedged. "You said you were going to tell me about your uncle's will.''

"Yes,'' Becky nodded. "Well—the will isn't only complicated, it's diabolical.''

"In what way?''

"In every way. It would take a lawyer to explain it to you properly. I don't understand all the ramifications of it myself, and even Tim shakes his head over it. To begin, the house itself was left to Aunt Maude. That is, it was left for her use, and for the rest of her life she'll get an income from a trust fund, which I'm sure is more than adequate. When she dies the trust fund and the property, which involves quite a bit of acreage as well as the house, will revert to the estate."

"In other words, your aunt can't leave anything to anyone herself?"

"Exactly. Even in death Uncle Horace has tied strings to her. I believe there's a clause that if she remarries she immediately loses the house *and* the income. Not that she's apt to remarry. Aunt Maude's pretty well along in years, and after being married to Uncle Horace I can't imagine her even thinking about trying it with anyone else!"

"So, then," Midge said, "what about the rest of the estate?"

"There's the *Valley Voice*, of course. It was Uncle Horace's favorite of all his holdings—his sounding board. A local newspaper can be surprisingly powerful, and of course he reveled in power. There are many other business holdings besides the *Voice*, though, plus a great deal of property in addition to the old family mansion and the land around it. Uncle Horace was an extremely wealthy man; I had no idea *how* wealthy until everything was listed."

"You still haven't told me who really benefits from all this."

"No one has, thus far."

"You mean the will hasn't been probated yet?"

"Oh, yes," Becky responded, "the legalities have been taken care of. Mr. Summers—Andrew Summers—is the Vandervelt lawyer, and he sends us regular reports. But so far there has been what he calls a probationary period. It's in effect for two

years from the day of Uncle Horace's death, so the
time is almost up. In fact it will be up in little more
than a month: the final estate settlement is scheduled
to take place the first of November.''

"Who's on probation? You?"

"No," Becky said. "Brian. I told you, remember,
that he took over as editor and publisher of the *Voice*
right after Uncle Horace died. Well, that's the crux
of the whole thing. According to Mr. Summers, the
terms of Uncle Horace's will required Brian to run
the paper successfully for two years. In other words,
to show a profit.''

"Has he?"

"From the latest reports he's doing very well. Mr.
Summers says both the advertising and the circulation have gone up since Brian took over, and they're
supposed to be the barometers of a newspaper's success. There doesn't seem much doubt that Brian will
pass the test, unless something radical takes place
within the next month.''

"What happens if he passes?"

"Brian will inherit the paper and a number of
other business holdings and properties, and when
Aunt Maude dies the house and adjacent property
will be his. The balance of the Vandervelt estate will
be divided between Brian and me, with a few bequests for employees like Clara and Tom Jennings.
Clara has been the Vandervelts' housekeeper for
longer than I can remember, and Tom, her husband,
is a combination chauffeur-gardener.''

"So," Midge said, "whether or not you inherit
anything depends on how Brian does in this probation period your uncle devised?"

"No. My stake, if you want to call it that, remains

relatively the same whether Brian passes his test or not. If he fails, however, he will be cut off with one dollar, and the paper will go to the department heads. There are four of them: the business manager, the advertising manager, the circulation manager and the mechanical superintendent. They will also divide the half of the estate that would have been Brian's, and the house and furnishings will be liquidated when Aunt Maude dies.''

''You mean your brother would be cut off with a *dollar*?'' Midge demanded incredulously.

''Yes. Go ahead and tell me you think it's fiendish—I couldn't agree more!''

The waiter approached. Becky asked, ''Do you think we could manage another daiquiri?''

''I couldn't.''

''Very well, then,'' Becky said, ''the check, please. No,'' as Midge started to protest, ''this is my treat.''

As the waiter left their table, she continued, ''Midge, can you see now why I'm so anxious to find out about Brian? Between this crazy will and the commitment he's been forced to make, plus the fact that I'm certain there has been something wrong with him since the accident, I'm close to frantic; and now with that November-first date getting closer all the time, the whole situation is coming to a head. Brian is going to need every bit of strength he can muster to get through the next month, and I just wish I had some assurance that he's able to handle all this. Can you imagine what a temptation it would be to those other men to...to sabotage him when the stakes are so high?''

The fear was back in her eyes again, and Midge flinched as she saw it. Becky, she knew, was imaginative, impulsive; these qualities were part of her essentially generous nature. Yet in this instance it had to be admitted that she had grounds for concern.

Unable to stop herself, Midge reached across the table and took Becky's hand in hers, and her words seemed to come involuntarily. It was as if she spoke in direct opposition to her own will.

"Becky," she said, "I'm not sure what, if any, good it will do. . . but I'll go to Coxsackie for you."

CHAPTER TWO

BECKY HAD SKETCHED THE MAP quickly, drawing it with a green felt marking pen on a scrap of pale gray paper, but it was clear enough. One aimed from New York City for the Tappan Zee Bridge, connected with the New York State Thruway, branched off at the town of Catskill onto Route 9W and from 9W drove cross-country to a state road that ran close to the banks of the Hudson River.

The Vandervelt mansion was between the villages of Athens and Coxsackie, on the river side of the road. "You've seen pictures," Becky said, "but even if you hadn't you couldn't possibly miss it. There are lots of big old homes along there, but ours is a monstrosity, all gabled and turreted and painted a horrible dark gray with rust-colored trim. It's funereal even on a sunny day!"

This was not a sunny day, so, Midge warned herself, the old house should be the epitome of gloom!

Clouds were threatening as she left the city, and it started to rain before she crossed the Tappan Zee Bridge. Now lightning bayoneted the massive bulk of the Catskills to her left, while Rip Van Winkle's thunder rumbled.

She stopped for coffee in Catskill, looked again at Becky's map, then put it back into her handbag.

From here on it would be almost impossible to get lost.

She had almost finished her coffee when a boy wearing an orange slicker struggled into the small restaurant carrying a load of newspapers that were protected from the weather by a sheet of clear plastic.

Midge asked curiously, "Is that the *Hudson River Valley Voice*?"

"Right off the press," the carrier boy answered with a nod.

"I'll take one," she said.

She ordered a second cup of coffee, then started to read the *Voice*, not pausing until she had scanned it from cover to cover, finally coming to the classified pages. Knowing that sooner or later she would be job hunting, she had developed the habit recently of looking through the ads, and as she did so now she could not quite believe her eyes.

The notice in the "Help Wanted" column seemed to leap out at her, the type clear and black. "Advertising copywriter needed," it read. "Layout experience a must. Apply to Trent Clayton, Advertising Manager, *Hudson River Valley Voice*."

What was it Becky had said in San Francisco? Something about more than half believing in fate. Although she considered herself an essentially practical person, Midge felt a twinge of empathy with Becky just now. Probably the Hudson River valley was no more rife with superstition than any other place, she told herself sternly, and coincidences, while seemingly inexplicable, could happen anywhere. Still, she would not have been surprised to see Rip Van Winkle himself saunter in, long white beard and all.

She folded up the paper, put it in her raincoat pocket and dashed out to her car. Once behind the wheel, with the windshield wiper fanning furiously, she paused for a thoughtful moment to tell herself that this was an absolutely idiotic excursion and that if she had any sense at all she would turn back to Manhattan right now!

Still, Becky was not the kind of friend who asked a favor lightly. It had been a true cry for help that afternoon in San Francisco, and Midge knew in her heart that she could not possibly fail to respond to it, especially now that she had come this far along the way.

To top things off, there actually was a job opening in her own field, on Brian Vandervelt's newspaper, which was more than slightly ironic. Would her friendship with Becky work for or against her if she decided to apply for it, she wondered. Not that she had any serious intention of doing so. No, she reminded herself, this was an exploratory mission, nothing more. She must complete it as quickly as possible, report back to Becky and then get on with living her own life again!

Now she followed 9W from Catskill to the Athens turnoff, drove cross-country for a relatively short distance and then took the river road that Becky had indicated on the map. It was only a few miles from Catskill to Athens. From there the road to Coxsackie hugged the top of the low yet steep hills that sloped down to the banks of the Hudson.

The countryside was an architectural miscellany. Midge drove by stately old residences that had been encroached upon by a variety of modern houses, most of their styles jarring upon her; for in her opinion the old homes suited this area far better than the new ones. From time to time she glimpsed the river, gunmetal today, its surface spattered by the falling rain. She had heard the Hudson likened scenically, to the Rhine, and although she had yet to visit Germany she now appreciated the truth of this from pictures and paintings she had seen, and would have been quite ready to accept a vision of a full-fledged castle on the distant horizon.

As the minutes ticked by she realized she should have asked Becky precisely how far the Vandervelt home was from Athens. Then, even as she wondered about this, she saw it looming ahead, and smiled. It was every bit as recognizable as Becky had promised it would be.

Traffic was no problem on this road; not, at least, at the moment. There was nothing ahead of her now, and, she verified with a glance in the rearview mirror, there was nothing behind her. Thus she was able to slow to a crawl as she approached the house.

It *was* a monstrosity, she did have to agree with Becky about that. Still, there was a fascination to it, a grandeur that could become magnificence if the drab charcoal paint were stripped away and replaced with white; if the trim and shutters were done in the darkest of greens, or blues, or perhaps black, lending an authority sadly lacking in the present rust color, which in the gray light of this rainy day reminded her all too much of dried blood.

Basically the house had good lines. The main section was square and rose to three full stories, with wings of equal proportion—later additions, no doubt—flanking either side. The center section was further augmented by a large square tower, its roof ending in a separate peak. The tower was completely enclosed by windows with semicircular tops that gave the effect of half-moons looking out upon the river to the east and the massive Catskills to the west.

The view from the tower room, Midge thought, must be sensational. She wished that Becky had garnered the courage to make this pilgrimage herself, for it would have been fun to tour the old house with her. As it was, there was something definitely formidable about it; it needed no Keep Out sign to convey that message.

Driving on slowly, Midge could not help but conclude that she simply had not been thinking things through when she had taken her slightly battered Volvo out of the garage today and decided to make this trip. Last night she had gone to dinner with friends who also knew John Pemberton, and that had been a mistake, for his name had entered the conversation again and again and she'd had the feeling that anything she might say would almost surely be conveyed back to him.

Not that there was anything *to* say. As she had told Becky, it was all over between John and her. After the better part of six years she was her own woman again, all the stronger for the experience. Of course, she and John had not been deeply involved for the total of the six years she had spent with the agency; their romance had evolved slowly. He was an account executive, a glamour figure to her in the beginning when she'd been low on the agency totem pole. Thanks partly to John's influence, though, she had advanced rapidly, for she had a real flair for writing copy.

John had been divorced and understandably was

cautious about marrying again. For a long time this had not concerned Midge. Actually, she had been career-minded herself—much to John's ultimate exasperation—and had not been at all willing to give up her job for him when he finally asked her to do so. She knew now that a break had been inevitable between them because neither was willing to make the kind of total commitment a good marriage demands. Nevertheless, when the break had come it hurt; it had not been easy for either of them.

There were still memories, there was still pain, and she had gone back to her apartment after the dinner last night in a peculiarly depressed frame of mind. She had needed something to take her out of herself, and the mission to Coxsackie on Becky's behalf seemed an ideal solution. She had spent a wakeful night, finally falling asleep close to dawn so that she overslept, and by the time she got up and breakfasted and attended to a few odds and ends it was nearly noon; really much too late to start out, yet she had done so.

Now it was three o'clock and would be growing dark in another couple of hours, especially on a day like this. Midge was glad she had decided at the last minute to toss a nightgown, robe, slippers, a change of clothing and a couple of other essentials into an overnight bag. The sensible course of action, she told herself, would be to complete her errand, then find a hotel in Coxsackie for the night and get a good rest before driving back to the city.

Having seen the house, though, she knew she couldn't possibly walk up to the front door, knock and ask to see Mrs. Vandervelt. *Coward I may be,* she admitted to herself, *but that's out of the question.*

The alternative was to present herself at the offices of the *Hudson River Valley Voice* and ask to see the editor-publisher. Just now the second course seemed almost as bad—worse in some ways—than the first one. Yet what else could she do if she were going to give Becky a report about her brother?

She could not imagine herself hanging around town trying to elicit information about the Vandervelts. Strangers would be noticed in a place like this; she would have no hope of remaining anonymous for long. No, she would somehow have to muster her courage and make contact with either Mrs. Vandervelt or Brian. And neither was a task she relished!

The road swung down a sharp hill, and ahead Midge saw a cluster of houses. This must be Coxsackie, she decided. The town had been built on the riverbank; its twisting streets led down to a main street that for the most part was lined on either side by red brick buildings with tall narrow windows, reminiscent of mill buildings in New England towns she had visited. Some of the buildings had been renovated and housed a variety of shops. Others were empty, For Rent or For Sale signs giving them an air of desolation.

She turned right at the first corner, driving along a street that paralleled the river. There were a number of the same type of brick buildings along here, too, some of them in use, some deserted. Then ahead on her left she saw a black iron fence enclosing a stretch of surprisingly green lawn, in its center a large black-and-gold-lettered sign reading Hudson River Valley Voice. The newspaper office itself was housed in a square well-kept brick building. Curious, Midge pulled her car over to the curb across the street from it and parked.

From this vantage point she could see a long addition jutting out from the back of the main building, which must, she concluded, house the printing plant. Since the paper was a weekly obviously gone to press, for she herself had just bought a copy in Catskill, most of the staff would have gone home by now, their week's work behind them. That would account for the paucity of cars parked in the vicinity. Yet lights shone through the grayness, so the building was not entirely empty. Possibly Brian Vandervelt, as publisher and editor, was still at his desk.

Midge thought of the mansion back on the Athens road, tried to imagine herself paying a call upon Mrs. Maude Vandervelt, and then looked at the building across the street. It was definitely the lesser of two evils.

She took a mirror out of her handbag and peered into it. She had thrown the hood of her raincoat over her head as she dashed out of the coffee shop in Catskill, but her long chestnut hair still curled obligingly, framing her face with soft waves. Her deep brown eyes looked questioningly at the reflection that met them. Usually after a long stint of work in the city she was apt to become a bit too pale, but she had been out of doors much of the time on the recent trip to San Francisco, so her color was good; there was still a glow to her complexion that was admittedly becoming. And her full well-shaped mouth needed only a touch of lipstick, which she now applied.

She had worn a pale coffee-colored blazer today with matching slacks, and a brown turtleneck accented with two gold chains, their links contrasting in pattern. All in all she was quite presentable. There was no need—or was she merely looking for an excuse, she wondered—to put off calling on Brian Vandervelt.

Four shallow marble steps led to the entrance of the newspaper office. Midge opened the heavy front door and found herself in a large square lobby. There was a reception area to the left, but it was unoccupied, so she walked on across the lobby and down a central hall. Offices branched off on either side. Advertising, Circulation...the names of the various departments were gold-lettered on frosted glass panels. Most of the doors stood half-open, revealing a series of empty rooms and deserted desks.

At the end of the hall a large double door bore the single word Editorial. She pushed it open and found herself in what was obviously the newsroom, as deserted at present as the rest of the place, but with desks still littered with paper and wastebaskets overflowing.

Distantly she heard a phone ringing, then it stopped, and she wondered if someone had answered it or if the caller had merely hung up. She listened for the sound of voices but could hear none. Nevertheless there might still be people out back, she decided, in the long addition that must house the presses. She debated making a safari to find out, then her eyes fell on a closed door at the far side of the newsroom.

The word Editor stood out in neat black letters, and yellow light was reflected through the frosted glass panel.

Was Brian Vandervelt in there?

Without letting herself pause to deliberate, Midge

walked across to the door and knocked, then stood back, waiting in a silence that suddenly seemed thunderous. Finally she knocked again, but there was no response, and she concluded that Brian Vandervelt must have gone home, leaving his office light on, which might or might not indicate that he planned to come back later. No matter; this provided an opening wedge. She would leave a note mentioning that she was a friend of Becky's passing through town and would phone him in the morning.

She opened the office door, so confident that the room would be empty that she gave an audible gasp of surprise when she saw a man sitting at a desk, writing rapidly on a long yellow scratch pad. His concentration, however, was so intense that he didn't move, and briefly Midge thought of beating a hasty retreat. Then, even as she opted to try to do so, he looked up and their eyes met in a moment of mutual shock.

His eyes were gray, really gray, without a trace of blue or green. She sought hopefully for something about his face that would remind of her of Becky, but their features were entirely different. He was blond, like his twin, but there the resemblance ended.

Becky was very pretty, true, but her brother was even more handsome than his photograph in a naval cadet's uniform had suggested. Also, there was a maturity to his face now, a kind of resolution about his features that only heightened his attractiveness. Midge had an overwhelming impression of a head that might have been sculpted by the ancient Greeks, with thick hair that could truly be called golden molding its contours and emphasizing the near-classical proportions of his forehead and finely chiseled nose. His strong chin was a direct heritage, she found herself thinking, from his Dutch ancestors.

The gray eyes became question marks, making Midge suddenly and painfully aware of the fact that she was staring at him. She said hastily, "I'm sorry. I knocked, but I guess you didn't hear me."

Eyebrows a shade darker than his hair arched upward. "No," he said coolly, "I didn't hear you. I was absorbed in my work."

He might as well have added, "And you, young lady, are an intruder!" Midge flinched, then, determined, gripped her courage and advanced farther into the room.

"My name is Marjorie Boardman," she began. "Probably it doesn't mean anything to you—"

"Should it?"

"No, of course not," she said, almost stammering over the words. She knew even as she spoke that she couldn't go through with this. It would be impossible to tell Brian Vandervelt that she was a friend of his sister's who just happened to be passing through town. She knew instinctively that he would never buy such a story.

No, Brian Vandervelt, she felt sure, would very quickly surmise that she was in Coxsackie because Becky had sent her; in other words, that she had come to snoop. So she hesitated only briefly, then said haltingly, "I'm looking for the advertising manager." She tried desperately to remember the name in the ad and suddenly did so. "Mr. Clayton, isn't it?" she asked.

Becky's brother stood up as if he had suddenly been reminded of his manners, brushing back a lock of hair with a swift smooth gesture, and Midge could not quite believe the impact he made on her. She was of average height herself and Becky was somewhat shorter, but now she saw, to her surprise, that Becky's twin towered over her, and once again she found herself thinking he would have been a Greek sculptor's delight. She was terribly conscious of a latent muscular power about him that was marvelously controlled. He literally exuded masculinity, in a way she had never encountered before, and the effect was staggering. He wore a white shirt with the sleeves rolled up, his arms still showing evidence of a bronze summer tan; where the shirt was open at the neck, his throat, she saw, was also bronzed. She became uncomfortably aware that once again she was staring at him.

He was watching her so closely that she flushed beneath his gaze, and he said almost wearily, "Excuse me, please. I was rather deep in thought when you came in. What did you say your name was?"

"Marjorie Boardman."

"And you're looking for Trent Clayton?"

"Yes."

"I'm afraid he's left for the day. Could I help you?"

Brian Vandervelt's words were cordial enough, yet there was no warmth in his manner. Also, there was again that note of weariness in his voice—or was it boredom?

No, she decided, it was fatigue. He looked tired, strained; undoubtedly he had been anxious to finish what he was doing and end his week's work, and she was serving only to detain him. She had never before appreciated what it felt like to be a trespasser!

She hesitated, then said, "I don't know whether or

not you could help me. I happened to see the ad for a copywriter in your paper, and it said to apply to Mr. Clayton, so I . . . I thought I would.''

''I see.'' The gray gaze was steady, so intent in fact that Midge's cheeks began to flame. It was one thing to be looked at, another thing to be stared at! Indeed, his scrutiny was almost downright rude.

''What brings you to Coxsackie?'' he asked now.

And there he had her!

She told herself that she should have invented a plausible story to take care of such a contingency, yet how could she possibly have foreseen this situation? She forced a smile, hoping that he might smile back in return, but he didn't.

''To tell you the truth,'' she said, ''I simply decided I wanted to get out of the city today. I knew I should go job hunting, but I felt like playing hooky, so I started driving. It was pouring when I got to Catskill, so I stopped for coffee and the newsboy happened to bring your paper along just then. I bought a copy and saw the ad.'' Most of this, she told herself, *was* the truth.

''You should have gone job hunting, but you decided to play hooky instead?''

''Yes.''

The gray eyes remained intent. ''That's a bit more understandable,'' he conceded. ''It stands to reason you surely wouldn't have come up *here* to job hunt. Not, that is, if you've been working in New York, as I presume you have.''

''Yes,'' she nodded, then remembered that Tim Ross, Brian's brother-in-law, once had worked for the same agency. Amazed at her own subterfuge, she quickly dispensed with the Anderson-Brent part of the title and said, "I've been a copywriter with John Pemberton Associates for the past six years."

Brian Vandervelt's smile was brief, touched with frost. "Then I hardly think you would be interested in writing copy for the *Valley Voice*, Miss Boardman. This is a long way from Madison Avenue."

"For personal reasons," she found herself saying, "I want to get away from Madison Avenue."

"Oh?" He didn't pursue the matter; in fact he made it entirely clear that he was not in the least bit interested in knowing why she had chosen to get away from New York. The effect was precisely like having a door slammed in one's face.

"I doubt this would be the place for you in any event, not with six years' experience in a New York agency," he said then, coldly. "However, I prefer my department heads to do their own hiring and firing. I'm sure Mr. Clayton would be glad to talk to you in the morning, if you plan to stay in town that long."

"Thank you," she said, and while she was still thinking about what to say next he sat down again, nodding curtly. It was a dismissal, and with her cheeks stinging Midge left the office, closing the door behind her.

It seemed to her that she could feel those level gray eyes boring into her back as she walked down the corridor, across the lobby and through the big paneled front door, and she shivered.

Brian Vandervelt was strange, there was no doubt about it. He was almost hostile, so completely the opposite of Becky that it was hard to believe they could be brother and sister. Yet, as Becky had said, there obviously was nothing physically wrong with him, nor did it seem likely that he could carry on his job if he were in the throes of any sort of mental illness.

What, then, was his hang-up?

It had started to rain again. Midge drove back across town to 9W—no need of going the river route by the Vandervelt mansion this time—finding her resentment at this disturbingly attractive man's attitude mounting with every mile she drove.

It was a dismal afternoon. Through the rain she saw a red neon motel sign, and she decided to stop. Admittedly dispirited because what might have been adventure had turned sour, she wondered now if she had stumbled on some sort of fleabag as a lodging for the night; but the motel, though small, was attractive, painted white with a cheery red trim, its windows faced with boxes abloom with bronze and gold chrysanthemums.

The woman at the desk in the lobby had a pleasant face and a plump motherly figure. Her smile was genuine, so welcoming after Brian Vandervelt's cool reception that Midge would have sworn she could actually feel the warmth of it. She was shown to a well-furnished unit and told not to hesitate to ask for anything else she needed.

"The Maples just down the road serves excellent meals," the motel manager added. "Same side of the road we're on. You can't miss it."

Midge thanked her, and as she closed the door of her room she glanced at her watch and saw that it was not quite four-thirty. It had been a long time since breakfast and she hadn't bothered with lunch, but four-thirty was still too early for dinner. The room boasted a small coffee-making machine, so she brewed herself a cup and settled down in front of the television, but she found it impossible to become interested in either the rerun of an old situation comedy or the bright shallow talk show, these the only two offerings of the moment.

She switched off the set, and as the picture faded the elusive fragment of a thought darted through her mind, leaving a lingering sense of annoyance. There was something elusive, too, about Brian Vandervelt; she had a feeling he was hiding something. Yet what could he possibly want to hide from *her*?

It was entirely too tantalizing to think that in the normal course of events she might never know, unless at some future time Becky herself unraveled this seeming mystery that surrounded Brian. True, she nevertheless could now write her friend and tell her, with a perfectly clear conscience, that she had seen Brian, and certainly there was nothing obvious the matter with him. Yet she knew very well that "obvious" was the catchword in this situation.

Restless, Midge paced over to the window to look out on a road empty of cars at the moment, the vista beyond of the massive Catskills effectively blocking the sky. Normally she was moved by magnificent scenery, yet just now she barely saw it, because she was remembering the astonishingly intense impact Brian Vandervelt had made on her, for all of his aloofness. Behind that cold, even unfriendly facade she had sensed a vibrancy quite at odds with his expressed attitude, and there also had been something else. Certainly Becky's brother was not issuing any cries for help, yet there had been something strangely troubled about him, something that she doubted had anything to do with his late uncle's will. Something personal.

She felt certain that Brian Vandervelt was a man with a problem. But what sort of problem?

She stirred restlessly, reminding herself that she had fulfilled her obligation to Becky. She had seen Brian, she would report back, then she could perfectly well return to New York and pick up the threads of her own life. And that was exactly what she *would* do, she told herself sternly, if she had any sense at all.

Yet although until this moment she had not seriously considered going back to the *Valley Voice* in the morning, she now knew it would be impossible to leave Coxsackie without making one further attempt to find out what really had happened to Brian Vandervelt.

CHAPTER THREE

A PRETTY DARK-HAIRED RECEPTIONIST was presiding at the desk in the lobby Friday morning. She pressed an intercom button and said, "There's a Miss Boardman to see you, Mr. Clayton, about the copywriting job."

Midge walked down the already familiar corridor and through the door with the frosted glass panel lettered Advertising, studiously avoiding even a glance toward the editorial office at the end of the hall.

The outer room, in which, she quickly estimated, perhaps three people could work in comfort, was empty just now, but as she entered it a man came to stand on the threshold of a smaller office just beyond. She judged swiftly that he was about thirty, tall and well built and decidedly attractive. He had smooth dark brown hair and hazel eyes, and was wearing plaid slacks and a dark green sports shirt; had he been dressed a bit more formally she would have been reminded, uncomfortably, of John Pemberton. They bore somewhat the same stamp, although John had already made it to the top on Madison Avenue, while this man was obviously on the way up.

Still, there was a familiar suavity to his manner as he came across to her, hand extended. "Miss Boardman?" he said. "I'm Trent Clayton." Even his voice

reminded her of John as he suggested, "Let's go into
my office, shall we?"

His private office was small but well furnished,
and he took his place behind the desk and motioned
her to a nearby chair with an air of assurance that
again was reminiscent of John.

His eyes, lingering on her, were approving, and she
knew that he was noting every detail of the burnt
orange knit suit she was wearing. She wished briefly
that she had chosen something that didn't emphasize
the curves of her figure quite so emphatically! Then
he asked, even as Becky's brother had, "What brings
you to Coxsackie?"

"The urge to get away from New York," she said
simply, which was not at all untrue. "It's an urge I
think I may want to satisfy permanently, so when I
saw your ad I decided to apply for the job."

"A spur-of-the-moment decision, eh?"

"Well, yes, I suppose so."

"What I mean to say is that I assume you weren't
actively job hunting when you came to this area?"

"Not exactly," Midge said carefully. "I drove into
Catskill yesterday afternoon when it was raining
quite hard. I decided to stop for a while and have
some coffee, and a newsboy happened to come in the
restaurant just then with copies of your paper."

"Are you staying with friends here?"

"No, I'm at the Springdale Motel on 9W."

"Mrs. Prescott's place," he nodded. "I stayed
there for a while myself when I first came to Coxsackie, until I found an apartment." There was still
approval in his eyes, but Midge saw that he was also a
businessman and a sharp one, and just now this
aspect of his personality was dominant. Like Brian

Vandervelt, Trent Clayton evidently could not entirely buy the thought of her seeking work on the *Valley Voice*.

"You have friends around here, do you, Miss Boardman?" he persisted.

"No, Mr. Clayton, as a matter of fact I don't," she told him. "Does it matter, though? I *am* an experienced copywriter, and that's what your ad asked for."

"True," he conceded. "Well, then, suppose you give me some idea of your experience."

"I was with the same agency for nearly six years," she said. "Pemberton Associates, on Madison Avenue near Forty-seventh," she added, and hoped he wouldn't realize she was giving him only part of the agency's name. Despite Trent Clayton's urbanity, Coxsackie was sufficiently removed from the New York City scene that it was not likely he would be familiar with all the agency names.

"Why did you leave?" he asked, and she tried not to let her relief show through, for evidently he was accepting the existence of Pemberton Associates at face value.

"I left for personal reasons," she said.

"You left—you were not dismissed?"

"I left," she assured him frostily.

"I see."

"In any event," she added hastily, before he could pose another question, "if I had known I'd be applying for a job up here I would have brought some samples of my work with me. As it is, I can go back down to the city and get them for you, or any references you might require."

And she could. Even though it would mean facing John.

Trent Clayton brushed this aside. "I see no need to ask you for references," he said. "You can do some sample copy for me, and if it's satisfactory that will be reference enough. I might add that I'm sure it's apt to be more than satisfactory—what I mean is that if you've been doing copy for a New York advertising agency for the past six years you are certainly over-qualified for this job. We have a good paper here, and we constantly strive to upgrade our work. But we are not Madison Avenue."

She nodded. "I realize that."

"I'm not sure you do. I'm not sure you'd be willing to settle for what we have here, Miss Boardman. The girl who held the job we're now advertising left last month when she and her husband moved out of town. She had come to the *Voice* right out of high school, and my predecessor and I taught her everything she knew about writing copy. She had a certain flair for it, she was passable, but she surely could never have made it in New York."

Trent Clayton picked up a long silver pen and thoughtfully tapped the surface of his desk with it. "Right now," he said, "I have a young man named Clem Thorne doing outside selling for us, and he shows a lot of promise. Then we have Ellen Brent, who is a local girl and does layouts for us. She's also staff artist for the whole paper. This, after all, is a weekly, not a city daily.

"Clem, Ellen and I comprise the ad staff at the moment, and our ranks will be complete once again when we hire a copywriter. There is every reason to believe that we'll be expanding, the way things are going with the paper. But this is still a small operation compared to what you've been used to, and I daresay the salary the job offers would seem small to you, too."

"It wouldn't cost as much to live up here."

He smiled. "True," he admitted. "I came here from Chicago myself, and the cost-of-living differential has been a pleasant surprise to me."

He leaned back, his eyes once again a little too approving for comfort, and Midge wished that she knew what his marital status was. Was he single, divorced, widowed, engaged? There would be a plus to having a married boss in a small town, she thought; at least she assumed it would be a plus. Scandal spread quickly, and so a discreet employer would surely try to avoid staff involvements. On the other hand, if Trent Clayton was relatively free of romantic entanglements there was the chance that working for him could present problems of a sort she definitely didn't need.

He said, "Believe me, it isn't that I don't want you on my staff. I would welcome you if I thought we had a chance of keeping you with us for a reasonable amount of time. I must be honest, though, and say I'm inclined to doubt we could. Once you'd recovered from this 'personal' matter that caused you to give up your last job, I fear we'd quickly lose you to greener pastures. So it's only fair to tell you that I'd prefer to have someone with less talent and more staying power."

This nettled her. "I don't take jobs lightly, Mr. Clayton," she told him, and found that she was intensely serious about this. "I can understand your feelings, but I don't think they're justified, nor do I feel you're being in the least fair in assuming that my wanting the job is a mere whim. I think there are times in everyone's life when it becomes desirable to change a situation or an environment. I've reached such a time in mine. I don't promise that I'll spend the rest of my life in Coxsackie, but I can't imagine you could make such a promise, either."

He smiled faintly. "That might depend upon a number of things," he remarked, but she sensed that she had scored a point.

"Well, then," she said, pressing the advantage, "all I can say is that if you'll give me a chance at the job I will surely give you my best work in return. Why don't we settle for a trial period? Three months, perhaps?"

There was decided admiration in Trent Clayton's smile. "You're on!" he told her.

IT WAS NECESSARY to make a trip back to New York to pick up extra clothes, arrange for mail to be forwarded and make sure that matters in general would be cared for during her absence, and by late Friday afternoon Midge was in her apartment. Before leaving Coxsackie she had booked a motel unit with Mrs. Prescott for Sunday, this for an indefinite stay. Later she could think about hunting for an apartment or even a small house, for she had every intention of honoring her three-month commitment to the *Valley Voice*.

Aside from her curiosity about Brian Vandervelt, she was finding an unexpected challenge in the thought of working for the newspaper. True, her salary would be far from stratospheric, but it *would* be cheaper to live in Coxsackie than in Manhattan. She had managed to save a bit these past six years, and there was an inheritance, thus far untouched, of a few thousand dollars from her mother, so she had no financial worries.

She thought briefly of subletting the New York apartment, then decided against it. She and Jennifer Lund had a lease that ran until the first of February; well before then she might be glad to come back to New York for a visit at least, and if so she'd appreciate still having the apartment. It would probably be wise to come back anyway after the three-month commitment to the *Voice* was over, so that she could carefully plan her next career step.

As she packed some heavy sweaters that would be useful when the weather in Coxsackie got really cold, she caught a glimpse of herself in the dresser mirror and smiled wryly. She had never considered herself wildly impetuous and was somewhat amazed at having decided to make this interim job move so quickly. Until now she hadn't realized that what her mother used to call her "curiosity bump" was quite so large.

"Becky, Becky," she said aloud, "you've really got me into something!"

The phone rang, startling her, and as she picked up the bright orange receiver all at once time whirled backward. She quickly sat down on the edge of the couch.

"Midge," John Pemberton said. The sound of his voice still had the power to stir her.

She pitched her own voice to just the right degree of lightness. "John?" she asked. "It *is* you, isn't it?"

"Thanks for remembering," he said, and she knew

immediately from his tone that he was well past the first martini. "Where the hell have you been?"

"Out of town."

"Out of town! Okay, it's none of my business. Look, are you free for dinner?"

"No," she fibbed. "I'm sorry, but I'm not."

"Then would you kindly shake whomever you're with around eleven and meet me at the place down on Lexington?"

"No, John," she said steadily. "I won't."

"Midge," he said with surprising gentleness, "this is stupid. We're both being stupid. At first I had too damned much pride to call you. Then I heard you'd gone out to San Francisco."

"Yes. To see my father."

"What are you doing now?"

"I've got a job—out of town."

"Where out of town?"

"I'd rather not say."

"I see." The pause that followed seemed eternal, then he said, "We can't let it end like this."

"It already has ended," she told him gently.

"Midge—" he began again.

But she said, "Good night, John," and hung up the receiver so carefully that it barely made a click, surprised at her own calm. Nevertheless, her hands were shaking and her cheeks were wet.

She yielded to impulse and mixed herself a Scotch and soda, but there was no pleasure in drinking alone. She finished packing, half hoping that John would call her back, for maybe she had been overly abrupt at that, but the phone didn't ring again.

She did some last-minute shopping Saturday, then met a friend for dinner, and on Sunday morning she gave the apartment a brisk cleaning and wrote a long and detailed letter to Jennifer about her plans. It was not until she had called the garage and told them to bring the Volvo around that she realized there was one thing yet to do. She must phone Becky.

In San Francisco the Rosses were having a late breakfast. Becky explained, "Just Tim and me. I got up and fed the kids hours ago and then went back to bed. We went to a party last night."

"Hedonists," said Midge. "Becky—I went to Coxsackie."

The silence was acute. Then Becky asked very cautiously, "Did you see Brian?"

"Yes."

"Well?"

"He looks terrific. There certainly doesn't seem to be anything wrong with him. He's not the friendliest person in the world, though. In fact I'd say he's almost hostile."

"Brian—hostile?"

"Yes."

"Then there certainly *is* something wrong with him," Becky declared firmly. "Brian has always tended to be aloof; I've told you that. But hostile... no. Did you see Aunt Maude?"

"No. Becky—that house! I simply couldn't walk up to the front door...."

"Yes. I can understand that."

Midge paused, wondering just how to phrase what she had to say next. "I'm going back," she said then.

"To *Coxsackie*?"

"Yes. I've got a job on the *Valley Voice*."

"You?" Becky's laugh was too high-pitched; it

sounded perilously close to hysteria. "Midge, you're crazy!"

"No, I'm not. I found out entirely by accident that there was a copywriting job open, and I applied for it. I start work Monday morning. I've agreed to a three-month trial period—after that we'll see what happens."

"Does Brian approve of this?"

"Not necessarily. He referred me to his advertising manager. He doesn't know I know you."

"Midge!" Becky's chuckle was ever so much more normal now. "I didn't know you had it in you. Such subterfuge!"

"Your personal spy," Midge said lightly. "Seriously, darling, I'm going to do a good job up there. They will get their money's worth, I assure you, and in the process I'll see what I can find out for you. Okay?"

"Okay," Becky said. But just before she hung up she added, "You know how worried I've been about Brian, but even so I didn't expect you to do anything like this!" Doubt crept into her voice. "I hope you're not getting in too deep," she finished thoughtfully.

MIDGE LEFT THE CITY toward midafternoon. It was another gloomy day, and darkness descended before she got to Coxsackie. On 9W the glowing red sign that marked the Springdale Motel was a welcome beacon.

Mrs. Prescott greeted her as if she were an old friend, and when they had exhausted the mutual topic of the miserable weather Midge, realizing she had not eaten since breakfast, drove down the road to the Maples. She was finding, though, that just as it was no fun to drink alone, it was no fun to eat alone. She finished her dinner quickly and, back at the motel, showered and slipped into her robe before unpacking the clothes she planned to wear to work in the morning. Her other things could wait until later.

She kept thinking about Becky's final statement. *Was* she getting in too deep?

She shrugged philosophically. She'd know the answer to that soon enough!

She switched on the television and settled down in front of it, only to doze off. When she awakened much later to find the now empty screen staring vacantly at her, she was reminded again of Becky's brother. It was a strange association, and it made no sense to her.

She switched off the set, slid into bed and let sleep overtake her before wakefulness had the chance to stake a claim.

THE PARKING LOT at the side of the *Hudson River Valley Voice* building was well filled with cars Monday morning. Midge did not add hers to them but instead chose the same parking place on the opposite side of the street that she had used on her two previous visits there. Entering the building, she nodded to the pleasant brunette at the reception desk, who was busy on the telephone, and confidently walked down the hall to the advertising department.

She was ten minutes early and wondered if she might have preceded her new boss, but Trent Clayton, as urbane as ever, was already in the outer office looking over the shoulder of a thin girl with carrot-colored hair who in turn was bent over a drawing board. The only other occupant of the office was a pallid young man with a shock of brown hair, thick glasses and a blotchy complexion.

Trent Clayton straightened and said, "Well, Miss Boardman, you're right on time!"

"I hope so," she responded, smiling, but to her surprise he did not smile back. There was, in fact, no welcome in his expression: the cordial interest he had evinced the other day was definitely lacking.

He nodded to the girl at the drawing board. "This is Ellen Brent, who does our artwork, and Clem Thorne, our ad salesman."

They mumbled greetings, then almost immediately Clem Thorne picked up his phone and dialed, and Ellen Brent returned to her layout. The advertising manager, frowning, said, "Come into my office, will you, Miss Boardman?"

"Of course," she answered, but she was perplexed as she followed him. Something had happened since Friday; something had changed.

Trent Clayton closed the office door, motioned her to a seat and took his own place behind his well-polished desk. Leaning back, he picked up the silver pen, and as he looked across at her Midge could not resist asking, "Is something wrong, Mr. Clayton?"

"Should there be?" he countered.

"Not that I know of."

His chair thumped as he sat forward. "You didn't tell me when you came in here Friday that you'd already had an interview with Brian Vandervelt," he said.

"I hadn't."

"Come on, Miss Boardman. The department heads hold a staff conference each Monday at eight, to start the week. This morning I told Vandervelt I'd hired a new copywriter, and when I told him who you were he said you'd been in to see him last Thursday."

"But I wasn't," she protested. "That is, I did see him last Thursday, but actually I had come here to see you, to answer your ad. He was the only person around at the time."

"But you did talk to him?"

"Yes."

"Why didn't you tell me so?"

"It never occurred to me," Midge said honestly. "Certainly I had nothing to hide. Mr. Vandervelt told me you did your own hiring and to come back on Friday, so I did."

"I wondered about that," he admitted.

"About what?"

"I *do* my own hiring; I wouldn't work any other way. But naturally the publisher has influence. Vandervelt didn't use it: in this instance there was no need. With your qualifications I would have been an idiot not to hire you, but if you're a friend of his I think I have the right to know it."

"A friend of Brian Vandervelt?" She didn't have to feign astonishment. "I never saw him in my life until last Thursday afternoon."

Unexpectedly, Trent Clayton smiled at her. "Then, that's that," he said. "I guess I still find it hard to believe an attractive girl like you would leave an agency job in New York to come up and work on a weekly paper in a town like this. It seemed to me you must have a friend around here, despite your denial, and that it just might be Vandervelt."

"Well, you were wrong," she answered frostily. "I told you I was leaving the city for personal reasons and that's all I'm going to say about it. I'm not asking any favors. I *can* write good copy, we've agreed to a three-month commitment, and unless you want to retract on your part of the bargain I'm prepared to go to work and give you my best."

"That's more than good enough for me," he assured her smoothly. "There's one thing you'll have to do before you start working, though."

"What's that?"

"Vandervelt wants to see you himself. He said to send you to his office as soon as you came in. I guess that's what set me to pondering a bit. His office is down at the end of the hall, through the newsroom, but I guess you already know that."

"Thank you," she said stiffly. "Yes, I do."

Clem Thorne and Ellen Brent looked up briefly as she went through the outer office, then quickly averted their eyes. Maybe, Midge decided, frowning, there was something about the late Horace Vandervelt's newspaper that bred suspicion and hostility. As she walked down the corridor to the newsroom, her pulse was hammering, and her mind raced backward to the time when she and Becky were students together at Pine Haven Junior College.

Brian Vandervelt had entered Annapolis the same year Becky entered Pine Haven, and thereafter they had seldom been in the same place at the same time, much to Becky's distress. She had always wanted her best friend and her brother to meet, but it simply hadn't happened.

After graduation Midge had gone to New York and had got the job at the agency. Becky had arrived in New York that fall to take an art course, somehow having wangled permission out of her uncle to do so.

In the winter Midge introduced her to Tim, and by the end of the following year they were married. After that Tim switched jobs, the Rosses moved to San Francisco, and although she and Becky had corresponded with each other occasionally there had been long periods of time when they were out of touch.

In the beginning, though, when they were both at Pine Haven, Becky might very well have written to her brother about Marjorie Boardman, the girl who had become her best friend. If so, could Brian have remembered the name since Thursday? Could he have connected it with the fact that she had worked in a New York advertising agency, as had his brother-in-law?

It was possible, of course, but it seemed unlikely, especially if one considered Becky's habits. Becky was casual, quick to use first names. In writing to Brian she would have been much more likely to say simply Midge than to mention Marjorie Boardman.

In any event, so much had happened in the intervening years, to all of them. It was unlikely Brian could have made the connection, she told herself, then recognized this as pure wishful thinking.

The newsroom was in full production today, typewriters clattering, phones ringing. A gray-haired man looked up from a desk near the door and asked, "Yes?"

She gestured toward Brian's door. "I'm from advertising," she said. "Mr. Vandervelt's expecting me."

He smiled too knowingly for comfort. "The new

copywriter?'' And at her nod he went on, ''Go on in.
Don't bother to knock.''

Nevertheless she did knock, and then, waiting, was
about to follow the gray-haired man's advice when
Brian Vandervelt called, ''Come in.''

He was standing behind his desk, and in a perfectly
tailored dark blue business suit with a crisp white
shirt and a dark blue tie he looked startlingly handsome. Again she was astonished at the impact the
mere sight of him had on her. There was an essential
masculinity about him that was entirely too disturbing! Then she saw that today his gray eyes were
glacial, and his full mouth was set in a tight uncom-
promising line. As she looked at him her heart sank.

''Sit down, Miss Boardman.'' He indicated the
chair nearest his desk, and feeling like a frightened
child she obeyed him.

He continued to stand, surveying her from what at
the moment seemed a near-Olympian height. Then he
said shortly, ''I suppose you wonder why I've sent
for you?''

She had to swallow before she could speak. Then
she admitted, ''Yes. Yes, I do.''

The gray gaze did not falter. ''Well,'' he said, ''I'll
admit I was surprised when Clayton said he had hired
you.''

''Why? Don't you think I'm qualified?''

''Obviously you are qualified,'' he told her impatiently. ''Both Clayton and I have indicated to you
that we think you are *over*qualified. What bothers
me is that I can't understand why you want the job.''

''Must there be a reason?'' she demanded.

''There usually is.''

''Very well, then, I have told Mr. Clayton and I

will tell you that my reasons for leaving my job in New York were purely personal. If you must know, I was involved with someone who worked in the same agency. I left of my own accord; I was not dismissed, if that is what you are afraid of. I can verify that for you if you wish."

"I beg your pardon?"

"If you think I was fired I can get proof that I wasn't," she said stonily.

"That won't be necessary." He turned away from her, toward the window, and his back seemed like a wall between them.

She said helplessly, "I can't understand why both you and Mr. Clayton are so concerned about simply giving me a chance at this job. I *am* a copywriter; I'm even a good one. Why won't you at least let me try?"

He swung around, and this time he sat down at his desk. He said, clearly preoccupied, "I'm sorry. What did you say?" Then, as she started to repeat herself, "No. It doesn't matter. I can understand your bewilderment. You are offering us more talent than we need, and we must seem peculiarly indifferent." He hesitated. "It isn't that, Miss Boardman. Actually, it is particularly important to me at this phase of the paper's development to maintain a good employment record. I'm against hiring people who wish to work for us for capricious reasons, no matter how high their qualifications, because I realize that it's unlikely they will stay."

Remembering the will and the probationary period nearly at an end made his concern seem more valid, and Midge informed him, "I've made a three-month commitment, Mr. Vandervelt."

He nodded. "I accept that."

"Then—" her words were touched with irony "—you *will* permit me to go to work?"

For a moment she thought he might smile, but he didn't.

"I won't delay you further," he assured her, and turned to some papers on his desk in a clear gesture of dismissal.

CHAPTER FOUR

By WEDNESDAY Midge had produced copy for three advertising accounts that "really sang," as Trent Clayton proclaimed with satisfaction. She had also been introduced to the various department heads, Clayton taking her around himself to do the honors. Abe Weissman, a jolly roly-poly man, headed circulation; Fritz Handel, stolid with a heavy Teutonic accent, was the mechanical superintendent, and though inclined to be irascible, according to Trent Clayton, he was reported to be an expert at keeping his end of the operation going.

The editorial staff tended to keep to themselves, but she did come upon Trent Clayton talking to the gray-haired man who had been in the newsroom Monday morning when Brian Vandervelt had summoned her to his office. He was introduced as Mike Stabler, the managing editor, and later she was told that he was one of the best in the business—or had been until he'd started a love affair with the bottle.

Midge found that insofar as her own department was concerned, she had no particular personal rapport with either of her immediate co-workers, yet they were not nearly as uninteresting as they had seemed at first; in fact both were surprisingly accomplished in their own fields. Clem Thorne, despite his unprepossessing appearance, was an excellent ad

salesman. He was a native of Coxsackie, married and
the father of a baby daughter; he knew everyone in
the area and had a disarmingly simple sales approach
that was being reflected each week in increased advertising linage.

Ellen Brent was also a native of the town. She'd
had little formal education in art aside from a course
she had taken in high school, but she was definitely
talented. Her layouts were provocative, novel, yet
still suited to the *Valley Voice*'s rather traditional
makeup, and she worked very hard. At least part of
the reason for this dedication, Midge surmised, was
Trent Clayton. The girl took every possible opportunity to seek his opinion, and her eyes followed him
almost hungrily every time he moved through the office. If Trent was aware of Ellen's infatuation with
him, though, he gave no indication of it. Outwardly
he was pleasant to his staff, friendly but not too
friendly, and although again his eyes tended to linger
appreciatively upon Midge, thus far he had been very
circumspect.

Occasionally Midge caught a glimpse of Brian
Vandervelt walking down a corridor or coming out
of an office, but the glimpses were few and far between, nor did they come within even nodding distance of each other. Still, even the sight of his tall
well-built figure at a distance had a surprisingly
chaotic effect on her senses. Although he might be
aloof, even hostile, his virility was an almost tangible
force, and she found herself wishing rather ruefully
that he was not quite so blatantly attractive!

Also, she could not repress a nagging sense of
disappointment. She felt sure that by now he must
have read some of her copy, and she yearned for the

kind of ego boost his approval would give her, even though it was ridiculous to think he would make a special trip to the advertising department to tell her how good she was.

Wednesday, after a solitary dinner at the Maples, she had a sudden desire for a candy bar to accompany a television program she planned to watch later in the evening, and so she detoured into town. There was already a touch of fall in the cool night air, and she shivered slightly. She lingered in the pharmacy, buying a lipstick she didn't really need and a new magazine she had been meaning to scan, and discovered that she dreaded going back to the loneliness of the motel room, pleasant though Mrs. Prescott tried to make it for her.

She was about to leave the store when she saw Brian Vandervelt pass by the entrance. He walked quickly, looking to neither left nor right, and she was certain he hadn't seen her. Despite herself she lingered in the doorway watching him as he started to cut across the street, the glow from the corner streetlight turning his hair to pure gold. She was tempted to go after him, for on neutral ground, away from either the newspaper office or—God forbid—his uncle's mansion, she felt she might actually be able to tell him she was his twin sister's best friend.

Hers was a harmless sort of deception, to be sure, something he should be able to understand her doing out of friendship; yet as she watched his retreating figure she wished fervently that she never had become involved in it. What was that old quote about the tangled web we weave when first we practice to deceive? Midge could not remember it precisely, but the thought was certainly valid.

If only she had told him that first day in his office about Becky's request that she look him up. In retrospect it seemed this would have been such a simple thing to do! But she knew only too well that it was too late to "confess" to him now. She could just imagine his reaction; she could virtually feel those glacial gray eyes sweeping her face!

As she continued to watch him, Brian Vandervelt, walking along the sidewalk now, paused beside a low white Jaguar, and Midge realized she had seen it in the parking lot at the paper. A moment later she heard its engine spring to life, and he drove off.

Thursday, with the paper off the press, Trent Clayton invited his staff to go over to Murphy's, a neighborhood tavern, to celebrate Midge's first week with them. Midge didn't particularly want to go, yet there seemed no gracious way to refuse in the face of Clem's and Ellen's quick acceptance. She suspected that Trent would try to maneuver matters so that the two of them could linger on in the tavern after her co-workers had left—an arrangement she was determined to forestall. Trent was pleasant, attractive, sophisticated, and it was impossible not to like him, but she had no desire to become involved with him. Perhaps it was because he reminded her so much of John, but she felt certain that it would be impossible to remain casual with him for very long.

Nevertheless, the small celebration at Murphy's was pleasant. Charming and relaxed, Trent bestowed his attentions equally upon Ellen and herself, for which Midge was grateful. There had been moments already when she had seen quick jealousy flicker across Ellen's plain face, and this was something else she wanted to forestall, especially since Ellen had no reason for it as far as she was concerned.

Now she graciously accepted the toast the others proposed to her and then toasted them in turn, thanking them for their cooperation. She was careful to compliment some of the artwork Ellen had done, and the girl's usually pale cheeks flushed with pleasure.

Clem was the first to leave, explaining that his wife had planned an early dinner, and when he offered Ellen a ride Midge was afraid the girl was going to accept it, thus leaving her alone with Trent. Ellen hesitated just long enough, though, for Midge to offer, "I can take you home if you like, Ellen," and she saw Trent Clayton's lips quirk.

"Let's have another round of drinks first," he suggested, and Ellen quickly agreed.

Midge was not averse to the idea herself. The mood was mellow, and it occurred to her that if she were careful enough about it she might find a way to ask Trent and Ellen some questions about Brian Vandervelt without appearing to be overly curious.

As it was, Trent shortly gave her an opportunity she didn't expect—nor did she want it when it came!

As he stirred his drink he said, "Vandervelt damn near got himself killed today!"

Midge, horrified, was too startled to speak immediately, but Ellen quickly demanded, "How?"

"He was out in the composing room. There was a box of some heavy metal stuff stored on a shelf near where he was standing. When the presses started, the vibration must have jarred it. The box fell within an inch of him...almost on top of him, as a matter of fact. It's a miracle he wasn't hit. At least, that's what everyone who was there at the time has been saying.''

"Didn't he hear anything?" Midge demanded.

Trent looked at her oddly. "Hear anything?"

"Yes. Or didn't someone try to warn him?"

"It wouldn't have made much difference if they had," Trent responded, "especially with the presses going." He frowned at her obviously perplexed. "I thought you knew," he said. "Vandervelt's deaf."

Deaf. It was a thunderbolt.

Midge stared at Trent dumbly, disbelieving, her mind reeling with shock. Brian Vandervelt, she thought dully, couldn't be deaf! One associated deafness with elderly people, or unfortunate children. Vital handsome men like Brian Vandervelt simply weren't deaf!

But even as she told herself this, Midge knew that Trent was speaking the truth, and it was as if in the process he had also given her a full explanation of all the things that had been so puzzling.

Of course there had been nothing in his pictures to warn Becky of her brother's affliction! He concealed his disability very well. But now that she knew, it seemed to Midge that she should have had some inkling of what was wrong with him herself. She should have *sensed* something. Last Thursday, for instance, when she knocked at the door of his office and there was no response, he had been as shocked as she was when they unexpectedly confronted each other.

Now that she thought about it, she could recall that in both of the conversations she'd had with him he had asked her to repeat herself at least once. She had mistaken this for preoccupation with his own affairs, or perhaps merely a lack of interest in her.

Then, too, there was that disconcerting gray gaze, his way of focusing so intently on people's faces that it was as if he were analyzing every word; this should have given her a clue. Herein also, she realized, lay the answer to that elusive something she had felt looking at the television set gone blank, suddenly devoid of sound.

Ellen Brent, as if reading her thoughts, told her, "Brian Vandervelt was hurt in an explosion several years ago. He hides it pretty well, though."

"Do you mean he's totally deaf?" Midge found herself reluctant to accept that fact, despite her own reasoning.

"Well, he wears hearing aids," Trent explained. "You don't notice them because of the way he keeps his hair cut: it's rather thick, and he has it contoured so that it camouflages very well. He does fairly well when he has the aids turned on, though I notice it's best to be right in front of him when you speak to him. But when he's working in his office he often switches them off. I've walked in on him sometimes when it doesn't seem as if he can hear a damned thing. So just what you'd call totally deaf, medically...I don't know."

Midge remembered a gesture of Brian's that first afternoon in his office. He had smoothed back his hair. Now she knew the reason for it: he'd had his hearing aids turned off and had switched them on in the effort to understand her.

She said, still shaken, "It's hard to believe. It's a...terrible handicap. He's so young and—"

"So good-looking?" Trent finished knowingly. "Look, don't feel too sorry for him! Brian Vandervelt is extremely self-assured, as you must have noticed, and why wouldn't he be? He's scheduled to inherit a fortune almost any day now; he'll have enough to keep himself in gold-plated hearing aids for the rest of his life!''

Midge ignored this last remark. "Someone told me the big old gray mansion on the Athens road belongs to the Vandervelts,'' she ventured. "Do Brian Vandervelt and his wife live there?''

"He hasn't got a wife,'' Trent said. "He lives with his aunt—the late Horace Vandervelt's widow.'' He swallowed the last of his drink. "I'll drop you off, Ellen,'' he announced almost abruptly, and there was no doubt that the previous mellow mood had thoroughly evaporated. "It's on my way, actually, and Marjorie would have to detour.''

Marjorie. Few people called her by her given name, but thus far Midge had kept her nickname to herself, just in case Brian Vandervelt might make a connection with his sister should he hear of it.

They parted outside the tavern, Trent and Ellen going in one direction and Midge in another. She was almost at her car when she remembered she had left her jacket back at her desk. It promised to be a chilly evening, so she walked across the street to the newspaper office, pushing open the front door with a pleasant sense of familiarity.

She had retrieved the jacket and was coming out of the advertising department with it over her arm when she heard a door close and saw Brian Vandervelt starting down the hall. She stood rooted to the spot, swept by a surge of conflicting emotions. Trent was right: there was definite self-assurance even in Becky's brother's walk, emphasized by that air of aloofness. But there was also a latent sensuality about him that was almost a danger signal, even at moments like this one when he was clearly not only preoccupied but extremely tired, for weariness etched his face, making him look much older than he was.

It must, she thought now, be exhausting to be forever striving to hear what people were saying to you, and she felt a swift pang of compassion for him.

He glanced up, saw her and stopped. "Well," he said. "Hello."

"Hello," she answered, almost stuttering, painfully conscious of the rosy color that she could feel flooding her face, making her seem as awkward as an infatuated teenager.

"You're working late, aren't you?"

"No," she said. "I came back for this." She fingered the jacket.

He nodded and fell into step beside her. They walked together to the front door, and as he opened it for her his arm brushed her shoulder. It seemed to her she could feel an instant response from him that matched her own near-convulsive reaction, this in itself making her heart thud.

They walked out into a perfect October night, the moon a sickle preparing for harvest, the polished stars firm in their settings.

Midge, taken aback at this swift surge of feeling he evoked in her, was overwhelmingly conscious of the wood scent of his after-shave lotion and the very warmth of his nearness. And, astonishingly, she was again possessed by the conviction that he was every bit as aware of her as a woman as she was of him as a man.

They crossed the street and came to her car, which was parked under a streetlight, and Midge wanted desperately to say something to him, yet found herself tongue-tied.

It was he who spoke first. "You've been doing some very good work for us," he told her.

"Thank you."

"Are you sorry you came back?"

"To get my jacket?" she asked, puzzled.

"No, to the paper—after that first afternoon I talked to you. Are you sorry you took the job?"

"No," she answered simply.

A smile came briefly to curve his lips; in fact it was so brief Midge thought for a moment she had imagined it. Then he said, "Good," nodded slightly and went on to his white Jaguar parked farther down the street.

As Midge drove back to the motel, she was unable to shut Brian Vandervelt out of her mind, the emotion she felt for him a wrenching thing. Later, eating a solitary early dinner at the Maples, she had visions of Brian dining at home with his aunt somewhere in the dim recesses of the Vandervelt mansion. It evoked a gloomy picture at best.

That night she had a vivid dream in which she found herself teaching a class of deaf children, and the dreadful part of it was that she was totally unable to communicate with them. She became exhausted, using all the tools at her command to no avail. Then she peered closely at the children and saw that all of them looked exactly like Brian, and at this point she awakened.

Her watch had a luminous dial, and the hands stood at 4 A.M. A ridiculous hour to get up—but she soon found she could not get back to sleep. Finally she rose and made herself a cup of coffee, then put

on a wool robe and snuggled up in the armchair, trying, among other things, to imagine what it must be
like suddenly to become deaf. One would have no
time for adjustment, no time to memorize familiar
beloved sounds, if in fact anyone ever could. On the
spur of the moment she turned on an all-night radio
station and put her fingers in her ears, but even so the
sound filtered through and she could hear distant
music.

Could Brian hear that well, even with mechanical
aids? A gust of wind rustled autumn leaves on the
trees outside her window. Could Brian hear sounds
like that?

I'm getting maudlin, she warned herself, *which
will be no help to anyone at all.*

Thinking about being a help to anyone reminded
her that she supposed she must write Becky and tell
her about Brian—a task she dreaded. Why, for that
matter, hadn't Brian long since written Becky about
his deafness himself? Unless he had decided to shut
her out of his life permanently, he must realize that
eventually she would be hurt by his having kept
something so very important from her. Surely when
you loved someone you wanted to share the bad with
the good.

Brian's sensitivity about his hearing was understandable but he certainly carried it to an astonishing
degree!

Horace Vandervelt must have known that Brian
was deaf when he made his last will and testament,
yet he had put him to a test that was not only
especially trying under such circumstances but
dangerous, as well. The Vandervelt inheritance con-
stituted a massive fortune; Becky had expressed her

awareness of this fact when she had indicated that greed could become an overwhelming thing. And if Brian Vandervelt were not around to inherit on the first of November his share of the estate would automatically go to the department heads at the paper.

Becky's worry about her brother was more valid than she realized, Midge thought now, for to add to the problem Brian, obviously determined to cope with his handicap entirely alone, had built a kind of wall around himself that could only help his enemies!

Midge shivered, possessed of a coldness that could not be warmed by wool robes or hot coffee.

TRENT CLAYTON had told Midge that she didn't need to come in on Friday, and so she decided to drive to Albany to investigate some of the shopping facilities.

First, though, she stopped for breakfast at the Maples. A plump young waitress led her to a booth by a window that looked out upon sere brown fields. The corn had been harvested, the sand-colored husks piled into slanting stacks; the Catskills, blotting the western sky, were a magnificent blend of blues and purples. It was a gorgeous day, much too beautiful to be indoors, and Midge decided that she might postpone her shopping expedition so that she could drive around and explore some of Rip Van Winkle's fascinating countryside.

She threw dietary caution to the wind and ordered pancakes and sausages, and had just taken the first delicious bite when someone said, "Good morning."

She recognized the low-pitched voice even before she glanced up to see Brian Vandervelt standing by her booth. Then despite herself she gulped, and he smiled faintly.

"I didn't mean to startle you," he said.

She swallowed hastily, nearly choking as she answered, "You didn't."

"May I join you?"

"Of course."

He sat down opposite her, and once again she could not seem to take her eyes away from him. He was dressed informally today, wearing a gray knit sweater that almost matched his eyes and also emphasized the muscular width of his shoulders.

"Where are you staying?" he asked her now. "Prescotts'?"

"Yes."

"Are you comfortable there?"

"Yes, thank you." Like a frightened schoolgirl she could hardly keep from wriggling under his steady gray gaze.

The waitress brought him a steaming mug of coffee and two sugar doughnuts, and when he said, "Thanks, Janie," the girl smiled at him as if he'd given her a medal.

He stirred sugar into his coffee, liberally laced it with cream, then explained, "I saw your car parked outside, so I decided to come in."

"Oh?" she said. "Then this isn't your usual stop?"

"Not regularly. I usually have breakfast at home."

"I see."

"I felt I could talk to you better here than at the office," he said. He hesitated, then flashed her a look that actually was reminiscent of Becky. "As I've already mentioned, you did exceptionally good work for us this week. I appreciate it, especially because I didn't encourage you on either of the occasions when we met in my office. That afternoon when I looked up and saw you standing in front of my desk—''

She said, without even thinking, "I *did* knock, you know," and then wanted to bite her tongue.

Briefly he looked away from her; then the gray eyes came to rest upon her face again, but it was as if they had turned cloudy. "Yes," he said, "I'm sure you did, and I imagine by now you know I couldn't hear you."

She flushed, willing her voice to stay steady. "Yes," she admitted.

"Did you surmise for yourself that I'm . . . deaf?" he asked, and she knew that "deaf" was a word that did not come easily to him. "Or did someone tell you?"

"Trent Clayton mentioned it yesterday," she said. "I . . . well, no, I didn't realize it myself." She hesitated, fearing his resentment, yet this was something she had to say. "You manage very well," she told him.

He shook his head, his smile rueful. "That's a matter of opinion," he said, so softly that she had to strain to catch the words. "If I'd had my hearing aids turned on the other day I might have heard you knock, but the presses had been going and sometimes the sound gets overpowering. It's rather like having a couple of extra radios hooked up to your head. Regardless, I apologize for my rudeness."

"Please—" she began, but she was to have no chance to continue. An interruption came in the form of a young man wearing the gray uniform of a New

York State trooper, who strode across the restaurant toward their booth.

Brian shook his head. "No!" he protested.

"Yes," the trooper nodded. "I hate to bother you, but it's Mike again."

Brian's lips tightened. "It's getting to be a habit," he sighed wearily. "Where was he this time?"

"At a dive in Albany. They had to lock him up. No choice. He was taking it out on the whole world to the tune of about eighty dollars' worth of broken glassware."

Brian agreed reluctantly, "Okay, I'll come. Miss Boardman, I'm sorry. This is Jerry Mueller."

The trooper grinned as he acknowledged the introduction. "Sorry to break in on your breakfast," he said.

"That's quite all right," Midge replied automatically. "We were just discussing business."

"Business?" Mueller's eyebrows rose.

"Miss Boardman is the new copywriter at the *Valley Voice*," Brian explained. "Jerry's wife also works for us," he told Midge. "Lucille—she's our receptionist."

"She's very pleasant," Midge responded, and Jerry Mueller smiled.

Brian, though, again seemed preoccupied, and his farewell was brief. As she watched him leave the restaurant, Midge remembered Trent's comment about the managing editor's love for liquor. It seemed there was truth to it, which meant that Brian Vandervelt had personnel problems to add to his other difficulties. Evidently he preferred to handle them himself, at least in the case of Mike Stabler.

Were the terms of the late Horace Vandervelt's probationary period so severe that it was necessary to camouflage any deviation on the part of the staff, as well as to show a profit?

Midge waited until she was sure that Brian and the trooper had left the premises and then asked for her check, only to be told that it had been paid.

Once in the Volvo again, she stared for a long moment at the tempting vista of fields and mountains, thinking that it would be terrific to have someone to drive up into the Catskills with. Especially someone like Brian Vandervelt. Dear God, but he was attractive! And he had made it plain enough that he had come into the Maples solely to see her.

Whoa there, she warned herself. *Don't jump to conclusions too quickly!* Maybe Brian Vandervelt had merely been playing the part of a good employer.

Regardless, the thought now of either shopping or exploring the countryside alone had lost all attraction, and Midge decided to go into the office after all and finish up some work she had started previously.

The advertising department was empty. Midge sat down at her desk and studied the block of copy she had been working on the day before, when Trent had invited them all out for a drink. She had been dissatisfied with it then and still was, so she started redoing it, first editing it with a pencil.

She had nearly got one stubborn phrase just the way she wanted it when someone interrupted her concentration. "Hey, is Clayton back there in his office?"

She looked up to see Abe Weissman, the circulation manager, standing in the doorway. Weissman, short and fat, seemed to be deliberately accentuating the negative in the outfit he was wearing. A bold black-and-white-checked suit with a bright red shirt made him look like a human barrel. A diamond ring sparkled on his right hand, and he held a well-chewed cigar between two stubby fingers.

"No, Mr. Weissman," she told him with a smile. "Mr. Clayton isn't here."

Weissman scowled and muttered something under his breath, then strutted into the room, the scowl fading. "You holding down the fort by yourself?" he asked her.

"At the moment, yes."

"You think Clayton plans to come in today?"

"I think he was here earlier."

"Yeah, he was trying to get out of seeing me, that's what he was doing," Weissman grumbled. "Did he tell you about this special section he's dreaming up for Halloween week?"

"No."

"That figures," the circulation manager said bitterly. "He'll spring it on you just like he planned to spring it on me." Weissman pulled out Clem Thorne's desk chair and sat down, the chair squeaking in protest as he did so. "Handel put me wise," he went on. "Clayton had to talk it over with him to be sure the composing room could handle it, with everything else they've got to do. 'Trick or Treat,' he plans to call it, a whole damned advertising section with specials for the kids and anything else he can think up, doctored up with pumpkins and witches. It's got to be printed separately, then inserted into the paper the Thursday before Halloween, and distributed. That's a hell of an extra job for my department," he pointed out.

"Yes, I imagine it must be," she agreed.

Weissman scowled again. "He'll have you working your fingernails off writing extra copy," he warned her. "Clayton's smooth, but he's also ambitious as hell." Then he hoisted himself to his feet and smiled at her—an unexpectedly charming smile.

"You're okay," he said. "You're good. You can hack it and handle Trent Clayton, too. I'd bet money on it."

And with that he left her.

She was smiling as she got back to work. Weissman, though flamboyant and blustery, *was* likable. Finally, alone and without further interruption, she got her copy the way she wanted it and was leaving the building when she nearly collided with Wilson Strathmore, the business manager, at the front door.

Strathmore was a tall dignified man who had come from Virginia originally and had never quite lost his Southern accent. Now he straightened quickly and said, "I'm sorry, Miss Boardman. That was nearly a real collision!"

"Yes," she admitted. "It was my fault, though—I shouldn't plunge through doors so quickly."

"No matter," he shrugged, "we're both intact." Looking down at her, he smiled a tight-lipped smile. He had a long narrow face that emphasized his thinness, with a high forehead and sparse white hair. His pale eyes, behind rimless glasses of a long-outdated style, were exceedingly sharp. It occurred to her that Wilson Strathmore didn't miss much.

"We're happy to have you with us, Miss Boardman," he told her.

"Thank you. I'm happy to be here," she said

politely in return. They nodded to each other and she went on through the door.

As she walked across the street to her car she found herself thinking of Wilson Strathmore, Abe Weissman, Trent Clayton and the fourth department head, Fritz Handel, the mechanical superintendent. She had encountered Handel several times when Trent had suggested she take her finished copy out to the composing room herself, and had found him the least likable of the four men. He was short and wiry with watery blue eyes, distorted by extremely thick glasses, and a dour personality. He looked like a man who had worked hard physically most of his life and had been prematurely aged, if not also embittered because of this.

What a strange quartet they were, she thought now, each distinctly different both physically and in personality. Abe Weissman looked as if he belonged at a racetrack. Trent Clayton was right next door to Madison Avenue, whereas Wilson Strathmore gave the appearance of a professor in an Ivy League college and Fritz Handel looked like an aging longshoreman.

These were the four who stood to inherit the *Hudson River Valley Voice* if Brian failed the probation period, and she wondered how they felt about that. Even if they had a high regard for Brian Vandervelt, it would be only human to harbor a nagging hope that he might fail, giving them a once-in-a-lifetime chance of becoming enormously wealthy. Yet all four men seemed to have been working in accord with Brian, as if in a mutual desire to help him. Circulation had increased, the advertising revenue was up, the copies of the paper that she had seen were extremely good editorially. It looked as if everyone on the staff was cooperating—or was this purely a surface appearance?

She thought of the box of metal that had nearly struck Brian on the head yesterday. Had it really been an accident, she wondered. The idea chilled her, for Trent had said that had the box struck him Brian would very likely have been killed.

Greed was one of the oldest of human motives and men had killed for far, far less than the Vandervelt inheritance. Also, the entire possibility of a plot against Brian Vandervelt was made all the more diabolical by the fact that while he could *see* an enemy, he couldn't *hear* one.

Midge sat at the wheel of her car for a long time, staring across the street at the newspaper building and wishing that there was something she could do. She had never felt so powerless, yet when she got right down to it she had to admit she knew very little about this whole complicated matter involving Brian Vandervelt and his inheritance. She had barely skimmed the surface of it. Becky had said it would take a lawyer to explain it fully, and undoubtedly she was right.

Now Midge wondered how Brian himself felt about the situation. Did he realize his uncle had made him a pawn in a very dangerous game? Did this account, at least in part, for his aloofness, the way he seemed to keep himself apart from his staff—or was his attitude primarily due to his deafness?

She found herself wishing there were some way she could get to know him better, some way to find a chink in the wall that Brian, according to Becky, had always been able to build around himself. She suspected that the aftereffects of the accident had made him even better at wall building than he had been before. That and his uncle's subsequent death, the strange will. . . .

She shook her head. No wonder Brian seemed years older than his twin sister! He had been given a great deal on his plate these past few years—far too much, really. No wonder he sometimes was hostile.

Yet, she remembered, this morning at the Maples he hadn't been hostile at all. He had come into the restaurant because he wanted to talk to her, and now she wished fervently that the state trooper—his name, she remembered, was Jerry Mueller—had not interrupted them. He must have spotted Brian's white Jaguar parked outside; it was a distinctive car, to say the least, almost impossible not to recognize.

She wondered what Brian might have said to her had they been left alone, and was frustrated that there could be no answer to such conjecture unless he sought her out again. And, needless to say, there was no reason at all to think he might do so. In a sense he had smoothed over what had been a rough beginning to their relationship, or at least that seemed to have been his intention. But if this latest encounter had left any thread at all between them it was a tenuous one, too fragile for comfort; she only wished she could think of some way of strengthening it, some way of getting closer to Brian.

Closer. The vision the word evoked had a strange effect. Midge's cheeks stung as if she'd suddenly become sunburned, and she waited for a long moment before she started up the car engine. It was ridiculous to feel like this about a man she scarcely even knew, and she told herself she should be hoisting up all sorts of warning flags.

I'm only letting myself in for something, she admonished herself. *And I of all people should know better!* She also, after all, had decided to foreswear men for a long, long time—and for that matter had prided herself on her powers of resistance!

But it was one thing to resist the Trent Claytons of the world. It would be something else entirely, she knew, to try to resist a man like Brian Vandervelt.

Not, she reminded herself as she drove across town to the motel, *that I'm ever apt to have the chance to put the matter to test....*

CHAPTER FIVE

IT WAS A LONG WEEKEND. Midge went into Catskill and did some necessary shopping, took several solitary drives through the countryside, napped, watched television and on six different occasions tried to write a letter to Becky to tell her about Brian, tearing up each attempt and finally abandoning the effort entirely for the moment. By Monday morning she was more than ready to get back to work, and when Lucille Mueller, the receptionist, looked up with a smile and said, "Good morning, Miss Boardman," it gave her an unexpectedly satisfying sense of belonging.

She was still smiling as she walked into the office, but her pleasure was short-lived. Trent Clayton, stony faced, was waiting by her desk, and the minute she came into the room Ellen Brent quickly bent over her drawing board and Clem Thorne busied himself at the telephone, as if on cue.

"Come into my office, will you, Marjorie?" Trent asked her.

Puzzled, Midge followed him, but this time he did not sit down at his desk, nor did he suggest that she take a chair. Rather, once they were over the threshold he lowered his voice, ostensibly so Clem and Ellen couldn't hear him, and said, "Vandervelt told me at the staff conference he wants to see you as soon as you come in. He seems extremely angry. What's happened?''

She was honestly shocked. Her last meeting with Brian, Friday morning at the Maples, had been their single pleasant encounter. True, he had left in an unhappy frame of mind, but that had been because of Mike Stabler.

"I can't imagine," she answered truthfully.

"Frankly, neither can I," Trent admitted. "I even sat down and went over every word of the copy you wrote for last week's paper, just in case there was something offensive there and he'd got feedback on it. But there's nothing—nothing I can find, anyway. Don't you have any idea what may have ticked him off like this?''

"No idea at all."

"Then I guess the only thing to do is go and find out," Trent concluded reluctantly.

She nodded, and said with a confidence she definitely didn't feel, "Maybe it just seemed to you he's angry about something I've done. Whatever, this shouldn't take long."

"I hope not," Trent told her. "We have a special section with a Halloween theme coming up, and I want to get you working on it as quickly as possible."

Briefly she thought of Weissman; the circulation manager had been right. "I'll be back as soon as I can," she promised.

She walked rapidly down the corridor and into the city room. To her surprise, Mike Stabler was again at the desk near Brian Vandervelt's office. It seemed to her he looked even grayer than he had the last time she had seen him; but that, she conceded, could be pure imagination.

He said curtly, "He's with someone. You'll have to wait."

Almost simultaneously the door opened and Wilson Strathmore came out. The business manager seemed upset, as if something had shaken him badly, but he forced a tight smile when he saw her. "Go right in," he told her. "He's expecting you."

Brian Vandervelt was standing behind his desk wearing the same dark blue suit he had worn last Friday. It had the effect of making him seem particularly austere, and his gray eyes were icy.

He didn't waste time. "Sit down, please," he said, and she had barely complied when he handed her a square gray envelope. Her heart sank as she saw the writing—Becky's peculiarly curved handwriting— and the name in the upper lefthand corner, "Mrs. Timothy Ross," with the Menlo Park address.

She nearly groaned aloud. *Becky,* she moaned silently, *how could you?*

The disconcerting gray gaze chilled her. Brian said coldly, "I think you owe me an explanation. Why didn't you tell me you know my sister?"

His voice was like a whip, stinging her, and suddenly she, too, was angry.

"I might ask *you,*" she said just as coldly, "what makes you think you have the right to intercept my mail?"

"I didn't," he said shortly. "I usually come in here on Saturdays and check the mail, among other things, but I skipped last Saturday. So when I came in early this morning—I was the first to arrive—and there was an accumulation of weekend mail on Lucille's desk, I went through it to see if there was anything of importance for me. I could hardly fail to recognize my own sister's name; in fact, at first I thought the letter was for me."

"Well," Midge said. "At least you didn't open it!"

"I don't usually open other people's mail, Miss Boardman," he told her, and his jaw was tight, his eyes stormy, belying the studiously cold tone of his voice. "However, I don't owe you an explanation; you owe me one. Again, may I ask why you didn't tell me you know my sister?"

Midge closed her eyes briefly, desperately trying to think of what to say to him—and finally settled for the truth.

"I couldn't," she said simply.

"You couldn't?"

"That's right."

"Why?"

"You admitted yourself the other morning that you weren't very friendly the first time I came in here," she reminded him, "and that was an understatement, believe me! You made me feel like the ultimate intruder. Actually, I *had* bought the paper in Catskill and I'd seen the ad, and I began to think it might be interesting to apply for the job, so I did."

"But in the process you deliberately concealed the fact that you know my sister."

"I don't like the word 'conceal.' "

"Call it what you want," he said indifferently. "It amounts to the same thing."

His gray gaze was unwavering, and suddenly she couldn't bear his eyes upon her. She moved past his desk to the window at the rear of the room, staring out at the rippled surface of the Hudson.

"Why must you always make me feel like some

sort of criminal?'' she demanded. ''You never *ask* me anything—you automatically accuse me!'' .

There was no answer, but a second later she felt her shoulders gripped by two strong hands, and he swung her around to face him so abruptly that briefly she lost her balance, actually stumbling toward him so that had he not already been clutching her, she literally would have fallen into his arms.

She could feel the rough wool material of his suit coat against her cheek before she pulled back slightly, and for an instant his pulse beat seemed to become a part of her, communicating a surging force that swept through her like a tide, quite impossible to hold back. As if to emphasize this, she saw that he was breathing unevenly, and his eyes now were quicksilver fire, blazing with a mixture of anger and something even more turbulent that she couldn't quite define.

''Damn it,'' he said, his voice ragged, ''I can't hear you when you turn away from me like that! Don't you have the guts to say whatever you have to say to me directly, so I can at least try to understand you?''

''That's not fair!'' she retorted hotly, and watched his lips tighten until there was a thin white line around their edges. He was still gripping her shoulders and it seemed to her that his touch was actually scorching her. Then, as if propelled by a force beyond his control, he bent his head and his mouth took possession of hers, lips that had been thin and taut only a moment before melting into a fullness that sent a cascading onrush of desire coursing through Midge.

She swayed so that she was tight against him, thoroughly, tremendously aware of every contour of his masculine body. Then, even as she waited for him to progress beyond a kiss, he literally thrust her away from him and she found herself reaching for the windowsill, to steady herself.

"That," he said bitterly, "is the very last thing I intended to do. I'm sorry."

"You should be!" she retorted furiously. "Especially since you're so horribly sensitive about your hearing that you go to all sorts of lengths to conceal your problem—"

She broke off, feeling with dismay that now she'd definitely gone past the point of no return.

"Go on," he suggested ominously.

"No," she said.

"So you *are* a coward!" he challenged.

"No!"

"Then suppose you explain to me what sort of lengths you think I go to...."

She looked up at him, her own dark stormy eyes connecting with his shimmering blaze so that for a moment it was as if they had been locked together.

"You haven't told Becky," she said to him then.

She saw him swallow hard. Yet his anger was unabated; his face was pale with it.

"No," he agreed coldly, "I haven't told Becky. For my own very good reasons, I might add, which are absolutely none of your business. But the reason for your coming here under false pretenses *is* my business. Would you care to explain it?"

Midge tightened her own lips. "Is that a request or an order?" she asked him.

"I don't appreciate your delaying tactics," he answered icily. "All right, if you won't explain why you didn't want me to know you're acquainted with

my sister, perhaps you'll tell me why you came here
at all.''

"Doesn't it occur to you that I might have *wanted*
to leave New York and get a job in a smaller place?''
she demanded.

His gaze didn't falter, but she saw that his anger
was evaporating and something astonishingly like a
flash of amusement came to flicker in its place.
"You're a very poor liar,'' he told her.

She glared at him. "I'm not a liar!'' she retorted.
"I did want to get away from New York. However, if
you want me to leave, I'll leave!'' Even as she spoke
she was heading for the door; then, as her hand
touched the knob, his voice stopped her.

"Midge,'' he said quietly, "once again I didn't
hear you.'' And as she swung around, startled, "You
are Midge, aren't you?''

"Yes,'' she admitted.

"Then you're not just an acquaintance of my sister's, you're her best friend,'' he said. "So suppose
you come back and tell me—fairly slowly, please—
just what this is all about?''

To her chagrin, tears started to her eyes, but she
brushed them away angrily as she strode over to the
chair by his desk and sat down.

She began slowly, carefully, "I came here because
Becky asked me to.''

"You saw her in San Francisco?''

"Yes.''

"She wrote me that she was going to see you
again,'' he said. "She writes fairly frequently as a
rule, and ever since she was at Pine Haven and I was
at the Naval Academy I have known of her friend
Midge. Naturally, I didn't connect Marjorie Board-

man with Midge. Nor did I connect Pemberton Associates with the agency my brother-in-law worked for in New York—where, if I remember correctly, he met you and you introduced him to Becky.''

''It was Anderson-Brent Associates,'' she admitted. ''Now it's Anderson-Brent-Pemberton. Call that a lie if you like.''

''Shall we say a fib?'' He hesitated. ''Did Becky really ask you to come here?'' he asked then.

''Yes.''

''Why?''

''Because she's concerned about you.''

''Oh?''

''She wanted me to. . .to see you.''

He was silent for a moment, then he said, ''So you did, and evidently I aroused your curiosity to such an extent you decided the only way you could satisfy it was to come and get a job on my newspaper. Is that it?''

It was so close to the truth that she squirmed, and before she could answer he remarked, ''I've already told you you're a poor liar. You would also make a terrible poker player!''

Glancing at him swiftly, Midge saw his lips twitch, as if he were suppressing laughter. But, almost immediately he was so impassive again that she wondered if she had imagined this. He leaned back in his chair and, being studiously calm about it, asked, ''Why is Becky concerned about me?''

''Can't you figure that out for yourself?'' Midge said impatiently, literally casting discretion to the winds. ''She feels that everything has been. . .different with you since your accident, and she can't fathom what it is.''

"And now you, of course, know what the difference is," he stated flatly. "Have you told her?"

"No."

He raised his eyebrows, obviously surprised. Then he said slowly, "I admit I don't write to Becky as often as I should, but when I do I try to make things seem normal...."

"Evidently you succeed, for the most part," Midge told him. "Even so, there's still been something."

"I see. What else did Becky tell you about me?"

"I don't think you have the right to ask me that," she said firmly.

"I admit I don't, but I'm going to ask you anyway, because what you say to Becky is very important to me. Perhaps I can help you get started if I tell *you* what I think she must have told you about me. She certainly must have mentioned that I was in my last year at the Naval Academy and went to a weekend party at a beach cottage on the Chesapeake Bay. Right?"

"Yes."

"I'm sure she told you there was an explosion in which a girl was killed, and that although I evidently escaped without injury, my career was ended as far as the navy was concerned. Still right?"

"Yes."

"Could you take it from there?" he asked with a detachment she found astonishing.

Somehow talking to someone who could remain so unemotional about a very personal issue was especially difficult for Midge. She found herself stumbling over the words as she said, "Well, Becky told me that for a long time after the accident you didn't write to her, and she tried to reach you by phone but never managed to do so."

Briefly his calm wavered, and he was unable to entirely suppress the bitterness in his voice. "At that time I couldn't hear at all, so it wouldn't have done much good for me to answer a phone call. Even now I can only use a telephone that has special amplifying devices. So. . . ."

His words trailed off, and the bleakness on his face struck her like a physical blow. She bit her lip, just beginning to realize the loneliness that must have been part of his suffering; the loneliness that, for that matter, was still very much a part of his life.

She went on gently, "Becky didn't know why she couldn't get you on the phone, and your uncle's explanations didn't satisfy her. She was about to have Timmy, and later, with a new baby on her hands, there seemed no way she could get East to see what had happened to you for herself.

"Then you went to work for the paper. By that time Becky was wondering if you had been badly injured in the explosion, maybe blinded or crippled, and didn't want her to know. But there were pictures of you in the paper from time to time, and obviously there was nothing wrong with you—"

"Obviously," he cut in, the word thick with irony.

"Then your uncle died," Midge continued steadily, ignoring this, "and Becky said that under the terms of his will you had to meet some sort of test in running the newspaper if you were to inherit anything. I gather the test time is nearly up, and this has intensified her worry. She's wondering where you stand now, how you're making out, and she's also still sure that something is wrong. So she asked me to come and see you, and your aunt, after I got back East."

"Have you made any attempt to contact my aunt?"

"No. On my way in to Coxsackie I drove by your house, and I admit it daunted me. I couldn't possibly have walked up to the door and asked to see Mrs. Vandervelt without a prior appointment. That's why I decided to come to the paper instead."

"And," he said, "I turned you off."

"That's a rather blunt way of putting it."

"The truth has a way of being blunt."

He toyed with a letter opener on his desk. "I suppose you must think it odd for me to be so reluctant to tell Becky about my hearing."

"Yes, I do," Midge answered frankly.

"Well," he said, "so you can be honest after all! Okay, I admit that at first I was sensitive about it. Very sensitive. It took me a long time to accept the facts, and I was...resentful. Also, I didn't want pity—Becky's or anyone else's. That still holds."

He avoided her eyes, fingering the letter opener. "I was in the hospital for quite a while," he said, "and then there were sessions at clinics and with specialists to make certain nothing further could be done. After that there were lipreading classes, then the matter of finding the right type of hearing aids for my particular kind of loss." He did not look at her as he spoke, but she felt nevertheless as if the wave of his unhappiness was washing over her. "After the experts supposedly settled on the right type of aids there was quite a period of trying to get used to them, if one ever does entirely, before I was ready to try to face *anyone*. Maybe this seems strange to you, but facing Becky would have been the hardest thing of all, and I knew that if she found out what had happened to me she'd come here somehow, new baby or not.''

"Yes, I'm sure that's exactly what she would have done,'' Midge agreed.

"Well, I didn't want to see her,'' he admitted, "and I'll confess that it would still be very difficult for me. Even now, I'm not sure I could stand the look on her face when she found out I'm deaf. But since my uncle's death there have been other, entirely different reasons why I didn't want Becky to come to Coxsackie. They are *my* reasons, and I don't intend to spell them out to you, but they are valid, believe me.''

Putting the letter opener back on the blotter, he continued thoughtfully, "For a long time, when we were kids, Becky and I were like two small ships adrift in an otherwise empty sea, so we became very close. We never knew many people our own age here in Coxsackie. We didn't come here until we were ten, and then we both were sent away to school. During summers we depended upon each other for the most part. I did get to know Jerry Mueller, the state trooper you met, and he still is my closest friend, but Becky never had that much contact with anyone around here, so it hasn't been too hard to keep my secret from her. The only person I know who keeps in touch with Becky is my Aunt Maude, and she's a romantic at heart. It wasn't too hard to sell her on the idea of not letting Becky know about my hearing until the time came when I could tell her myself, in my own way. Incidentally, I would prefer that you don't call on Aunt Maude. She's not too well, and she keeps very much to herself."

"I have no intention of intruding," Midge said coldly.

"I didn't intend to imply that you did," he answered, equally cool. "I also know that I can't censor whatever you decide to write Becky, and I'm well aware that there is no reason why you should defer to my wishes. I can only say that if you are as fond of Becky as you've always seemed to be, I wish you'd try to understand that just now I'm trying to keep her away from here for her own sake. However, you've made me realize that I am not being fair to her, and I will do something about it as soon as possible. Perhaps a family reunion at Thanksgiving."

"And you're asking me not to say anything to Becky in the meantime?"

"I haven't the right to ask favors of you," he admitted flatly. "I can only ask you to consider my request, and then to use your own discretion."

"Very well," she told him, "I shall do that."

She stood, to find that her knees were wobbling. Trying to be very calm about this, she said, "I suppose you'll want my resignation."

"Not unless you wish to submit it," he said surprisingly. "As you have pointed out, there was a bona fide job vacancy here, you had more than enough experience to fill it, and your initial work has been excellent. Also, you mentioned earlier that you and Trent Clayton have made what amounts to a three-month contract, though perhaps not a formal one.

"Whether you stay or leave, Midge," Brian Vandervelt told her, "is entirely up to you."

MIDGE WAS TREMBLING as she walked back down the corridor to the advertising department. Once in the office, she felt her agitation must be so apparent that she was glad Clem was talking on the telephone, his head averted, and Ellen seemed totally absorbed in a layout.

It took effort to sit down at her desk and put paper in the typewriter, and it didn't help when almost immediately Trent appeared at her shoulder to ask, "How did it go?"

"All right," she said, forcing herself to sound casual. "It was purely a personal matter."

Trent's look was skeptical, but he merely turned on his heel and went back into his office without further comment. Shortly afterward he called her in to discuss the special Halloween section and the copy he wanted her to do for it, but he did not again refer to Brian Vandervelt.

Abe Weissman had been right: by the end of the day Midge *did* feel as if she had typed her fingernails off. She took time only to snatch a milk shake at lunch, and it was not until she got back to the motel that night that she had a chance to read the letter from Becky that Brian Vandervelt had intercepted.

Midge, I never should have sent you up there in the first place. As you know, I've been terribly worried about you, too, especially since you went and got a job on the paper.

There is a lot of money involved here, and much as it shocks me to think about it, I realize that there are people who will do anything for money. I don't really know any of the department heads who stand to inherit if Brian fails.

Maybe I met them back in the days when once in a while Uncle Horace would take us down to see the paper go to press—I guess he thought he was giving us a big thrill. I wouldn't know any of them today, though, if I fell over them, so when it comes to trying to single out the villains from the heroes I'm helpless.

You didn't tell me where you were living, so I'll have to send this to the paper. I hope by now you have seen enough of Brian that you can tell me a little bit more about him, and that's all I'm asking for. In other words—I wish you'd get out of there!

In a couple of weeks it will be two years since Uncle Horace died. Whatever is going to happen, *if* anything is going to happen, will have to happen by then. It's bad enough to have my twin brother in the middle of this, but I don't want my best friend involved, too. Also, there is absolutely nothing you can do about it, any more than I can.

Brian must be aware of the whole situation. He has always been a very sharp person, so I am just going to have to assume that he still is and can take care of himself.

As for you, Midge, please go back to the city and forgive me for disrupting your life in the first place. Just write and tell me what you can about him.

Write me and tell me what you can about him.

It seemed like such a simple request, and yet it was so incredibly difficult. Midge knew now that she could not possibly tell Becky of Brian's deafness. To

do so would be wrong; this she felt strongly. He
deserved the opportunity to explain everything to
his sister himself, and though in her opinion that was
something he should have attended to long ago, she
could understand his reluctance. Becky's pity, she
sensed, would be almost harder for him to face than
his own affliction.

Well, he had indicated that as soon as possible he
was going to tell Becky; he had admitted that Midge
had made him see the necessity of doing so without
waiting any longer than he had to because of something that had nothing to do with his own physical
problem. Now she felt she had to accept his word.
Whatever criticism she might have of Brian Vandervelt's attitude, he was a person, she found herself
thinking, in whom one could put total faith, total
trust. . . .

Midge paused to make herself a cup of instant coffee, still not really content to leave matters alone; yet
she realized that anything more she might do just
now would come under the heading of rank interfer-
ence. Later, though, there was a part she certainly
could play. She would write Becky her own version
of the story, after Brian made his announcement, for
she felt sure there were all sorts of things he would
never tell his sister.

Becky should know without any doubt at all that
Brian's deafness had in no way diminished him as a
person. Midge suspected that actually it had made
him even stronger in character, and she had the conviction that he would be able to cope with just about
anything that might come his way, with very little
help. Brian, in fact, had already been through so
much that she doubted there was anything that would

really throw him. Though just briefly he had shown a trace of bitterness in talking to her today, she had to admire the overall manner in which he had handled the terrible blow that had been dealt him. She had to admire his strength.

Yes, she thought, surely Becky should be told that her brother was a total man in every sense of the word, overwhelmingly attractive, extremely competent, with a commendable loyalty to his employees and his friends. He had demonstrated this both in affirming his friendship for Jerry Mueller and in so quickly going to Mike Stabler's rescue for what was clearly not the first time. Becky should know that under no circumstances could her brother be considered helpless, and that he was someone of whom she should be very, very proud.

As she stirred powdered creamer into her coffee, Midge reflected that there was something else she must also make Becky understand at some point. It was ironic, true, but she liked working for the *Valley Voice*, in fact she liked it very much and had no desire at the moment to go back to the city.

The special Halloween section she was working on, for example, was a challenge, strange though that might seem to the people who had known her on Madison Avenue. She was being given a chance to explore her own talents in her work on it, to be as innovative as she wished to be.

Also, it would raise quite some havoc with the advertising schedule were she to give up her job now, with or without Brian Vandervelt's approval. She could imagine Trent's consternation if she walked in and handed him her resignation at this point!

But regardless of that, the fact was that she didn't want to give the job up. She *wanted* to stay for her three months. She wanted to prove herself, and after today's "exposé" there was no reason why Brian Vandervelt should be concerned with her or she with him.

She fought back the memory of his kiss, and of the chaotic moment when in far too true a sense she had been rendered helpless by the power of an attraction that she tried to dismiss now as a totally chemical reaction on both their parts; something, she told herself firmly, that would not happen again. For that matter, she felt reasonably sure that Brian himself did not intend to let it happen again. He had made it very clear at the end of their session today that he didn't give a damn whether she stayed or left. But now she became determined not to give him what she suspected would be the real satisfaction of having her quit. She wasn't going to let him force her to do something she didn't want to do that easily!

Her course, it seemed to her, was obvious. She would stay at the motel, which was warm and comfortable, she would work at the paper, and from now on she'd leave town on the weekends and go to New York, or to visit friends in Boston, or somewhere, so that there would at least be a temporary respite from the thought of Brian Vandervelt's disturbing, impelling presence.

Meanwhile, there was just one thing that remained to be done. She did have to write Becky something, and she did so after another solitary dinner at the Maples, keeping the letter short by stating at the beginning that she had put in a full day of copy-writing and was tired.

Actually, though, I love it. I've committed myself to staying three months, Becky, and find there's a definite plus to it. It's clearing out all my own cobwebs. When I leave I'll be able to make an entirely fresh start, and I feel sure it will be a good one.

In other words, I don't *want* to leave Coxsackie, darling, and stop worrying about either your brother or me. You're being melodramatic! Although our chemistries don't seem to gibe particularly well, your brother is a very self-assured man, and he certainly is in complete command of himself. I am sure he is fully aware of any "situation" that exists, and he is more than able to cope with anything that may come up. For that matter, the paper is doing extremely well, and the four department heads seem to be working in perfect harmony with Brian. I don't think you have a thing to worry about.

For myself, I don't want to presume on my friendship with you where your brother is involved. I would much rather just keep things going in my own way. I had thought of calling on your aunt, but I understand she has become something of a recluse, and quite frankly I've avoided it. There still is something about the Vandervelt mansion that I find awesome.

I am living at the Prescotts' motel, and since I only plan to be here till January I'm not going to bother trying to get an apartment in the area. So write to me here.

BY THE TIME the paper went to press on Thursday Midge had put in the hardest workweek of her life. She had written copy for the regular edition plus a

major part of the "Trick or Treat" section that
would be coming up toward Halloween. Although
Trent Clayton tended to conceal his own drive he
could be very demanding, and there were moments
during the week when Midge wondered if he was taking out his frustration on her because she had refused
his first invitation to dinner and clearly wasn't
responsive to him, as he'd made it plain he would
like.

Although with deadlines passed his approbation
made up for the long wearying hours she had put in,
still she was exhausted. She knew it wasn't rest she
needed, however, as much as a change of pace, good
company. When Trent suggested an after-work drink
she was tempted to say yes, but knowing very well it
would only lead to more than she wanted to handle
just now, she invented a quick excuse.

After freshening up at the motel, she drove into
Catskill, did a little shopping, ate in a restaurant not
nearly as good as the Maples, then went to an indifferent movie. It was nearly eleven when she left Catskill, opting to drive back along the Athens road. A
somewhat longer route, it was nevertheless the more
peaceful one, lit tonight by a benevolent moon.
Finally she felt herself relaxing.

She slowed almost involuntarily as she neared the
Vandervelt mansion, then at the last moment pulled
over to the side of the road and parked well off the
edge, staring at the huge old house. Silhouetted
against the moon-washed sky, it was like an illustra-
tion on a Gothic novel; there was an eeriness about it
that made her shiver.

A few dim lights were visible on the first floor, but
everything above it was in darkness, and she won-

dered which of what must be a vast number of rooms
was Brian's. For that matter, she wondered what part
of the mansion Maude Vandervelt might be in right
now. Becky had also mentioned servants, a man and
his wife: did they live in the house, or were there
separate quarters somewhere on the grounds?

It was impossible not to be curious, and she wished
she could summon up the nerve to call on Maude
Vandervelt despite Brian's request. But she had the
feeling that if she were to do so he would be sufficiently annoyed to put an end to her working for the
Valley Voice.

She was about to start the car up again when in her
rearview mirror she saw headlights bearing down on
her at a frightening speed. A white car veered close to
her side, passing her, then, its brakes screeching,
pulled diagonally in front of her, blocking her way.

Her pulse began to hammer. True, the driver of the
car obviously was an expert, but the approach had
been much too close for comfort. For a moment she
had thought he was about to slice off the side of her
car. Also, although she was not about to panic, it was
hardly pleasant to think of facing a possibly crazy
stranger out on this lonely road under the circumstances. Then she recognized the Jaguar and
stared incredulously as Brian Vandervelt got out and
walked over to her.

She had switched on her headlights, and now, as he
was caught in their light, she saw the rage etched on
his face; his gray eyes seemed to glitter. As he came
to the side of the car the odor of whiskey was strong
on his breath, and she shrank away from him.

Before she knew what he intended doing he had
flung the door of the car open and with pure brutal

strength dragged her out to stand beside him. Then, as she started to tremble, overwhelmingly aware of her own weakness in comparison to his frightening physical power, he demanded harshly, "What the hell are you doing here?"

For a moment she could not speak, and when she did so her words seemed to run one into the other. "I was driving home," she said, her teeth chattering, "and I just stopped for a moment."

He glared down at her. "What?" he asked.

She shuddered but forced herself to speak more distinctly. "I said I just stopped."

"You mean you just decided to snoop, don't you?" he grated. "Look, I can't force you to leave town, although I'll admit I could make it uncomfortable enough for you that you might want to do so. But I'm damned if I'm going to have you spying on me!"

Now the words came clear, cool, distinct. "You flatter yourself," she said.

"Do I?"

"You're damned right you do!" she snapped, and started to get back into the car, but in an instant his restraining arm forestalled her.

"Little bitch!" he hissed. "Do you really expect me to believe you are a *friend* of Becky's? What are you here for, anyway? Whose game are you playing? Trent Clayton's?"

She stared at him, astounded, but before she could speak he said, "I'll wipe that innocent look off your face!" Then in a terrifying second he seemed to loom over her, and as his hands grasped her shoulders she had the horrible feeling that they were going to move to her throat, that he was going to choke her.

But instead he clutched her closer, his hands moving to clasp her waist and draw her to him. His mouth found hers, crushing her lips against her teeth so that she wanted to cry out but couldn't, because he was probing deeper, his tongue demanding, possessing, as she tried to struggle against him.

It was a pagan kiss, hot, intense. She felt as if she were being devoured by his fervor; his body was so close that the potent maleness she'd been aware of ever since she'd first seen him now became a tangible thing. It was as if he had set her on fire; she could feel the glowing coals of her own mounting desire burst into a series of swift darting flames that turned any logic she might have mustered to ashes, making of her resistance a weak and flimsy thing.

She couldn't fight him. Though she despised herself for it, she could not keep her lips from meeting his willingly. And while she could not have said at precisely what point the tempo between them changed, there came a moment when what surely had begun as an outraged desire to vindicate on his part merged into something entirely different and far more treacherous: a forging, searing, mounting passion.

Once again it was he who stopped it, and she could only begin to appreciate the effort it cost him. He held her away from him, staring at her through the moonlight, his eyes seeming dark now rather than quicksilver, his face very white.

"I seem to have said this before," he told her, the words coming raggedly, "but I *am* sorry!"

Scalding tears that stemmed from a mixture of pain, frustration and rage came to fill her eyes. "Sorry?" she echoed scathingly. "You don't know what it is to be sorry! You've accused me of all sorts of things. Well, suppose I ask you what *you're* trying to do? Why are you so anxious for me not to see your aunt? Does it involve Becky? Are you trying to cheat Becky out of her rightful inheritance?''

He stepped back as quickly as if she had slapped him, staring at her without responding, and though she would have given anything to retract her words the instant she spoke them, she flung out impulsively, ''What's the matter—didn't you hear me? Or is it that you just don't want to listen?''

His voice coil tight, he said softly, ''Yes, I heard you. And I'll try to remember that you're speaking out of an anger to which you're fully entitled.''

With this he turned his back on her and went over to the Jaguar. It was a tellingly effective action, for she knew that even were she to call out to him he really wouldn't hear her now. He had removed himself from all possible communication.

As she watched, he swung the white car around and drove up the driveway that led to the mansion, and she heard the sound of his brakes as he came to a quick stop. A moment later the thud of a closing door echoed in the distance between them, and she felt as if it had been slammed on her own heart, the hurt was that intense.

CHAPTER SIX

IT WAS A LONG TIME before Midge could settle down, and when she finally drifted into sleep it was a restless sleep, filled with dreams that verged on nightmares. She awoke early in the morning, tired and irritable and wishing this were a working day rather than a Friday, for she really had nothing to do at the office: she had finished all the copy she'd been working on, so there was no point in going in. And beyond that she faced an empty weekend.

She had no wish to go back to New York so soon. She thought of calling a friend in Boston and suggesting they get together, but this didn't appeal, either. The memory of her blazing encounter with Brian Vandervelt was too much on her mind, and it became worse with each passing hour. She didn't see how she could possibly return to the paper come Monday and risk facing him again.

The weather was beautiful, so beautiful that it only underlined the misery of her own mood because there was no one to share it with, and she had never felt more alone. She spent much of the weekend exploring the Albany area, for the state capital was but a short drive from Coxsackie. She found that the city itself had been founded in 1624 by French-speaking Walloons from Holland, as well as a number of Scots, Germans, Norwegians and Danes, but the

Dutch emphasis held, for the area at the time had been under the patroonship of Kiliaen Van Rensselaer. Idly she wondered if he might be an ancestor of Brian's.

Albany, she also discovered, was literally an inland seaport, with a full mile of dock wall built to accommodate oceangoing ships. She had already wondered at the huge freighters she had seen passing by Coxsackie, which was some twenty miles downriver, and had been surprised that the Hudson was capable of handling this sort of navigation so far from its mouth.

She took time to visit Cherry Hill, which had been in the Van Rensselaer family until the early 1960s. The charming old residence still contained many of the original furnishings, china, silver, documents and family portraits. She found herself searching for cool gray eyes and thick smooth blond hair in the portraits, and decided, this on Sunday afternoon, that she'd better get out in the fresh air and take a walk in the sun to try to banish the ever present and very live ghost of Brian Vandervelt from her consciousness!

By the time she got back to the Maples she felt considerably more in control of herself. She had come to the conclusion that the only possible course of action was to go to the office as usual the following morning—and hope that she wouldn't encounter Brian Vandervelt for a while at least. If she did, she promised herself, she would match his mood, which was certain to be a cool one.

Her newfound confidence was short-lived, though, when she opened the door of her motel unit, then stopped short, appalled.

The television set had been pulled out so that it

faced her squarely as she stood in the doorway. Across the screen had been painted a crude red cross, its dripping edges horribly reminiscent of blood. A note on top of the set, written on what looked like common typing paper and held down by an ashtray, was crudely lettered with the same red marker.

"GET OUT WHILE YOU STILL CAN," it warned.

Midge sat down on the edge of the bed, both her knees and her hands shaking. It took a full moment to begin to think coherently again, and first she wondered how anyone had gained entrance to the unit. But a little investigation determined that. The bathroom window, which faced toward the back of the motel, was wide open. Someone had cut through the screen, pushed it up and climbed in, certainly without being seen by Mrs. Prescott or anyone else.

Still wobbly, Midge moistened a towel and started to scrub the television screen. Fortunately the red stuff was washable, and she worked at getting it off until the job was done. It was only then that she sat down again, drew a long breath and reached for the Coxsackie phone book.

As she flicked through the pages she told herself that the Vandervelts probably had a private number, but to her surprise they were listed, although the phone was still under Horace Vandervelt's name.

She put through a call, and her pulse began to hammer all over again when she heard the phone start ringing at the other end of the line. A woman answered on the third ring. "Vandervelt residence," she said primly, and Midge decided this was probably the elderly housekeeper Becky had mentioned.

It took all her willpower to keep her voice steady. "May I speak to Mr. Brian Vandervelt, please."

"Mr. Vandervelt's not in."

"Do you know where he might be reached?"

"He's over at the newspaper office." The information was volunteered cheerfully enough. "Would you like to leave a message?"

"No, thank you," Midge said. "I'll contact him later."

She hung up the receiver, annoyed to find that her fingers were still trembling.

So—he was working on a Sunday afternoon.

She lost no time about it. She folded the red-lettered message, put it in her handbag, then marched out to her car and drove across to the village and down to the office. It was only as she pulled into the parking lot, stopping next to the white Jaguar, the only other car in the lot, that she realized this might not be the most sensible move in the world.

But that was not about to stop her.

Midge did not waste time today pausing to knock. She walked right in on him, and when he failed to look up she literally pounded on the desk.

The vibration reached him. He at once stood, quickly smoothing back his hair in the gesture that, she knew now, meant he was turning on the hearing aids.

"Midge!" he said, and astonishingly he seemed glad to see her. "I tried to reach you by phone all day Friday, then I stopped at the motel, but Mrs. Prescott said you'd gone sight-seeing."

"So you left a message, didn't you?" she accused him. She took the red-lettered note out of her handbag, unfolded it and tossed it on the desk in front of him.

He picked it up and frowned as he read it. "Where did you find this?" he asked her.

"Don't you remember where you put it?"

He stared at her, the color literally seeming to drain from his face. "Do you seriously believe I had anything to do with this?" he demanded.

"Who else?" she asked him coldly. "You're the only person who would like to see me leave Cox-sackie. Let's say you have a vested interest in scaring me off."

"I? You're jumping to conclusions when you say that."

"Am I? Well, it seems to me that you jumped to quite a few conclusions the other night," she told him, and nearly put a hand to her lips. They still felt bruised from the savagery of his kiss.

"I was trying to get in touch with you to apologize for my behavior the other night," he said steadily. "I'm sorry, very sorry, about what happened."

"If it's any consolation to you, I have a beautiful bruise on my wrist, among other places, and it aches like the devil," she replied tautly.

She pulled back her sleeve, then shrank from the misery in his gray eyes as he stared at the place she indicated. Speaking carefully, as if it were an effort to keep control, he said, "Perhaps you can imagine how that makes me feel."

"I can't imagine how anything makes you feel," she retorted. "I don't think you feel things the way most people do."

Briefly the gray eyes sparked with an anger quickly

suppressed. "You seem to be saying," he told her, "that my...affliction...has caused me to become demented. Deranged to the point of leaving a crazy threatening note like this," he added, flicking the red-lettered paper contemptuously.

"I don't think this has anything to do with your deafness," she said stormily. "It's entirely to do with you. You're...."

"What am I, Midge?" he challenged.

"Arrogant, autocratic, opinionated," she began, and to her surprise he smiled faintly.

"No wonder you're such a good copywriter," he said irrelevantly. "All right, suppose I'm all those things you list, and a few more. I don't think I'm childish in the bargain, and this—" again his scorn was directed at the piece of paper "—falls under the heading of a stupid prank. If we were a bit closer to Halloween I'd go so far as to call it a Halloween prank. At that, maybe someone's getting ahead of himself a bit. Where did you find it? On your desk?"

"No," she said, "in my motel room, on top of the TV. And someone went to the trouble of cutting a screen and climbing through the bathroom window to leave it there."

His eyebrows arched upward disbelievingly. "That doesn't make sense," he observed. "Did you talk to Mrs. Prescott about this? Did she see anyone hanging around the place?"

"I haven't spoken to her yet," Midge admitted. "It seemed to me she would have left a note for me to get in touch with her if she'd seen anyone or knew anything about this. I will speak to her, but I think it will come as a total surprise to her. Quite an unpleasant surprise, I'm sure, since it's her premises, after all, that have been violated. I found the note and the face on the TV all smeared with red stuff that looked like blood when I got back from Albany this afternoon. I tried to phone you—"

Again that echo of a smile flickered across his face. "Because I was your prime suspect, eh?"

"Yes," she confessed, her cheeks beginning to flame. "I couldn't think of anyone else."

"Neither can I," he said, "which makes it something of a problem. I can't think of any reason for anyone wanting you to leave Coxsackie. You're not involved in the Vandervelt affairs, and certainly anyone who's concerned with them would realize that. Nevertheless, when someone has gone to the trouble of climbing through a back window to deliver his message I think we have to consider it a definite threat; and I can speak with authority on that subject because I've been living with threats for quite some time myself."

"Oh?"

He shrugged. "I'm not sure just how much you really know about my uncle's will, but suffice it to say that if I died before the first of November quite a few people would stand to benefit substantially who wouldn't if I were alive to inherit. I'm not so crass as to say I seriously believe any of them would try to do away with me for the sake of money, but stranger things have happened, as we all know. So when something occurs like that box full of metal that nearly hit me on the head the other day in the composing room, I do tend to wonder whether it was by accident or design."

She stared at him, her eyes wide, her anger toward him evaporating. "Do you think somebody was trying to kill you the other day?'' she demanded.

"No," he said. "I think it was an accident, and so does Fritz Handel, whom I trust implicitly. Nevertheless, a situation like this creates an uneasy environment, to say the least. I admit it keeps me on edge. One tends to become paranoid."

Midge felt her throat constrict with her fear for him. True, he was extremely capable, but he was also deaf, and so much of the time he seemed to be alone. It would be relatively easy to arrange an "accident" when a person was alone, and that much easier when that person was also deaf.

He was watching her curiously. Now he asked, "What is it?"

"Nothing, really," she hedged, but then could not resist saying, "I know you're not going to like my suggesting this, but shouldn't there be someone with you until this. . .this probationary period involving the will is up?"

Again he raised his eyebrows, but this time there was pure irony in his expression. "Are you saying you think I need a keeper?" he demanded softly.

"No. I'm just saying that there should be someone. . . ."

"Someone who can hear?" he finished for her.

She tightened her lips. "Look," she told him, "I'm sorry I mentioned it."

"Don't be," he said, but the irony was still there in his tone. "I appreciate your concern."

"Brian. . . ."

It was the first time she had called him by his given name, and she saw that this fact registered with him. There was very little, she decided, that *didn't* register with him, and at times that posed difficulties.

"Let's get back to your message," he said. "I'm going to turn this note over to Jerry Mueller."

"All right."

"I'm glad you agree. Meantime, tell Mrs. Prescott about it. I think it might be wise for her to move you to another unit."

"Oh, come," she protested.

"I'm serious, Midge. Whether you choose to believe it or not, I had nothing to do with this, and I still can't understand why someone should have gone to such trouble to do something so essentially juvenile. Yet someone did do it—and must have had some sort of motive."

He surveyed her carefully. "You're a very attractive girl," he said, while she felt herself flushing under his scrutiny. "There are a lot of weird people in the world; maybe one of them has become infatuated with you, just seeing you around town, and this is his way of showing it. Because we may be dealing with a situation like that, I want you to promise me to be careful."

"Very well," she said, feeling as if she'd been relegated to the status of a schoolgirl, "I will be."

"I'm going to call Mrs. Prescott myself and talk to her about this," he added, "and we'll see what Jerry suggests, as well. I'll get back to you about it by phone later tonight—or perhaps you could come in a few minutes early and we'll talk here in the morning."

"Very well."

Brian stood towering over her, and as always she was intensely aware of the sheer magnetism of his physical presence. He was wearing a cream-colored sweater and dark brown corduroy slacks, and both

.emphasized his broad shoulders and his strong muscular thighs. Midge, remembering entirely too well how it felt to be pressed against both those shoulders and those thighs, could feel her palms growing damp.

Much of the time Brian seemed so cool, so aloof; yet she was deeply certain that he wasn't really cool at all. Hadn't he already given her evidence that there were distinctly passionate depths to his nature?

She only wished that right now he would forget about everything except the fact that at this moment they were alone together. She wished he would take her in his arms, and at the mere thought she shuddered so that he asked, "What is it, Midge?"

"Nothing," she said quickly. "I think I'd better be going."

"I'll walk you to your car," he offered unexpectedly.

"That's not necessary." She was not at all sure she could bear much more of his company just now.

To her surprise he smiled, and she caught her breath because he looked so very much younger when he smiled like this. The weariness in his face seemed to dissolve, and she discovered that the gray eyes were not always glacial, that in fact they could be quite warm.

Still, there was a kind of sadness to his smile that tugged at her already overburdened heart as he said gently, "I know it isn't necessary, but I don't want you wandering around the streets by yourself just now. Midge...."

She could feel her pulse thumping. "Yes?"

"About the other night—"

"There's really no need to go into it," she told him stiffly.

"I think there is," he corrected her. "I can't blame you for anything you might think after the way I behaved."

"You were drunk," she said flatly.

"No," he told her gravely, "I wasn't drunk. Perhaps it would have been better if I had been, because then I could use intoxication as an excuse. It happens that on Thursday nights the Valley Men's Club has its dinner meetings. Uncle Horace organized the club, he was president, and when he died they elected me in his stead.

"Frankly, it's hell every Thursday. I can seldom understand half of what people are saying, especially when we have a speaker, and it's quite a strain. This past Thursday I came out with a mammoth headache, and I felt so uptight I stopped and had a drink on the way home. It was just one drink, but I'm sure I must have seemed to you to reek of liquor."

"Yes," she admitted, "you did."

"Well, as it happened I was sober. Sober, but pretty well exhausted, and with a throbbing head that made me feel as if someone was pounding me with a hammer. When I saw your car parked across from the house it did something to me. I'll admit I was furious. You haven't exactly leveled with me from the very beginning, you know."

"I realize that."

"Well, when I saw your car I assumed you were deliberately being defiant, snooping where you had no business to snoop. I suppose I felt you were Becky's spy—and that galled me because I couldn't believe Becky would have intended for you to go where you weren't wanted."

This hurt. It hurt so much it would have been very

easy for the tears to come, but Midge was determined not to cry in front of him if she could possibly help it.

Her voice unsteady, she admitted, "I suppose I've been going where I wasn't wanted ever since I came to Coxsackie."

"Perhaps you have," he said, which didn't make her feel any better. "I realize it was Becky who got you started on all this, but I guess Thursday I thought your own curiosity had taken off from the point where Becky, if she had any sense, would have had you stop."

He sighed. "I can't blame Becky," he went on. "I suppose it's my own damned fault because I've been trying to keep her out of the picture—and my Aunt Maude, too, as much as possible—until this business of the will is settled... just in case there *is* someone around us who has been motivated by the prospect of a big inheritance to do things I don't even like to consider.

"What I did resent Thursday, though, was the idea that you were poking around on your own, and I suppose I have to admit that of late I've been developing a nasty suspicious nature. If I could hear what's going on around me it might be different. As it is...."

He caught himself up short, then went on, without any particular intonation, "That sounds pretty self-pitying, doesn't it? I don't mean it that way, and I think we've said enough about the whole thing anyhow. Again, I apologize for Thursday night."

After a moment, when she didn't answer, he asked, "Did you say something?"

"No."

"I thought I might have missed it."

"No," she said, then added, "Should I say something?"

His lips twisted. "You might tell me whether or not you accept my apology," he suggested.

It surprised her that this mattered to him, yet clearly it did. She said, almost formally, "Yes, I accept your apology, and I'd like to say that I'm sorry myself for some of the rather miserable things I've said to you."

"Very well." He seemed satisfied with her answer. "Shall we say that at this point we're even?"

She nodded, not trusting herself to speak, because there was entirely too much danger of telling him that they weren't even at all. No, even though he seemed completely unaware of it, she was entirely too much in his power.

I've fallen in love with him, she thought, *absolutely incredible though that is!* How could anyone fall in love so quickly, and so completely?

Now he came around the desk and asked, crooking an elbow, "Ready to go?"

There was a sense of companionship between them Midge wouldn't have believed possible as they walked arm and arm down the corridor and out into the pale amethyst twilight. There was also the scent of burning wood in the air: someone had made a fire on his hearth, and Midge sniffed appreciatively.

She didn't try to speak to Brian because she knew it would be unlikely he could hear her, nor in this dim light could he read her lips. But there was a warmth to the silence between them; just now it created no chasm.

At the car he said, "Look . . . please take care, will you! Talk to Mrs. Prescott, and if you go out to get

something to eat, go straight to the Maples and
straight back, will you?''

She nodded affirmatively.

He bent toward her, and now his kiss was so tender, so brief yet ultimately expressive, that she was
stunned by it.

She couldn't hold back the tears that came to fill
her eyes, and once she turned the corner onto Main
Street she pulled over to the curb because just now
her visibility was decidedly limited.

As she wiped her eyes with a handkerchief that
soon became sodden, she found it difficult to believe
that something like this could have happened in the
space of a couple of weeks.

Oh, Becky, Becky, she thought, *whatever did you
do when you persuaded me to come to Coxsackie!*

MRS. PRESCOTT was appalled. She called her husband, who worked at a concrete plant in nearby Ra-
vena, and he came to listen, perplexed, to Midge's
story. At the conclusion of it they agreed that she
should move to a unit closer to their own quarters.

''Nothing like this has ever happened to us before,'' Mrs. Prescott complained, her usually cheerful motherly face perturbed.

A corridor led from the unit chosen for Midge to
the motel lobby, and now Mrs. Prescott ushered her
through a connecting door into her own, pleasantly
furnished living room. ''You can come to us directly,
without going outdoors at all,'' she said. ''And I
want you to have your supper here with us tonight.''

''Please,'' Midge protested. ''That's not necessary. I don't think there's the slightest chance that
whoever left the note is going to come back here. It's

like anonymous letters—the kind of people who resort to such things don't have much basic courage.''

"I suppose you're right,'' Mrs. Prescott conceded, but clearly she was still doubtful. "I told Brian Vandervelt you were going to have supper with us, though, and he was very pleased about it. Anyway, we'd like to have you, Midge.''

The incident had put them on a first-name basis, Mrs. Prescott insisting that Midge call her Dora and her husband Bob.

"Well, I'd like to join you,'' she said now.

"We have a daughter about your age,'' Bob Prescott told her. "She's married, lives down in Georgia, so we don't get to see much of her.''

They had gone from the living room into a bright yellow-and-white kitchen, and Mrs. Prescott said, "Bob, pour us out a glass of wine while I get things ready. It will do our digestion good.''

She turned to Midge. "Yes,'' she went on, "our daughter was about the same age as Brian Vandervelt and his twin, and she was in the same class at school as Grace De Witt, the girl Brian was going to marry. When Grace got to high-school age, though, her folks sent her away to private school. Sort of a finishing school, I guess you'd say. After that she and our Jenny never saw much of each other. If you ask me, things went to Grace's head—''

"Mother,'' Bob Prescott said warningly.

"Well, it's the truth,'' Mrs. Prescott affirmed. "She ditched him, you know.''

"Brian Vandervelt?'' Midge asked.

"Yes. They were to be married when he graduated from Annapolis, but of course his accident changed all that. The wedding had to be postponed—post-

poned indefinitely, they said at the time. And once
Grace found out Brian was going to be deaf she ran
off with a man from Albany. He's lots older than she
is...wealthy, though. But I heard the other day
they're not doing so well together."

"They live here?" Midge asked.

"They live the other side of Albany," Mrs. Prescott said. "Winters, they spend quite a bit of time
away...Florida, other places. Like I say, he's
older."

So, to add to everything else that happened to him,
Brian had been jilted by his fiancée. Midge pondered
this, but although she deplored the action itself she
could see another side to the coin as far as Grace De
Witt was concerned. According to Becky, Brian had
been with another girl down at a cottage on the Chesapeake Bay when the accident happened. Under
those circumstances one could not entirely blame
Grace for whatever she might have done. How gall-
ing it must have been to find out the man you were to
marry in just a few weeks' time was having a rendez-
vous....

Mrs. Prescott was putting steaming dishes full of
marvelous-smelling food on the table, and now she
said, "Please help yourself."

Midge did so, and found that there was nothing
wrong with her appetite. The chicken and dumplings,
green beans specially prepared with bacon, and warm
apple tarts all tasted ambrosial to her.

Later, while Bob Prescott went to watch a sports
event on television, she insisted upon helping Mrs.
Prescott with the dishes, and the older woman
seemed happy to have someone to talk to.

"Keeps you confined, running a motel," she said

as if in explanation of this. "Sometimes I think if Brian Vandervelt weren't the kind of person he is I'd tell Bob I wanted to give it up and just get a little place of our own."

Puzzled, Midge asked, "What does Brian have to do with it?"

"Why, he owns the place," Mrs. Prescott said, as if it had not occurred to her that Midge didn't know this.

"Brian owns this place?" she echoed, incredulous.

"Yes. Bob and I just run it for him. I'm here mostly, of course, because Bob has his own job. Brian's uncle bought the motel years ago; he was always buying up investment property. You'll find the Vandervelts own a lot of things around here."

Becky had said that there were various business properties in the family besides the newspaper, and considerable real estate and other assets, as well. Midge could only dimly begin to realize what all this meant. Money, she thought. Lots of money. The *Valley Voice* was really just one part of it all.

Finally she bade the Prescotts good-night and went back to her new unit, unpacked and was about to take a shower when the phone rang.

The sound froze her. Thoughts of the crudely printed piece of paper urging her to get out of Coxsackie flashed through her mind. Could it be the author of the note phoning her?

She picked up the receiver on the third ring, her voice trembling slightly as she said, "Hello."

"Dora told me you were in," Brian Vandervelt greeted her. "Were you asleep?"

"No."

"Midge, are you all right?"

"Yes, I'm perfectly all right."

"I'm glad you agreed to have dinner with the Prescotts."

"It was very kind of them to invite me."

"They're kind people, but this wasn't altruism on their part. They miss their daughter, Jenny, very much, and I'm sure they were more than pleased to have you around for a while. I spoke to Jerry...."

"Yes?"

"He's sending the note into the state police lab for analysis, but he doesn't have much hope anything will come of it. It's an ordinary piece of cheap typing paper; it could have been purchased anywhere, and so could the red marker that was used. It's doubtful there will be any fingerprints of value at this point— too many people, myself included, have handled it. You don't know anyone around here you haven't mentioned, do you?"

"Of course not!" she almost snapped.

"You needn't sound so angry about it," he observed mildly. "I just wondered if you might have had more of a reason than I realized for coming to Coxsackie."

"I suppose you're thinking of a man?" she suggested coldly.

"Yes, I suppose I am. This could be a jealous-lover sort of thing."

"Please, Brian!"

"All right, maybe now I'm the one who's being overly imaginative. What about the man in New York, though—the one who caused you to give up your job?"

"In the first place," she said, "he didn't cause me to give up my job. I resigned from the firm because I thought it would be difficult for both of us if I continued to work for him. I might add that he'd be happy to take me back at any time.''

"I see.''

"Do you? I'm not sure you do. In any event, I can assure you he isn't the type to drive for a hundred and some miles to climb through my bathroom window and leave me a sick childish note. John is far too sophisticated for anything like that, and much too direct, I might add.''

"I see,'' he said again, then after a moment added, "Are you still in love with him?''

She had not expected this. "What?''

"I asked you if you're still in love with him.''

"Do you have to know everything about everybody?'' she countered. "Does it really concern you?''

"As your employer, I suppose you mean?'' he queried. "No, when you put it in that light I guess it doesn't. To get back to the note: Jerry agrees with me that it has echoes of Halloween, and we both doubt anything like it will happen again. We don't think whoever did this would make any overt gestures toward you, either.''

"That's what I told Mrs. Prescott,'' Midge said. "People who write anonymous notes are usually cowards.''

"I agree. Nevertheless, don't be foolish, Midge. For the next few days, until Jerry checks around a bit, stay close to the motel or the office, will you? Stick to the Maples for meals.''

"I'm not a child, Brian.''

"Aren't you?'' he asked, chuckling. And it occurred to her that with a specially amplified telephone, such as the one he must be using now, he could hear quite well indeed. Certainly he didn't seem to miss anything; in fact he probably realized that she was coming to the simmering point and that annoyance would soon give way to anger on her part if they said much more to each other. This, she suspected, would only amuse him. She could picture him at the other end of the line, his blond head slightly tilted, that faintly arrogant thrust to the line of his jaw, and she moistened her lips. The thought came unbidden that she still had a good two and a half months left on her "contract" with Trent Clayton.

How could she bear to be so near and yet so far from Brian Vandervelt all that time?

THERE WERE PROOFS of the special Halloween section on Midge's desk when she arrived at work Monday morning, and Trent Clayton came out of his office almost immediately to look them over with her.

As they scanned the pages Midge said enthusiastically, "I love the way Ellen has done these black cats especially. They really have personality." She looked around the office. "Where *is* Ellen?" she asked.

"She called in sick," Clem Thorne volunteered from his nearby desk, where he was getting his own material ready to go out and do some ad selling. "Sore throat or something."

Trent said, "I want you to take a set of these proofs with you, Clem. We still have time to add a few pages to this section now that we have the basics down, if you can sell enough linage to justify it. I think when your advertisers see what we're doing here you'll have no problems. Midge's copy sparkles.'' Trent and the others had discovered her nickname, and now used it.

He had put his hand on her shoulder as he leaned over her, and his grip tightened—just slightly, but there was an air of possessiveness to it. ''I don't know how we ever got along in here without you,'' he said softly, bending so that his lips were entirely too close to her ear.

The curtness in the voice that came from the doorway caused both Trent and Midge to start and look up like guilty children. ''Excuse me,'' Brian Vandervelt said, surveying them with an ice-water gaze.

Midge could feel herself flushing and bit her lip, knowing that this would be tantamount to an expression of guilt when there wasn't anything at all to feel guilty about.

Trent asked quickly, ''Did you want me, Brian?''

''No,'' Brian said tersely, ''I want to speak to Miss Boardman. Come out into the lobby, will you, please?'' he asked Midge.

She followed reluctantly, noting Lucille Mueller's surprised gaze as they passed the reception desk. She also noticed that Lucille seemed rather pale today, restrained, as if she had something on her mind. Was there nothing simple about life on the *Valley Voice*, Midge wondered.

Brian took her over to the wide windows that looked out onto Main Street. There was a long deacon's bench underneath them, and abruptly he motioned to her to sit down.

She did so, aware of his displeasure; she knew very well what had caused it, ridiculous though that was. Obviously Brian liked his staff to stick strictly to business during working hours, and the little scene he had interrupted between Trent and herself had undoubtedly seemed entirely too intimate for his taste. To go into it, though, and tell him so would only give the whole episode more importance than it merited, she decided, so she folded her hands in her lap and faced him, and waited.

He sat down, keeping a fair expanse of bench between them. The plaid jacket he was wearing today was a blend of brown and beige and deep gold, and it enhanced the color of his hair. His shirt was beige and his tie picked up the tricolor pattern of the jacket, while his slacks were a very dark brown, perfectly tailored so that they were snug but not overly so. He was frowning, and he seemed very austere. At the moment theirs was entirely an employer-employee relationship, a world apart from the intimacy between them when they'd walked through this very same lobby together only last night.

"I talked to Jerry this morning," he began.

"Yes?"

"As we expected, they couldn't come up with any worthwhile prints on the note; there were just a lot of smudges. Jerry wanted me to ask if there's anyone around here at all who you feel may have taken a dislike to you."

She thought about this, then shook her head. "Ellen was a bit resentful at first," she said, "or she seemed to be, but we work very well together so we've been getting along better and better. I can't say I've had any vibes at all from Clem, but then he's a quiet sort of person; which surprises me, because you don't usually think of salesmen as being so reserved."

"And Trent?" Brian Vandervelt demanded. "But then I don't really need to ask that, do I? He seems to be making his feelings toward you pretty plain."

"Trent and I were merely going over the proofs for the Halloween section when you came by," she snapped.

"Indeed?"

"Yes," she said, sparks in her own eyes now. "Indeed!"

"Do you date him outside the paper?" he asked.

This was too much! "I don't think that's any of your damned business," she said frostily, and made up her mind that she would accept Trent's very next invitation.

"What my employees do does come under the heading of my business if it begins to interfere with their work," he told her infuriatingly.

"Are you implying that my relationship with Trent has been interfering with my work?" she demanded.

She felt as if she had been doused with water from a deep icy spring. "Then there is a relationship," he said quietly.

She seethed. "Damn you, Brian Vandervelt," she said between gritted teeth, "you are too much! Just because you own almost everything around here you think you can own people, too."

He was watching her mouth intently, which meant he was not relying upon the hearing aids alone but wanted to be doubly certain of understanding exactly what she was saying. This indicated, certainly, that whatever she had to say was really important to him, which surprised her. There were moments when he seemed so insufferably sure of himself that she couldn't believe he really cared what anyone else in the world said or thought.

He said levelly, "I suppose you've found out that my family owns the Prescotts' motel, among other things. That really has nothing to do with the present situation, Midge. I would certainly never presume to imagine I could own you, in any sense of the word."

"Wouldn't you?"

"No, I wouldn't, and there is no point in going into this any further," he said shortly, effectively cutting her off. "Think about it a bit, and if you come to any conclusions that might be helpful to Jerry I suggest you call him directly. Lucille can give you the number."

With that he stood, nodded coolly and started back to his office. She was miserable as she watched him go. Again he had turned his back on her; again he had filled in all possible chinks in the wall with which he had surrounded himself.

CHAPTER SEVEN

MIDGE PLUNGED HERSELF INTO HER WORK during the week that followed. There was plenty to do, for Clem Thorne was even more successful than Trent had expected him to be in selling additional advertising linage for the special Halloween section. This meant that quite a bit more copy needed to be written for it, with an imminent deadline on the whole project.

When Trent suggested they have a drink together after the paper came off the press Thursday afternoon, Midge accepted, to his evident delight. They left the advertising department first, both Clem and Ellen lingering to finish up various details of their own; Ellen very seldom came in on Fridays, and Clem's own work load had been increased by the special section, causing him to fall slightly behind with his regular accounts.

As she walked through the lobby with Trent, Midge felt as if Brian Vandervelt were in the shadows somewhere looking after her, and she told herself defiantly that she hoped he was. He would surely disapprove of this example of fraternization, and she was in a mood to displease him!

For that matter, even Lucille Mueller seemed disapproving just now. There was an odd expression in her lovely dark eyes as they passed her desk and she bade them both good-night.

Midge had assumed that they would go to Murphy's Tavern, as they had on the one other occasion when they'd gone out together for a drink, but Trent had other ideas.

"There's a new place up on 9W," he told her. "They call it the Flamingo, which I admit is rather ridiculous for this part of the world, but I hear it's pretty good. They have a cocktail lounge and an adjoining restaurant that's supposed to be excellent, so if we get hungry enough we can have dinner there."

Trent, she sensed, was deliberately being low-key in the interest of forestalling her usual refusals. Well, she decided, this time she just might surprise him!

The immediate question was what to do about her car. She still parked it across the street from the paper, and now Trent suggested that she leave it there. "I can do all the chauffeuring tonight, and I'll pick you up at your place in the morning," he promised.

This seemed the logical way to handle things, and so she agreed. She thought briefly that she might have a bit of difficulty with Trent at the motel, if he decided she should ask him in, then realized that could be taken care of easily enough by having him drop her right at the lobby entrance. She couldn't imagine him trying to so much as kiss her good-night under Dora Prescott's watchful eye.

The cocktail lounge at the Flamingo proved to be surprisingly attractive, and Midge ordered their drink specialty, a piña colada that was quite a creation, frosty and garnished with slices of fresh pineapple and bright red cherries.

Trent was pleasant, very pleasant. He was careful still to keep things casual, but in the process he told her quite a bit about himself, his early life on a farm in Illinois, college and then his first advertising job in a town not far from his home. Later he had spent time with an agency in Chicago, and when she expressed surprise at his coming from a large city to a town as small as Coxsackie he smiled a bit ruefully and said, "I had to do my bit at getting over a broken romance, too, Marjorie."

"Midge," she said absently.

"Of course—Midge. In my case, it was a marriage, though. We married when we were both just out of college, and—" he spread his hands wide and smiled disarmingly "—it didn't work out. Not her fault, not my fault. A mutual mistake, that's all."

"Did you have children?"

"No, which is just as well," he admitted. "For a while I couldn't imagine thinking about marriage again," he added slowly, "but I've begun to feel differently." He didn't pursue the topic, but nevertheless Midge was uncomfortably certain she was involved in this change of philosophy on his part, and it was an involvement she didn't want.

It would be folly to encourage Trent, especially if her prime reason for doing so was to spite Brian Vandervelt, she told herself now, and was sorry she had agreed to go out with him tonight. But then it occurred to her that there was another angle to this entire matter. Trent was one of the department heads at the paper, one of the four who would stand to inherit should disaster befall Brian. He must know a great deal about the will, the probationary period and all the rest of it. If she could manage to keep him from getting too intense with her....

She began carefully, "How long have you been with the *Valley Voice*, Trent?"

"Four years," he answered readily.

"Then you knew Horace Vandervelt?"

"Yes, he hired me. Why? You seem surprised."

"I am. I suppose I imagined Brian had hired you, because you're younger than the other department heads."

"True, but Horace was not averse to an accent on youth, despite what you may have heard about him. He was a tough old man, very difficult to work for, and I always had the feeling he'd have my head on a platter if the advertising linage started dropping. When my predecessor died, though—and he was an elderly man who'd been with the paper many years— old Horace sent out feelers to all the major papers in the country, and he made a very attractive offer from the financial point of view. Obviously he wasn't willing to settle for hometown talent where advertising was concerned. His plan was to convert the *Valley Voice* into a daily instead of a weekly paper, but Horace never did anything quickly; he felt out every step of the way to be sure it was economically sound. So he died before that particular dream was realized."

"Was Brian on the paper when you got there?"

"No. He came not long afterward. He went directly into the editorial department. I understand that during his high-school years—prep school, I guess you'd call it in Brian's case, for he went away to school—he worked on the paper as a cub reporter. He has a good writing style. As you probably know, he writes the editorials; in fact last year he got an award for his editorial writing. I think Mike Stabler has had quite an influence on him. Stabler evidently took him under his wing when he was a kid and taught him a lot of things. Whatever else you can say about Stabler and his personal habits, he's a first-rate newspaperman."

"When Brian came back to the paper was it as a reporter?"

Trent shook his head. "No. He became assistant to his uncle as both editor and publisher."

"In other words, he was put right over Mike Stabler's head?"

"Yes, but Horace was not above nepotism. In fact he considered it his natural right to do as he wished about almost anything. He was the ultimate auto-crat."

"It seems to be a Vandervelt characteristic," Midge commented wryly.

Trent shot her a glance that was a bit too discern-ing. "Oh?" he queried. "Well, as far as Brian is con-cerned I don't think he could have handled reporting any longer anyway because of his hearing, and there's no doubt Horace was grooming him for an eventual takeover as publisher. I suppose Stabler could have been promoted to the post of editor, but Horace always kept his own finger on the editorial pulse, and I think this was an area he was not about to let anyone outside the family get into.

"I would say," Trent went on, "that Brian has justified his uncle's confidence. He's fair with his employees and a lot easier to get along with than Horace ever was. I admire his keeping things on an even keel the way he has despite this tension over the will."

"What about the will?" she asked ingenuously.

Now it was Trent who was wry. "Well," he said, "were it not for Brian Vandervelt I would be a very rich man come November first, Midge. So would Abe Weissman, Wilson Strathmore and Fritz Handel. If Brian had put the paper in the red during these two years since Horace Vandervelt died, the four of us would have inherited it, and some chunks of the rest of the Vandervelt empire, the end of this month."

"And Brian hasn't put the paper in the red?"

"Very much the contrary," Trent told her. "He enlisted our cooperation from the very beginning, which was quite a feat in a sense. There's something else about the will, though."

"Oh?"

"Should Brian not be alive the morning of November first, the four of us would also inherit," Trent told her. "I don't blame you for looking shocked! It's a hell of a way for a man to leave anything. It's worse than the apple in the Garden of Eden!"

"Yes, I can see that," she said faintly.

"Temptation," Trent said. "It's a lousy thing, evil, corroding. You couldn't blame Brian Vandervelt if he went around thinking we're all hoping he'll break his neck before the end of the month!"

She drew a long breath. "Do you?" she dared to ask.

Was she imagining it, or was there something veiled now in Trent's hazel eyes? He spoke carefully, though, without giving any evidence of having been affronted. "I think I can speak for the other department heads as well as myself when I say that we wish Brian no harm," he told her. "We don't like the situation we're in any more than he does. Suppose something *did* happen to him? Each of us would be an instant suspect, and even if we were found blameless, how do you think we could live with ourselves afterward? It would be as if we'd killed him by wishful thinking...."

She shuddered, and Trent assured her swiftly, "Don't worry, Midge. Nothing's going to happen to Vandervelt. He may be deaf, but he's sharp, cautious and completely in control of his situation. As for the rest of us, as I started to tell you, Brian enlisted our cooperation right after Horace died. He spelled out his situation for us—he was very frank about the whole thing—and what he did was to offer a very substantial bonus to each of us if we pulled together so that the paper came out of these two years in the black. True, the bonus is in no way comparable to what we'd stand to inherit, but it's more money than most of us would be likely to see in many a year, and we prefer it this way. We'll have enough to feather our own nests, and we'll also be able to live with our consciences."

He stirred restlessly. "Enough of business," he told her. "Shall we adjourn to the dining room and have dinner?"

Midge was tempted to refuse, then changed her mind. Why not have dinner with Trent, after all? There was no joy in going to the Maples by herself.

They talked about many different subjects over dinner, including their own varying experiences in the agency business, and they found things to laugh about, things they had in common. It was good just to *be* with someone, Midge decided, and Trent could be excellent company. She was almost sorry when they finished their demitasses and liqueurs and he asked for the check.

They were relatively quiet on the drive down the road to Prescotts', and at the door of the motel Trent's kiss was almost brotherly, which came as a surprise. She was sincere when she thanked him for the evening, and he responded lightly, "Let's do it again soon, then."

There was no reason to say no to this.

When she had agreed that Trent could pick her up and take her to work the following morning, Midge had forgotten it would be Friday, when usually there was not much reason to go into the office. She knew that Trent himself normally checked in on Fridays only to take care of any really pressing details and to go over his mail. But if calling for her interfered with any other plans he had made he gave no indication when he arrived at the motel precisely at eight-thirty, as he had said he would.

"Had breakfast?" he asked cheerily, and when she shook her head he suggested, "Let's stop at that place down the way, then. I'm famished."

A moment later they were drawing up in front of the Maples, and Midge hoped fervently that Brian would not decide to come by today as he had on a previous Friday.

He didn't. As they were leaving, though, a state police car swung into the parking lot, and she saw Jerry Mueller at the wheel. This, then, must be a favorite coffee-break place for him, too! She hoped he wouldn't recognize her, but he did.

He came across to Trent's car, leaning down as Midge opened her window.

"I've been intending to get in touch with you, but

these past few days have been hectic," he told her. "I imagine Brian has kept you posted, in any event."

"Yes, he has," she said quickly.

"Look, if you have any thoughts call me, will you? I'm in and out of the barracks, but Lucille can tell you when you'd be apt to catch me at home."

She promised she would, then rolled up the window again, knowing she couldn't possibly hope to sidestep Trent's questioning. She was right, for he immediately asked, "What was that all about?"

"Nothing of any importance, really," she answered.

Trent's glance was quizzical, and she could not blame him for doubting her at the moment. But he said only, "Mueller and Vandervelt seem to be pretty close."

"I gather they've known each other since they were children," Midge told him.

"Oh? Then you know more than I do about them." Trent's tone was still curious.

"I don't know much about them at all, Trent," she responded somewhat wearily. "I don't think anyone knows very much about Brian Vandervelt when you get right down to it. Nor is anyone apt to. Look—" she sought a change of subject "—you really didn't have to go into the office today, did you?"

"Not if you can think of something else for us to do," he said agreeably.

"No, I want to work awhile myself," she hedged. "I want to go over some of the Halloween copy again."

"Midge," he reproved her, "you're not writing for the *New York Times*."

"It doesn't matter," she said stiffly. "I like to try to do my best no matter where I'm working."

"Such dedication," he teased. "Well, then, if you don't mind I think I'll drop you off and come back later to check the mail. I've a lunch date in New York. I was hoping I could persuade you to drive down to the city with me, because it won't be a long one and afterward there are all sorts of things we could do. Perhaps we could get tickets to a play—"

"Not today," she said. "But thanks all the same."

"A rain check?"

"Perhaps."

He smiled at her. "At least you've stopped saying no," he commented.

He left her at the door of the *Valley Voice*, and she walked slowly into the lobby, greeting Lucille absently. There was no one in the advertising department, so she sat down at her desk and got out the Halloween proofs and the additional copy she had been working on, scanning them thoughtfully, yet without having her mind really on them.

She was toying around with a few ideas but getting nowhere when someone knocked on the door. Before she could respond the handle turned and Brian Vandervelt walked in.

As he glanced down at her, she felt as if she were being examined under a microscope, and it was clear that he didn't like what he was seeing. Then as she watched he reached into his pants pocket and withdrew a slip of paper, which he silently passed to her.

To her consternation, she saw that it was a parking ticket.

"There's a ban on all-night parking in your favorite place," he told her coolly. "Evidently our police sergeant marked your car around nine last night, and it was still there at eight this morning."

"And it still is," she finished for him.

"Mechanical trouble?" he asked lightly.

"No."

"Then why did you leave it there?"

"Because it seemed the simplest thing to do."

He raised his eyebrows. "I guess that depends upon one's definition of simple," he said. "Did you walk back to Prescotts' last night?"

"You know very well that I didn't," she told him. "What is this, an inquisition?"

"I have a right to ask some questions, Midge, when one of my employees gets a ticket for leaving a car out on the street all night," he said firmly. "How were the police to know what had happened to you? How was *I* to know? I tried to get you at Prescotts' after Sergeant Dolan brought the ticket in to me this morning, but Dora said you'd already left."

"Well, then?"

"She said Trent Clayton had picked you up."

"Is everyone a spy?" Midge demanded, infuriated.

"Did you spend the night with him?"

She stood, her eyes blazing. "If I did, I'm damned if I'd tell you," she flared.

"Perhaps you'd better." There was an ominous note in his voice. "If you did spend the night with Clayton, you may consider your employment at the *Valley Voice* terminated!"

She stared at him. "That," she said, her voice choked with anger, "is the most ridiculous thing I've ever heard of!"

"I really don't give a damn about your opinion," was his indifferent response.

"No," she agreed, almost dangerously calm now, "you don't really give a damn about anyone's opinion, do you! Well, if Mrs. Prescott saw me leave with Trent this morning she certainly should be able to tell you whether or not I was at the motel last night."

"She was not keeping tabs on you," Brian said wearily. "She happened to be glancing out the window when Trent's car drove up, that's all. What you do or don't do isn't as interesting to most people as you assume it to be."

"Oh?" she retorted, stung. "Then why is it so interesting to you?"

"Because you are my employee, and I require a certain moral code among the people who work for me. What you do away from Coxsackie is none of my business, but this is a small town and I can do without a lot of needless scandal."

"You're so afraid you might lose your precious inheritance, aren't you?" she taunted him.

"It has nothing to do with my inheritance," he said evenly. "Stop vacillating, Midge. Why did you leave your car across the street all night? Where were you?"

She stared at him, meeting an expression that was closed against her. There was no encouragement in his face at all; in fact she had the feeling he had already been judge and jury in the case he'd built up against her, and come into a verdict entirely his own.

Well, if that was the way he wanted it, that was the way it would be!

"Find out for yourself," she defied him. "I'll

never tell you. If that means you're going to fire me, go ahead!''

She turned away from him; it was her turn to put an end to communication, she thought joylessly. She swept the Halloween copy into her side desk drawer and picked up her handbag. In a swift furious gesture she opened it to add the parking ticket he had put on her desk and then she started to brush by him, since he made no move to let her pass.

At once he thrust his arm out, blocking her, and she said tightly, "Let me go, damn you!"

"Midge...."

"Let me *go*!" she insisted.

"I will, in just a minute. Look, I—"

She shook her head, determined not to listen to him, obsessed with trying to convince herself that she hated him more than she had ever hated anyone in her life. But it was hard, if not impossible, to switch emotions so violently when the man involved was Brian Vandervelt. She fought to free herself of his arm, not wanting to look at him, knowing that if their eyes met just now it would be much too easy to reveal her own weakness where he was concerned.

"Midge, were you with Trent all night?" he demanded huskily, and now her scorn came to her rescue.

"Would you believe me no matter what I said?" she challenged him. "Let me by, Brian. You don't have to fire me. I quit."

IT WAS A MISERABLE DAY. Midge stopped at a supermarket in West Coxsackie on her way back to the motel and bought bulky rolls and ham and cheese and a bottle of milk. She made a thick sandwich for lunch and another one for supper, and spent the rest of the time watching television or trying to read a book that failed totally to capture her interest. For a while she napped, but she was so restless that she tossed and turned in doing so, plagued by bad dreams.

During the evening Dora Prescott came to visit for a few minutes, bringing some fresh-baked brownies. There was concern on the older woman's face, and Midge could not help but wonder if Brian Vandervelt had called and asked her to look in on her tenant. She wondered for that matter if Brian might call her himself before the evening was over, but he didn't, and she went to bed with a nagging sense of disappointment preempting everything else.

She woke to the sound of rain on the roof Saturday morning. It was a bleak chilly day, dark low-hanging clouds obscuring the mountaintops to the west. She had thought of going to Boston for the weekend, but the weather sapped incentive when it came to travel, and in any event there were problems to wrestle with. Now she wished very much that she could retract those two words, "I quit," which she had flung at Brian in the heat of temper. Nevertheless she had said them, at the time she had meant them, and she was not about to muster the humility it would require to go to Brian and tell him she hadn't meant what she said.

True, they had both overreacted. He had been ridiculously arbitrary in demanding that she account to him for her actions; yet in retrospect she could see that she had been equally stubborn. When she and Brian became angry at each other neither of them made very good sense, she thought dolefully.

She sighed. The passage of time was making things

more difficult between them, rather than easier, it seemed. Of late Brian appeared to have adopted a rather strange hands-off policy toward her, and she wondered if he regretted his earlier impetuousness.

At moments it would have been easy to think that he actually was jealous of Trent. Of course that was ridiculous; yet she doubted that he believed her story about why she'd left the car parked across the street all night, and this was infuriating. There was absolutely no need for Brian to be suspicious!

"Damn!" Midge said aloud.

She finished the last of the ham and cheese for lunch on Saturday, watched an afternoon movie on television, dozed and then awakened after dark to find that she really was hungry. It was still raining out; in fact the rain seemed heavier if anything. There was nothing for it, though, but to get somewhat wet and drive down to the Maples, where she could order a good hot dinner.

She slipped into her raincoat, fixed the hood over her head, then made tracks between her motel unit and the space in which her battered Volvo was parked. The old car balked sometimes in weather like this, not that she could blame it. It had already performed trusty service for many thousands of miles before she'd acquired it, and had done considerably more duty under her ownership.

Now it sputtered, coughed, but finally started, and she swung out onto 9W, making a left turn.

After that everything happened so quickly she never could remember the events clearly. She saw a flash of white that seemed to appear from nowhere to become a car that careered dangerously close as it sped past her, virtually forcing her off the road. She fought frantically for control as she saw trees looming directly in her path, and she tried desperately to swerve away from them, only to realize at the final instant that she was heading straight into a ditch.

Then there was blackness.

CHAPTER EIGHT

THE BLUE LIGHT REVOLVED, brilliant sapphire in the darkness. Midge heard voices and was conscious of vague shapes bending over her.

Someone said, "She's opening her eyes...."

Then someone else said, "Here's the doctor," and she felt gentle hands touching her.

"How is she?" yet another voice asked, and it seemed to her there was anguish in the tone, but she was sure that the speaker was Brian and she couldn't understand why he sounded so torn when it was he....

She stirred, forcing memory away, and tried to speak. But words wouldn't come, and someone said, "There now, take it easy. Here's the ambulance."

She didn't want an ambulance. She tried to tell them that, but again the words wouldn't come, and shards of pain shot through her as she was lifted onto a stretcher. She turned her head and, ironically, a single object came into her line of vision: the white Jaguar, parked to one side.

Brian, Brian! Why would he do such a hideous thing?

The mere thought of it made her start to retch, then mercifully the blackness came again, descending like a welcome velvet curtain.

When consciousness returned she was in a hospital

bed, in a room dimly lit by the small lamp on a table at her side. She ached, yet, experimenting, found that she could move everything. She opened her eyes tentatively, and someone at her side said anxiously, "Midge?"

She closed her eyes again quickly, squeezing the lids together. Just now she could not look at him.

He said again, "Midge," and reached out to touch her, but she shrank away, and he drew back as if she had stabbed him. Now she did look at him, flinching from the agony in his eyes.

He said disbelievingly, "You think I ran you off the road!"

"I don't know *what* to think," she began. "I'm so totally confused. But even so," as logic came to the fore, "No...no, I don't think you tried to run me off the road. Brian—"

She started to reach out to him, but he had turned away from her. He didn't see her hand, and she realized that she might as well have been talking to herself. He had gone beyond her.

He said tightly, "I'll get Jerry," and left the room.

Jerry Mueller, wearing civilian clothes tonight, came in almost immediately, but his first question was not for her. Rather, he said quickly, "What's wrong with Brian?"

She said miserably, "He thinks that *I* think it was he who came at me. And I did at first. But—"

He stared at her. "Brian! You can't be serious! Good God, hasn't he been through enough hell—" He paused. "I'm sorry," he said. "You've been through quite an experience yourself. But to set your mind free about one thing, Brian was with me."

She swallowed hard. "As far as I'm concerned, he doesn't need an alibi."

"Well, I'm going to give him one anyway! Brian and Lucille and I planned to have dinner at the Maples, and that's where we were heading when we came upon the accident scene. Brian recognized your car immediately. The police were already there and they called my uncle—he's a doctor. They picked up the guy who sideswiped you a couple of miles down the road. He was heading for the Thruway and one of the other troopers had stopped him for speeding. He actually took some of the paint from your Volvo with him, so I wouldn't say there's any doubt about his being the right one."

Midge leaned back against the pillows and closed her eyes. Tears started to come; she couldn't suppress them.

Jerry said helplessly, "Miss Boardman, please." He found a box of tissues on the bedside table and thrust it at her.

She wiped her eyes, but the tears wouldn't stop. She said, sniffing, "I feel so terrible about this! Brian has enough problems without my adding to them. I'll admit I was horrified when I saw the white car because I thought it was his Jaguar, but once I came to my senses—"

"Look," Jerry consoled her, "it's understandable! Come on now, stop crying, will you!"

"I can't. Brian didn't need this. He *really* didn't need it! Don't you think you should go find him?"

"Yes, in a minute," he said. "Look—you were lucky. My uncle says there's no serious damage, but you're bruised, you'll have some aches and pains, and he wants to keep you here overnight just as a precaution. Later the police will be coming around to ask you some questions. Meantime, is there anything either Lucille or I can do for you?''

"No, thank you.''

"Midge—I hope you don't mind my calling you Midge—don't punish yourself. You were in a state of shock. You saw the white car passing you and later you saw Brian's white car parked at the scene. It was a natural conclusion to jump to.''

The tears were starting up again. "You don't have to try to make excuses for me,'' she sniffed.

"I'm not, and I would like to see you calm down and get some rest.''

"I'm all right,'' she insisted.

"I don't know,'' Jerry shook his head. "If my uncle weren't the doctor on your case and if I weren't with the state police, I probably wouldn't even be allowed in here. As it is, I've overtaxed you. Look, I'm going to get the nurse; I'm sure my uncle's left an order for something to make you sleep.''

"I don't care about that,'' she said. "What about Brian?''

"I'll find him,'' Jerry promised. He smiled. "I've found him before,'' he told her. "Quite a few times before. Now don't blame yourself so much.''

But she did blame herself.

Jerry's uncle had left a sedative, and in due course it took effect; but also, in due course, she awakened. It was morning and she did indeed ache, as Dr. Mueller had said she would. However, her physical bruises were not nearly as painful as that other nagging ache that was quite beyond the realm of medical science.

Midmorning a state police officer came in to talk

to her, and she answered his questions, which were routine ones.

Dr. Mueller came in soon after the police officer left. He was shorter than Jerry, older, of course, yet there was a family resemblance. He told her she could go home in the afternoon if she would promise to take it easy. He added that he would expect her at his office for a checkup Wednesday morning. Until then she must promise not to go back to work.

She asked about her car, because there was the matter of transportation between Catskill and Coxsackie. He smiled and said that even if the Volvo were salvageable, which it wasn't, he would not think of permitting her to drive until after he had seen her in his office Wednesday. But she had no cause to worry on that score: transportation would be arranged, and he understood there would be a substitute Volvo delivered to her Tuesday. In the meantime. . . .

Dr. Mueller smiled almost conspiratorially. "I think," he said, "we'll let Mrs. Vandervelt tell you about the meantime herself."

Midge stiffened, completely dismayed, but there was no way out. Even as she wished that she could somehow disappear among the sheets and pillowcases, Maude Vandervelt came into the room.

Midge had pictured Brian's and Becky's aunt as a tall, thin, austere woman, but actually she was short and plump, with very little of the grande dame about her. Her well-corseted figure was encased in a brown wool suit of a much earlier vintage, and her iron gray hair was swept into a French knot. Diamonds twinkled at her ears and on her fingers, and she obviously was still using cake rouge. She came across the room extending both hands; there was something almost hungry in her greeting.

"Midge," she said. "I can't believe it! Our Becky has been writing to us about you for years!"

She took the chair the nurse placed for her at the side of the bed, then remarked with an appraising glance, "Becky said you were pretty, but you're considerably more than that! I'd say you are downright beautiful."

Briefly, Maude Vandervelt almost pouted. "It was very naughty of you not to get in touch with me promptly when you came to Coxsackie," she chided. "Brian says you've been living at Prescotts', and although I think the world of Dora and Bob Prescott I'm distressed that you didn't come to us immediately.

"But—" she brightened "—I'm not here to scold you; maybe later perhaps, but not now! I've promised Herman Mueller that I will hold my tongue until you are strong again. The main thing is to have you come to us *now*. Later, much later, we can talk about why you didn't in the first place."

Midge stared at her disbelievingly. "Mrs. Vandervelt," she began, "you're not suggesting that I go to your home...?"

"Indeed I'm not," Maude Vandervelt said airily. "I'm insisting upon it. In fact," she added, looking very much pleased with herself, "Herman Mueller has released you into my care."

Despite an aching head and a number of other assorted pains, Midge salt bolt upright. "I can't," she said. "I mean, I really *can't* go to your house. Your nephew would never agree to anything like that."

"On the contrary," Maude Vandervelt said, "it

was Brian who suggested it. Now come on, my dear; let's get you dressed and out of here. Tom is waiting downstairs with the car."

The car, a vintage Rolls-Royce, was parked directly in front of the hospital entrance. Midge would have expected the gnarled little man at the wheel to be dressed in impeccable chauffeur's livery, but instead he wore a rather drab charcoal suit of a vintage akin to that of Mrs. Vandervelt's own clothes.

He sprang out of the car door with more dexterity than she would have believed him capable of, saw to it that she was settled in the back seat, then helped Mrs. Vandervelt in beside her. "We'll go directly to the house, Tom," Mrs. Vandervelt instructed. "You can pick up Miss Boardman's things at the motel. Dora Prescott has promised to pack up everything for her personally."

Again Midge wanted to protest, but she found herself subsiding meekly. The accident had taken more of a toll physically than she had realized at first, even though there had been no serious injuries. Both emotionally and mentally she felt numb.

It seemed unbelievable that Brian would have suggested Mrs. Vandervelt bring her into his home when he had made it so clear previously that he didn't want her trying to contact his aunt. Yet it seemed equally impossible that Maude Vandervelt could even have learned of her existence unless Brian had told her.

She ventured feebly, "Mrs. Vandervelt...are you sure your nephew knows about this?"

"Of course," Maude Vandervelt said stoutly, "and there's no reason at all for you to worry about coming to us. Child, Brian and I rattle around in that old house. You're doing us a favor."

"But Brian—" Midge began again.

"Don't worry about Brian. He tends to keep to himself. He's not much for conversation, as you probably know. He lives in the tower—"

"In the tower?"

"Yes. It's fixed up very comfortably, but it's about as far away from everything as a person can get. That's the way he wants it."

Maude Vandervelt's dark eyes were unhappy. "It's not that there are any bad feelings between us," she explained quickly, "although I suppose we've never been as close as I would have liked. My husband and I were middle-aged when Brian and Becky came into our lives, and Horace was set in his ways. Too much childish laughter around the place irritated him. That's why Brian and Becky were sent away to school, and at vacation time they were outdoors more than inside. They were both full of fun. I always wished I could do more things with them."

She sighed. "Well," she said, "it's too late. At least before the accident I could *talk* to Brian. Now he's like a closed book." She smiled wistfully. "Maybe if you come to stay with us you'll be the one to open it."

Tom had taken the river road out of Catskill, and they passed through Athens without Midge's even realizing it. Now the Vandervelt house loomed ahead of them, and she was gripped by a sense of total unreality as Tom swung the car into the circular driveway and came to a stop at the front entrance.

He helped her out, and she found to her horror that her knees were so wobbly she staggered when she walked. Tom promptly took her arm, and Maude Vandervelt said, "Careful now, my dear." Slowly

they approached the massive front door just as it was
drawn back to reveal a birdlike little woman wearing
a faded black uniform.

"Clara," Maude said gaily, "this is Midge Boardman. She's just seen Becky in California, so as soon
as she's feeling stronger she can tell us all about her.
Won't that be a treat?"

Clara nodded, her smile revealing at least one gap
where a tooth should have been. "Indeed it will be,"
she agreed.

"Clara has always loved Becky," Maude told
Midge. "Look, my dear, I'd suggest you stop with
me first for a glass of sherry, but Herman Mueller
made me promise we'd take you directly to your
room."

"I think that might be best," Midge agreed weakly.

"Clara," Maude continued, "can you and Tom
help Midge upstairs?"

"Of course, ma'am."

"Then," she concluded, "I shall see you later."

She disappeared into the recesses of the house, and
Midge, still leaning on Tom's arm with Clara leading
the way, followed slowly. She found herself in a large
square foyer carpeted with Oriental rugs. The wide
staircase directly ahead led to the center of the second
floor, where rooms branched off from the corridor
that ran on either side of the stairwell. As they slowly
started up the steps, Midge saw that yet another staircase led to the third floor. The way to Brian's
quarters in the tower must be even beyond that.

At the top of the stairs Clara said, "I can manage,
Tom. Why don't you go on over to the motel and get
Miss Boardman's things?"

"That I will," he agreed.

"Mrs. Vandervelt's given you the master suite," Clara volunteered as she guided Midge toward the front of the house.

Despite her weakness, Midge found she still had sufficient strength to be thoroughly appalled at the thought of living in quarters that might once have been occupied by Horace Vandervelt. "Mrs. Vandervelt shouldn't have done that," she protested.

"Oh, she has no need for it," the housekeeper assured her. "Since Mr. Vandervelt died she's lived downstairs. Brian converted two large rooms into an apartment for her, fixed them up with her own furniture, bed and all. Her heart's not too good, and Dr. Mueller said she's not to go up and down stairs any more than necessary. The shock of Mr. Vandervelt dying like he did took a lot out of her."

"Was his death sudden?"

"Sudden?" Clara echoed. "I should say!" She peered up at Midge, then paused in mid corridor, pointing out over the stairwell to the graceful curving flight they had just climbed. "Fell down right there. Broke his neck—" she snapped her fingers graphically "—just like that!"

Midge shuddered. "How horrible!"

"It *was* pretty bad," Clara admitted. "Happened just about two years ago. He'd been at a meeting in town—and went upstairs to change his clothes. Mr. Vandervelt always took off his good coats and put on an old jacket around the house. Mrs. Vandervelt was in the library, watching TV like she always did when he was out. She switched it off when she heard him come in, because Mr. Vandervelt couldn't abide TV, and she was just about ready to pour out the glass of port he always took when she heard this awful crash.''

''Was their nephew here?'' Midge asked.

''Brian? Yes, but he didn't hear nothing. When he's up in that tower he turns them hearing things off most of the time—says they get on his nerves. That night Tom had to go up and fetch him. Tom and me, we were having our supper in the kitchen when Mrs. Vandervelt screamed. As soon as Brian came downstairs he told Tom to call Dr. Mueller, but it was too late.''

They had slowly resumed their walk along the corridor. Now Clara pushed open a door and announced, ''Well, here you are.''

Midge stepped into a room that was pure Victorian in decor. The wallpaper was a deep tan with gold overlay, and the draperies were brown velvet. The furniture was dark, the tables heavy, the chairs stiff, and there was a small bronze plush settee that no one could possibly want to sit on. Everything in the room, Midge thought, emphasized the worst of what had been an uncomfortable age at best.

Clara led her on into a bedroom that was furnished with a massive carved walnut bedstead, a matching dresser, an enormous dressing table and large overstuffed chairs. The bedspread was dark blue, heavily patterned, with floor-to-ceiling matching draperies, and the effect was overpowering.

''Mrs. Vandervelt said to make yourself right at home,'' the housekeeper told her. She drew back the bedspread, turned down the blankets and plumped the pillows as she spoke. A blue satin dressing gown had been thrown over one of the chairs, and she said, ''Here—let's slip you into this. Mrs. Vandervelt said she thought it ought to fit.''

It more than fit. It was, in fact, voluminous, and Midge wondered how Maude Vandervelt could possibly wear it without tripping over the hem.

"Now," Clara said, "let's get you down for a while. I'm going to draw the shades, and you just go off to sleep for as long as you want. Tom will bring up your suitcases later. If you need anything meantime, just pull that rope bell over in the corner."

"Thank you, Clara," Midge responded gratefully.

The little woman paused in the doorway. She looked back, birdlike and oddly appealing. "Miss Midge," she said, "I'm awful glad you've come to us!"

MIDGE WOULD NOT HAVE BELIEVED that she could sleep peacefully in the late Horace Vandervelt's bedroom. Yet she did.

When she awakened it was dark, and she was spared ringing the rope bell by Clara, who came bearing a tray with soup and hot rolls. Tom followed directly on her heels with the suitcases.

She ate the soup, changed into her own nightgown and promptly got back into bed and fell asleep again, without the assistance of the pill that Dr. Mueller had left as a precaution. When next she awakened, sunlight was etching golden edges on the window shades.

She stretched, and found that her aches and pains had diminished remarkably and her headache was gone. Under the circumstances she had no intention of ringing and asking Clara to bring breakfast upstairs to her. She was quite capable of going downstairs and finding the kitchen for herself.

Still, it took a while to get dressed, for she did have to maneuver carefully. She found green slacks and a matching turtleneck and opted for a pair of old sneakers, and then she made her way along the corridor, eyeing the long curving stairs with a definite feeling of distaste. She negotiated them cautiously and, once on the ground floor, headed for the back of the house, which seemed a logical place in which to find the kitchen.

Indeed it was. The kitchen was a big square room, but in contrast to the rest of the house it was unexpectedly bright and cheerful. There were white curtains patterned with blue windmills at the windows, and a long wooden table dominated the side of the room, to serve, Midge suspected, both as a work surface and a place for casual dining.

Although the equipment was not strictly modern, it was a long way from the Victorian era. There was a substantial stove and a large refrigerator, she noticed. Just now Clara was standing in front of the stove, stirring something in a huge pot. She turned quickly when she saw Midge and was unable to repress a quick smile, but she said reprovingly, "Now then, you should have rung for me. There was no need for you to come downstairs yet."

"I'm fine," Midge insisted. "A little stiff and sore but otherwise fine, so I'm not having you continue to carry trays of food all that way up to me."

Clara grinned. "Well," she said now, "I've fresh muffins and orange juice, and it'll take only a minute to scramble some eggs—"

"Please," Midge protested. "Just the muffins and orange juice and maybe some coffee will be fine. It must be almost lunchtime for that matter."

"Ten-thirty," Clara said promptly. "Mrs. Vandervelt's already left for her garden-club meeting; it's about the only thing she goes to these days. She'll maybe have lunch with friends, but she thought you ought to rest anyways. She said to tell you she'd see you at dinnertime tonight.''

Clara was bustling around setting a place at the wooden table as she spoke. She motioned Midge to sit down at it and a moment later placed some tempting apple muffins and a big pat of butter in front of her, quickly adding a large glass of orange juice and a cup of steaming coffee.

''Now,'' she said, having seen to it that Midge was settled, ''if you'll excuse me for just a minute I'll go call Brian. He wanted to know as soon as I heard from you.''

''There's no need to bother him,'' Midge cut in quickly. ''He's probably in a staff conference anyway. This is Monday, if I haven't lost all track of time.''

Clara shook her head. ''He went down earlier and had his meeting,'' she conceded, ''but then he decided to come back and do his work here today.''

''Here?'' Midge echoed, aghast.

''Yes,'' Clara nodded. ''Sometimes when he's thinking out one of them editorials he likes to work here at home; he's got a desk and everything in the library. Says there aren't so many interruptions so he can think better.''

''Then don't bother him now,'' Midge said swiftly. ''I...I think I'll go back upstairs as soon as I eat anyway, Clara. You and Mrs. Vandervelt are right, probably; I guess I should rest today.''

Clara cocked her head to one side, the birdlike gaze inquisitive. ''You feeling all right?'' she demanded. ''Maybe Brian should call Dr. Mueller.''

"Oh, no," Midge said hastily. "I'm feeling fine, really I am. I even thought about taking a walk out-doors, it looks so beautiful out. It's just that—"

"That's all right, then," Clara interrupted, and added sagely, "Brian wouldn't want me *not* to inter-rupt him this time!"

CHAPTER NINE

THERE WAS NO CHANCE of stopping Clara, Midge realized to her horror. She thought of trying to escape either upstairs or out-of-doors before the little woman returned, undoubtedly bringing a peremptory summons from Brian to come to the library. But escape, she knew, would only be a delaying tactic. Sooner or later she would have to face him, and it was an encounter unlikely to become any easier with the passage of time.

She heard footsteps and looked up to see Brian entering the kitchen, then saw to her dismay that he was alone. Evidently he had changed his clothes since returning from the morning's editorial conference, for now he wore snug faded jeans and a yellow sweater that nearly matched his hair, which for the first time since she'd met him was tousled, as if he'd been running his fingers through it.

The outfit made him seem younger, but when she looked at him more closely she saw that fatigue had left deep shadows beneath his eyes. In fact weariness lay like a thin mantle upon his features.

Midge was seized by a weakness that had nothing to do with her recent accident, and found herself completely tongue-tied in the bargain. She'd had no opportunity to rally whatever forces she might have been able to muster before facing him, and she was at a total loss for words. What *could* she say to him after this latest, terrible contretemps between them?

Because she wasn't quite sure she could manage being alone with him without saying or doing something very foolish, she blurted, "Where's Clara?"

"Well," he said, "Tom was ready to go shopping, and so she went along with him. She said she'd left coffee for both of us. You'll have another cup, won't you?"

"Yes, thank you," she stammered.

As he got a cup out of a cabinet for himself and then refilled her cup and filled his, Midge's eyes lingered upon his hands. They were beautifully formed, his fingers long and shaped as she imagined a concert pianist's should be. She already knew that they could be either bruising or very tender, and she swallowed hard as she remembered his touch upon her, the astonishingly treacherous feelings he had so easily evoked in her.

"I suppose Clara told you my aunt is at her garden-club meeting," he began. "She's never been much for social activities beyond those forced upon her by my uncle in earlier years, but this is something she really seems to enjoy, and Dr. Mueller has no objection to her going."

Brian was talking faster than he usually did, and watching him Midge became aware that he was as ill at ease as she was. She reached for the coffee cup he had just filled, only to find that her fingers had started to shake. Fumbling, she knocked the cup over, then stared helplessly at the stream of hot brown liquid flooding the wooden table surface.

Brian quickly found dish towels, and a moment later the mess was cleared up. He refilled her cup for her, but she couldn't face more coffee just now. She knew she was going to cry and she knew also, with a certain sense of resignation, that there was absolutely nothing she could do about it, so she stood and turned toward the window to hide her tears. In an instant he was at her side, and she could feel those intent gray eyes upon her face.

Shuddering because she wanted so terribly to reach him, the words coming brokenly, she said, "Brian, I feel like such a fool! What must you think of me? I'm so very, very sorry!"

Unconsciously she had averted her face as she spoke, and now he gently tilted her chin to turn her toward him. "I didn't get it," he said, but for once that mask of assumed indifference he was apt to don at such moments didn't fall into place. "At least, I didn't get all of it," he added, "but I would guess you were making some sort of an apology. There's no need for that, Midge."

She shook her head, unable to speak, and now the tears would not be restrained. They began to flow and kept flowing as she sobbed uncontrollably. Without even being aware of it, she walked into his arms and felt their strength as they folded about her.

"Dearest Midge," he said, his voice incredibly soft. "Look, I don't even have a spare handkerchief! You'll have to settle for a paper napkin."

But instead of getting the napkin he kept her close to him for a very long moment, and she felt an incredibly precious kind of communion between them; his strength seemed to flow into her. Then slowly he released her. "You've been through quite an experience, and you're still shaky. Sit down, and I'll pour both of us some fresh hot coffee."

She obeyed, because she was indeed shaky. But she had never wanted coffee less, even though she sipped some under his watchful eyes and even tried to eat another one of Clara's muffins when he insisted that she needed food.

He sat down at the table opposite her, buttering a muffin for himself, and finally he said, not looking at her now, "Look, there's absolutely no need for you to apologize. This time around it was my fault, if anything. I wouldn't listen to you in the hospital, and Jerry said you tried to tell me I was wrong...."

"Yes, you were," she managed, "and I did try to tell you. But you turned away from me."

She couldn't look at him, but it seemed to her she could feel his gray eyes flicker swiftly across her face. "For God's sake, don't cry again!" he said tautly. "Midge, it's over, and you're all right, and that's all that matters. When I saw your car in the ditch...."

For a moment his voice sounded as unsteady as she felt. Then he told her, "There's no point in going back over it," and there was a finality to his tone. She had the distinct impression that their moment of closeness had passed.

"Probably," he said, finishing his muffin, "you should go back upstairs and rest, and I suppose I'd better try to get on with my editorial."

She nodded listlessly, for her heart was not in leaving him. No, she thought unhappily, her heart was *with* him; it seemed to have become a part of him. She felt herself inextricably interwoven in his destiny, even though just now he was surveying her in a manner that seemed almost remote.

He had developed an ability to turn himself away from people mentally and emotionally as well as physically, she decided. An ability to retreat at will into his own silent world, and a way, in doing this, of indicating that he had no intention of letting anyone follow him. She wondered dispiritedly if there was any way of getting on the same path once he'd started down it with his back to everyone.

She suspected that although he had said there was no need to apologize to him, her rejection in the hospital had been more than a little daunting to him. What was it Jerry had said, almost flinging the words at her? That Brian had been hurt enough? That certainly was true. She felt a swift stab of resentment toward the girl who had jilted him at a time when he needed love so much, probably more than he ever had before. Or had Brian always needed love? He and Becky both had been deprived of their parents at such an early age. Becky seemed to feel that Brian had adjusted better than she had, but now Midge suspected he was merely more adept at emotional camouflage. Also, Becky now had Tim; she had found a wonderful blend of passion and support in her marriage. Whereas Brian. . . .

She realized she was staring at him again, and there was a curious expression in his eyes as they met hers.

"What is it?" he asked.

She flushed. "I was just thinking," she evaded. "Your aunt told me it was at your suggestion she invited me here."

"My suggestion?" he asked, and when she nodded he said, "That's true."

"Why?"

"Well," he answered slowly, "because it would

seem that you've become my responsibility for the moment."

He said it without emphasis, but she noted only that while he expressed no displeasure at the thought of having her in his care, neither did he seem to be deriving any pleasure from it! She told him quickly, "There is no reason at all for you to feel a sense of responsibility toward me!"

"On the contrary, there is," he corrected her. "You came here because my sister asked you to, and now your car has been totaled and but for the grace of God you'd have been seriously injured—"

"You had nothing to do with that," she interrupted.

"No," he agreed levelly. "However, you also had a warning of sorts about getting out of Coxsackie in the note that was left in your motel room. When I think back on it, I feel I should have insisted then that you move in here."

"The note certainly didn't have anything to do with the accident, did it?" she asked, puzzled.

"It wouldn't seem so," he admitted. "The police will check the whole thing out thoroughly, of course, but Jerry tells me the driver who sideswiped you had been drinking, and there doesn't seem any reason to think the incident was anything other than it appeared to be. An accident."

"And the note?"

"I still call it a sick sort of prank," he said. "Nevertheless, I have to take into consideration the fact that the probationary period concerning the will is rapidly coming to an end. Someone around here may think that because you're a friend of Becky's you are somehow involved. In any event, there is no point in taking chances. I'd rather have you safe under my own roof."

He hesitated, then added slowly, "There's another reason, too. Perhaps a selfish one on my part."

She held her breath. "Oh?"

"My aunt has been failing ever since my uncle died," he explained. "Except for her garden session once a week, she's very much alone. It's true that her heart is not too good and her energy gives out easily, but there's more to it than that. She was kept in the background by my uncle for so many years that it isn't easy for her to get used to the idea she can do anything she wants to do now."

He looked across at her levelly. "Uncle Horace was quite a tyrant," he said. "I imagine Becky already has told you that."

"She's indicated it," Midge admitted.

"Well, I couldn't help but notice how much Aunt Maude brightened up when she knew she was going to have you to fuss over. I think it would do her good just to have someone young and...responsive around this house." He hesitated briefly, then added quietly, "I realize I'm not much company for her."

He said this simply, entirely matter-of-fact about it; definitely it was not a bid for pity. Yet Midge felt as if something deep inside her had been twisted and would never be quite intact again.

She felt words surging up within her, all sorts of words, and yet she held them back. Though there was so much, so very much, she wanted to say to him, she knew that in touching upon this particular subject her choice must be entirely right.

He was watching her closely; she could feel his eyes

upon her lips. He asked almost abruptly, "Will you stay?"

"For the present, yes," she said. "Later you may change your mind about my being here."

A slight smile curved his lips. "Later you may change your mind about being here," he countered, then quickly he sobered. "I've got to work on the editorial," he told her, "and you'd better go get some more rest."

She wondered if this was merely a polite ploy to avoid getting into what he might well sense could become an emotionally intense situation; for she surely felt that way about it. In any event, she was not ready to have him set her aside again, not quite yet. She had been looking through the kitchen window at a vista of green lawn eclipsed only by the vivid cerulean sky, and she said almost wistfully, "Do you think your aunt would mind if I wandered around the grounds for a while? It's so lovely out."

"Of course not," he told her promptly. "Are you sure you feel up to it, though? Wouldn't it be better to wait a couple of days?"

She smiled at him. "It might be raining a couple of days from now," she teased, then added quickly, "Honestly, I think the fresh air and sunshine would do me good."

"Very well, then," he told her. "I'll come with you."

This was the last thing she had expected. "There's no need," she protested quickly. "I mean, I know you have work to do."

He shrugged. "It can wait awhile longer," he said. "Come along."

They went out the back door, passing through a

small herb garden. Just beyond this was Clara's kitchen garden, where, Brian explained, she grew tomatoes, lettuce, radishes, cucumbers and a number of other vegetables, principally for salads.

"Tom also has a really big garden," he said. "Bigger than we've ever needed. But that's one extravagance Uncle Horace permitted."

He led her through an apple orchard where a few dark red fruit still clung to the almost bare branches, then on to a wide sloping lawn. To the right she saw an octagonal summerhouse, and she exclaimed in delight. Brian, following her gaze, said, "The gazebo—Becky always loved it. Summer afternoons I'd come back from sailing or playing tennis and often she'd be sitting on the steps looking out at the river...."

She turned to him. "May I go in?"

"Of course."

He followed her up shallow wooden steps, across the wide planked floor and then down the steps on the river side. For a long moment she stood very still, looking across the cobalt Hudson to the far shore, which was dressed for fall now with maples and oaks wearing Halloween shades of orange and rust and scarlet. A soft breeze rustled the tree leaves, and somewhere a bird sang. Midge murmured softly, "It's beautiful," but Brian didn't answer, and she knew that he hadn't heard her. She wondered if he ever did manage to hear the rustle of tree leaves or a bird singing.

She swung around, surprising such an expression of sorrow in his eyes that it dismayed her. Quickly she said, "I only mentioned that it's...beautiful."

He nodded, his face a mask again, the gray eyes dark. "Yes, I know," he answered, but it seemed to her that he had gone miles away from her.

Almost desperately she pleaded, "Brian, please don't!"

He seemed honesly puzzled. "Don't what, Midge?"

"Don't retreat like that! I realized you hadn't heard what I said, so I repeated it. Was that wrong?"

Unconsciously she reached out to clutch the sleeve of his yellow sweater as she spoke, and now he took hold of her hand and said gently, "Of course it wasn't wrong. And the problem wasn't with you, it was with me. For a while I...forgot. Then you turned away from me and it all came back." He tugged at her hand, attempting a smile. "Come over to the top of the bank. I want to show you something."

Holding her hand, he led and she followed. A path wandered down the bank to a place where graceful willows, draping low, nearly blotted out the view of a cove with a small dark-sanded beach.

"Becky and I used to sneak off and go swimming down there," Brian told her.

"She's mentioned it to me," Midge said.

He chuckled. "Uncle Horace found out once and was downright choleric about it. I guess he thought we'd been polluted."

"Could we go down?"

"It's steeper than it looks," he warned. "You should be a bit past the convalescent stage before you try it. Later, maybe."

Later. There was hope to the word.

CLARA WAS IN THE KITCHEN when they got back, unpacking her groceries. "Mrs. Vandervelt wants me to make my special chicken dish for dinner," she reported happily. "Brian, have you been wearing Midge out?"

"I hope not."

"She's supposed to take it easy," the housekeeper chided.

"I will, I will," Midge promised.

And she did. Brian went back to the library to work on his editorial, and once more Midge slowly climbed the stairs to the suite that had been Horace Vandervelt's.

She was more tired from the morning's excursion than she had thought she would be. She made no protest when Clara brought a sandwich lunch up on a tray, and she spent the better part of the afternoon napping.

At six o'clock she went down to join her hostess for a predinner glass of sherry, Clara having conveyed Maude's invitation to do so. She had brought no really formal clothes to Coxsackie with her, but she slipped into a gold wool dress that was simple and very becoming, adding an antique topaz pin and topaz-and-gold earrings. The color of the stones seemed to echo the lights in her chestnut hair.

Maude's sitting room was a jumble of chairs, settees and marble-topped tables, stern "ancestor" portraits in ornate gold frames, a grand piano in one corner and two enormous bookcases amply filled with a variety of volumes. The draperies and upholstery were dark in tone, the fabrics plushy, and there was something that Midge suspected might actually be a rubber plant on a table in a corner.

Maude suited the room. This evening she was garbed in full-skirted plum satin that touched the floor. She greeted Midge with a hug, her pleasure in having company almost pathetic.

Clara brought sherry in a decanter with facets that captured a thousand shimmering lights, and Maude carefully poured it into beautifully fragile long-stemmed glasses. She gave a nervous little laugh. "I suppose it's old-fashioned of me, but I like a glass of sherry before dinner."

Midge sipped, then responded sincerely, "It's excellent sherry."

"Thank you, my dear. That's one thing I did learn from my husband—a taste for good wines." She made the statement matter-of-factly; there were no overtones of bitterness.

A fire was burning on the hearth. Midge sat back and watched the flames curling around the edges of the logs, waiting for Maude to continue the conversation, which she did after another nip of sherry.

"I was sorry to leave you this morning," she said, "but Clara tells me Brian looked after you."

"Yes, he did," Midge replied. "He was very kind."

"The garden club had a special demonstration, an ikebana expert from New York," Maude explained. "If it had been anything else I wouldn't have gone."

"Ikebana?"

"The Japanese school of flower arrangement. I've been taking classes."

Midge could barely repress a smile; she could not think of two things in the world more totally disparate than the decor of Maude Vandervelt's sitting room and a classic Japanese flower arrangement.

Although Brian did not join them for sherry, he did appear when Clara summoned them to the dining room for dinner. He had changed to gray slacks and a dark green turtleneck, and his thick blond hair had been carefully combed.

There was a formality to his manner as he took his place at the head of the table, and the conversation was admittedly sparse and stilted. Midge suspected, however, that this had little to do with Brian's hearing problem. He seemed distracted and rose at once when the meal was over, almost immediately excusing himself. Shortly afterward she could hear him going upstairs.

Briefly Maude looked disappointed, then she brightened and asked Midge if she'd like to watch television. For the next two hours they watched a series of programs in which Midge had little real interest—but she feigned enough to satisfy her companion.

Finally Maude said, "It's my bedtime, dear, but you go right ahead and watch something else if you like."

"I think I'll go to bed myself," Midge said. "Would you mind if I took a book up with me?"

"Take anything you want." Impulsively Maude patted Midge's cheek, adding, "It's wonderful to have you here," and as she turned away Midge saw that her eyes were filled with tears.

Her own eyes misted; for all of the Vandervelt wealth, what a miserable life Maude must have led under Horace's domination! Now, as Brian had pointed out, she was finding it hard to accept freedom. She still seemed to be looking over her shoulder, as if expecting the ghost of her husband to emerge from the shadows.

I'd like to meet up with Horace's ghost, Midge thought bitterly. *I'd give the old miser a piece of my mind.* Yet she had to concede, as she looked over the contents of the bookshelves, that either he or some of the other Vandervelts had surely had excellent taste in literature.

She took down Stendhal's *The Red and the Black,* which she had always wanted to read but had put off for one reason or another. Then she saw an encyclopedia on a lower shelf and, setting Stendhal aside for the moment, picked out the volume marked Corot to Deseronto and turned to the section on deafness.

There was considerably more than she would have thought there would be; on another occasion, she decided, she would go over it thoroughly. But just now, as she skimmed, one section seemed to leap out at her. It was headed "Problems of the Deaf," and she read the first paragraph through once and then again.

Although man has traveled a long torturous road from the pre-Christian era in evolving an enlightened understanding of the problem of deafness, a large portion of society still looks upon the deaf as queer, dependent and somehow ridiculous. Since their handicap is not as visible as that of the blind and the crippled, the deaf often find themselves in embarrassing and humiliating situations because others do not understand their special problems....

She thought of this morning with Brian, when he had said, "For a while I forgot. Then you turned away from me and it all came back."

I must never turn away from him, she found herself thinking. *I must never turn away from him again.*

CHAPTER TEN

THE WEATHER HELD CONSTANT. Tuesday was another beautiful October day. Waking to sunlight that brought cheer even into her gloomy bedroom, Midge found to her amazement that it was past nine o'clock. She seldom slept so late.

She had not thought to ask if there was a specific time for breakfast. Probably there wasn't. Except for dinner, meals seemed to be quite informal in the Vandervelt household; something, she felt sure, that had been initiated since Horace's time.

She dressed in a comfortable pair of beige slacks and an orange pullover sweater. The outdoors beckoned; she wanted to walk, to explore, and she wished she could think of a way of asking Brian to go with her. But he'd doubtless already gone into the office today.

Clara was in the kitchen making piecrust. "Well, now," she chirped upon seeing Midge, "you *did* get your beauty sleep!"

"I never stay in bed this late ordinarily," Midge told her.

"It was good for you," Clara said firmly. "Let me wash this flour off my hands and I'll fix you some breakfast."

Despite Midge's protests that she could pour coffee and fix toast for herself, Clara insisted upon doing it, adding a jar of strawberry jam. She was briefly disapproving when Midge again refused scrambled eggs.

Breakfast before her, Midge settled down at the big kitchen table and watched Clara roll out the dough with expert fingers and fit it into a pie plate, chattering meanwhile about a variety of things. Maude Vandervelt, she confided, always stayed in bed until at least noon, often later. She had her own television set in her bedroom and seemed content to watch the programs for hours on end. Usually she combined breakfast and lunch into a single meal, which Clara took in to her on a tray.

"Says it's better for her heart," the housekeeper went on, "but I don't necessarily hold with that. Seems to me, from what I've seen on TV myself, that it's better for your heart if you get a little exercise. I guess both Tom and me feel, though, that we should do whatever she wants from here on in. She couldn't even breathe for herself while *he* was living."

He. The late Horace Vandervelt again. Tom and Clara obviously hadn't liked him, either; in fact Clara gave the impression that they had stayed with the family only for Maude's sake, living in an apartment over the big garage, which was actually a converted carriage house.

"After Mr. Vandervelt died, we got us an intercom," Clara explained. "If she needs us any hour of the night all she has to do is push a button. We've rested a lot easier since Brian had it put in."

Midge was torn between a personal aversion to prying and an almost burning desire to find out all she could about Brian, his aunt and the mansion. Clara, of course, was an invaluable source of information, but she soon switched to talk about the harvest this year, her favorite recipes and the cooking she planned to do through the fall in preparation for Thanksgiving and Christmas.

"I wish Becky and her family would come for the holidays," she said wistfully. "Can't quite imagine Becky with children of her own. I'd like to see them here."

"Brian mentioned something about having a family reunion at Thanksgiving," Midge ventured, and saw Clara's eyes widen.

"Did he now," she observed thoughtfully.

"Clara," Midge said, "maybe you'd better not tell him I told you that. He might not like it. I mean, I don't think he's yet made up his mind and—"

Clara smiled conspiratorially. "Mum's the word," she promised with a wide smile.

Finally Clara went off to the laundry room to do a wash, and Midge wandered through the first floor of the house. Her footsteps seemed to echo behind her as she explored a formal drawing room and a more intimate parlor and then came finally to the library where Brian evidently worked when he was at home. On those walls not covered with bookcases were hung ornate gold-framed paintings of Hudson River scenes, very old, she imagined, and undoubtedly quite valuable. She supposed the huge mahogany desk that dominated the room must once have belonged to the late Vandervelt, but seeking now for any sign of Brian's use of it she was disappointed to find nothing at all reminiscent of him. Certainly he had left nothing behind him here in the library; in fact the house, or as much of it as she had thus far seen, in no way reflected Brian's personality. It was a cold place, she decided, as austere as Brian in his most aloof moments.

The morning wore on, and she wished Maude Vandervelt would wake up and send Clara to fetch her. There was a stark quality to the loneliness she was feeling, so perhaps she was more friendly than she might otherwise have been when Clara told her there was a phone call for her and she heard Trent Clayton's voice at the other end of the wire.

"Midge!" he said. "My God, how are you? Vandervelt just told me that you're up and around again. I tried to get you on the phone yesterday, but the housekeeper said you were resting."

Clara had not relayed a message from Trent, but then, Midge thought, very possibly it had slipped her mind. She'd had to put up with far more than the usual quota of excitement around the Vandervelt household in the past couple of days.

Now Midge said, "I'm fine, Trent. As far as I'm concerned, I could have come into the office this morning, but I have an appointment with the doctor this afternoon and he's not about to let me go back to work until he's seen me."

"Then you may be in tomorrow?"

"I hope so," she said, and laughed. "Time's hanging rather heavily on my hands," she confessed.

"The minutes have been dragging like hours for me," he told her. "And to make it worse, I can't help feeling they're keeping you prisoner out there in that god-awful house."

"That's not so at all, Trent," she protested.

"Maybe not. But couldn't you have gone back to the motel from the hospital?"

"Well," she began, "Brian thought—"

"Yes," he interrupted, and she didn't like the cynicism in his tone, "I'm sure Brian has thought about quite a few things. Look, have dinner with me tomorrow night, will you? We can make it early."

"I honestly can't make any commitments until I see the doctor," she hedged. "He said I had a mild concussion, and he did want me to take it easy for a few days."

"All right, darling," Trent responded with a rueful laugh, "I suppose I'll have to wait for his verdict. I'll hope to see you tomorrow, though."

"I hope so," she agreed.

The rest of the morning passed slowly. Her appointment with Dr. Mueller was for one-thirty in his office on Mansion Street in Coxsackie, and she imagined that Tom would drive her over although, she recalled, the doctor—or had it been Jerry—had mentioned there would be a replacement car supplied for her use. She felt sure that if it arrived in time she could drive herself.

To her surprise, though, as she was coming back from a walk shortly before noon she saw Brian pulling up at the front entrance in the Jaguar. It was as if she'd become rooted to the spot; her legs suddenly felt entirely powerless. She stood on the side lawn waiting for him to bridge the space between them with long even strides, wishing fervently that the mere sight of him didn't have quite such a traumatic effect upon her.

Evidently he mistook her reaction to his appearance for fatigue, for he said swiftly, "You look pale, Midge. You haven't been overdoing, have you?"

"No." She could feel a telltale surge of color

sweeping into her cheeks. "I just walked across to the river, that's all."

"You didn't climb down the bank?"

"No," she repeated, and ventured to add, "I'm waiting to do that with you."

"Good." As he fell into step by her side he asked casually, "How's Aunt Maude this morning?"

"I haven't seen her yet," Midge confessed. "Clara says she stays in bed until quite late; in fact I understand she often has a combined breakfast-lunch in bed, with the television on. I thought of going in to see her, but I felt I shouldn't disturb her."

He had been watching her attentively as she spoke, and now he said, "I don't think you would have disturbed her. As a matter of fact it would be good for her to have someone or something interrupt the routine she seems to have fallen into. I'll look in on her myself for a few minutes before we leave."

"Leave?"

"Yes. I've come to take you to Dr. Mueller's," he explained. "We've plenty of time, of course. We'll have lunch first."

He had called her a responsibility—now it came to her that he surely was taking this particular responsibility seriously, perhaps too seriously, in a way that made her feel she might be a burden to him. "Tom could have driven me over, couldn't he?" she suggested.

"I suppose so," he acknowledged. "Why? Would you rather go with Tom?"

Was she imagining it, or was there actually a teasing note in his voice? She glanced at him swiftly and saw the laughter in his eyes, although his face was almost deceptively bland, and she said rather sharply, "Of course not. But I realize you're busy."

"I finished the editorial last night," he told her, "and Mike's been in good form of late, so I feel it's safe to leave things in his hands at present. He seems to have climbed on the wagon at least. How long he stays aboard, though, is a matter of conjecture."

They had come to the front door, and to her surprise it was unlocked. As he turned the knob Brian said, "The house seems forbidding enough to turn people off all by itself. Clara and Tom never bother locking up during daylight hours. We have few visitors."

Clara fixed a lunch of sandwiches and soup for them. They ate at the big wooden table in the kitchen, and Midge was midway through one of the soft molasses cookies Clara served for dessert when she was struck by a sense of total unreality. She felt she should be pinching herself to be sure that she really was here, making herself very much at home with Brian Vandervelt, who was sitting across from her and occasionally exchanging a quip with Clara. The housekeeper obviously doted on him.

He raised a quizzical eyebrow as she met his eyes. "For a moment there you seemed perplexed," he commented.

"Not exactly," she hedged, and added quickly, "Should you be taking so much time away from the paper on a Tuesday, even if Mike Stabler is doing a good job just now?"

"Well," he said, and she sensed that he was amused, "one advantage of running an organization is that despite the overtime hours you're often forced to put in, when it gets right down to it you can do what you wish. Just now," he went on, to her astonishment, "I'm doing what I want to do."

Lunch over, they both stopped in to see Maude, this at Brian's suggestion. She was propped up in bed against a mound of pastel satin pillows, looking thoroughly comfortable and quite happy. Still, it didn't seem to Midge that this was a very healthy sort of life for anyone to live.

Immediately after, Brian drove Midge into Coxsackie. Dr. Mueller's office was in his home, which proved to be a big white frame house with wide porches and an intriguing old stained-glass window to one side of the front door. The doctor pronounced himself pleased with Midge's progress but still insisted she rest for a few more days before going back to the paper on a full-time schedule.

"If you must work on your copy, let Brian bring it home to you for the present," he suggested. "Just promise me you won't burn any midnight oil."

"I won't permit her to," Brian said firmly.

As they drove back to the Vandervelt mansion, Midge remarked, "He's such a nice man. Has he always practiced in Coxsackie?"

"Yes," Brian nodded. "He came back here after he finished his internship—that was years ago, of course. He was born here; so was Jerry, for that matter."

"It's a fascinating town," she commented.

"Coxsackie? I suppose it is. We tend to take places and things for granted once we become accustomed to them. Coxsackie is an old town, though; this area was founded by Peter Bronck in the 1660s. New York's famous Bronx, incidentally, is named after the Bronck family."

"Was his the old Bronck house over on 9W?"

"Yes," Brian confirmed. "You might like to go visit it sometime—it's quite representative of its period. If I remember correctly, the house was built in 1663 and then enlarged a couple of times afterward during the eighteenth century. Speaking of the eighteenth century, Coxsackie wrote its own Declaration of Independence back in May 1775, a couple of months before the more famous version was proclaimed at Philadelphia. It was engineered by Hudson River valley Dutchmen who had resolved never 'to become slaves,' and after its issuance they considered themselves Americans rather than British subjects."

"I suppose some of your ancestors were among them?" she asked.

"Yes, they were. This entire part of the countryside was extremely Dutch in those days, and there are many Dutch echoes, as you've probably already noticed, even today. As a matter of fact, Coxsackie was originally known as Kock's Hackie, and that's the way you should pronounce it, with a broad *a* on the Hackie. Most people say Cocks-sacky. Catskill was spelled with a *k*—a kill is a brook, or creek in the Dutch language. Both the towns of Coxsackie and Catskill were originally part of vast farms, big country estates owned by the Broncks and the Van Bergens, and...." He broke off. "I must be boring you."

"But you're not," she protested. "I've always loved history."

"Nevertheless," he said, "that's enough of a lesson for today. Look, Midge, I see no reason why Trent can't handle any copy that needs to be written for the next few days. He was doing the job himself before you so conveniently walked in the door.''

She frowned. "I've come to consider the Halloween section as my own thing," she admitted.

"Very well, then," he said, "we'll compromise. Forget about doing anything for this week's paper, and I'll bring home your 'Trick or Treat' file. Then you can drum up all the witches and ghosts and goblins to fill in that you like."

He was turning into the Vandervelt driveway now, and Midge hated to have the car draw to a stop in front of the main door. She wished that she could extend the moment, that she could go right on being with him forever.

He reached across her to open the car door on her side, and his hand brushed her breasts as he did so. She knew at once that he was as aware of this inadvertent contact as she was, for he paused briefly, and the second between them was an electric one. Then he flicked the door latch and said, smiling, "Out you go. I have to get back to the paper, and I want you to promise you'll head directly upstairs and take a nap.''

"Even if I'm not sleepy?''

"Even if you're not sleepy," he said, then leaned over to give her the briefest of kisses, accompanied by a slight but positive little push, so that she climbed out reluctantly.

MIDGE HAD FULLY EXPECTED that Brian would join her and his aunt for dinner that night, but when she went down to have a glass of sherry with Maude she found that this wasn't to be.

"Brian is tied up at the paper," Maude reported.

"Some kind of a problem; it seems to me he's always having to solve problems. Sometimes I think the men he works with deliberately make things hard for him."

Unfortunately there was no way of knowing whether this was fact or Maude's imagination, but Midge could not get the thought out of her mind that maybe the department heads weren't being as cooperative toward Brian as they appeared to be. Even Trent had made it clear that there was a great deal of money at stake. True, he had said he preferred getting the bonus Brian had promised in lieu of an inheritance that would be his only if Brian met with some terrible misfortune, and she believed him. Still, one could not expect any of the department heads to be objective about the situation. It was, to say the least, a terrible way for a man to have left his fortune.

Again Wednesday night Brian did not come home for dinner, and on Thursday Maude pointed out that this was his night to attend the Valley Men's Club meeting. He had brought home the Halloween copy, leaving it with Clara to give to her, and Midge was thankful to have it. Each evening she watched television for an hour or so with Maude, then was able to leave the other woman engrossed in a favorite program while she went upstairs to revise and polish her work until she knew it was by far the best thing she had ever done.

By Friday, though, she had done all she could do toward the section, and she went downstairs in the morning hoping that Brian had decided not to go into the office today. If so, perhaps she could ask him to climb down to the little beach with her and walk along the river front, or maybe if he was in an especially good mood he might even be prevailed upon to go for a drive up into the Catskills. It was another perfect fall day; the looming mountains, hazy blue in the morning light, seemed to beckon.

Midge sat at the wooden table in the kitchen talking to Clara as she drank her coffee and munched an English muffin, and when she heard footsteps in the hall outside it seemed for a moment as if her wishes were going to come true. As if on schedule, her pulse started to pound, but it wasn't Brian who came into the kitchen. It was Jerry Mueller.

He was out of uniform today, wearing faded jeans with a blue sports shirt and a nylon jacket that had seen better days, and he was carrying a tennis racquet.

He smiled when he saw Midge. "How are you doing?" he asked. "Brian said you'd moved in here, and I think it's great."

"I'm fine, thanks," she told him. "Getting a bit restless, though. I'll be more than ready to go back to work Monday."

Clara's eyes, Midge noticed now, were lingering on Jerry's tennis racquet, and she asked abruptly, "Isn't he going to play?"

"No," Jerry said ruefully. "He wanted to, but he's not up to it."

As Midge looked at him inquiringly, he explained, "Brian and I play tennis together whenever we have a chance, and I have the day off today so I came over thinking we might have a few games, since Friday isn't usually busy for him. Every now and then he gets a rough headache, though, and unfortunately that's the case this morning." He hesitated. "You don't play by any chance, do you?"

"Very indifferently," Midge answered.

"Feeling up to batting a few balls?"

"Why not?" she smiled.

"See here," Clara protested, "she's just out of the hospital! What are you thinking of, Jerry Mueller?"

"She doesn't look as if it would hurt her," Jerry grinned. "If she starts getting tired we'll quit. Wait a minute, Midge, and I'll go find a spare racquet."

Looking after him, Clara shook her head. "No sense at all, either one of you," she grumbled, then smiled crookedly, revealing the missing tooth. "Jerry's a fine boy. He married a fine girl, too. Jerry and Lucille are the only ones around here who are real friends to Brian. I wouldn't give a fig for any of the rest of them."

Midge took her courage in hand. "What about the girl he was engaged to?" she asked.

"Grace De Witt? I wouldn't give *half* a fig for her," Clara snorted. "Minute she heard he was deaf she walked right out on him and married someone else!"

She was about to say more, but Jerry returned with an extra racquet. "We can go out this way," he said, indicating the kitchen door.

"Where's the court?" Midge asked, preceding him through it. "In town?"

He laughed. "No, on the other side of the garage. The Vandervelts have all the conveniences—except a swimming pool. I keep telling Brian he should have one put in, but he says he's going to take one thing at a time. He just had the tennis court built last year and old Horace probably has been turning in his grave ever since!''

This was a part of the estate she and Brian had not explored the other day. She walked around Tom's vegetable garden, past the garage and saw the chain-link fence that enclosed the tennis court.

''Jerry,'' she asked, ''did *anyone* like the late Horace Vandervelt?''

''I doubt it.''

''Was he really so terrible?''

''You'd better believe it!''

''What about the girl Brian was engaged to?'' she went on, and was a bit appalled at herself; because she'd had no intention of posing this question to Brian's best friend. ''Maude and Clara don't seem to have thought much of her, but surely she had her side of the story, too?''

Jerry stopped short, his eyes narrowing. ''I suppose so, if you can justify walking out on someone you've been about to marry at the precise moment in his life when he needs every bit of love and understanding he can get,'' he said coldly.

''I wasn't thinking of that,'' Midge told him. ''I was thinking of...well, of what precipitated the whole thing. Brian *was* with another girl at the time of the accident, wasn't he?''

''I don't know what kind of a story you've been told,'' Jerry said. ''However, the truth of the matter is that it was a house party Brian was at. Three or four couples were there. They were building a bonfire on the beach—it was April, still cold on the Chesapeake once the sun went down. They were going to roast hot dogs, and Brian went to get more beers out of the fridge. The girl whose family owned

the cottage had gone back to it a few minutes before; she must have decided to light a space heater
they had in the living room, to take the chill off.
The heater hadn't been used for quite a while,
though, and it was faulty. Something went wrong,
and it blew up.

"Brian was knocked flat by the force of the explosion. When he came to, he was in the hospital. He
says he gradually realized that the people around him
were talking, but he couldn't hear them."

Midge winced. "It must have been terrible."

"Brian's had his share," Jerry said tersely.

"Isn't there anything that can be done for him?"
she asked. "I mean—he's young, and money is no
object. With all the advances being made in medicine, don't you think there could be some kind of
operation—"

"No." Jerry's tone was firm. "The damage to his
ears was the result of a blast injury. It's permanent.
He was just outside the beach house when it exploded. As I understand it, when something like that happens it's almost like being hit by a tidal wave, except
that in this case it's a sound wave. A sharp pressure
rise causes the wave, and when it comes into contact
with the human body it plays havoc with such things
as eardrums."

"So," she reflected slowly, jolted despite herself,
"he will *always* be deaf."

"Yes." There was a strangely questioning look in
Jerry's eyes. "Always." He shrugged then, as if trying to cast off a mood, tossing his racquet into the air
and catching it. "Okay, Miss Boardman," he said,
his voice deliberately light, "how about it?"

Midge had not played tennis for quite a while, yet

she acquitted herself reasonably well. Still, she began to tire after a relatively short time and Jerry, noting it, insisted upon calling the game off, saying that his uncle would probably raise hell with him if he knew he'd been letting her play at all.

Jerry glanced at his watch as they walked back toward the house, saying, "I think I'll drop by the paper and invite Lucille to have lunch with me. One of these nights, when we all have a free evening, do you suppose the four of us could get together and go out to dinner? There's a French place in Albany we've been wanting to try."

Midge realized that by the four of them Jerry meant his wife and himself and Brian and herself, and she was not at all certain that Brian Vandervelt would welcome this kind of pairing.

Before she could answer, though, Jerry went on, "We may have to work on Brian a bit. He doesn't go out very much. I keep telling him he's going to turn into a hermit if he doesn't watch it." He smiled as he spoke, then sobered quickly. "He thinks he's rotten company because of his hearing."

"That's not true," Midge denied quickly.

"I agree, and so does Lucille," Jerry told her. "But we've got to convince Brian. Let's work on it, shall we?"

With that he left her.

Clara suggested that Midge join Maude for lunch today, and took trays into Maude's bedroom for both of them. Obviously Clara had mentioned that Brian's headache had forestalled the tennis game with Jerry, because Maude said after a time, "I worry about Brian. I know he's had expert medical attention, but even so. . . ."

"Probably they have something to do with tension," Midge ventured. "The headaches, I mean. It must put an awful lot of pressure on him, trying to hear all the time."

Maude nodded uncertainly, and Midge managed to switch the conversation onto other topics; but when Maude suggested that she still looked a bit tired and probably needed a nap, she was quick to agree. Once in Horace Vandervelt's bedroom though, she could neither concentrate on Stendhal's *The Red and the Black*, nor nap.

She could only think of Brian, alone in his tower....

THE AFTERNOON WORE ON. Even the weather seemed to respond to the oppressive silence in the house. By three o'clock it had clouded over: the sky was surly, and from Midge's window the Catskills were like dark bruises against a distant gray horizon.

If Brian was still isolated in his tower it must mean that the headaches were so severe Maude's concern was justified, Midge decided; and certainly he should do something about them. Also, she wondered, had Clara taken both breakfast and lunch up to him? It was a long way to the tower, and Clara was not young. This must be a difficult chore for her, whether or not she would admit it.

Midge stirred restlessly. She had no right to invade Brian's privacy, she reminded herself, yet he had been very kind to her since the accident; there had been a definite rapport between them. Now the thought of him in pain and literally out of touch with the world up there in his tower, because of his hearing, was too much.

"*Damn* his privacy," she said out loud, and the die was cast.

She opened the side door that led from her bedroom into the corridor, more than half expecting to hear someone or something, and she did. Downstairs the old grandfather clock in the hall chimed four o'clock. Then all was still again.

Feeling as if she should walk on tiptoe, Midge made her way down the corridor alongside the stairwell, then slowly, cautiously, went up the steps to the third floor. Here the main staircase terminated. Windows lined a rear wall, and a corridor ran on either side of the stairwell with doors leading off it, following the pattern of the second floor. Were there guest bedrooms behind the closed doors, she wondered, or were these rooms originally designed for servants' quarters?

She wondered, too, how long it was since any of this part of the house had been used. Even more important, where was the stairway that led to the tower? It was not visible, which meant that it must be behind one of these closed doors—which meant in turn that she must go from door to door until she found it.

This was beginning to seem like snooping at the least, if not downright trespassing, and it gave her an uncomfortable feeling. Nevertheless, she paused to sketch a mental picture of the outside of the house. The tower sat in the middle; it must be directly over the stairwell itself. Thus, she reasoned, it seemed likely that access to it should lie behind one of the middle doors, either to the left or to the right. She tried the right door first, and she was in luck. It opened onto a narrow steep flight of stairs with a door at the top; the door was closed.

She faltered briefly and nearly turned back, but she had come too far at this point, in a distance that was definitely more than physical. She started up the steps slowly, flinching when one creaked, then reminding herself that it was highly doubtful Brian would be able to hear such a sound.

There wasn't much point in knocking on the door at the top, but she did so anyway. Then, when there was no response, she faced up to the fact of maximum intrusion, opened the door and went in.

Once over the threshold, she stopped in astonishment, momentarily transfixed by the view. It was like being at the top of the universe. There were windows on all sides, opening onto a world that stretched in every direction. To the west she saw the majestic bulk of the Catskills; to the east the Hudson was a charcoal ribbon. Vistas unlimited—no wonder he loved it up here.

And Brian? He lay on an oversized studio bed, so still that for a moment her heart contracted. Then she moved closer and saw the steady rise and fall of his chest, and felt a ridiculous surge of relief.

A lock of blond hair had fallen forward over his forehead, while sleep had tinged his cheeks with a faint flush. He looked both young and very vulnerable, and as she stared down at him she thought, *I love him. Oh, dear God, I love him so much, and the whole situation is absolutely impossible!*

She was a responsibility to him at the moment, true, but that responsibility would end with the month of October. *Then,* she thought, *he will inherit the Vandervelt fortune—there's no good reason to think he won't—and in every possible way I will be out of his world. All this can lead to, Marjorie Boardman, is hurt.*

Watching him, she decided that if she had any sense at all she would leave Coxsackie as soon as possible!

But even as she was thinking this she became aware of cold gray eyes watching her steadily. "What in hell do you think you're doing?" he said in a voice thick with anger.

She turned away, so acutely embarrassed that she forgot he couldn't hear her as she stumbled over words of explanation. She didn't hear him get up, either, for that matter, and when he gripped her from behind and swung her around roughly, she was so startled that she nearly lost her balance.

"Don't *do* that!" he commanded.

She stared at him, chagrined, thoroughly annoyed at herself for turning away from him, for this was the one thing she had promised herself she would not do again. She started to speak, but before she could say anything his grip tightened and she inadvertently cried, "You're hurting me again!"

Now it was he who turned away, standing with his back to her by a window facing the river.

"Brian!" she pleaded, but he made no movement. She touched his arm tentatively, and when he still didn't respond she tugged at his shirt sleeve.

He looked down at her, his gray eyes miserable. "Go away, will you, Midge?" he murmured.

She shook her head stubbornly. "No," she told him, "I won't! You asked me what I was doing up here, and I'm going to tell you."

He was watching her intently. "Okay," he said. "Tell me."

"I came up because I was worried about you."

He frowned. "What?"

"I said I was worried about you."

"*Worried* about me? Why should you be?"

She started to answer, but he said, "Hold it," and went across to a large chest of drawers against the wall. Returning, he smiled, but it was a twisted smile. "Go ahead," he sighed wearily. "I'm wired for sound."

"Well, I was in the kitchen having breakfast when Jerry Mueller came in and said you couldn't play tennis with him because you had a bad headache," she told him.

Brian raised his eyebrows. "So," he said, "this worried you so much that you went out and played tennis with him yourself. Right?"

She responded stiffly, "I did play tennis with him for a while, yes."

"The two of you did quite a lot of talking, too, didn't you?" he observed caustically. "What did he say to you about Grace?"

She stared at him, her anger rising. "You *do* have a grapevine, don't you? Did Jerry call you as soon as he left here?"

"No, I don't have a phone up here. Most of the time when I'm here I don't wear these damned hearing aids, so I wouldn't know whether a phone rang or not anyway." He indicated a pair of binoculars on a window ledge. "It was those," he said.

"What do you mean?"

"I got up to take some of the pain-relieving junk the doctors have prescribed for occasions like today.

I saw you and Jerry over by the tennis court, so I went and got the binoculars and watched you. I couldn't see Jerry's face, just yours.''

Suddenly she understood. "You lip-read!" she accused.

"Yes, I did," he admitted. "I try it at a distance sometimes, just to see if I can make anything out. Usually I'm not too successful, but you have very clear diction."

Scorn blazed in her eyes. "That was a *vile* thing to do!" she told him furiously.

"That's a matter of opinion," he said indifferently. "As far as I'm concerned, if people are talking behind my back I see nothing so outrageous about trying to find out what they're saying."

"It wasn't a matter of talking behind your back!"

"So you say," he retorted coolly, as glacial now as he'd been when she first met him. "What is it with you, Midge? Do you have to try to impress every man you meet? Trent Clayton's been infatuated with you since the day you walked into his office; now do you have to try to stir up Jerry, too?"

"What are you saying?" she demanded. "Jerry's married!"

"Does that mean so much to you?" he countered. "The man you were involved with in New York was married, wasn't he?"

Her voice shook as she answered, "John was divorced."

"Before or after he fell into your web?"

She glared at him, but before she could speak he said, "Jerry is married, yes, but right now the marriage isn't on the firmest of foundations. Lucille saw that letter my sister sent to you at the paper."

"What is that supposed to mean?"

"She put two and two together. She realizes you are a friend of Becky's, and as it happens Jerry was very much in love with Becky when we were growing up here. If it hadn't been for my uncle it might have led to something."

"Becky never mentioned him."

"No? Well, perhaps she meant more to Jerry than he did to her. Whatever, having you on the scene has stirred up an old ghost for Lucille. She's also quite aware of your charms, shall we say, and she knows Jerry. He has an eye for beautiful women, even though I've no doubt it's Lucille now whom he really loves. But I'd appreciate it if you'd cool it nevertheless."

She closed her eyes tightly, wanting to strike out at him, wanting to do or say something that would unsettle him as thoroughly as he had just unsettled her. But before she could speak he asked, the words caustic, "*Now* will you leave?"

"Not until I've told you how...how absolutely wrong you are!"

"I don't want to listen," he retorted roughly, his eyes narrowing as he looked at her. "But if you won't leave, let's at least make good use of our time together."

Before she realized his intention he had swept her into his arms, and she felt as if she were caught in a vise. His lips crushed hers as savagely as they had the night he had come upon her parked outside the house, but there was an urgency to his kiss that hadn't been there that other time, an urgency that was communicable. She could feel something deep within her ignite, and thin streaks of fire seemed to flame through her body, merging together in a molten blend of pure desire that astonished her by its quick intensity.

He loosened his grip, but now his hands were exploring her body, probing beneath her sweater, unfastening her bra so that he cupped first one bare breast and then the other. Then, in a single propelling move, he half carried her across the room to his low daybed and thrust her down upon it.

She made no resistance when he edged the sweater over her head, removing the bra with it. Her pulse thundered as she lay before him, her breasts upthrust, the nipples swelling to rose tightness, ready for the caresses of first his fingers, then his mouth.

He had unbuttoned his shirt and now he shrugged out of it impatiently and lay beside her on the bed, his body so close that he left her no doubt of the intensity of his own desire, his maleness flagrant as he thrust himself against her.

She moaned, wanting him so much that she could think of nothing else. Then she saw his hand reach for his belt buckle, and in that instant she looked up, straight into his face, to find that passion had turned him white. There was a glitter to his eyes that was almost frightening, and there was something else, too. She could think of no other word than "contempt" for this thing she saw lurking in Brian's face, and she was sickened by it. Suddenly it was as if everything that had flamed within her just a second earlier turned to ashes. She felt as if she had been burned out, and she caught her teeth on the sob that forced its way through her lips because of this dream become a nightmare.

She pushed him away from her, staggering to her

feet, feeling as if she were going to be sick. Slowly, painfully, she shrugged into her bra and sweater, moving to one of the big crescent windows as she did so. Then she stared out at Brian's wonderful view without even seeing it as other sobs came to join the first one and she felt herself racked by them.

She fought for control, fought for steadiness. Then she heard his step behind her and felt his touch on her shoulder. She shrugged away from him as if he were branding her, hysteria nearly coming to edge her sobs with laughter as she realized the analogy was not far from the truth.

"Look," he said, his voice ragged, "why this, for God's sake? You want me as much as I want you—do you deny that? Ever since that first time in my office we've been moving toward this moment—does that come as any surprise to you? God, it's not as if you were a virgin!"

Shock came with glacial coldness. Shock and bitterness—oh, God, what bitterness! It was true that she was not a virgin, but this didn't mean that she had ever in her life been promiscuous. On the contrary, she had given herself to only one man, and how she had regretted it!

Brian was actually smiling at her now; she saw this as if through a mist of shame—shame she didn't deserve. "You're not trying to tell me that you *are* a virgin, are you?" he challenged. Each word was a mockery.

She reached out blindly, slapping him with all the force she could muster, and she saw his head reel back, saw the shock on his face.

Then he groaned, "Midge! Oh, my God, Midge... please!"

But she shook her head, not wanting to hear anything at all from him now, neither apologies nor explanations.

She turned and bolted through the door, running down the narrow flight of stairs, knowing that she might very well fall, and not caring.

She was nearly at the bottom when she heard him call her name again, but she neither looked up nor turned back.

CHAPTER ELEVEN

THAT FRIDAY EVENING Brian came down to dinner, to Midge's surprise. He looked tired and pale, but when Maude asked him solicitously about his headache he managed a smile and insisted he was fine again.

He made an attempt at conversation as they ate, picking it up quickly when Midge mentioned that the mountains to the west, with their wonderful color interplay of lights and shadows, were a source of constant fascination to her. "There's a solidity to them," she said. "They're always the same and yet forever different."

"The Catskills are very old," Brian told her. "They're composed of thick layers of shale and sandstone—the rocks date back to the Paleozoic era—and they've been the delight of geologists for longer than any of us can imagine. Actually, they're not very high, as mountains go. Slide Mountain and Hunter Mountain are the two highest in the whole group, and they're both just a bit over four thousand feet. But I agree with you: they give an impression of permanence; you get the feeling they've been there forever and are going to be there forever, though I'm sure the scientists wouldn't agree with that latest premise. The earth is forever changing, altering its face. Then, of course," he added, flashing a surprisingly impish grin, "there are legends."

"Like Rip Van Winkle, do you mean?" she asked him.

"Rip's the most famous one, I suppose," he conceded.

"Was he a real person?"

Brian lifted his eyebrows, looking across at his aunt. "What shall I tell her?" he asked.

Maude laughed. "You shouldn't ask me," she said gently. "As far as I'm concerned Rip has always been very real."

"I might have known you'd say that," he teased. "I can't tell you a lie, Maude; on the other hand maybe Rip *was* a real person, but under another name. The Rip Van Winkle we've all heard about was a character in a story by Washington Irving."

"*The Sketch Book*," Maude put in.

"Yes. He wrote it in 1819, I believe, so Rip has been around awhile; but as I say, maybe he *was* a real person hereabouts, because Irving supposedly adapted an old local legend for his plot. According to the story, Rip was a Dutch colonist, and he was a casual sort of individual. He was plagued by a nagging wife and took whatever opportunity he could to escape her scolding tongue. And he wasn't averse to taking a drink or two.

"Not long before the American Revolution began, he went off hunting in the mountains. He was wandering around out there somewhere," Brian continued, waving vaguely toward the west, "when he met some very odd little men. They were playing ninepins, and Rip was happy enough to join them, particularly as they had a good supply of liquor on hand, which they shared with him. He knew there was something strange about them, though, and this was reinforced when they told him they were members of Henry Hudson's crew. Rip at once realized they were ghosts, because Hudson had died some one hundred and fifty years earlier, but this didn't bother him particularly. Evidently there was nothing unearthly about their liquor, and he continued to drink up until he finally fell asleep.

"Well, of course, as we all know, Rip Van Winkle's nap lasted for twenty years, and when he woke up he found he had a long white beard and wasn't quite as agile as he used to be. He came back down from the mountains to the village where he lived, to find that it was now part of a new country, the United States of America. Further, his wife had died in the interim, and their daughter was married.

"When Becky and I were youngsters and there was a thunder-and-lightning storm," Brian added, "Clara always used to tell us that the thunder was the sound of Rip Van Winkle playing ninepins up there in the mountains. Remember that, Aunt Maude?"

"Yes," she said, "I do indeed. Brian, you ought to take Midge for some drives through the Catskill country. There are some beautiful places to visit up in the mountains," she added, turning toward Midge.

Brian's lips curved in the semblance of a smile that was not echoed in his eyes as he said, "I'm not sure Midge would want to go driving in the Catskills with me."

Then, before she or Maude could reply, he went on, "Speaking of transportation, I've asked them to deliver another Volvo to you tomorrow morning."

"My car really is unsalvageable?"

"Totally," he said. "But I've a friend at a place in

Albany that specializes in foreign cars, and he found one somewhat newer than yours that I expect you'll find satisfactory.''

"You rented it?"

"No," he said, clearly surprised. "I bought it."

"Brian," she began, "I can't possibly—"

He held up a restraining hand. "Later, please?"

But he gave her no opportunity that evening to go into the matter again. For a while he sat in Maude's sitting room and watched television with them, then he slipped away so quickly that Midge had no time to detain him.

She hoped he might come into the kitchen while she was having breakfast the following morning, but he didn't, and when finally she asked where he was, Clara said he'd gone to the office earlier.

The substitute Volvo was delivered at ten o'clock, and Midge was dismayed when Clara called her and she went out to accept the keys for it from the garage mechanic who had driven it over. It was indeed of a newer vintage than her trusty old car had been; it was, in fact, just next to new in her opinion, and she knew that paying for it would make a real dent in her finances. Yet there seemed no alternative now *but* to pay for it, except to send it back wherever it had come from and then try to find a cheaper car by herself. She certainly wasn't about to accept any presents from Brian, large or small!

As she stared at the little car, which was a very pretty shade of blue, her annoyance with Brian mounted, and she told herself he had absolutely no right to be so high-handed about something like this. True, the money involved probably didn't mean very much to him, but he should at least be able to realize that not everyone was a Vandervelt.

Her cheeks stung now as she remembered the scene between them the previous day in the tower room. Brian had been entirely right when he said that she wanted him as much as he wanted her. What made her feel so terribly cheapened, what made her despise herself, was the knowledge that he could so easily have taken her had she not seen that expression on his face. The contempt.

Oh, at that moment, she thought bitterly, he had been very much a Vandervelt. A throwback to a real patroon, the ultimate aristocrat. She tried to tell herself that she hated him, then admitted sadly that this would be merely self-deception. His attitude, perhaps. Brian himself—never.

Now, without testing the Volvo, she pocketed the keys and went back into the house and upstairs to her room. She was in no mood to talk to either Clara or Maude just now, nor did she want to face Brian should he suddenly come back from the office.

The Victorian decor of the suite was particularly oppressive today. Midge felt as if she were being smothered by heavy furniture, thick upholstery and the draperies that blocked so much of the wonderful view even when pulled to the side as far as they could go.

She had become very fond of Maude in this short space of time, and of Clara and Tom, as well, but it seemed to her that it was impossible to go on living in the Vandervelt house any longer. No, she told herself firmly, the best course of action would be to move back to the Prescotts' motel. Then, once this month was over, she could talk to Trent about getting out of the balance of their verbal contract.

She would not go until then, though. Regardless of the situation between Brian and herself, there was no way she could consider leaving Coxsackie until after November first. She had to wait it out until the probation period had passed and she was sure he was all right.

Then....

AS SHE WALKED THROUGH THE FRONT DOOR of the *Valley Voice* building Monday morning, it seemed to Midge that she had been away much longer than a week.

Lucille Mueller, already at the reception desk, smiled and asked some solicitous questions, but now Midge was painfully aware of the threatening impasse between Lucille and Jerry, and her replies were stilted.

Trent was alone in the advertising department, and he came to her quickly, drawing her to him and hugging her in a way she was not apt to encourage. Then, perhaps sensing her lack of response, he stepped back and looked her over from head to foot.

"Well," he concluded, "you don't seem to be any the worse for wear. Am I ever glad to have you back! There's something, though...." He hesitated, then walked over and closed the glass-paneled door that led into the main corridor.

"I'm glad you got here this morning before Clem and Ellen," he told her while she looked at him, puzzled. "Midge, I hate to say it, but you've still been holding out on me."

She frowned. "What are you talking about?"

"Well, now it comes out that you're a friend of Brian Vandervelt's sister, and that's why you've moved into the old family homestead," he said with more than a touch of sarcasm. "And I, of course, was the last to know."

"There hasn't been anything to know," she told him, impatient because she'd had more than enough of this sort of thing. "I moved into the Vandervelt house because they felt I shouldn't be alone after the accident."

"How considerate of them!" Trent responded coolly.

"Trent, please," she said, "spare me the irony! I've had enough grief recently; I don't need any more from you."

"Care to elaborate on that statement?"

"No, I don't."

"Has the Vandervelt heir been making unwelcome advances?" he persisted.

"Oh, for God's sake," she said, annoyed. "Is that all you can think of?"

"When I'm with you, darling, perhaps it is," he told her. "I'm jealous as hell of you, I admit it. Vandervelt may be deaf and dumb, but he's a handsome devil and—"

She bristled. "That's a rotten thing to say!"

"That he's handsome?" Trent asked, feigning innocence.

"No, of course not. You know perfectly well what I'm talking about. As it is, that 'deaf and dumb' phrase is dreadful and should be abolished from the language, but even so it doesn't apply to Brian."

"How defensive you are where he's concerned!" Trent observed.

"And how obnoxious you can be," she finished. "I'm beginning to be sorry I came back."

"I was afraid perhaps you wouldn't," he said. "A life of luxury can become habit-forming very quickly, I understand. Nice habit, too—"

"I'm not going to listen to you," she interrupted. "This is ridiculous." She handed him a large manila envelope. "Here's the Halloween copy."

He took it from her, clearly surprised. "So you did work on it!" he commented.

"Yes," she snapped. "What did you think I was doing with my time? No, don't answer that question. With your poisonous mind, it could lead in only one direction."

He was leafing through the copy. "This looks terrific. Midge, darling, cool down, will you? Ellen and Clem will be walking in the door any minute, and you look as if you'd like to stab me in the heart."

"Perhaps I would."

"You already have," he said succinctly, and she shook her head in dismay at him. "Have dinner with me tonight and I'll convince you."

"I don't want to be convinced," she retorted. "To go back a bit, though, before the others do get here, it's true that Becky Vandervelt is one of my dearest friends, and I admit one of my reasons for coming to Coxsackie was to see where she used to live. The job on the paper, however, is an entirely different matter. I think it's fair to say that I got it and am holding it purely on my own merit."

"That's true enough."

"Then I don't see why the fact that I know Becky or am living temporarily in the Vandervelt home should have anything to do with my work here. Did Brian Vandervelt speak to you about this?''

Had Brian spoken to Trent about her? She shrank from the thought and yet had to admit that it was possible. It seemed second nature to sow seeds of suspicion here at the *Valley Voice*. Brian might well be as guilty of this kind of game as some of the others.

Trent, though, looked decidedly startled, she saw with satisfaction. "Of course not," he said hastily. "Brian Vandervelt hasn't said anything to me about your knowing his sister or your moving into his house. We're not on quite that cozy a basis!"

"I don't especially like the word 'cozy' used in that context," she said sharply.

"Midge—" Trent looked at her imploringly "—it seems as if everything connected with you has put me in a strange position," he confessed. "Ellen accused me the other day of having fallen for you." He smiled wryly. "I didn't know it was that obvious. I've never mixed business with pleasure before, or maybe I should say pleasure with business, and I can see readily enough that it's not a good idea. I wish you and I had met somewhere on neutral ground, but as it is I have to admit that in addition to being one hell of an attractive lady you're the best copywriter I've ever worked with, and I would hate to lose you. I suppose that's what worries me every time I hear about the Vandervelts having you in their clutches."

"The Vandervelts do not have me in their clutches," she said coldly.

"Midge," he began again, but this time he was interrupted by Ellen Brent, who knocked once before turning the doorknob and coming into the office. Midge felt her cheeks go warm, because it was not usual to keep the outer door closed; one look at Ellen's suspicious face told her that the girl had put the worst possible interpretation upon the whole situation.

"Hi, Ellen," Trent greeted her, recouping with remarkable ease. He turned back to Midge. "As I was saying, if you've finished with the Halloween copy you might go to work on a new account Clem brought in the other day. Some people from New York have opened a combination restaurant-boutique in Athens, which seems rather unusual, and they want to see what we can do for them."

She nodded. "I'll talk to Clem about it as soon as he comes in," she promised, and later she did so, but her heart was not in her work today. She had not seen Brian since Friday evening, and without actually going up to the tower again—and she had no intention of doing that—there had seemed no way to get in touch with him to work out something about payment for the Volvo.

Somehow she had "just missed" him all weekend, at least according to Clara and Maude. She realized he was avoiding her and resented the fact.

This situation continued throughout the week. It seemed to her that she had occasion at one time or another to talk to almost everyone on the *Valley Voice* except Brian, and by the time the paper went to press on Thursday she was convinced that could only be becuase he didn't want to see her. He had not come down to dinner any of the evenings, and since neither Maude nor Clara seemed to expect him she refrained from asking questions.

Once again Trent asked her to go out with him, this time to a German restaurant-nightclub near

Catskill called the Berghof that was, he promised, always a lot of fun. He suggested the following evening, and after contemplating spending another dreary evening alone in her room she agreed to go.

The garden club was holding its fall banquet that Thursday night and Maude had asked her to be a guest, but she sidestepped, saying she had some shopping she really needed to do and so planned to go to Catskill since the stores would be open late. Actually, she didn't care in the least whether she got to Catskill before the stores closed. She merely wanted to be alone tonight, and in this case being alone meant getting away from both the *Valley Voice* and the Vandervelt mansion. So when she left the paper she drove directly across 9W to the Maples.

A waitress whom she'd never seen before led her to a window booth, and she was consulting the menu when a familiar voice said, "I hope you don't *really* want to eat by yourself."

She looked up into Jerry Mueller's laughing face. "All right, I plead guilty," he added. "I saw your car turn in here and I followed you. May I join you?"

"Of course."

"How about a drink before dinner?"

"Yes. A Manhattan on the rocks."

"Make it two," he told the waitress.

He was wearing civilian clothes, a blue tweed jacket that was extremely becoming and an open-throated sports shirt of a deeper shade. But he said, "Believe it or not, I'm on duty; I have a special job to do later tonight. I'll have worn off one drink long before then, though. It's a piece of luck, running into you. I've been wanting to talk to you."

"Oh?"

He smiled ruefully. "I couldn't very well call you at the paper because Lucille answers the incoming phone," he explained. "And I decided it would be just my luck to get Brian if I tried to reach you at the Vandervelt house."

Midge frowned and Jerry averted his gaze, toying with a fork, his voice low.

"Brian thinks I'm not being fair to Lucille lately, which doesn't happen to be the truth," he said slowly. "I think he's also somewhat blinded where you are concerned." He looked up now, his dark blue eyes serious. "I know it's none of my business," he told her, "but I can't help being concerned about Brian. He doesn't need to be hurt again!"

"And you think I'm apt to hurt him?" she asked, more than a little incredulous.

"You seem to reach him as no one else does."

"You're mistaken," Midge said firmly. "I don't think anyone reaches Brian, especially a woman. Certainly you know how Brian feels about women. He's built quite a wall. I'll be honest: at first I wished I *could* knock it down, but now I'm quite sure there's no chance."?

Jerry said quietly, "So it's like that, is it?"

"Yes," she answered. "No. It was, but it's not going to be!"

"Do you have a choice?"

"Yes," she said with more firmness than she felt. "I've been through one unhappy romance. That's why I quit my job in New York and went out to San Francisco—that, and because my father remarried recently and I wanted to meet his new wife. I also wanted to see Becky again, of course, which was wonderful—except for getting me into this."

"So you really did come here because of Becky?"

"Yes. She's felt all along that something serious happened to Brian at the time of the explosion, and she asked me to find out what it was. She has two little children, so she hasn't been able to come East herself."

"Have you told her what really did happen to Brian?"

"No."

"Why not?"

She raised her eyes to his. "It really *is* Brian's business," she said. "He's the one who should tell his sister about his deafness. But also I've come to agree with him that it would be best if Becky didn't come East until this whole strange affair is over."

"Why do you call it a strange affair?" Jerry asked curiously.

"Because it is! It's unreal, at least to me. I simply can't understand why anyone would leave such a fiendish will. It puts temptation on a platter!"

"You didn't know Horace Vandervelt," Jerry told her. "You asked me the other day if there was anyone left who liked him. Well—it was more than a matter of 'like' and 'dislike,' Midge. For instance, when I was a kid and we used to read Dickens's *A Christmas Carol* in school I was sure that Scrooge and Horace Vandervelt were one and the same...except that Horace never had a change of heart. I suppose a good psychiatrist might have been able to analyze him, but I think Horace would have burned up the couch first.

"I never knew him personally, of course, until Brian and Becky came here to live after their parents were killed," Jerry continued. "They went away to school, but they were here on vacations and by some miracle we managed to get friendly despite Horace. My only brother died when he was four, so I guess you could say Brian became like a brother to me. He still is, even though—'' Jerry smiled his engaging smile ''—he's rich, scheduled to be *very* rich, while everything I've got comes via my salary from the State of New York.

''But being a Vandervelt, with everything that means around here, never seemed to matter to Brian. When we were kids he used to look out at the river and watch the tankers heading for Albany, and he said that's what he wanted to do—to go to sea. I think he felt it was the one way he could get away from Horace!

''He applied for the appointment to Annapolis all on his own and got it, and the old man was furious. He had always assumed Brian would go to the college of *his* choice and then come back and be groomed to take over the paper and manage the estate if anything so mortal as death ever happened to Horace Vandervelt. That's why after the accident, when Brian was at his weakest, both physically and emotionally, Horace took full advantage of the situation and forced him into the contract.''

''The contract? Is that this probation thing Becky has talked about?''

''Yes. Brian signed a contract agreeing to remain with the *Hudson River Valley Voice* for a period of two years after Horace's death. During that time it would be necessary for the paper to show a continuing increase in both advertising and circulation, and a minimum turnover in personnel. In this interim period the responsibility for handling Vandervelt

Enterprises—which comprises not only the *Valley Voice* but also all sorts of other properties and businesses that Horace got in his clutches over the years—would remain in the hands of Wilson Strathmore, the business manager, and Andrew Summers, who lives in Catskill and has been Horace's attorney for years.

"Well, Brian signed the contract, a year or so later Horace died, and next came the will. You obviously know about the will."

"Enough about it, I think," Midge interrupted. "I gather that if Brian fulfills the terms of what you call the contract he'll inherit the paper and eventually the mansion, upon his aunt's death, and half of everything else. If he doesn't fulfill the contract, then he's cut off with a dollar, the four department heads will inherit, and there are some others who would get fairly substantial bequests. Becky stands to inherit fifty percent of Vandervelt Enterprises, I suppose you'd call it, no matter what. Right?"

"Essentially," said Jerry. "But if both Becky and Brian were to die before the contract time is up, the department heads would inherit the whole package. That," he finished soberly, "is why Brian wants to keep Becky away from here."

CHAPTER TWELVE

MIDGE WENT ON TO CATSKILL and shopped as she had
planned to do, but it was purely necessary shopping,
stockings and some makeup, and she was glad to finish and start back to Coxsackie.

Jerry's conversation had disturbed her, and as she
drove along the Athens road she felt strangely troubled for Becky, Brian...and for herself, as well.
There was such a sense of unreality to the whole matter of the Vandervelt will, making it seem more fic-
tion than fact. Now she felt she had been lulled into a
state of false tranquillity, and for the first time really
the sharp edge of danger came to give her pause. She
felt herself grow cold as she thought of Brian Vandervelt's terrible vulnerability.

She sighed. She had become entirely too involved
here in Coxsackie, yet she knew only too well that
once the month was up and Brian—please God—was
safe there would be no further part for her to play.
She did not belong in Brian Vandervelt's world, she
thought sadly, and never before had she felt so lonely.

Turning into the Vandervelt driveway with a sense
of habit, she noticed that Brian's white Jaguar was
already parked to one side of the entrance, and she
pulled up behind it. As she got out of the Volvo she
inadvertently glanced first at the tower, then at her

watch. It was not even ten, but the tower was in darkness. Brian, then, must already be asleep...but she was wide awake.

The moon hung lopsided in the sky, touching the lawn and the treetops with minted silver. Midge wandered toward the back of the house, wondering if it had also given the Hudson a Cinderella touch, and there ahead of her was the gazebo, a symbol to her now of Brian's and Becky's childhood.

She walked across to it and was mounting the steps when she saw Brian, sitting on the side that faced the river. A ray of moonlight turned his hair to white gold, and he was statue still.

She started to backtrack and was about to slip out the same way she had come in when he said, "Midge?"

She stopped, and would have sworn that her heart was thumping so loud it must be audible even to him. "Yes?" she answered.

He stood and slowly walked across to her. He was wearing a light-colored jacket, and temporarily his face was lost in the shadows.

"Where were you?" he asked. And when she didn't answer, "Okay. Tell me I've no right to ask!"

It was like igniting anger's spark. She forgot about everything except the fact that, unable to help herself, she had been looking for him all week, subconsciously wondering and worrying about him.

"Never mind about rights!" she blurted now. "Where have *you* been?" Then she stopped, horrified, actually hoping he hadn't heard her. But this time he fooled her.

"By any chance does that imply that you missed

me?'' he asked. Sensing her surprise, he added, ''There are no distracting noises, so my substitute ears are doing very well. Am I right in thinking you want to know where I've been?''

Midge nodded, unable to trust herself to speak because she loved him so much it seemed impossible that she would not in some way communicate this to him.

As it was, silvery moonlight was highlighting her face and he was watching her much too closely as he told her, ''Well, Monday and Tuesday I had to go to New York on business. Wednesday I holed up in my office to make up for lost time. After the paper came out this afternoon I went to look for you, but you had left. I had that damned Valley Men's Club dinner meeting, but I skipped out early and came home. Only,'' he added, sounding amazingly vulnerable about this, ''you...weren't here.''

She closed her eyes tightly, her senses swimming, and after a very intense moment of silence he said gently, ''Well, I've told *you*. How about a return performance?''

She swallowed hard. ''I thought I'd go shopping in Catskill,'' she answered. ''First I stopped at the Maples for dinner, because I'd told Clara I wouldn't be here. Then Jerry Mueller came in—''

''Just by chance?''

''No. He saw my car—your car, I should say. You shouldn't have done that.''

''Midge,'' Brian said, ''please. Don't make an issue of it. If you hadn't come up here in the first place your own car would still be intact. Anyway, it was very little to do for you.''

''I don't agree, but we'll go into it later,'' she

responded stiffly. "As I was saying, Jerry saw the car, so he came in. We had dinner together."

"Just the two of you?"

"Look," she snapped, "don't sound so damned disapproving. He was on duty actually, and anyway I can assure you he's not being unfaithful to Lucille with me or anyone else!"

"Whoa!" he said. "Slow down, will you! I didn't mean to be critical, though I do think that it would be bad timing for word to get back to Lucille that Jerry was dining out with a beautiful girl. Not that I blame you for seeking outside companionship: living here must seem like being shut up in a tomb at times. The house, God knows, is something out of a horror story, and Aunt Maude, bless her, does have her hang-ups. And as for me...."

"Yes? What about you, Brian?"

"I've mentioned before," he said quietly, "that I'm fully aware I'm not the best company in the world."

He said this emotionlessly, as if it were a simple fact not to be disputed, and his attitude infuriated her.

"You know damn well that's not so!" she exploded.

"On the contrary," he said levelly, "I believe it's absolutely so!"

She shook her head. "You couldn't be more wrong. There is no reason for you to be so damnably defensive! There in the tower room...."

"Yes?"

She could feel herself flushing. "I don't want to talk about it. But I *am* sorry I invaded your privacy. I shouldn't have."

"All right," he agreed easily. "There is one thing I'd like to know, though."

"What?" Midge asked suspiciously.

"You mentioned being worried about me. Why?"

She hesitated. "Jerry told me you have bad headaches occasionally," she answered. "I wondered if you should do something about them."

"Playing the mother hen?" he asked lightly. "As a matter of fact, I *have* done something about them. Sometimes trying to hear can create considerable tension, and it's augmented by extraneous noises that drive you slightly out of your mind when you have to depend on hearing aids. I'm doing better, though I still get headaches now and then. But it's nothing fatal. I'm not about to succumb to a brain tumor or something equally dramatic. Is that what you wondered?"

"I don't know," she said, her voice so small that he sighed.

"I detest the question," he told her, "but I'll have to ask it. What did you say?"

"I said I didn't know what I wondered, but I really meant...."

"Yes?"

"I don't want anything else to happen to you."

A shaft of moonlight slanted through the gingerbread curlicues trimming the gazebo, touching them both. Through it they stared at each other, and it seemed to Midge as if time had stopped, as if they would forever be bathed in silver light, both of them speechless and barely breathing. Then he took her in his arms, and this time his kiss was entirely different. It seemed to her a distillation of love's purest essence, and she was so tremendously moved by it that it was a long moment before she realized he had released her and she was standing alone.

Before she could believe what he was doing, he strode across the gazebo and down the steps, walking with rapid strides back across the lawn. She heard a car engine roar and saw headlights flash on, and a moment later the white Jaguar swung out of the driveway and turned onto the road in the direction of Athens.

AFTER A TIME Midge strolled slowly back to the house, undressed and went to bed, but she lay awake for a long while hoping to hear the Jaguar come back. Finally she slept, then awakened with the dawn and ran at once to the front window. The white car was parked in its usual place, and she found that it was entirely possible to go weak with relief.

She went back to bed and back to sleep—and overslept. This wasn't particularly important, because once again Trent had told her not to come into the office unless she wanted to. She had already more than made up for the lost days after the accident.

Nevertheless, there were several small details she preferred to attend to before the beginning of the new week, so toward midmorning she drove over to the office. Brian's Jaguar was not in the driveway when she left, nor was it in the newspaper parking lot, and she could not help but be anxious. She reflected ruefully that she *was* getting to be a mother hen about him.

She had been working about an hour when her

desk phone rang. To her surprise it was Jerry, sounding brusque and almost angry.

"What happened with Brian?" he demanded.

"What do you mean?"

"After I left you last night I handled the detail I was assigned to, which took me to the other side of Catskill. I drove along 9W on the way back—this was around midnight—and I saw Brian's Jag parked outside a bar—"

"The world seems to be full of bars," she interrupted.

"True. Anyway, I decided to go in, and Brian was by himself downing one Scotch after another. All I could get out of him was that he'd been talking to you in the gazebo."

"That's so," she admitted.

"Well, what in hell did you say to him?"

"Nothing," Midge told him. "Nothing, that is, that hadn't been said before in one version or another."

"*Something* must have happened," Jerry insisted. "I stayed with him until the place closed up, and by then he could hardly stagger. I've never seen Brian in such shape. I know the bartender, so I drove Brian home in the Jag and he followed and took me on home. I went back with Lucille this morning and redeemed my own car, all of which represents quite a bit of hassle for a drunk friend, especially when he didn't appreciate it."

"And he didn't?"

"I'll say he didn't! He was resisting so much, in fact, that I told him if he didn't knock it off I'd arrest him."

"Would you have?"

"You're damned right I would have," Jerry said darkly.

"What happened when you got back to the house?"

"His house?"

"Yes."

"It can be a long, long way up to that tower," Jerry informed her. "Have you seen him this morning?"

"No."

"I imagine he's still sleeping it off, then. Midge, I don't expect you to be his keeper, but it isn't the safest thing in the world for him to be acting like that right now. Try to take it easy with him, will you?"

He hung up before she could express her resentment at the last statement. And as far as being Brian Vandervelt's keeper was concerned—she laughed derisively at the mere thought.

The conversation with Jerry had interrupted her creative flow. She had to force herself to get back to work, and it was past noon when, after struggling through a final paragraph, she knew she'd had enough. She was restless, she was hungry, and so she decided to stop at a small coffee shop up the street for a sandwich.

She had told Clara that morning that she'd be out for dinner, and had been surprised at the housekeeper's visible disappointment. Clara had at once suggested she join Maude first for a predinner glass of sherry in the library, and this she had promised to do. She was touched by the thought that Maude truly welcomed her companionship, for it was about the one thing she had she could offer the dear woman, and it seemed very little; she wished there could be something more.

She was thinking of this as she walked into the coffee shop—only to stop short when she saw Brian sitting alone in a corner booth. At precisely the same moment he looked up, and their eyes meshed.

He was wearing a gray tweed suit with a white shirt open at the throat. She appraised him frankly and decided he looked terrible. Although he had shaved, he was unusually pale, his eyes red rimmed.

She summoned up sufficient nerve to walk across and slide into the booth, taking the bench on the other side of the table and asking simultaneously, "May I?"

"You already have," he pointed out, "though I wasn't sure you wanted to, from the look on your face!"

There was an empty glass by his plate, and a cup of black coffee that had barely been touched. As she noted the glass he said, "That was something Joe swears will cure a hangover." He nodded toward the chunky dark-haired man behind the counter. "Maybe it will, but it tastes god-awful!"

"Don't expect *me* to have any sympathy for you," she said sternly.

Joe, wiping his hands on a dish towel, called out to her, "Want a menu?"

"No, thanks," Midge told him. "I'll have a cheeseburger and a strawberry shake, please."

Brian grimaced, moaning, "Ouch."

"If it upsets you to watch me eat, just look the other way," Midge told him firmly, and then stopped, briefly horrified, remembering that she was talking not only to Becky's brother but to her employer, who, God willing, would also soon be the inheritor of the Vandervelt empire. But to her amazement he smiled, and it was such a natural and totally wonderful smile that she could only stare at him disbelievingly, even as she felt the throb of an unexpectedly tumultuous pulse in the hollow of her throat.

Brian's laugh rang out, an uninhibited, surprisingly youthful laugh. "You're almost worse than Mueller!"

"What do you mean by that?"

"Well," Brian said, "despite the fact I'm sure he'll tell you I wasn't in shape to remember anything, I remember very well that he was giving me hell all the time I was trying to finish up what started out as a pretty good job of getting drunk. Then he dragged me home against my will and berated me thoroughly before he let me go to bed, and about fifteen minutes ago he popped in here just to be sure I wasn't thinking of heading for any of the hair of the dog that bit me."

Joe brought the cheeseburger and the milk shake and asked, "Brian, how about you? Maybe a BLT or something like that?"

"A little later, maybe," Brian said cautiously.

Midge took a bite of her cheeseburger. "You're chicken," she accused him.

"No, prudent," he corrected. Then he went on soberly, "Midge, about last night...."

"Yes," she said, avoiding those disconcertingly direct gray eyes.

"I had to leave you just then," he told her frankly. "I'm not going to try to explain my actions. I'll only say that it was such a...a tremendous moment I suppose I was afraid that if I tried to prolong it I'd only ruin it. So I took off. After a while I saw a bar and I stopped and went in. I hadn't started out with the thought of doing a lot of drinking, but the further along I got the better idea it seemed. When Jerry came in...."

He virtually forced her to look at him. She did, and he said, "Look, I know it was juvenile. Or just plain foolish. Or... chicken."

She couldn't resist it. "But not prudent?"

The corners of his mouth twitched. "No," he agreed, "not prudent."

She finished her lunch, and still avoiding Joe's suggestion of a BLT, Brian walked outside with her. At the curb he glanced at the Volvo. "Is it running all right?"

"Yes," she said, and began, "Brian..." but he held up a protesting hand.

"Not now," he told her wryly.

"Where's your Jaguar?" she asked him.

"Down the street. There wasn't any place out here in front when I came along. I've got to go over to the paper for a while, but...."

He seemed oddly hesitant, and she looked up at him curiously. "What is it?" she asked.

"Jerry mentioned that he said something to you about the four of us going to a French restaurant he wants to try, up in Albany," he said to her astonishment.

"Yes, he did," she agreed cautiously.

"Would you like to try it tonight?"

Disappointment stabbed her. "I can't," she nearly wailed. "Trent asked me yesterday if I'd go to a German place with him over near Catskill."

"The Berghof?"

"I think that's the name of it, yes."

"It's a fun place," he said casually, but she felt as if he'd closed a door in her face, and she was sick at heart as she left him.

CHAPTER THIRTEEN

THERE WAS A STRANGE CAR in the driveway at the Vandervelt house when Midge arrived back there, so she walked around to the kitchen entrance and inside found Clara busy setting out cups and saucers on a silver tray.

"Good!" the housekeeper announced. "I was hoping you'd get back. Mrs. Strathmore stopped by, and Mrs. Vandervelt said she'd like you to join them for a cup of tea."

The thought was not at all appealing, yet Midge had been lecturing herself about doing something for Maude.

Despite herself she sighed and said, "Clara, I *would* like to freshen up first. Is there a way to get upstairs without using the main staircase?"

"Sure is," Clara assured her, and leading her to the far end of the kitchen she opened a door that revealed a narrow steep flight of stairs, much like the ones to Brian's tower.

Up in her room, Midge dabbed on some lipstick and gave her hair a quick brushing. She seldom saw Wilson Strathmore, but on those rare occasions when they met she was always struck by his courtesy; there was an air of old-fashioned gallantry about him.

He had been studiously polite, she remembered, even on that occasion when she had almost bumped into him coming out of Brian's office. But he had been visibly troubled that day, too, and now she wondered why.

She went back down the main staircase and at the threshold of the library found that Maude and her guest were so deeply engrossed in conversation they did not immediately notice her. This gave her a chance to get a good look at the business manager's wife. Midge found that she was petite with white hair, her prettiness faded but still somehow very appealing.

Maude, looking up, said, "Well, there you are, my dear! Moira, this is Midge Boardman."

Moira Strathmore's smile was quick and sincere, and her voice had soft Southern overtones. "I'm delighted to meet you, my dear," she said. "I understand everyone is happier since you joined the staff of the *Valley Voice*. I think the only thing that worries the executives is that one of these days you'll up and leave," she added in what evidently was meant to be a touch of humor.

Maude, though, at once looked apprehensive and interrupted quickly, "Nonsense! Midge is here to stay." But there was a question mark to her statement.

Midge, trying to keep it light, responded with a smile, "Actually I'm on a trial period. We'll see what happens at the end of it."

"You've nothing to worry about, believe me," Mrs. Strathmore assured her.

Maude brightened. "Moira brought me her latest ikebana arrangement," she told Midge, indicating a floral arrangement that had been placed on the coffee table. "Isn't it lovely?"

Studying it, Midge found it exquisite. Moira Strathmore had arranged autumn leaves with just three bronze-toned chrysanthemums in a low gray green container. The effect was striking.

Maude, tracing a flower with her fingertip, said, "See, the tallest one, in the center, represents Heaven. Then the next highest is Man, and the third is Earth. Heaven, Man and Earth. That's the philosophy of ikebana. It takes in everything there is, and yet it's so simple. That's what I like about it. The lines are so clean and uncluttered."

The sentence was oddly revealing. Maude, Midge felt, was unconsciously saying that ikebana, like staying in bed as late as she wanted to and watching television, was a protest on her part, a form of revolution, for her own life had been cluttered, stuffed to the bursting point, with Horace Vandervelt's Victorianism. Although she still lived in Horace's shadow in this house crammed with the trappings of a more hypocritical era, Maude had turned to an art form that emphasized simplicity to the point of starkness. It was surely one of her first acts of self-expression, and Midge found it poignantly significant.

Then a terrific idea came to possess her, and with a growing sense of inner excitement she thought, *perhaps this is what I can do for Maude!* She could gradually assure the twins' aunt that she should do what she probably had always wanted to do: redecorate the entire mansion. But first she had to be convinced that to do so would not cause Horace to rise from his grave. And it shouldn't be done in Japanese modern, to be sure; that would be an anachronism. But if one started on the outside with fresh white paint and did the doors and the shutters and the win-

dow frames in a contrasting color, what a difference
it would make!

She warmed to the plan. The rooms should be
done over one by one with new paint, new wallpaper
and in most instances new draperies. A lot of the furniture should be retired, the good pieces should be
revitalized, and everything upholsterable should be
redone in vibrant new colors. It would be a lot of
work, she conceded, but the results would be fabu-
lous!

She became so enraptured over the prospect that it
took all her willpower not to bring the subject up on
the spot. Instead she forced herself to sit back and
listen as Maude and Moira chatted about their garden club, their ikebana instructor, who actually had
lived in Japan, and a potpourri of other subjects.

Moira left, and while Maude was still in a flush of
excitement over having had a guest, Midge told her
she was going out for dinner with Trent Clayton.
When Maude gave her a look like a child who has
suddenly had a chocolate bar snatched away, she
added hastily, "But I'd love to have a glass of sherry
with you first."

This was acceptable, and Midge went upstairs to
change. Deciding to dress up tonight, she chose a
long red-and-black-banded skirt with a black scoop-
necked top, adding an intricate silver medallion and
silver earrings. Finishing with a touch of her best perfume, she decided that despite a poor night's sleep
she really didn't look bad at all!

She ran down the long staircase feeling surprisingly
carefree, and was nearly at the bottom when she became aware of Brian standing off to one side, toward
the corridor that led back to the kitchen. Automati-

cally she slowed her pace, and as he came toward
the stairs she realized anew how tall he was. She had
to stand on the third step to be on a level with him,
and it seemed strange to meet his gaze on the same
plane.

He said softly, "You look terrific!"

"Thank you," she managed, and knew that if he
kept on looking at her with gray eyes that were anything but cool at the moment, it was going to be
impossible to continue down those last three steps.

"Is Trent coming for you this early?" he asked.

Midge shook her head. "No, he won't be here for
nearly an hour. I promised your aunt I'd have sherry
with her before I left." Suddenly she felt as heady as
if she'd been infused with champagne, and she let her
smile shine forth in all its brilliance. "Hangover
gone?" she teased.

Brian laughed. "Yes," he said, then added ruefully, "though I'll admit I've felt better."

He was watching her very intently, but she was becoming used to this; she knew that with him it was a
necessary way of communication. Yet now she realized that there was something entirely apart from a
need to lip-read in his expression. His eyes seemed to
darken, and suddenly he reached out his arms, quickly swinging her off the steps to floor level, so that her
head came barely to his shoulders. Then his mouth
descended and she felt the beloved warmth of his
lips, and everything within her surged to meet and
match his ardor.

As their hands moved mutually to caress, to explore, they seemed to be suspended in time, and it
was a moment that Midge wished could be eternal.
Then Brian said huskily, his lips against her hair, "If

I don't let you go you'll have to go back upstairs and get ready all over again!''

"Brian..." she moaned.

But he cut her off shakily, "No, darling. Don't make it harder...please.'' He straightened and added, almost abruptly, "You'd better go have your sherry with Aunt Maude.''

Midge obeyed him like someone moving in a trance, reality returning only when she actually stood on the threshold of the library and saw Maude sitting in her favorite chair. Then she came down to earth with a thud. Maybe it was only a trick of light, but it seemed to her that Maude looked ghastly.

She's ill, Midge thought. *She's really ill!*

At that moment Maude looked up and smiled brightly. "I had Clara bring the sherry in so I'd be ready for you. Don't you look lovely!'' she added admiringly.

The flower arrangement had been moved to one end of the coffee table to make way for the silver tray with the cut-glass decanter and two long-stemmed wineglasses. Maude's hands became busy now pouring the wine.

"Brian stopped in a little while ago,'' she remarked. "I asked him if he'd join us, but he isn't much for sherry. Matter of fact, he said he's dead tired tonight and thought he'd just take a thermos and some sandwiches up to his room and get to bed early. He does that sometimes.''

The protest was involuntary. "Then you'll be alone!''

Maude handed her the sherry and spoke factually, obviously with no intention of making a sympathy bid. "I don't mind being alone, dear,'' she said. "I guess you could say I'm used to it. Most of my life, when I come to think about it, I've been alone—one way or another.''

THE BERGHOF WAS FUN, and Trent was an entertaining companion. He knew the German words to a lot of the songs the lederhosen-clad band played, and Midge found that he could do a very authentic waltz.

They feasted on sauerbraten and red cabbage and potato dumplings, with a sinfully rich Black Forest cake for dessert followed by small glasses of a caraway-flavored liquor. Trent was on his very best behavior with her, and under normal circumstances it would have been a delightful evening, but something was lacking and Midge knew he was astute enough to realize it just as much as she did.

It was nearly midnight when they left. The weather had turned colder, dark clouds scuttled across the moon, and the swaying trees seemed to be moaning softly.

Trent, looking skyward, said, "Frost-on-the-pumpkin weather. It's almost the first of November, and somehow that's a dividing line. Afterward it always seems more like winter than autumn."

She was wearing a knitted wool cape and now drew it closely about her. "Cold?" he asked.

"Only psychologically. You make winter sound frightening."

They were walking across the parking lot; now they reached his car and he opened the door for her. "Well, winter's not *frightening*," he said practically, "though they do get some hard ones around here. There's usually more snow than I really care to see, even though I ought to be used to it, coming from Illinois."

He closed the car door on her side, walked around and got in behind the wheel. The car was a low-slung Alfa Romeo, and the instrument panel, Midge thought, looked like something one would find in a jet plane. But then, she remembered, Trent had mentioned once that he'd raced cars for a while when he lived in Illinois. This probably was a kind of compromise, an adult toy.

He started the engine revving, then looked across at her. "Midge," he asked softly, "where are you and where have you been all evening?"

She tried to smile. "Has it been that bad?"

"No. Having you around physically is better than not having you around at all. I do admit, though, that I wish it could be the whole you in residence!"

"I'm sorry."

"Don't be." He put the key in the ignition switch but didn't turn it, trying to force a smile as he went on, "I can appreciate the way you feel. These are not things one necessarily wishes upon oneself. What I'm trying to tell you, I guess, is that I really have fallen in love with you."

"Oh, Trent!" she protested.

"It's Brian Vandervelt, isn't it?" It was more a statement than a question.

There was no use hedging. "Yes," she said simply.

"*Why*, Midge?"

"I don't think that's a question anyone can ever answer satisfactorily, Trent."

"It just happens, eh? Okay, okay," he relented as she glanced at him suspiciously, "I'm not arguing the point. It certainly just happened to me. I didn't intend to fall in love, seriously in love, ever again.''

She was tempted to tell him that she doubted he had fallen seriously in love, even with her, but she held her tongue, and after a moment he started up the car, flicking on his headlights as he drove out of the parking lot and onto the main road.

"What is there about Vandervelt?" he asked then, as if there were some sort of rhetorical question involved. "All right, we've both conceded that he's handsome, but I don't think that would be enough for you. Personalitywise, I've seldom come across anyone cooler. He comes on to me like a winter blast off the Hudson, though I suppose your experience in that line may be entirely different—"

"Stop it, Trent," she cut in sharply.

"Okay," he said, "call it sour grapes. If it weren't *you*, though, Midge, I'd wonder if maybe it's that great big fortune that dazzles your eyes and makes your heart beat faster."

For a moment she actively disliked him, and evidently he sensed it. "I'm sorry," he said, "I really am. I guess I'm a bad loser, that's all. Don't think I'm going to step out of the picture, though. I'm hanging in until the last countdown, Midge."

She stared at him, wondering just what he meant by that, but was oddly hesitant to ask him.

They were near the outskirts of Coxsackie when he suddenly said, "Damn!"

"What's the matter?"

"I think I'm getting a flat. In fact, I think I've got one."

Briefly she wondered if this was a hoax, a rather adolescent ruse to park by the side of the road with her. Then she saw the diner ahead, its lights still on, and Trent suggested, "We can go in there and you can have some coffee and keep warm while I change the tire."

MIDGE WAS SIPPING A CUP OF COFFEE and appreciating its warmth when she sensed someone standing at her side.

"Miss Boardman," a man said, and she turned to face Mike Stabler.

The managing editor's face was flushed and she suspected he'd been drinking, yet he said clearly enough, "How about bringing your coffee over to my booth while Clayton's fixing his tire? I've been wanting to have a word with you."

She nodded agreement and moved across to the booth Mike had been occupying. The ashtray on the table was littered with cigarette butts, and an empty coffee cup stood next to it. Now Mike ordered more coffee and brought it with him. He was evidently trying to sober up, and Midge felt a surge of pity for him.

Clem Thorne had mentioned one day that Mike Stabler had been considered a first-class journalist in New York not too many years ago. Evidently there had been personal problems; he had taken refuge in alcohol. Now he was like so many newspapermen of an older school who moved from paper to paper and were called "floaters" in the trade. In his case, however, he seemed to have found a permanent berth in Coxsackie, due at least in part, she felt sure, to Brian's generosity.

He lit a cigarette with shaking fingers and said, "I never get a chance to talk to you in the office."

The statement came as a surprise—she'd had no idea that he'd ever wanted to talk to her. But she said only, "Well, our departments are rather separate."

He nodded. "Advertising's not my thing, but I know a good job when I see it, and you're doing one."

"Thank you."

He smiled crookedly. "You're a pretty girl; I can see why Brian Vandervelt's so taken with you." Then before she could answer he told her, "Look, if you think I'm some kind of kook I don't blame you. I'd think the same thing if I were in your place!"

"I don't think you're a kook," she found herself saying, to her own surprise. "In fact, I have a feeling you're probably the one true friend Brian has on his staff."

"You're right," he said solemnly, then asked abruptly, "Did you ever know Horace Vandervelt?"

"No."

"No loss. He could have given the Marquis de Sade lessons." She realized suddenly that his rheumy eyes were sharper than she would have believed possible. "You care about Brian, don't you?" he said without further preamble.

He had no right to ask her such a question. No right at all! Yet she found herself answering, "Yes. Yes, I do."

"Then," Mike told her gruffly, "don't let him put you off. Brian's got some crazy ideas about himself, and he's going to have to get over them one of these days, but it isn't going to be easy. He gives the impression that he has everything in the palm of his hand, but the book isn't always like the cover, you know. When he lost his hearing he lost a hell of a lot of self-confidence, as well, and sometimes he isn't nearly as sure of himself as he seems to be. There are moments when it takes a lot of reaching to get to him.''

''I know that,'' she said, ''and I'll admit there are times when I find it very...discouraging. I think Brian lost his faith in women when the girl he was engaged to walked out on him, but there's more than that involved.''

''Such as what?''

She faced up to something she'd been trying to thrust to the back of her mind. ''The girl he was with that awful weekend was killed. That's a memory he'll have to live with for the rest of his life, too.''

Mike shook his head impatiently. ''Brian wasn't involved with the girl who was killed,'' he told her.

Perplexed, Midge recalled now that her suggestion had met with a similar response from Jerry. But the circumstances of Brian's accident were still not clear to her, so she persisted, ''What do you mean?''

''The girl who was killed was with one of the other midshipmen,'' Mike explained. ''Brian's told me the whole story, and what happened is that she'd gone up to the cottage—her parents' cottage—because it was chilly, and decided to light the space heater. It was one of those obsolete things with no safety devices; Brian said it hadn't been used for a long time, since the cottage was generally occupied only in summer. Anyway, I don't know all the technical details, but it seems to me there must already have been gas escaping or the place wouldn't have gone up the way it did.

''No,'' he continued, lighting another cigarette, ''Brian's date was down on the beach with the others at the time of the explosion. Seems to me her name was Sally something or other; while he was at the Naval Medical Center in Bethesda, Maryland, she used to come over to see him. He'd gone up to the cottage to get some more beer—he walked in just when the whole place blew up.''

Midge shuddered, then asked, ''Did they expel him from Annapolis?''

''No. As a matter of fact he stood so high in his class that he was graduated even though he couldn't take his final exams. Both of our senators went to bat for him on that. His diploma was presented to him while he was still in the hospital. Obviously, though, there was no chance of his ever having a career as a naval officer.

''He took it remarkably well,'' Mike continued. ''He's taken most of the things that have come his way remarkably well.''

''I understand the girl he was engaged to is married now and lives right in Albany,'' Midge said miserably.

Mike eyed her narrowly. ''So I've heard. I've also heard that the marriage isn't going so well; in fact someone mentioned she phoned Brian just the other day.''

A hard little knot formed somewhere in the region of Midge's heart and slowly, painfully, turned over.

''Look,'' the managing editor said, still watching her closely, ''don't jump to conclusions. Brian isn't a fool, and he has a surprisingly good sense of values, considering he was brought up during his adolescent years by Horace Vandervelt. If you ask me,'' he went on, ''he was never that deeply in love with Grace. When she walked out on him, I think what was hurt was his pride more than anything else. They met at a regatta here on the Hudson, then she went South to college, and I've heard that when he was at Annapolis she really latched onto him. He proposed to her at Christmas, his last year there. I had the feeling at the time that it was mistletoe and champagne talking. If he'd cared more about Grace, he wouldn't have gone down to the beach that April with another girl."

He switched the subject abruptly. "What bugs me now," he said, "is that Halloween is one week from today. Do you know about the will?"

"Yes."

"Do you know about the meeting coming up?"

She frowned. "Not really, no."

"It's scheduled for noon, the first of November, in Brian's office at the paper." Mike snuffed out his cigarette and promptly lit another. "Everyone mentioned in the will is to be there," he said. "That means all the department heads, Maude Vandervelt, the whole caboodle. That sister of Brian's should get herself East, also, if she wants to protect her own interests."

Midge said carefully, "I don't think Becky plans to come."

"Maybe you could convince her otherwise," Mike suggested, adding at her look of surprise, "Yes, I know the two of you are friends. Brian confides in me quite a bit, Midge, and I've never betrayed his confidence. I never will. I've talked to you more about him just now than I ever have to anyone else. He's a fine person, a very fine person. He doesn't deserve this deal he's been handed. I just hope he lives through it. Greed is a hell of a thing!"

She stared at him, suddenly cold, marrow cold.

With just a few words Mike Stabler had made the danger that hung over Brian seem more tangible, more real, than it ever had before.

"If Brian's still alive on the first of November," he went on, "he stands to inherit a hell of a lot. If he's dead, then his sister will get her half and the four department heads will get the rest. Oh, I guess there'll be a couple of other beneficiaries, but not me, you can be sure of that. I wasn't one of the old man's favorites."

He snuffed out his cigarette. "If Brian's sister is *also* dead by the first of November, then the four department heads will split the whole thing, even the house and the trust fund, once old Maude is gone. If only three of them are still alive, they'll split three ways. And so on."

And so on. Mentally she continued the premise. *If only two are alive, they'll divide it. And if only one is alive. . . .*

Her eyes widened as she stared at him. The concept was fantastic, almost beyond grasping.

Mike appraised her, then nodded. "Yes," he said, "you've got it. I've covered a lot of things in my time, and I don't think I've ever come across a better motive for murder. I've been trying to convince myself that maybe no one is that ambitious, but what's the point of being naive? No matter how you put it, this is a crazy game. It makes Russian roulette look like tiddledywinks."

Stabler finished his coffee, even though it had long since turned cold. "You know Jerry Mueller. Talk to him, will you?" he suggested. "I don't think he'd buy any ideas from me. I have what you might call a credibility gap with the cops," and his admission brought to mind the first time Midge had met Jerry Mueller, when he had come into the Maples to tell Brian that Mike Stabler was in trouble yet again.

"Brian should have protection this next week. Everybody who's scheduled to be at that meeting should have protection, for that matter. Make Mueller see that, will you?"

"I'll try," she promised.

Mike slumped back in his seat and closed his eyes, and as she studied his face Midge realized that once he must have been a handsome man. Time had taken more than a fair toll of him.

Trent came in and raised his eyebrows when he saw her companion. Rallying, Mike rose and said, "Hello, there, Clayton. Take my place. I'm about to leave."

This he did, weaving his way out the door in a fashion that led Midge to think he was more drunk than she had realized. Yet surely he had spoken almost too coherently.

"I've got to wash the grime off my hands," Trent told her, "then I could use a cup of coffee, if you're not in too much of a hurry to get home. It's cold out there!"

A moment later he was sitting across from her in the booth stirring sugar into his coffee. "How did you come to join up with Stabler?" he asked.

"He invited me to."

Trent frowned. "He's a lush," he said tersely, "yet for all his drinking he's sharper than you might think. And he's very much in the know about the Vandervelts' affairs.

"Stabler is Andrew Summers's brother-in-law," he continued, without waiting for her reaction to his

statement about the managing editor's sharpness.
"And Summers, remember, is the lawyer who drew
up Horace Vandervelt's whole insane will—though
not without considerable protest, I understand. He
knew, of course, that if he didn't do it someone else
would. I imagine, too, that he thought maybe he
could eventually persuade Horace to amend it, but he
never got the chance. Horace died before that ever
came to pass.

"Anyway," Trent went on, "Stabler was married
to Summers's sister. They had a daughter who
drowned when she was eleven or so, at a summer
camp up in the Adirondacks. His wife went all to
pieces, and he thought it might do her good to come
back to Coxsackie. Summers got Stabler the job on
the *Valley Voice*. He wasn't drinking so much then,
and he was a damned good editor—far better than
Horace ever deserved.

"His wife developed a heart condition, and she
died about the time Brian got out of the hospital. Actually, Brian was still convalescing when Horace
made him editor of the paper. It was an awkward
situation, but I have to hand it to Stabler. He'd
known Brian since he was a kid, and evidently he'd
taught him a lot about journalism when he worked
on the paper during summers. When Brian was ap-
pointed editor over his head, Stabler didn't take it
out on him; he helped him all he could. Meantime,
though, he kept drinking more and more.

"But Brian was his champion. He kept Stabler's
drinking hidden from his uncle as much as he possibly could and many times he took it on the chin for
something that was Stabler's fault. The two of them
built up a very close relationship. I'd say," Trent

finished somewhat cynically, "that Brian trusts him more than he does all the rest of us put together."

Trent paid for their coffee, and Midge walked out with him into a perfect harvest night. But just now she barely noticed the moon or the stars or the beauty. She was thinking of the things Mike Stabler had said, and hoping she'd have the chance to talk to Jerry Mueller before long. But more than anything else she was worrying about Brian....

CHAPTER FOURTEEN

NATURE SEEMED DETERMINED to outdo herself in her final color presentation of the year, for the last Saturday in October was truly spectacular.

Midge awakened, wishing she were more rested, so that she really could enjoy the day. She convinced herself, however, that it could be a tonic just to get out in the fresh air, so she put on jeans and a pink sweater and went down to the kitchen.

Clara was not there this morning, but Brian was. He was wearing jeans and an old blue sweater that had seen better days, and just the sight of him was enough to make her knees start to wobble.

Scanning her face, he said, "You look as if you might have a touch of the same problem I had yesterday."

"No." She shook her head. "I just haven't been sleeping very well."

His glance was sharp, but he said only, "Share my toast, and I'll make some more." And despite her protest that she could fend for herself, he poured orange juice for her and coffee for both of them.

"Did you have a good time at the Berghof last night?" he asked her.

"Yes."

"I really don't know Trent socially," he continued,

"but I should imagine he's an interesting person to be with."

"Yes," she agreed lightly, "he can be fun to be with. We had a flat on the way home, though, which didn't overjoy him."

"I thought you were pretty late getting in," he commented, to her surprise. Noting her expression he added hastily, "I wasn't keeping tabs on you. I couldn't sleep well last night myself, and I happened to be looking out the window when Trent's car pulled in the driveway."

She smiled; a smile that he evidently took for skepticism, because he said again, "I wasn't watching the clock, Midge."

"If I thought you were, I'd be flattered," she told him impishly.

She spoke lightly, but his mouth tightened and he said, "I'm afraid I don't quite buy that. No," as she was about to speak, "let's get on another track, shall we? I'm not much for word games."

This piqued her. "Strictly a man of action, eh?" she taunted.

He frowned. "I suppose I had that coming. And if you mean that I don't seem to be able to keep my hands off you, I admit you're right. But you don't exactly discourage it, you know. Is that your way of being charitable by any chance?"

Her eyes narrowed. "What's that supposed to mean?"

"Well," he said, "possibly this has been declared Be Kind to the Handicapped Month, and I've been unaware of it."

Midge resisted the impulse to throw her orange juice at him, but her eyes were snapping and her voice choked with exasperation as she accused him, "Must you misinterpret everything? Life would be a lot easier for you if you'd learn not to be so damned defensive!"

His eyes swept her face, and she felt as if she'd been struck by shards of gray metal. "I'm not defensive," he said coldly. "However, I *am* realistic."

"Are you?" she demanded. "It seems to me you probably spend half your time brooding about your misfortunes. Mightn't it be an idea to stop and count your blessings once in a while?"

Gray metal flared into white heat. "So," he responded in a tone that made her flinch, "evidently now you've decided to become an amateur analyst."

She knew him well enough to know that her remark had struck deep, that there was hurt beneath his anger. "Brian, I'm sorry!" she said quickly.

"Are you?" he challenged, then before she could answer added, "I know what you're getting at, Midge. Like a lot of other people, you think I'm lucky because unless I meet with some sort of catastrophe within the next week I stand to inherit my uncle's money."

Each word he spoke seemed to be encased in chilled crystal, and his expression was grim as he continued, "I'd like to set you straight about a couple of things. As a matter of fact, I do feel I'm lucky in many ways, but inheriting my uncle's money—if indeed I do inherit it—isn't necessarily one of them. Money really *doesn't* buy everything, though I'll admit it does pretty well in most cases. For instance, it could probably buy me a wife, but she surely wouldn't be the kind of wife I'd want. She would be a paid performer, for she'd have to be a very good actress to make me believe she wasn't fed up to the teeth with living with someone whose standard expression is 'What?' I'm sure you know my fiancée walked out on me when she found out I was deaf. Well, I have no regrets about it; it was better for both of us to end it then."

This was an unusually long speech for Brian, and he had just finished it when Clara came in from the laundry with a pile of freshly washed dish towels in her hands.

Midge was frankly thankful for the interruption. Once again it would have been entirely too easy to say the wrong thing to him.

Clara scowled at both of them and put her hands on her bony hips. "Land sakes," she said, "a beautiful day like this! Why don't you two get outside and play tennis or something?"

Brian looked across at her. His jaw was still set, but he asked in an almost normal tone of voice, "Would you like to?"

"Yes," Midge responded, reminding herself that one of these days she truly must bless Clara.

Brian got the racquets, and they went out the kitchen door together. In the sunlight his hair looked like freshly minted gold, and she found herself yearning to touch it but restrained herself, for she could imagine his reaction were she to do so.

She warned quickly, "You're probably going to be bored to death playing with me. I'm not very good."

"Well, I haven't exactly tried out for Wimbledon myself," he teased her.

In fact, however, he was an even better player than Jerry Mueller and beat her all too easily. When they had finished two sets she moaned, "I told you it wouldn't be much fun for you."

"But it has been," he insisted. "Actually, if you'd just modify your serve a bit. . . ."

He came around to her side of the net and stood in back of her, changing the position of the racquet just slightly while holding her arm. Feeling that telltale pulse begin to throb, she knew that in another minute her blood would be turning to quicksilver, and she was relieved when a familiar voice speaking loud and clear observed, "What a cagey way to operate!"

She turned to see Jerry Mueller standing by the chain-link fence that enclosed the tennis court. Again he was in civilian clothes, but the state police car was parked out in the driveway.

Brian grinned. "When opportunity knocks, I believe in taking advantage of it," he said lightly.

"My philosophy exactly," Jerry responded, but the smile on his face did not quite reach his eyes. He strolled toward them. "I guess in my job I ought to get used to being the bearer of bad news, but somehow I never do. It's Mike Stabler, Brian. He was killed early this morning."

Brian was still holding her arm, and Midge could feel him grow tense with shock. "What happened?" he demanded hoarsely.

"Hit and run," Jerry told him, adding, "Not that it's much help, but they say he died instantly."

Man-made clouds had been injected into a near-perfect day. Brian left with Jerry, and Midge went and sat in the gazebo, thinking about last night and her conversation with Mike Stabler, and mourning his loss especially because he had been such a friend to Brian.

Most of the leaves had fallen now to make scattered patterns of gold, amber and scarlet against grass that was still faintly green. The river today was indigo. She saw a tanker heading upriver for Albany and thought of Brian watching the ships as a child, dreaming of finding freedom at sea.

Brian still had not returned by lunchtime. Maude was in her room, and so Midge had her lunch alone at the kitchen table. Clara gave her homemade pea soup and chicken-salad sandwiches, and as she ate Midge declared, "I'm afraid to get weighed. I think I've gained a pound a day since I've been living here."

"Nonsense," Clara snorted. "You've got nothing to worry about. Me, I never gain. Used to think it came from running up and down stairs, but I don't do much of that anymore. You—insisting on making your own bed and doing your own straightening! You're as bad as Brian. I don't think he'd ever let anyone in that tower of his if he had his way."

Midge said, "I wouldn't want to run up and down all those stairs if I could help it. Especially the first flight."

"Well," Clara pointed out, "I never use the front stairs any more than I have to, even though they're not as bad as they were when Mr. Vandervelt was alive. He wanted everything waxed to a fare-thee-well, and those stairs were mighty slippery. I used to tell Tom he'd slip and break his neck one day, and that's what happened. Thought nothing could ever stop him, Horace Vandervelt did, but there's a force bigger than any of us," she added firmly. "Caught up with him just like it will with all of us one day. Sometimes I get to pondering about that."

So do I, Midge wanted to say, *so do I,* and thought of Brian.

IT WAS MIDAFTERNOON when Brian came home. Midge was sitting at the front window of the upstairs parlor when she saw the white Jaguar pull up, and immediately she went downstairs and ran outside to meet him.

He looked as haggard as he had yesterday, but now for totally different reasons, and her heart went out to him. "Do you know what really happened yet?" she asked.

He shook his head wearily. "Not exactly. We figure he must have gone back to the paper. It was after midnight, certainly."

"Yes, it must have been," she agreed. "I told you Trent had a flat tire last night. We were near a diner down the road and I went in and had some coffee while he changed it. Mike was there—we talked awhile."

"Oh?" Brian raised his eyebrows. "Well, I guess he'd gone from the diner to the paper, then. All the police can come up with is that he must have been heading back across the street to his car when someone ran him down." He went on miserably, "I still can't grasp it. Mike was a good friend and a super newspaperman. He saved my skin many times when Uncle Horace was still alive and I first took over. I'm going to miss him. I...."

His words broke off, and as she looked at the bleak expression on his face she wrapped her arm through his and said, "I think you could use some of your aunt's sherry."

"I could use something stronger than sherry," he

assured her. "Why don't we invade my late uncle's private stock?"

"I didn't know he had one."

"That corner cupboard in the dining room hides a well-furnished bar," he told her. "Incidentally, does Aunt Maude know about Mike?"

"No. She's still in her room." Midge frowned. "It doesn't seem to me she should be cooped up so much."

"I know," he said, "and I really must talk to Dr. Mueller about it. I'm still not sure whether this is a way of life he prescribed or one she's taken up on her own." He glanced at his watch. "It's nearly three-thirty. No reason to be in bed at this time unless she's actually not well!"

Midge followed him into the huge formal dining room. She had imagined previously that the corner cupboard he'd mentioned was used for china storage, but now as he swung it open she saw an array of bottles.

"Well!" she said, coming closer to read the labels. "Haig and Haig Pinch, Jack Daniels, Tanqueray, Benedictine and Brandy—your uncle did believe in the best, didn't he?"

Brian, bent over the cabinet, had retrieved a bottle of Scotch and a bottle of bourbon. Straightening, he asked, "Did you say something?"

"Yes. I was admiring your uncle's taste in liquor."

She saw his mouth tighten and that mask of aloofness he was so adept at donning begin to descend, as it always did when he was reminded of his deafness. "Brian, please!" she pleaded quickly. "Don't go away again!"

He paused, a bottle in either hand, and shook his

head. "Midge, please," he said. "I don't want to get into—"

It was her turn to be stubborn. "No," she insisted, thoroughly determined. "I'm going to talk about it. You retreat whenever something comes up about your hearing. You really do seem to go away...and I can't follow you."

"You wouldn't want to follow me," he said shortly. "There's nothing to be said for the silent world, believe me."

"But your world *isn't* all that silent," she protested.

"True—I do have my substitute ears. But hearing with electronic aids isn't the real thing, believe me. Also, some sounds can send you right into orbit, like a dog barking nearby, or a whole bunch of people chattering at a party, especially in a room where the acoustics are bad. I'm grateful for my mechanical ears, but sometimes I can't wait to turn the damned things off."

He smiled down at her wryly. "That's enough, all right?" he suggested. "It's not my favorite subject."

"Yes," she agreed, "you do rather convey that idea!"

He hesitated, then shrugged slightly. "All right. I'll admit there's a reason why I must seem at times to...go away from you. Often when I'm with you I come close to forgetting I'm deaf. Then something happens that causes me to remember, and it only makes it seem worse. Can you understand that?"

"I think so." Now it was her turn to hesitate. "You know," she reminded him, "when I first met you I thought you could hear as well as anyone."

He looked at her quizzically. "What's that supposed to mean?"

"Only, I suppose, that I reacted to you without any preconceived notions."

To her surprise he grinned. "When I remember our first encounter, I don't know whether to put that on the debit or the credit side!" He waved the bottles he was holding. "I can't tolerate our stuffy Victorian decor, which is why I spend so much of my time in this house in the kitchen," he admitted. "Shall we opt for it?"

They opted.

DUSK CAME as they sat together at the kitchen table. Brian said, "I love it as it is, but I suppose if I'm going to be sure of what you're saying I'd better put on a light."

As he switched on a lamp he remarked, "If Aunt Maude doesn't appear pretty soon I'm going to storm her fortress. Have you heard her stirring?"

"No," Midge told him. "Let's give her another fifteen minutes, then I'll go call her if we haven't heard from her."

They were spared doing this by Clara, who came in to announce cheerily, "Well, Mrs. Vandervelt just buzzed on the intercom. What are you two up to?" She peered. "Brian—hard liquor! Your uncle would turn over."

"It's his liquor," Brian said mildly. "Clara, does Aunt Maude often stay in her room as late as this?"

Clara thought about this, then concluded, "Yes. Seems to me it's getting later and later, except on her ikebana days."

"What does she do with herself?"

"Lies abed and watches TV and eats chocolates," said Clara. "I take her in her brunch, but she doesn't care too much for it. Rather have her candy."

"But that's unhealthy!" Midge protested.

"Mrs. Vandervelt ain't thinking about health, not at this stage of the game," responded Clara. "She's making up for lost time."

She flounced out of the door, and Brian said, "I'll *have* to speak to Dr. Mueller."

Midge nodded. She felt an odd sense of shock, thinking of Clara's statement about Maude's strange brand of newfound independence. "Your uncle must have been a terrible tyrant," she said slowly.

"He was."

"It's sad in a way. It must be dreadful not to have anyone to mourn you." She was speaking almost to herself.

"What?" Brian asked, and added hastily, "I heard you. I'm just not sure what you mean."

"Well, it's terrible to think that someone could die without leaving a single person in the world who was really sorry. In other words, it's frightful that anyone should have been so totally unloved."

"Uncle Horace brought it on himself," Brian assured her. "Now—shall we sample just a wee bit more of his private stock?"

Midge and Brian both had dinner with Maude that Saturday night and later Brian stayed with them and watched a comedy show on television, to Maude's delight.

Sunday was a quiet day. Brian went off with Jerry, and Midge surmised that it was in connection with Mike Stabler's death. She wrote a few letters and spent the balance of the afternoon reading, but she was really waiting all the while for the Jaguar to come back.

Brian returned in time for dinner, but he bowed out before the evening television programs started. As he left the room he bent and kissed Maude on the forehead, and she flushed with pleasure. When he had gone the old lady remarked to Midge, "Brian is so much more himself lately, and it's all because of you. You make a handsome couple, you two."

Midge said quickly, "Mrs. Vandervelt, you mustn't think—"

Maude brushed her objections aside. "I'm not jumping to any conclusions, young lady," she insisted, "but I do have eyes!" Then she smiled knowingly and switched the subject to ikebana before Midge could reply. The next thing Midge knew she and Maude were discussing ikebana versus Victorian American, and she was proposing her ideas about what could be done with the house.

When she had finished, Maude's eyes gleamed. "If only I thought I could get away with it," she breathed.

"Is there any reason why you couldn't?"

"Horace," sighed Maude. Seeing Midge's face, she said, "Don't look so startled, my dear. It isn't that I believe in ghosts; it's just that I can't imagine Horace ever allowing himself to die. I keep looking over my shoulder, half expecting to see him behind me."

"Mrs. Vandervelt." Midge hesitated, then probed cautiously. "Was he always so difficult?"

"No," Maude told her. "No. Horace was never an outgoing person; it was never easy for him to make friends. But in the beginning, when we were first married, he was not the bitter twisted man he became later. I made him that way...."

"You?"

"Yes." Maude lowered her eyes, then raised them again and looked directly at Midge. "I was unfaithful," she said simply.

It was unbelievable. It was also none of her business, Midge reminded herself firmly.

"Mrs. Vandervelt," she said quickly. "I'm *sorry*. I shouldn't have asked such a question."

"No," Maude responded, "I *want* to talk about it. I've never told anyone before, but under the circumstances I'd like you to know."

She smiled faintly. "I wasn't always such a mouse," she began. "This happened a long time ago, during the early days of the Second World War. Horace and I had been married several years; we had no children, and I wanted children desperately. He was immersed in his business and I was lonely, rattling around in this big house. Then Mark came back here on a furlough from the army at Christmas. Mark Vandervelt—he was Brian's father, Horace's younger brother.

"Horace was never a handsome man, but Mark— well, Mark looked like Brian. The day after Christmas Horace found us together. Mind you, I was ten years younger than Horace and Mark was younger than I was, which made it all the more scandalous. Also, *I* was the married one. I blamed myself for the whole thing—but Horace blamed both of us. He never permitted Mark to come into this house again!

"Several years later Mark married a young lady from Richmond, Virginia, and after a time the twins were born. They were only ten when Mark and his wife were killed. Horace was all for putting them in a private institution, but I swore that if he did I would leave him.

"He had his pride, he cared what the community thought, and it would have been a disgrace for his wife to walk out on him. So we compromised. We agreed the children would go away to school but would come here summers and on holidays.

"I think now that whenever Horace looked at Brian all he could see was Mark. Until that Christmas we had always shared the front rooms you have now, but afterward we never lived together again as man and wife. I moved across to the other side of the stairwell, a room that looks out over the river. Then, after Horace died, Dr. Mueller said that because of my heart it would be better if I stayed downstairs."

Maude sighed. "Don't let this go beyond these walls," she warned, "ever!"

"I won't," Midge promised, deeply moved.

Maude's smile was wistful. "I loved him," she said. "Mark, I mean. When he married Brian's mother I cried for days. Foolish, wasn't it? But even now, sometimes when I look at Brian I feel as if I'm seeing Mark all over again!"

CHAPTER FIFTEEN

MONDAY WAS ALWAYS A BUSY DAY at the paper, with everything gearing toward Thursday's press run, and this Monday was no exception. But today there was an added tension.

Mike Stabler's death had put a pall on the place. The atmosphere was subdued, people tended to speak in hushed voices, and Midge noticed that even Lucille Mueller had worn an especially severe dark dress, close to charcoal in color. Whether this had been by accident or design, she didn't know, but the effect was sobering.

Lucille, for that matter, looked more strained than ever, and there was a reserve to her manner as she said, "Good morning," with none of her usual cheerfulness.

She doesn't like me, Midge thought suddenly, and was shocked by the realization. She felt someone should tell Lucille that the way to hold a man was *not* by becoming instantly suspicious anytime he so much as spoke to another woman.

She didn't know Jerry very well, true, but he was Brian's best friend; she was certain of Brian's confidence in him. Despite Brian's remark that Jerry had always had an eye for attractive women, she felt sure he would agree that Lucille was overreacting. Jerry didn't deserve this sort of treatment at his wife's hand.

As she went into the advertising office, Midge had a nagging sense that someone had told Lucille about Jerry's joining her for dinner at the Maples the other night. She resented any implication that might be drawn from their having shared the same table. The encounter had been entirely unplanned; at least, she corrected, he had come in to see her because he wanted to talk about Brian, and that definitely was all there was to it!

If Becky still lingered in Jerry's mind it was because she represented something to him, perhaps the aura of youth too quickly lost, a romantic escape into the golden dream of an earlier time. She smiled to herself as she thought this. Figurewise, Lucille was considerably more glamorous than Becky; actually, she could be prettier than Becky, too, if she would relax and let even a modicum of joy shine through an expression that had become entirely too tense. Lucille had been pleasant, outgoing when they first met, Midge remembered. But it seemed incredible that she could have had any possible part in her ensuing personality change, or that Becky in absentia could be blamed for it.

Clem and Ellen were both in the office when Midge walked in. Clem was never particularly outgoing, which always seemed odd to her because he was such a good salesman, and today he was running true to form. But Ellen was absolutely dour. Her eyes were red rimmed, she looked as if she'd been crying, and Midge wondered curiously if her tears had been shed for Mike Stabler. She wouldn't have thought that Ellen and Mike could ever have been that close, but one never knew, she mused. One never really knew too much about anyone, especially in a setting such as this one. It seemed strange, for that matter, that one could work with people on a day-to-day basis for a much, much longer period than she had been at the paper and yet maintain a relationship that was only surface deep. She knew that Clem was married, and it had been mentioned once that Ellen still lived at home with her parents and three brothers, but these two people with whom she shared so much of her time were nevertheless essentially strangers.

Now, as she settled in at her own desk, she discovered a copy of the special Halloween section in front of her. It had been printed on the weekend and would be distributed with this week's paper; it looked very good, she thought, very good indeed. She thumbed through it, pleased with her own copy in print and genuinely enthusiastic about Ellen's artwork. But it didn't seem the moment to tell Ellen so. Lately Ellen had withdrawn into a shell of sorts; occasionally Midge had seen the girl's rather small pale blue eyes darting in her direction with a look of suspicion in them that was quickly camouflaged once Ellen realized she was being observed.

Why? What did Ellen have to be suspicious about where she was concerned? Trent? True, Ellen was infatuated with Trent; at least it seemed so. *But I can't blame myself for that,* Midge thought dully. You can't always choose the people who tend to fall in love with you.

Thinking of Trent, she realized he must still be at Brian Vandervelt's Monday-morning staff conference, and this was confirmed when he came in a few minutes later, looking stern and preoccupied. He nodded perfunctorily at his staff, then went directly to his own office, and Midge had the feeling that while he hadn't slammed the door behind him this was precisely what he had felt like doing.

A moment later he called to her, and she went in reluctantly to sit down in the chair by his desk. "Damn Vandervelt!" he scowled.

She looked up, startled, and Trent remarked caustically, "Excuse me! I forgot about your feelings for him."

"Trent, please. . ." she protested.

"Never mind," he said, waving a deprecatory hand. "This is nothing personal, Midge; nothing personal about Vandervelt, that is. It's just that he's already fouled up this week's paper."

"In what way?"

Trent ran an agitated hand through the sleek dark hair that was ordinarily never out of place. "He wants to print a special tribute to Mike Stabler in this week's issue, and it's going to raise hell with the advertising linage. I'm going to have to kill more ads than I like to think about in order to conform to the editorial budget he's set for himself. The guy is blockheaded when something like this comes up. I mean, what the hell. . .Stabler is *dead*!"

This wasn't the first time Midge had been stirred by a feeling of dislike for Trent. Carefully restraining herself from saying what she really would like to say, she pointed out, "I think he deserves a bit of a memorial, Trent."

"Why?" he demanded, pounding his fist on the desk for emphasis. "You saw him yourself last Friday night. Hell, he slobbered all over you there in the diner. He couldn't have walked a straight line when he left the place if he'd been offered a thousand dollars. My guess is that he blundered right into someone's car, and that person is scared to hell and doesn't dare report it."

Midge surveyed him coldly. "That's your opinion," she said. "I don't think personally that Mike Stabler was all that drunk. Tired, maybe, and he'd had a few drinks, but that doesn't mean he was as totally intoxicated as you seem to think he was."

"Do you always stick up for the underdog, Midge?"

The implication was clear to her that Trent also put Brian Vandervelt in the underdog class, in some ways at least, doubtless because of his hearing problem, and she felt resentment flare. She said steadily, "No matter. Whatever you think, or whatever I think, won't bring Mike back to life again, and it seems to me that the least the paper could do is to have some sort of memorial page or section for him."

She was tempted to point out that Trent himself had described to her the other night how close the bond had been between Brian and the managing editor, but she halted these particular words. As she looked across at Trent and noted the good-looking face already beginning to show the marks of cynicism and a driving kind of ambition that amounted to personal greed, she realized it would be wiser not to get into the matter further just now, and so she switched the subject.

"I've seen the Halloween section," she told him, and at once he brightened.

"Looks terrific, doesn't it?" he said, and she concurred. "I've been thinking we might do something similar, but perhaps a bit larger, for Thanksgiving. Pilgrims, turkeys, all the rest of it, but done in an entirely new kind of style with your verve for copy and Ellen's art.''

Midge followed along on this thought, even though Thanksgiving at the moment seemed centuries away to her. But she was glad to have Trent turn his attention away from Brian and toward almost anything else.

As the day passed, however, Midge began to realize that a new, uncomfortable awareness had been introduced into the atmosphere at the *Valley Voice*. Mike Stabler's death had somehow underlined the fact that, insofar as Horace Vandervelt's will and the probation period were concerned, time was running out. Although she flinched from the thought, there was no doubt that Horace Vandervelt had put temptation on a platter, and now every hour was a reminder that by Saturday there would be feast or famine for the four department heads, depending upon what happened to Brian in the interim. The paper certainly had prospered under Brian's leadership; he had passed Horace Vandervelt's test. But rather than spelling success this left implications so hideous that just thinking about them gave Midge a growing sense of panic.

Tension became a tangible thing, and she tried to force herself to concentrate on her work, which just now involved doing her very best for the new Athens restaurant-boutique account Clem had secured on a trial basis. But it was hard to concentrate, because Trent was being patently obvious and most annoying today with his very presence; he seemed to be riding herd on all of them.

He was uptight, this she realized. But so, she discovered, was Fritz Handel. When she went out into the composing room late in the morning with some copy, the mechanical superintendent was downright surly instead of merely dour!

She knew that Handel, too, was a man in whom Brian placed considerable confidence; but just now, as she met the unfriendly glance he gave her from behind his thick glasses, she came close to actively disliking him. He looked like a man who had worked very hard all his life, but he also appeared to have more than one chip on his shoulder. She found herself wondering what inheriting a fortune would mean to someone like Handel, and it was not a pleasant thought.

Later in the morning Wilson Strathmore walked right past her without even seeming to see her, let alone pausing to bestow a formal but friendly greeting as he usually did; and when she went out for lunch Abe Weissman was equally distant, driving past her as she walked along the street. She stared at his chunky silhouette hunched over the wheel and wondered about him, too. He tended to be loud; in fact, he was a thoroughgoing extravert, or at least he seemed to be. Yet he was actually her favorite of the four department heads, and it was unthinkable that he could be plotting Brian's death.

Brian himself stayed locked behind the glass door marked Editor all day. Midge didn't even get a glimpse of him, and by the time she left the office in the late afternoon she felt drained, physically and emotionally. She was so tired, in fact, that when she pulled into the Vandervelt driveway she did not at first realize his white Jaguar was right behind her.

"You sneaked up on me," she accused him.

"That'll be the day," he said mockingly, then inspected her more closely, frowning. "You look done in," he observed.

"I am," she admitted.

"There's no need for you to work so hard," he told her. "Is Trent pushing you?"

"Not really."

Those eyebrows of his, which could be so eloquent on occasion, rose slightly, conveying his disbelief. "You don't have to hedge for him," he said.

"I'm not hedging for him, Brian."

"I suppose," he went on, opening the front door for her, "that he told you how much I upset him this morning because I cut down on this week's advertising linage."

There was no point in dissembling with Brian; she long since had learned this. Hesitating only briefly, she answered, "Yes, he did tell me about it."

"And what were your feelings on the matter?"

"I think Mike Stabler deserves a special tribute," she said carefully.

Those intent gray eyes swept her face. "Thanks for that, Midge. When I made the decision I couldn't help but wonder what your vote would be."

"You doubted it?"

"Not exactly. But there's an age-old difference between the advertising and the editorial viewpoints. We have to consider revenue, of course, and so ordinarily I try to keep a logical ratio between the two, but there are moments when profit ceases to be the most important thing in the world to me."

There was a significance in the way he said this, and she looked up at him swiftly to note that he was looking down at her as if he wanted to make very sure she got his message. Then he added carefully, "Trent doesn't agree with that."

"No," she said slowly, "I suppose he wouldn't. His philosophy is different."

"At the least," Brian said curtly. "Midge. . . ."

"Yes?"

To her surprise, Brian muttered something short and impatient under his breath and then seemed to gaze at some empty space above and beyond her head. She saw that his mouth was taut, and a telltale muscle twitched along the side of his jaw. The tension was communicable; he more than anyone else must be feeling it to the hilt, she knew, and wished there were a way she could ease the situation for him.

If only he would make love to me, she found herself thinking. *If only he would take the first definite step toward what we both know we want, because it's there all the time beneath everything we say to each other, everything we do. If only he would take me in his arms and blot out the rest of the world. . . .*

Brian, however, was not about to blot out the rest of the world. He said abruptly, "Trent's not the man for you, Midge," and then, while she stared at him in amazement, added almost nastily, "But then that's none of my business, is it?"

It took her a moment to rally, and by then it was too late to answer him because he had turned his back on her and was heading for the library. This was not the time, she knew, to try to intercept him. The wall, she thought dismally, would be firmly in place, every stone cemented; just now there would be no chinks in it.

She wondered if he would join her and Maude for

dinner, and doubted it. This time he fooled her, however: he came to the dining room directly after Clara called them. But one look at his face told Midge that this still was not the time to reach him. Seldom had he seemed more aloof. He said very little, and there were points when the silence became so strained that Midge felt as if her own nerves were about to snap.

Maude had been told now of Mike Stabler's death; Midge imagined that Brian had told her himself. She spoke a bit about him, but Brian responded only in monosyllables and now and then seemed almost deliberately not to hear what was being said to him.

He told Clara that he was skipping dessert tonight, and Clara's face fell because she had made a very special pumpkin soufflé. Normally, Midge knew, Brian would have been persuaded by the little woman's expression to change his mind and linger at the table, but tonight he couldn't seem to wait to get out of the dining room and back to his lonely tower.

She had the feeling, too, that much of his present attitude stemmed not so much from Stabler's death, deeply though Brian unquestionably felt it, but from something to do with Trent Clayton and herself, and this perturbed her.

TUESDAY MORNING Midge awakened to the sound of rain, and when she went downstairs she found Brian alone in the kitchen finishing breakfast. To her relief, his mood had evidently improved. At least, he greeted her in a reasonably friendly fashion and insisted upon pouring her some coffee.

As he handed her the steaming cup, he glanced out

the window and remarked grimly, "What a day for a funeral!"

"Today?" She was dismayed.

"Yes. Two o'clock."

Undoubtedly, she told herself, she was going to be rebuffed, but that wasn't going to stop her! "If you like," she offered, "I'd be glad to go with you."

His gray eyes lingered on her face for what seemed a very long moment. Then he said, "I appreciate that, especially as I suspect you feel just about as I do about funerals. There's no need for you to go through it, though. Matter of fact, the department heads plan to go as a kind of delegation from the paper."

He poured another cup of coffee for himself and observed ruefully, "We may be the only ones there. Ourselves, that is, and Andrew Summers, our lawyer. He was Mike's brother-in-law, but Mike didn't have any other family, nor did he have many friends. These last years of his life he was pretty much of a loner."

The word seemed to echo. Brian, she thought bleakly, was in danger of becoming "pretty much of a loner" himself, and now he seemed to sense what she was thinking. His mobile lips twisted.

"I'm not a misogynist, Midge," he said finally, and then added, "But that implies hatred only of women, doesn't it? Well, I don't hate either women or men, and I'm not a hermit at heart. In fact I should imagine I've pretty well demonstrated that to you. But—" he stirred his coffee as if this required total concentration and then frowned as he put the spoon aside "—sometimes one has to go it alone."

She swallowed hard, then dared the question, "And that applies to you?"

"It would seem so," he said after a moment, and

looked away from her—with much the same effect as if he had turned his back on her.

She wanted to shake him, to shake him violently until his teeth rattled. She wanted to berate him for his obstinacy and then throw her arms around him and kiss him passionately. She wanted to lure him to some wonderful oasis where they could be together away from everyone else.

She wrenched her thoughts back to the present. "People weren't meant to live alone," she said huskily.

"What?" he asked, with what she suspected might be calculated blankness.

"Nothing," she retorted hastily, then saw the wave of pure frustration that came to sweep across his face.

She didn't expect him to comment on this, but he surprised her. He said stiffly, "When I can't hear what you say the first time around, I'd appreciate it if you'd repeat it. I know it's annoying, but...."

He tightened his lips as he broke off the sentence, and now she glared at him, thoroughly impatient. "Look," she told him, "haven't you ever said something you wished immediately you could take back?"

"Yes," he conceded, "but most of us don't have that option. The person we're speaking to *hears* what we say the first time."

The coolness was there again; it seemed to her that she could feel the brittleness of his reserve, and she sighed. Mike Stabler had said that Brian could be a hard person to reach, and at moments like this one she despaired of ever getting through to him completely. He had a way of putting a distance between himself and others, a chasm seemingly incapable of being crossed.

But, she discovered, just as ice melted in above-freezing temperatures so he seemed now to thaw slightly as she sat silently sipping her coffee, until finally he asked, with an odd little note of asperity, "Are you or are you not going to tell me what it was that you said?"

"Very well," she responded, trying to match his own aloofness. "It was an observation, that's all. I said people weren't meant to live alone. I think that's true, old cliché though it may be, whether or not you believe it."

"I don't think I've ever indicated I didn't believe it," he retorted.

"So the solitary state is ideal only when it applies to you, is that it?" she demanded. "You have the right to be unto yourself in your ivory tower, regardless of anyone else."

"That's a stupid thing to say," he accused, and she saw with some satisfaction that she had at least shaken him to the point where the wall didn't seem quite so high now. "Damn it, Midge, you know very well what I'm talking about! For God's sake, I—"

He broke off abruptly, and she thought that once again he was going to turn his back on her, figuratively at least. Instead he said levelly, "Unfortunately, anything I say about myself is almost bound to reek of self-pity. That's not what I want to convey, believe me. I neither need nor want pity from anyone, nor do I make it a practice to go around feeling sorry for myself. I've come to grips with my life—"

"Have you really?" she interrupted nastily.

To her surprise, he actually flushed. "Well," he said then, "until recently I thought I had!"

Once again they were interrupted. This time it was by Tom, who came to say that Clara had sent him to find a shopping list she'd written the day before, since he was going into the village and so could pick up the things she wanted.

Midge nearly groaned aloud from pure frustration. Increasingly, it seemed to her, whenever she and Brian came close to getting down to certain basics between themselves someone came in to bring a halt to progress. Did Brian really want such a thing as "progress" between them, though? Did he really *want* anyone else in his life, or had simply being the Vandervelt heir imposed upon him a desire for isolation. It was only too true that he neither needed nor wanted pity from anyone. In fact, most of the time he was almost unbearably self-sufficient!

With Tom gone, Brian glanced at his watch. "I'd better be getting on to the paper."

"So had I," Midge said.

Again he gazed out the window, observing, "The rain's really coming down. Look, there's no need to take two cars today. Why don't you ride over with me? I'll be back from the funeral before you're ready to leave for the day."

She tried to conceal her astonishment, but this was an offer to which she had no intention of saying no. A few minutes later she was beside him in the front seat of the Jaguar, and being beside him at all seemed so entirely right.

He was wearing a beige raincoat cinched at the waist by a fairly wide belt, and it emphasized the width of his shoulders. She watched his strong capable hands on the steering wheel and knew even before they were out of the driveway that he was an excellent driver; he handled the powerful sports car with commendable ease.

As far as she was concerned the ride to the *Valley Voice* was entirely too short; she only wished they could go on driving through the rain together for hours and hours and hours. She only wished, for that matter, that they could go on together for what would amount to eternity.

Brian parked the car in the side lot, then looked down at her quizzically. "You seem very pensive," he commented.

Again she took a conversational chance with him. "I was wishing that we could keep on going," she confessed. "I mean, I'd like to go on driving through the rain, and maybe later stop for lunch at some little place where there's a fire going...."

She broke off when she saw the expression that came into his eyes. There was no remoteness in their gray depths now, no aloofness. Saying softly, "I was thinking the same thing," he bent to brush her lips gently with his. "Maybe," he told her, "some other time." Then before she could respond he exclaimed impatiently, "That was stupid of me!"

Did he mean the kiss, she wondered, and asked, "What was?"

"I should have let you off in front of the door, so that you wouldn't get wet." And when she looked blank, "It's pouring, remember?"

There was a teasing note in his voice, and as he smiled at her she forgot, for the moment at least, about the rain, about fears, about funerals.

But the moment passed. They got out of the car, running toward the entrance, and it was only at this final moment that she thought of the picture they would make walking into the building together. She hung back, and he turned to her. "Do you *like* getting wet?" he demanded.

She hesitated. "People," she said then.

"Are you thinking about the people on the paper and the public-opinion poll this is going to stir up?" he asked her.

"Yes," she admitted.

"So let them enjoy it!" And he laughed out loud at her expression.

Still, she could not help but be self-conscious as she walked through the front door with him. She said good-morning very brightly to Lucille, then forced a smile and nodded when he left her at the door of the advertising department, with the reminder, "I'll pick you up later."

Ellen was eyeing her covertly, and Midge knew that even Clem had not missed this particular byplay. As she hung up her raincoat and walked across to her desk she looked directly into Trent Clayton's face and saw that he was glaring at her with a jealousy he didn't even attempt to suppress.

She more than half expected that he would think of a reason to summon her into his private office, but he didn't. Throughout the morning, for that matter, he seemed tense and completely preoccupied, and there was an almost audible sigh of relief in the air when shortly after lunch he went to join Wilson Strathmore, Abe Weissman, and Fritz Handel and Brian, since all of them were going to the funeral together.

As it happened, though, Brian did not go with the others. The outer door leading into the main lobby was open, and through it Midge saw Trent, Handel, Strathmore and Weissman standing together talking desultorily. Finally they left, and it was at least ten minutes later when she saw Brian hurry across the lobby, slamming the main door behind him in his haste.

She plunged into work, trying to keep her mind off the funeral because all funerals reminded her of her own mother's funeral, and that was something she still found difficult to think about. It was after three o'clock when she heard voices in the lobby and looked up to see the four department heads again standing in a group.

They separated and Trent slowly came into the office. "Well, that's that," he said grimly. "Ashes to ashes, dust to dust. I could use a drink," he told her, and went on into his private office, closing the door behind him.

Midge paid little attention to him, for her own nerves were on edge. She found herself watching the lobby, listening for the sound of the big front door closing, wondering where Brian was.

Another hour passed, and Trent came out to say, "I'm going to call it a day. You people clear out as soon as you can. We'll catch up in the morning." He paused, and Midge was afraid for a moment that he was going to ask her to accompany him, but to her relief he didn't.

Shortly after, both Clem and Ellen put their work away and silently departed, and Midge was left alone in the office. She could hear a typewriter in the distance, which meant someone must still be in the city room. A phone rang and was answered. But still her sense of desolation grew, and with it there was a clutching, almost sickening sense of fear. Finally she wandered out into the lobby, to find that Lucille

Mueller, too, was about to close up the reception desk for the day.

"Lucille," she asked, "have you heard anything from Brian?"

For a moment Lucille looked at her suspiciously; there was something close to hostility in Jerry's wife's beautiful dark eyes. Then miraculously she softened. "No, Midge," she said, and it was the first time Midge remembered Lucille ever calling her by her first name. She hesitated. "He got a long-distance call just as he was about to leave for the funeral with the others," she explained, "so he told them to go on...said he'd follow them. Probably he's stopped off somewhere."

"Probably," Midge conceded, flashing Lucille a grateful smile. But once she was back at her desk again her restlessness only increased as the minutes ticked away.

The clock on the wall had just reached five when she heard the front door slam, and she sighed with relief. But it wasn't Brian who appeared in the office doorway. It was Jerry, and he was in uniform.

She took one look at his face and cried out involuntarily, "No!"

"Take it easy," he said swiftly. "He's out in the cruiser, slightly banged up but okay."

She was shaking. "What happened?" she demanded.

"He intended to go to the funeral with the rest of the department heads—they were all going in Strathmore's car," Jerry told her tersely. "Then at the last minute Brian got a long-distance call from San Francisco."

"Becky?"

"He thought so. Then the operator said something about a delay, so he sent word to the others to go on without him. By the time he left, he decided the quickest way to get to Catskill, where the funeral was being held, would be to cut across to 9W instead of taking the Athens road all the way. So he did, but as he started around a curve he found out he had no brakes, and he wound up in a ditch."

"It's lucky he's a damned good driver. Even so, if he'd gone into a wall or a tree the odds are pretty high that at the speed he was going he would have been killed. It would have made a nice verdict of accidental death, skidding on a slippery road in a hurry to get to a funeral. Neat, isn't it?"

She asked, knowing the answer even before she voiced the question, "Couldn't it have been an accident?"

"I doubt it."

"But the car was all right this morning," she persisted.

"Then someone got to it in the parking lot," Jerry said. "It's been raining all day; there haven't been many people around outdoors. There would have been opportunity."

She stared at him, feeling herself begin to sway. "Oh, dear God!" she moaned softly.

"Hey, there," Jerry said, but his tone was gentle. "Don't pass out on me! He needs you, Midge."

She moistened her lips. "Jerry," she asked, "is he *really* all right?"

"A little banged up, like I said, but okay. Get your raincoat and come on."

The state police cruiser was parked just past the front entrance. Brian was sitting next to the driver's seat and he started to get out when he saw her, but she said quickly, "No. Don't move. I'll sit in the back."

He shook his head. "No," he told her. "I probably wouldn't be able to hear you. Get in the middle."

There was a square of gauze over his right eye, fastened with adhesive tape. She saw it and moaned, "You're hurt!"

"It's just a superficial cut. Come on—get in!"

She slid across the front seat and Brian got in beside her. Jerry, at the wheel, picked up his microphone and spoke into it, but his words at the moment were merely a jumble to Midge.

Brian said, "Midge—you're trembling!"

She nodded, her teeth chattering. "I know it."

"Come on," he said softly.

He put his arm around her, and now she saw that his knuckles were scraped and bruised. She winced, as if this were her injury rather than his, exclaiming, "You've hurt your hand, too!"

"If I could arrange to get shot in the line of duty," Jerry interrupted, "I wonder if Lucille would react like that!"

Midge said sharply, "That isn't funny!" then added more calmly, "Were you the one who found Brian?"

"Only after I told him where to look," Brian said succinctly.

Jerry growled, "That's gratitude for you! I come and pull you out of your damned ditch and what thanks do I get for it?"

"It's all in your line of duty, chum," Brian told him, "but you've got to admit I helped." He turned to Midge. "The Jag's equipped with a radio transmitter," he explained. "I had thoughts at one time of doing a sort of roving-editor bit, but frankly life hereabouts is too peaceful—at least on the surface."

"Purely on the surface," Jerry observed bitterly.

"Well, evidently I blacked out for a minute after the crash," Brian went on. "Then things settled down and I decided to give the state police a call, and who do you think answered?"

He was trying to speak lightly, but despite himself his voice roughened. "All I could think of was what might have happened if it had been this morning, when you were with me," he told her, and his arm tightened, pressing her closer to him.

Now she reminded him, "Brian, Jerry said Becky telephoned you."

"No," he said. "No, it wasn't Becky. It was a hoax. The supposed operator kept me stalling for a good fifteen minutes, then she told me the party in San Francisco would place the call later. By then the others had gone on. . . ."

Jerry frowned. "That means there's a woman involved in this. Somehow I hadn't considered that possibility."

A woman. If a woman was involved in what clearly seemed to have been an attempt on Brian's life, then she was either an accomplice or a good mechanic, that stood to reason. Midge could not imagine knowing how to tamper with a car so that the brakes would fail within a certain length of time, but she had to concede that it could be simpler than she thought. Also, because she was not mechanically apt herself didn't mean that a great number of her sex couldn't star in that department as well as men did. Still, why would a woman want to do such a ghastly thing to Brian?

Grace De Witt came to her mind, but she dismissed the thought at once. After all, as she understood it, Grace had been the one to put an end to that relationship; in any event it had all happened a long time ago, more than four years ago, and Grace had since married someone else. True, the marriage was not going well, and Mike Stabler had said that recently Grace had contacted Brian. Had he seen her in the interim?

But what if he had, Midge asked herself, forcing logic even as she felt a pang of what could only be termed pure jealousy at the thought of Grace's seeing Brian at all. Such a meeting would certainly not be likely to result in a murder attempt!

The only other women she could think of who were involved in Brian's life were Maude Vandervelt and Clara, and the mere thought of their being embroiled in a sinister plot was so ludicrous that it brought her to the edge of hysteria. She nearly laughed aloud and had to bite her lip to keep from doing so.

Still, she made an odd sort of noise, and Brian looked down at her curiously.

"It's not like you to be so silent," he commented. "Or so pensive."

She said vaguely, "Jerry said there must be a woman involved...."

"There haven't been that many women in my life of late," he responded dryly.

Lucille, Midge thought, paying no attention to this statement and still going through her own private roster. But Lucille had no reason to be against Brian; if anyone, it was Becky, for whom she would feel antagonism. No, the very idea of Lucille's being involved with this went way beyond credibility.

Then there was Ellen. But if Ellen was annoyed with anyone just now, it was Trent.

Trent... or me, Midge found herself thinking.

"A silver dollar?" Brian suggested. "For your thoughts, that is."

"They're not worth it," she told him, and then added reflectively, "It would have to be a woman who... could stand to benefit, wouldn't it? Someone connected with one of the four men."

Jerry nodded. "That's what I've been thinking," he admitted. "Brian, did you recognize the voice at all?"

He shook his head. "No. But then, it could have been disguised somewhat. In any event, I'm a poor judge of voice tones. It's usually difficult enough just to hear what someone's saying."

"But there are accents," Jerry persisted, "or a special way of pronouncing a word, maybe."

"Moira Strathmore has a Southern accent," Midge said suddenly.

"You've met Moira Strathmore?" Brian asked her, his eyebrows rising.

"Yes. Didn't I mention it to you? She came over to visit your aunt one day—last week, I guess it was. I'm beginning to lose track of time; everything seems to have become all strung together lately."

As she spoke she was again remembering that brief encounter with Wilson Strathmore the day she had met him coming out of Brian's office. He had seemed shaken; clearly he had been deeply disturbed about something. She wished she could ask Brian what it had been, but this was not the moment. Later, maybe, there would be an opportunity. But just now....

"What about the others?" Jerry asked. "Clayton and Weissman and Handel?"

"Let's stay with the Strathmores for just a minute," Brian suggested. "I would say that Wilson is really what one would call a gentleman of the old school, a very fine man who has had his problems. Moira has always been a somewhat fragile person; Wilson has been faced with more than his share of doctor bills over the years, and in the earlier days there wasn't the kind of medical and hospital insurance that's available today to help people foot their bills. At least, let's say that my late uncle wasn't too advanced in his thinking when it came to employee benefits.

"Handel was born here in Coxsackie. His father came here from Germany because the Hudson River valley reminded him so much of the countryside in his own homeland. There are lots of people of German descent throughout this area, as Jerry can testify. In fact I'd say they far eclipse the last of the Dutch.

"Handel is a widower, but he has a daughter he dotes on. She went to teacher's college and she works upstate in Plattsburgh. But—" he shook his head reflectively "—Handel is a man of simple needs, simple tastes....

"Abe Weissman," he continued, "is an entirely different personality. He comes from Brooklyn originally; he could head the circulation department of any big-city daily, and I've sometimes wondered why he settled for a place like this—no disparagement meant to your hometown and my adopted one, Jerry. Weissman has a showplace of a house, though, up toward Greenville, and he's married to a woman who is considerably younger than he is. He has to keep up with her life-style, which I suspect isn't always easy for him. Abe follows the ponies, too— sometimes wins, sometimes loses. But there's a kind of exuberance about him: he likes flashy clothes, flashy cars, lots of rich food and good whiskey. Abe takes in life as if he were always going to a feast...."

Brian's voice trailed off momentarily, and then he said, "That brings us to Trent. I think you know more about Trent than I do, Midge. I know he's divorced, but perhaps you could fill us in a bit?"

"Not really," she said uncomfortably. "Trent has never spoken much about his ex-wife, except to say it was a marriage that simply didn't work. I don't think there's any particular animosity between them. Brian, I actually don't know Trent that well...."

"No?" he asked softly, and she caught the note of disbelief in his voice and was chagrined by it. Even worse, the mood that had stretched between them like a shimmering golden thread suddenly seemed to snap, and he loosened his touch upon her, then a moment later leaned back, sighing, and removed his arm from her shoulder.

Jerry, glancing across at them, asked, "Are you okay, Brian?"

"Yes," he said, but weariness was heavy in his voice. "I could do with a drink, though. Can I tempt you, Jerry?"

"Not tonight. I'm in uniform, but aside from that I want to keep my wits about me. I'll admit I'm not going to rest comfortably until this week is over and you've had your blasted meeting and the question of the will is settled once and for all. In the meantime, try not to be a damn fool, will you?"

"What is that supposed to mean?"

"Face up to the fact that someone may want that inheritance enough to kill for it," Jerry said bluntly. "It doesn't have to be one of the principals. Anyone *associated* with one of your department heads closely enough to benefit by what they'd gain could be paranoid enough to try something. Take Trent, for instance. He may have no designs on the money himself, but for all you know he may have a girl friend."

"Yes," Brian said, his tone dull, "for all I know he may have." And his gray eyes lingered broodingly on Midge.

CHAPTER SIXTEEN

JERRY TURNED INTO THE VANDERVELT DRIVEWAY and pulled the state police cruiser up in front of the main door. "I've got things to do," he said, "but I'm going to check around here from time to time until I go off at midnight, and then Bill Cleary will be relieving me.

"Don't hesitate to contact either of us for any reason whatsoever," he added. "In fact, put your pride in your pocket for the next few days, Brian, will you? If you need help, ask for it. The same thing applies to you, Midge. After this episode with Brian today, I'm wondering if there may be a connection with your own accident that we've missed."

It was a sobering idea.

She trailed after Brian into the house, just as the chimes of the clock rang out. Six, she noted, counting automatically. Time to join Maude for a glass of sherry in her sitting room, an occasion she usually looked forward to but dreaded tonight.

Brian looked awful. Fatigue had etched shadows under his eyes and all traces of his summer tan seemed to have vanished, or else had been usurped by a pallor that alarmed her.

At the foot of the stairs she asked, "Can I get you something?"

"Thanks, no. All I want to do is lie down for a while."

"Do you have to go all the way up to the tower, Brian? Isn't there another room upstairs where you could rest without being so far away?"

"Yes," he told her coolly, "but I prefer the tower." And that was that!

He started up the stairs and she looked after him, dispirited and more than a little resentful. She'd had her own share of shock this afternoon, and she'd certainly taken no pains to hide the way she'd felt when she saw him with the bandage on his head. Then for a time, with his arm encircling her, she had felt so very close to him. But the feeling had dissipated with astonishing speed once Jerry started speculating about a woman's involvement in the attempt on Brian's life.

Brian had replied that there were few women in his life at present, but had he been dissembling? Had Grace again become a more important part of his life than he was willing to admit? Could he fear, perhaps, that if he were not careful her husband might name him in a divorce suit? Midge could imagine the rocking scandal that would ensue if something like that happened to the Vandervelt scion, especially now with the day of judgment in regard to the inheritance so close at hand.

And was there something else in Horace Vandervelt's will that no one had said anything about? Horace had been an intensely moral person, and his own wife's infidelity had burned him, cruelly stamping his personality for the rest of his life. Had he put a clause in his will to the effect that Brian would inherit only if there were no hint of scandal attached to the Vandervelt name?

Speculation, speculation, Midge thought wearily,

and started for Maude's sitting room just as Tom appeared in the corridor that led to the kitchen.

"Brian just rang," Tom told her, and Midge saw that he was perturbed. "We got kind of a priority system," he admitted. "If he rings three times quick, in a row, it means to get on up there, that it's kind of important." He frowned. "Would you know what might be wrong?"

Midge hesitated, wondering how Brian might feel about her discussing his affairs with Tom, and then decided to be honest but discreet.

"He had an accident this afternoon, Tom," she said, then added hastily upon seeing the man's expression, "but he's all right. He got a cut on the head that isn't too bad, and some scrapes and bruises, but evidently nothing too serious. I think I'd better let him tell you about it himself."

Tom nodded, but he moved closer to her and said urgently, keeping his voice low, "That's all right, but don't say anything to Mrs. Vandervelt about it, will you? That heart of hers is tricky; she dotes on Brian, and if she thought there was anything wrong with him...."

"Don't worry," Midge promised. "There again, I think Brian should talk to his aunt about this himself. Tom...."

"Yes, miss?"

"If there's anything he wants, I can help you and Clara take it up to him. Those are a lot of stairs to climb."

He nodded his thanks, but left her with the strong impression that he'd be attending to Brian's wants himself. As he started up the stairs with an amazingly spry step for a man his age, Midge reflected that he must be more than seventy.

Maude was already watching a quiz show. "Pour the sherry for us, will you, dear?" she asked. "This man is really funny. I think you'll enjoy him, and I imagine that after today you need a laugh as much as I do."

After today? For a moment Midge wondered if Maude had already heard about Brian's accident, then realized she was referring to Mike Stabler's death and recent funeral.

The quiz-show guest was amusing and she tried to escape in his humor and to laugh at the right intervals, but it was impossible. Tired and unhappy, she felt relieved when Clara came to say that Brian wouldn't be joining them for dinner—something Maude seemed to accept without surprise—adding that perhaps they'd like it if she brought them their own dinners on trays. This was an excellent compromise as far as Midge was concerned, for she had no desire tonight to sit alone at the dining table with Maude. There was a formality about the room that made casual dining an impossibility.

After dinner she continued to watch television with Maude for a time, but midway through a movie she pleaded fatigue, kissed the old lady lightly on the forehead and then told her she was going up to bed; which was a fib, but only a slight one. She was exhausted enough to tumble into bed immediately, no doubt about it, and that was precisely the action she intended to take after a good soaking hot bath and...a visit to the tower. For she knew she could not possibly sleep unless she first went to see for herself how Brian was, no matter how much he might resent her doing so.

Her footsteps dragged as she climbed that final narrow flight of stairs. Once more she paused outside

Brian's closed door, hoping she was not making a dreadful mistake in coming, yet certainly with no intention at all of turning back. It took a moment to work up the courage to knock, and even when she did so she wasn't at all sure he would hear her, but he did.

"Come in," he said, and she turned the knob and stepped over the threshold, unable to remember when she had ever felt more timid.

He was propped up on the daybed with a book in his hand, but she doubted he'd really been reading. There was a tray on the bed table with a bowl of soup and some rolls on it, barely touched. He looked ghastly, and she had the impulse to go back downstairs and call Dr. Mueller, but she could imagine what Brian would have to say about that!

Flicking her eyes from the tray of food to his face, she saw he was staring at her with a blankness that was disconcerting to say the least. There was neither approval nor disapproval in his gaze, yet the aloofness was back again as he asked, "What is it?"

She frowned down at him. "You look terrible," she told him frankly. "You should have been asleep hours ago."

"There's too much to think about," he admitted. "I hauled down a volume of Poe because I thought it might be a good diversion, but just now my concentration leaves something to be desired."

"I don't wonder," she said testily. "I suppose, among other things, you have a headache?"

His lips twitched ever so slightly, whether with annoyance or humor she couldn't be sure. Suspiciously docile about it, he answered, "Yes, ma'am, as a matter of fact I do have a headache. But I took some medication a while ago, and it's easing off."

She could feel his gray eyes intent upon her face and wanted to wriggle beneath their scrutiny. She was entirely too aware of the length of him stretched out there on the daybed, and despite the fatigue and the bandage on his forehead there was a basic masculine essence to him that made her understand fully what it meant to be stirred to the very fiber of one's being. Brian stirred her as she never had been stirred before; she thought dismally that never, for the rest of her life, could she hope to be free of the effect he had upon her, even were she never to see him again.

The sudden thought of never seeing him again was so appalling that she glanced swiftly and directly into his eyes, unknowingly mirroring such a dark agony that he asked quickly, "What is it, Midge?"

She latched onto the first thing she could think of. "You haven't eaten your soup," she said, and at once felt she couldn't have been more inane.

Now there was no doubt that the twitch to his lips spelled humor. He asked whimsically, "Is that enough to warrant such a tragic expression? Dearest mother hen, it's potato soup in any event, and potato soup grown cold becomes vichyssoise—so I can eat it cold."

"You're ridiculous," she began, but the end of "ridiculous" turned into a sob.

Instantly he reached up to her, pulling her down by his side, his arms going around her to bring her close to him. She rested her head against the soft wool of his sweater and felt the hard firm muscles of his chest underneath, and just now his embrace became a sanctuary, so that there was no longer a need to repress anything at all, and the hot tears that had been scalding her eyes began to flow freely in a veritable flood. He let her cry, somehow finding a handkerchief in the process, then gently wiping her eyes with it when she was done.

"I think," he said at length, "that you needed to do that hours ago."

"Many hours ago," she agreed.

"What is it, darling?" he asked her gently.

Again her eyes found his. She had no idea at all that they were like drenched pools of rich brown velvet. . . .

His arm was still around her; now it tightened as she said, her voice trembling, "I'm so terribly afraid for you!"

Their eyes met, and it seemed to Midge, strange though this thought was, that it was as if they were fully seeing each other for the first time.

Brian said huskily, "I won't be an idiot. Jerry's right. The only thing to do for the next few days is play it safe. So I promise you I'll take care, if that's what you're asking of me. Then, after Saturday. . . ."

After Saturday. At the moment "after Saturday" seemed an eternity away to her. She was so concerned just now with merely getting *through* Saturday that the implications of what it would mean if everything went smoothly for Brian had not yet really registered.

"Midge," he told her, "I hadn't intended to do anything, say anything, till after Saturday. But. . . ." She saw yet another kind of intentness in his gray eyes, and then he sighed helplessly, "Oh, my God! How can I possibly. . . ."

It was, in its way, an invitation. Now it was she who drew his blond head down until it was so close that she could reach upward to find his mouth with

her own, and as their lips met she experienced an entirely different feeling within the circle of his arms.

Was this still a sanctuary? Perhaps so, she told
herself, even though he was holding her so close to
him that it seemed as if the cloth separating skin from
skin must melt. He had kissed her before, to be sure;
in fact she could have said that his previous kisses
had held their own definition of ecstasy. But now
possession fused with passion and it seemed to her
that Brian was infiltrating the very depths of her being, leaving nothing unplumbed, nothing untouched.

Hazily she was aware that after today she would be
his forever; she would be entirely his even were he to
cast her away, as he already had cast her away at
times. She told herself this through the fog of sweet
sensations that assailed her as his hand found and
cupped her breast so that it lay round and warm
against his palm. Dimly it occurred to her that nature
had made every part of man and woman specifically
so they could merge together in this fashion, each
contour, each entity, fitting perfectly against another
contour, another entity.

Now she began to help him, divesting him of his
clothes even as he was divesting her of hers, until his
maleness became a tangible thing and she was set
afire by it.

She felt as if she were melting into a source far
beyond herself as he traced her eyes, her lips, the
pearly inner recesses of her ears, and then her nipples, taut now, proudly upthrust. There was a tenderness to his aggression, blended with an innate
maleness, and these qualities served to make a combination from which, as far as Midge was concerned,
there could be no possible escape.

He was beautiful, this Greek god of hers; she knew that, too. She was intensely aware of the pure magnificence of his body, the vital strength of him; and now he took her on a journey that was in its own way an odyssey. In fact she felt as if she'd gone to dwell on Olympus itself until he swept her up on yet another wave of passion, conveying her to a still higher peak until it seemed to her that all the gods were smiling down on her, and she was giddy beneath their gaze. Culmination came in a miracle of purely wonderful ecstatic sensation that left her clinging to him, suffused by love as she whispered things that made no sense at all. Then slowly he sealed his possession of her with one last encompassing kiss.

For a time the silence between them was fraught with wonder. Then he said slowly, "Dearest, you'd better go and try to get some rest."

"Brian," she began, but he put his finger gently across her lips.

"You might remember," he said, "that I stayed wired for sound tonight, because if you came up here I didn't want to miss your knock on the door. You see," he added, his voice little more than a whisper, "I wanted you to come here tonight, Midge. You've no idea of how much I wanted you to come!"

BRIAN INSISTED on going into the office Wednesday morning, this over protests, but when Tom said he'd take him in the Rolls-Royce he flatly refused. Turning to Midge, he suggested, to her surprise, "How about you driving me over?" and she quickly agreed to do so.

Some of the color had come back into his face, and he was wearing a dark gold pullover that brought out the deep glints in his hair. Midge had been inspecting him as she fitted the keys of the Volvo into the lock and turned the switch, but she was unaware that he was watching her until he asked, more than a hint of mischief in his tone, "Well, do I pass?"

"You...you look a lot better," she said, flustered.

"So do you," he complimented her, taking in her russet wool suit, enhanced by a gold-and-carnelian pin with matching earrings that she had inherited from her mother. "You look very chic today." For just an instant something not entirely pleasant flickered across his features. "Do you have a special date?"

"No," she said, puzzled by the question until she realized that he was thinking she might be going out with Trent. "I just felt like dressing up a bit this morning. I was rather depressed when I first got up, and sometimes there's no cure for it like gilding the lily."

She had started the car as she spoke and was turning out of the driveway onto the Athens road, determined to do an especially excellent job of driving under his scrutiny.

He was silent for a moment, and then he said soberly, "Midge, I'm sorry!"

"What for?"

"Getting you involved in this," he told her, "even to the point of possibly putting you in danger." He drew a long breath. "I don't think I have to tell you that if even a hair of your head were harmed—"

"Brian," she interrupted firmly, "not a hair of my head is going to be harmed. Nor, for that matter," she added with a confidence she didn't feel, "a hair of yours."

"Jerry came up last night after you left while on a

routine check," he said. "We talked for a while, and I told him maybe it's paranoia to think that yesterday's accident was caused by anything other than faulty brakes. The police have checked out everything connected with your accident, and even Jerry is convinced that it's just what it seemed at the time. It's true I keep the Jaguar in pretty good shape ordinarily, but I admit these past few months I've had my mind on a lot of other things."

"Can't they tell if the car was tampered with?"

"It's getting a thorough going-over this morning," he told her. "We'll have an expert opinion after that. I've come to realize, though, how easy it is to get caught up in all these potentially sinister events. It can make a person overimaginative."

She glanced at him sharply. "Would Jerry concur with that?"

"Not necessarily," he admitted. "But I want to be very sure, Midge, before I start casting suspicion on anyone. I've known some of these men for years, and I've worked with all four of them since before my uncle died. I suppose," he continued wryly, "that I don't like the whole concept. I'd rather be a disbeliever."

For this she couldn't blame him. It was a terrible cloud he was living under; in fact there was still an unreality to it for her. She, too, wanted to be a disbeliever, and yet she could imagine what Jerry Mueller would say to both of them were she to voice such a thought, and of course, he would be right. There were so many old clichés to cover the situation.

Better safe than sorry, she found herself thinking, and sighed.

They were almost into the village of Coxsackie at

this point, and she noted that Brian was gazing out the window. He seemed abstracted, far away from her, and she knew he hadn't heard her sigh. That was just as well: he needed no further concern about *her* at the moment; he had more than enough to contend with!

Again they walked into the paper together, but it seemed aeons instead of a mere twenty-four hours since he'd driven her to work in the Jaguar the previous morning. Lucille smiled at both of them with a friendliness that now included Midge, which was heartening. But once inside the advertising department she found that the atmosphere was extremely tense.

Trent was riding herd today; she had never seen him so demanding. In addition to drawing up ideas for Clem's new Athens account, Midge was already working on thoughts for a special Thanksgiving section, and there were a variety of other accounts that demanded her attention, as well. Thus she decided to cut her lunch hour short, so she went down the street to Joe's for a quick hamburger and malt, more than half hoping that she'd encounter Brian.

When she got back to the advertising department she found that Trent, Clem and Ellen were all still at lunch, and she settled down to work, quickly becoming absorbed in some ideas for the Athens restaurant-boutique. For one thing, she decided, the lovely glass flowers the boutique specialized in could be used as table centerpieces in the restaurant, and of course it would be made clear that they were for sale. In fact, it seemed to her that the whole theme for the advertising could revolve around these glass flowers, which were French imported and really quite unusual. It might even do to name the restaurant The Glass Flower, or maybe The Glass Chrysanthemum, or The Glass Bouquet.

She considered the last name and rather liked it, although, she mused, it might smack too much of a tearoom and so turn off potential male customers. But in any event, a glass flower could be used as the motif for the placemats and napkins, and as an identifying logo in all the ads. . . .

She was putting down ideas for all of this when Trent at her elbow said tautly, "Midge, I must speak to you."

She looked up, startled. "I didn't hear you come in," she told him.

"Obviously you were deep in thought," he responded, showing no appreciation at all of the fact that this indicated dedication to her work. "Look, will you have dinner with me tonight?"

"No," she said. "I'm sorry."

"Can't you get permission to leave the Vandervelt castle?"

"Don't be silly, Trent," she said shortly, and wished either Clem or Ellen or both of them would get back from lunch. "I don't need permission. I don't want to have dinner with you, that's all."

"Well," he said dryly, "that's frank enough. Midge, come into my office."

"Why?"

He glared at her, exasperated. "For God's sake, I can't talk to you here."

"As far as I'm concerned," she replied, "you can say anything you have to say to me in public. As a matter of fact, I wish you'd stop singling me out—"

For answer he reached over and pulled out her

desk chair, with her on it, so suddenly that she nearly
lost her balance and toppled over. Next he lifted her
to her feet, and before she could realize what had
happened she was in his arms, struggling to push him
away from her while his grip tightened until she
couldn't move at all.

She felt his lips hard upon hers, forcing them apart,
and she recoiled from his kiss, all the small moments
of distaste she had felt for him merging together into a
single entity of active dislike. Suddenly, savagely, she
clamped her teeth down on the tongue he had thrust
into her mouth, despite her efforts at resistance, and
he stepped back, his face contorted by pain.

"You bitch!" he exclaimed, half under his breath.

He was facing her, his back to the door that
opened into the lobby, and so his words did no good
at all, she realized when to her distress she saw Brian
standing on the threshold. He could not possibly
have heard them.

She felt the twin stabs of gray eyes turned to silver
metal and saw the terrible look of unadulterated contempt on his face. Then he turned on his heel, his
footsteps thudding back down the corridor toward
the editorial office, and for a moment she thought
she literally, physically, was going to be sick.

She turned on Trent, blazing. "Never touch me
again!" she warned him. "Never, do you hear!"

She realized as she spoke that he was completely
unaware of Brian Vandervelt's appearance, and she
intended to keep it that way. Still running his lips
over his injured tongue, and wincing as he did so, he
said thickly, "What put you off so, Midge?"

"Doesn't it occur to you that perhaps you did?"
she asked icily.

To her surprise, he said, "I apologize. It was poor behavior on my part. But sometimes you nearly drive me crazy. I . . . ."

This time it was Clem who came to interrupt them, and Midge turned back to her desk, thankful that the conversation had gone no further. She felt as if Trent's kiss had soiled her; she touched her hair, thinking that she surely must be disheveled after his embrace. A moment later she went to the rest room to wash her face and put on fresh makeup and to look at herself for a long moment in the mirror, as if her reflection might be able to give her some clue about what to do next.

Then suddenly she made a decision, and before she could even think about changing her mind she walked down to the end of the corridor and through the doors of the editorial offices and on to that final glass panel marked Editor.

As she did so, she was painfully aware of Mike Stabler's empty desk near the door. Brian, it occurred to her, must be doing at least part of the managing editor's work himself until he could find a replacement, which was an added load he didn't need at the moment. Undoubtedly he also didn't need a scene with her just now, but that didn't prevent her from turning the knob and walking in on him. No chance, she thought grimly, of pausing to knock and possibly being refused entry!

She found to her amazement that he was slumped forward at his desk, his head resting within the circle of his arms. For a horrible moment she was afraid that something terrible had happened to him, and the fear was so intense that the whole world rocked around her.

Then she saw that he was breathing evenly. Instead of speaking his name she bent forward, touching him lightly, but it was enough. He sat bolt upright as if someone had uncoiled a spring, and in an instant that mask of aloofness slipped down over his face, but not until she had glimpsed the stark misery in his eyes.

"Brian," she began, but he waved a hand.

"I have nothing to say to you, Midge," he told her flatly.

She gritted her teeth. "Perhaps," she acknowledged, "but I have a few things to say to you."

"Suppose I choose not to hear them?"

"Then," she said, "I will wait until you change your mind—even if I have to wait forever!"

Dramatic, yes. Probably overly dramatic, she conceded, yet she meant every word; she had no intention of retracting. And as if to underline her point she pulled out the chair at the side of his desk and sat down on it firmly, folding her hands, her lips tight and her chin jutting out defiantly.

Silence came between them, at first cold and brittle, then beginning to thaw in an oddly subtle way. His mouth twitching ever so slightly, he said, "My God, I believe you mean it. . . ."

"I do mean it," she assured him.

"Then—" a strange expression that was at least remotely related to a smile flitted across his face, only to be quickly suppressed "—I suppose I'd better listen to what you have to say."

"Let me ask you a question first," she countered. "Do you think I was enjoying myself with Trent?"

He didn't reply at once. Then he answered slowly, even reluctantly, "If you're asking me to look back on the scene objectively, I suppose I'd have to say no. On the other hand, sometimes it's hard to know what gives a woman pleasure. Trent's obviously attractive, and I'd say from the episodes I've happened to witness between the two of you that he's pretty adept at playing love scenes. I—"

"You're dodging the issue!" she accused.

Their eyes meshed, hers imploring, his clear and incredibly gray and, just now, very direct. "No," he said levelly, "you didn't look as if you were enjoying yourself. But you were in his arms. You were letting him kiss you."

"I didn't have much option," she told him. "Except that just before you came in I bit his tongue. I don't think he'll be eating anything solid tonight."

"You bit his tongue?" Brian echoed incredulously.

"You heard me!" she snapped without even pausing to think about her choice of words, but it didn't make much difference anyway.

He smiled, and his smile as always was a transformation; she felt as if the sun had come out in the midst of a stormy day. Then he laughed, and she'd never heard him laugh like this before: it was totally infectious, and she found that she was laughing with him. When finally he subsided he shook his head ruefully. "Poor Trent!"

A moment later he said, "Actually, I went down to your office to see if you'd like to go up to that French place in Albany tonight with Jerry and Lucille and me. Jerry phoned a while ago—he thought it might be a good idea for us all to get a change of scene and relax."

"Do you think you're up to it?" she asked him.

"Yes, are you?"

"I didn't crack up in a ditch yesterday," she reminded him. "Headache?"

"No, mother hen," he grinned. "Do I take it your answer is yes?"

She smiled, "Yes, my answer is yes."

"Then will you forgive me for such a blatant display of jealousy?"

"I'll think about it," she promised, matching his near-flippant tone.

But as she walked back down the corridor to the advertising department, the word he had used came back to haunt her.

Jealousy! She couldn't think of anything more wonderful than truly believing Brian Vandervelt was jealous of her.

CHAPTER SEVENTEEN

MIDGE HAD SUGGESTED that Maude might find the ensuing evening less lonely if they had sherry with her before going out to dinner, and Brian agreed, providing that she substitute Scotch and soda for him.

When she appeared in the sitting room, he had exchanged the gauze dressing on his head for a fairly large bandage, and when Maude asked him about this he told her he'd accidentally struck his head on the side of a file cabinet and got a small cut. Nothing to worry about, he assured her, and she was satisfied.

Maude was quite willing to have them leave her tonight because, she explained, she had an ikebana class in the morning and wanted to get to bed early. So they were both ready and waiting when Jerry and Lucille came for them at seven, Jerry having opted to use his own station wagon tonight for transportation.

Midge and Brian sat together in the back seat, and she found it relatively easy to work out a kind of communication system with him so that he missed very little of the conversation. A way of doing this, she discovered, was to repeat the key part of whatever the previous speaker had said, as if she were only emphasizing it. She thought she was being so adroit about it that Brian didn't realize what she was doing, but as they walked behind Jerry and Lucille down the street toward the restaurant he smiled down at her and said, "You're a great translator."

She flushed. "I didn't mean to be so obvious," she told him.

"You're not—to anyone but me," he assured her. "I realized what you were doing, and I appreciate it, believe me. It makes trying to keep up my part in a conversation a thousand times easier." He took her hand, pressing it, his clasp warm. "You're a very thoughtful person," he said softly. "Thank you."

She felt as if she'd suddenly acquired a lump in her throat, and her lips trembled. She glanced up at him, his profile turned to her so that again it occurred to her how easily he could pose for a classic Greek coin.

He was so very handsome and yet, despite that sometime air of arrogance that could annoy her completely, there was a singular lack of conceit about him. She found herself reflecting that he was entirely different in that way from Trent.

Jerry had booked a corner table in his name, so they were a bit out of the main hum of activity, and she gave him a grateful smile for this. It would make hearing easier for Brian, and she was sure Jerry had requested such a seating deliberately. The restaurant was charming, very intimate, very French, candles flickering on every table and a perfect waiter, with just the right hint of a Gallic accent, to attend them. Brian and Jerry huddled over the wine list, then ordered the *pâté de la maison* for the first course.

Looking around, Lucille remarked, "It's like a breath of Paris."

"One of these days," Jerry told her, "I'm going to take you to Paris on a delayed honeymoon. Ever been to Paris, Midge?"

"No," she said.

"Becky and I were there with our parents a year or so before they were killed," Brian volunteered, surprising Midge, for Becky had never mentioned this. "I remember that Becky was scared to death on the first stage of the Eiffel Tower; she wouldn't go up to the second stage, but I did, and I felt pretty brave about it. Then we had lunch on a *bateau-mouche*, those boats that go down the Seine. It was a misty day; I've always remembered glimpsing Notre Dame; you can imagine how gray and imposing it looked to a kid, especially in that kind of weather. The food on the *bateau* was terrific. I ate my first snails; matter of fact, I ate all of Becky's too. Have you ever eaten snails, Jerry?"

"I've never had the nerve," Jerry confessed. "Hey, why don't you and Midge come to Paris with Lucille and me, and you can be our tour guide!"

Brian laughed. "The tour would be conducted strictly from a nine-year-old's viewpoint," he pointed out.

"Nevertheless, you're on," Jerry told him.

They were lighthearted, remarkably lighthearted, Midge was to think later, considering the mounting ominous cloud on Brian's horizon. Brian tasted the wine they'd ordered and pronounced it excellent, and Jerry grinned.

"I've always wished the taster would wrinkle up his nose, say the wine's terrible and send it back," he confessed.

"I did, one time," Brian told him. "But if you want to do it we'll order another bottle."

"Thanks, but no thanks," Jerry protested.

They were enjoying delicious *paupiettes de boeuf*,

with another wine that Jerry *had* tasted this time and pronounced very good, when Midge became conscious of a woman standing by their table. A kind of sixth sense told her who it was even before Brian said, "Grace!"

He got to his feet, his face expressing a blend of surprise and—was it delight or was it dismay? Perhaps, Midge thought ruefully, a mixture of both.

She tried not to stare at Brian's ex-fiancée, but it was difficult to wrench her eyes away from this statuesque blonde, for she was beautiful. There was no other word to describe her. She was really beautiful. She and Brian, Midge thought dismally, were perfect for each other, each with shining golden hair, classic features and an air of autocracy that set them apart, put them in an automatically exclusive little world that belonged to very rich, very handsome people.

She didn't need to be told that it was not *her* world. This was a truth that never had been more evident to her than it was at this moment!

Brian said, "Grace, this is Midge Boardman. I think you know Lucille and Jerry Mueller."

"Yes." Grace acknowledged the introduction to Midge and the reference to the others with only the briefest of smiles. "Brian, darling, I've tried to get you on the phone three different times—"

"I know," he said. "I got the messages, and I've intended to return your call. This has been a very hectic time, though."

Midge saw the tight line of his mouth and knew how hard he was striving to hear everything Grace said to him. This was a time when he really would despise having to ask, "What?"

He smiled, a smile that was perhaps a bit too bright, and added, "I'll call you next week. We've some catching up to do."

"A great deal of catching up to do," Grace replied archly. "Well, I shall have to run along. I'm with friends, and I see they're already being seated. You *will* call, Brian?"

The last word, Midge found herself thinking desperately. *Latch onto the last word, my dearest, and you'll know what she's talking about.*

Evidently this was exactly what he did, for he said, "As soon as things straighten out, Grace."

She lingered for yet another moment. "You look wonderful, darling," she told him. "Really wonderful!"

He didn't try to answer this, nor was there really a need to. Grace reached up and brushed his cheek with her lips, then went on to join her companions, leaving the echo of her perfume behind . . . and a very dull ache in the region of Midge's heart.

Brian sat down again, but he reached for his wine before eating anything else, and it was impossible to guess what he was thinking. He was far too adept at camouflaging his thoughts and feelings to be transparent at a moment like this.

Lucille broke what threatened to become an uncomfortable silence. "Grace sure is gorgeous!" she exclaimed. "She's always been very attractive, but now—"

"She's an expensive product, honey," Jerry countered. "Everything from her hair to her makeup to her clothes to her jewelry has been bought, and it's cost a great deal. I don't call that real beauty."

"Jerry's right, Lucille," Brian told her, and Midge

noted that within their own intimate little circle he was managing to hear quite well tonight. "Beauty isn't merely an external thing—not that you have to worry about that, any more than Midge does. You both have an inner beauty, as well, which can never be bought. Neither of you needs gilding."

Lucille flushed with pleasure at the compliment, but Midge took it in context; it occurred to her that Brian was directing his remarks primarily to Lucille, realizing how easily her jealousy was aroused. It would not do to have Lucille think Jerry might find a woman like Grace De Witt fascinating, so such a diversion did have merit. Still, Midge found herself wishing that Lucille would gain more confidence in herself, that something would happen to make her surer of Jerry's love.

As for herself. . . last night had proven the intense physical attraction between her and Brian, and though neither of them had today referred to the interval in the tower, she knew he was every bit as aware of it as she was. Yet she was also wise enough to know that because she appealed to him sexually did not mean he didn't still love Grace.

She finished the rest of her own wine and didn't object when Jerry reached over and filled her glass for her.

THERE WAS A CHILL in the air when Midge woke up Thursday morning, a grayness to the sky that matched her spirits. She put on warm leaf-green slacks and a matching sweater, then, despite Brian's comment that she needed no gilding, took extra pains with her makeup and gave her hair one last brushing before going down to breakfast.

Brian was not in the kitchen; Clara explained that he'd had his breakfast earlier and was in the library. "He said to come along there when you're ready," she reported, "but to take your time."

Despite this last admonition, Midge quickly finished her coffee and toast. She found Brian seated at the big mahogany desk, working over the inevitable stack of papers that never seemed to dwindle; but that, of course, was a part of any work that involved writing.

He was wearing a particularly becoming cream-colored Irish knit sweater this morning, and it was hard to take her eyes away from him. The large bandage was still in place on his forehead, but he looked surprisingly fit, considering his recent experiences.

"I enjoyed last night," he told her after inquiring if she'd slept well. "Did you?"

"Very much," she said, which had been true until Grace De Witt had come to stand by their table. After that the evening had plummeted for her; it had been impossible to recapture her earlier mood.

"I talked to Jerry a while ago and he said he thinks the outing did Lucille a lot of good. Despite that luscious dark exterior Lucille's a shy person. She was brought up by a couple of maiden aunts who were very repressive; Jerry says he sometimes marvels that he ever got close enough to her to ask her to marry him. Jerry's always been as popular and outgoing as Lucille has been introverted. People are surprising...." He smiled across at her. "Sometimes very surprising," he finished enigmatically.

This was not a subject Midge wanted to get into. She asked quickly, "Are you planning to work here today?"

"No," he said, and seemed surprised. "Did you think I was?"

She hesitated. "It might be wise," she conceded. "This is Thursday, Brian."

"I know it's Thursday, mother hen," he told her indulgently, "but I don't intend to go into hiding. I'll be reasonably cautious, yes. But I'm not going to cringe."

She had to smile at this, for she couldn't imagine him ever cringing about anything.

"Anyway," he continued, "Dr. Mueller wants to take a look at the cut on my head this afternoon, so I told him we'd stop by his office about three. It wouldn't be a bad idea for him to go over you, too, to be sure you're up to par again."

"I'm fine," she protested.

"I'd like to be sure," he said, getting up to stretch. There was a lithe power to his movement, a surprising grace; that comparison with a Greek god inevitably came to mind, even though Midge could imagine how thoroughly he would hate it were she ever to voice it.

But there was nothing classic about him when he said, "Don't tell Clara, but I'm hungry. Let's stop at the Maples for coffee and doughnuts."

"I don't think it's the time to flaunt yourself in public places," she said flatly.

"I don't intend to put on any exhibitions," he answered. "Anyhow, Jerry is going to meet us at the Maples. He has something to tell me."

Again he let her do the driving, but he seemed much more relaxed this morning. Glancing toward the mountains as they went out to the car, he observed, "Looks like a storm brewing. Maybe we'll even get some thunder, and you can hear Rip Van Winkle playing ninepins.''

"I want to get a book about the legends of the Hudson River valley and the Catskills," she said.

"We have quite a few local-history books in the library," he told her. "Some of them are very old and quite fascinating. My uncle collected material about the Hudson, especially the section of it between Catskill and Albany. For decades the river governed the life of this whole area."

"In what way?" she asked curiously.

"Well, for the towns around it the Hudson was like a front door to the whole world. It's only one hundred sixty miles or so from Albany to New York, with deepwater navigation all the way. River commerce began to flourish shortly after the Revolution, and by the early 1800s the towns along the Hudson were experiencing great spurts of industrial growth. Coxsackie, for example, became a brick-making center: there was an abundance around here of the kind of sand and clay that make good bricks, and all the transportation potential needed to get them to market with the Hudson right at the foot of Main Street."

"How long did the brick industry last?" she asked.

"The better part of the whole nineteenth century. Finally the supply of clay and sand gave out, but at the height of it all there were more than twenty brickyards operating in the village, if you can imagine such a thing."

She shook her head. "It's hard to picture it."

"Yes, it's difficult to imagine a town as quiet as Coxsackie being such an industrial center a hundred years or so ago," he conceded. "They estimate that more than fifty million tons of bricks were manufactured here during the period from 1800 to 1900, and in the course of it the entire contour of the land was changed.''

''How?''

''Well, the land sloped more gently toward the river, for the most part. Taking out the sand and clay for brick was, in its way, like strip-mining in other areas. The whole terrain was gouged out. Now the steep hills and narrow streets that go down to the lower level in the village are about the only reminders left of the brick-making era.

''By 1850, though,'' Brian continued, ''Coxsackie was already into another big business. Harvesting the ice each winter, when the Hudson froze over, was a major industry. They say that Coxsackie in those days was the major ice supplier for New York City. There were big ice-storage houses in town, each with a capacity of something like four hundred thousand tons. Workers came here from all over once the river froze. They built special barracks for some of them; others boarded in homes around the village. Hundreds of horses were brought in to scrape the ice. The area farmers had no objection to that extra source of income, you can be sure.''

Brian laughed. ''Rumor has it that Coxsackie was a pretty wild town back in the ice-harvesting days,'' he told her. ''In fact it's been recorded that it was the wildest town all along the Hudson River.''

''I suppose,'' Midge interjected, ''the Vandervelts were involved, financially at least, in the brick making and the ice harvesting?''

Brian glanced at her sharply, but he said only, ''Yes, and in the mushroom growing, too, which also became a very big industry. Actually, the Knaust Brothers were the first mushroom growers in the Hudson River valley, and they had a very large enterprise. In addition to growing mushrooms commercially, they did a lot of experimentation with them—in one of the old ice houses, incidentally. This led to mushroom canning and also to the production of streptomycin during the 1940s, about the time of World War II. Coxsackie became famous for its mushrooms, and while mushroom growing isn't the big business it once was, you can still get some of the world's finest mushrooms in the area. Many small mushroom businesses are in operation here today.''

He paused, then, ''Again, I'm rambling on about things you may not find very interesting.''

Midge shook her head. ''On the contrary, I find them fascinating. Learning about the history and people of a place gives it an entirely new dimension. I'd never get tired of having you tell me things like this.''

They had come to the Maples, and she swung the Volvo into the parking lot. The state police cruiser was already there, and Jerry was waiting for them in a booth, his face grim.

''The brake line was cut,'' he told Brian as soon as they had ordered coffee and jelly doughnuts. ''There's no doubt about it: I went over to the garage a while ago and saw the car for myself. No chance that it was an accident, Brian.''

Brian nodded absently. ''I was afraid of that,'' he admitted. ''Still, I hoped—''

''Look,'' Jerry interrupted, ''I'd like you to keep a low profile today. We'd like you to keep a low profile—that means my superiors as well as myself.

Go back to the house, both you and Midge, and tell Tom and Clara you don't want to see any visitors for the next forty-eight hours.''

"Oh, come on, Jerry," Brian protested wearily.

"He's right, Brian," Midge interposed. "Look, there's nothing you have to do today—or tomorrow, either, for that matter—that can't be done at home in the library."

"True, but I'd prefer to be in my own office," he told them. "You can only get the feel of things when you're on the scene. There's atmosphere; you could call it a pulse beat."

"The smell of danger?" Jerry suggested somewhat caustically.

"All right, then, the smell of danger. I'm not going to smell it at home, Jerry, but if it's around at the paper I'll know it."

"This isn't the time to play hero," Jerry pointed out.

Brian's gray eyes flashed. "For God's sake," he said disgustedly, "this isn't a game, Jerry. Not as far as I'm concerned."

"You're quite right," Jerry replied levelly. "It's a matter of life and death. As simple as that."

His words hung between them, and Midge pushed away her doughnut, her appetite gone. Brian sighed, then said, "Jerry, I'll tell you exactly where I plan to be and when. As a starter, Midge and I will go from here to the paper. There's quite a bit I want to catch up on, so I'll have Lucille get me a sandwich at lunchtime. At two Midge is going to drive me over to your uncle's to keep an appointment with him. We'll go back to the house after that. Then tonight there's the Valley Men's Club—"

"To hell with the Valley Men's Club," Jerry said irritably.

"Wilson Strathmore is going to speak on business trends, at my invitation," Brian told him. "I feel I have to be there. You can come as my guest if it will make you feel any better."

"It will make me feel better."

"Okay, after the Valley Men's Club—and you can drive me there, if you will—you can take me home and I promise to lock the door after me. All right?"

"I hope it's all right," Jerry agreed glumly, and they had to leave things at that.

Brian was silent as they drove to the office. Midge thought of saying something about the brick-making days as she drove down the steep hill to Main Street, but he seemed so preoccupied that she remained silent. Still, on the village's lower level she was conscious for the first time of the effects of man on the contour of the land, and knew she would never come this way again without trying to picture the time when brick kilns had loomed like large beehives against Coxsackie's horizon.

Trent was standing by the reception desk in the foyer talking to Lucille when they entered the *Valley Voice* building, and he nodded curtly to both Brian and Midge before going on into the advertising department.

Lucille declared happily, "That was such fun last night!"

"We'll do it again," Brian promised her, then turned to Midge. "Be ready to leave a bit before two, will you?"

"Yes," she nodded.

She went to her desk, deciding that since her part

in this week's *Voice* was finished, for this was the day when the paper went to press, she would once again do some work toward the special Thanksgiving section. But almost immediately Trent came over to her and, glancing down at the material she was surveying, said, "I'd like to talk to you about this, Midge. Come into my office, will you?"

She caught a flash of resentment in Ellen's eyes as the girl looked toward them, but then Ellen swiftly returned to her own drawing board while Clem, busy on the phone, paid no attention to them at all. Still, there was nothing for it but to do as Trent had asked, so she reluctantly picked up her folder of material and joined him.

To her consternation, he swung his office door shut behind him, then stood, arms akimbo, staring down at her sternly.

"My tongue still hurts like hell!" he told her.

"I'm sorry, Trent, honestly I am." In this she was sincere. "You did put me off, though."

His smile was wry. "I'm well aware of that,". he answered. "I apologize, Midge. I had no right to force myself upon you, and I promise it won't happen again. With that in mind, will you join me for a drink after the paper comes out? There's something I want to talk to you about."

"Can't you talk to me about it here?" she asked him.

"Not really," he evaded. "Look, I won't keep you long."

"I'm sorry, Trent," she told him, "but I'm going to have to leave early."

"Oh?"

"Brian Vandervelt and I both have doctor's appointments," she explained, fibbing only slightly.

"I see," he said coldly, but then a hint of anxiety came into his eyes and he asked, "There isn't anything wrong, is there, Midge? You haven't had any aftereffects from your accident?"

"No," she said.

"You and Brian Vandervelt both creaming your cars in such a short space of time," he mused. "It's an odd coincidence...."

She nearly said that it would have been an odd coincidence, except that the incident involving her had been an accident whereas the one involving Brian had been purely by malicious design, but she held back the words. It wasn't that she was suspicious of Trent, she told herself, but simply that this wasn't the time to talk about very much of anything with anybody!

The morning seemed to pass very slowly. Toward noon Midge asked Lucille if she'd bring her back a sandwich when she went to get one for Brian, and Lucille seemed pleased to do this for her. She found that she could eat only a portion of it, though, and could barely manage to consume the coffee milk shake Lucille had brought with it. Anxiety was taking its toll, and she had no appetite.

She had no desire for another meeting between Trent and Brian today, so she was waiting for Brian in the lobby when he came out of the editorial office shortly before two o'clock.

She had been chatting with Lucille, and as she and Brian went out to the car she remarked, "Lucille seems so much friendlier."

Brian nodded, but Midge had the feeling he was thinking of other things as he answered, "I believe she's getting a bit more self-confidence." Not that she could blame him: the pressure at the moment must be tremendous, and she marveled at his outward calm.

Dr. Mueller was ready for them, attending first to Brian.

"I can have the stitches out in a couple of days," he told her as he came to rejoin her in the waiting room. It was the first time she realized that the cut had required stitches, and her consternation showed plainly on her face.

"Hey, there," Brian said softly. "It's not all that bad. I'll have a scar, I suppose. Will that bother you?" He laughed, a rather short laugh. "It's not much when you take everything else into account," he added enigmatically, but she had come to know Brian Vandervelt very well, and she understood he was referring to the deafness that would always be a handicap to him. Still, it was a handicap to which he was adapting more than he realized, she found herself thinking. His biggest problem was his own mental block about himself; in a sense he needed confidence almost as much as Lucille Mueller did, although in an entirely different way, of course. In so many areas of his life Brian was supremely self-confident. But....

He was eyeing her narrowly, "Midge," he said, "Dr. Mueller's waiting for you."

She got to her feet with a guilty start, to go on into the doctor's office. It was a big room, with shabby furniture that had seen better days, but there was a comfortable air about it that gave a patient confidence, as did Dr. Mueller himself. He seemed like a friend to her now, and she found herself blurting, "I know I shouldn't ask you this, but is Brian's head injury serious?''

The doctor surveyed her with wise blue eyes and she had the feeling he was seeing a lot more than she might want to reveal. For just now love for Brian Vandervelt could easily become much too transparent to someone with Dr. Mueller's acumen.

He answered, smiling slightly, ''Brian's a very strong young man, Midge. I'd say after my examination today that he's fine. The cut is healing nicely. There will be a scar, but it won't be unsightly. In fact, I'd say in time it will fade to a fine line and won't be particularly noticeable at all.''

Midge closed her eyes tightly, knowing that the tension she was feeling must be communicable, and Jerry's uncle said softly, ''I hope you won't object to my being personal, Midge. I've known Brian a long time, and I think as highly of him as I do of my own two sons and my nephew. You care a great deal about him, don't you?''

She found that she didn't even want to hedge. ''Yes,'' she replied, ''I do.''

Looking at her thoughtfully, the doctor went on, ''You do realize, don't you, that his deafness is permanent?''

''Yes,'' she said, her voice very small. ''Jerry told me.''

''Medicine is constantly making advances, Midge,'' he continued slowly. ''Don't misinterpret what I'm about to say, because the last thing I would want to do is hold out false hope. Someday, though, some of these advances may result in valid hope for people like Brian. Just now there's nothing further that can be done for him, but I would venture that he will handle his problem better and better as time goes on.''

''I'd say he already handles it very well.''

''Yes,'' Dr. Mueller agreed, ''that he does...outwardly. Psychologically, though, Brian considers himself a burden to other people. I think you've already helped him a great deal in that respect.'' He flashed her a surprisingly attractive smile. ''Keep up the good work, my dear,'' he told her.

Brian a burden? She could not get this thought out of her mind as she drove him back to the Vandervelt house. She thought again of the sentences she had read about the deaf in the encyclopedia, and she wished more fervently than ever that she could somehow convince him he was entirely wrong in his feelings about himself.

As they strolled away from the car, Brian broke into Midge's thoughts. ''I'm about to offer you that silver dollar again.''

''I'm sorry!'' she said quickly.

''What is it, Midge? Dr. Mueller didn't tell you anything about yourself that distressed you, did he?''

''No.''

''Or about me?'' he continued, and she felt herself flushing.

He laughed. ''I think I've mentioned before that you'd make a terrible poker player,'' he remarked, ''or if I haven't, I should have. You have such a transparent face...a very lovely transparent face, I might say.''

A long arm came to draw her close to him, and before she quite knew what was happening he kissed her parted lips, his mouth warm upon hers, this a kiss of love and deep affection that was sweeping in its tenderness.

It seemed to her that his hands were trembling slightly as he released her, and there was a rough edge to his voice as he said, "The rain's held off, but to judge by those clouds that are hanging over us I'd say it's still coming."

His words had a double meaning to her as she reflected that there was only a single day left now between tonight and Saturday morning, and she shivered.

"Cold?" he asked swiftly. She shook her head.

"Good," he said. "I was going to suggest we take a walk across to the riverbank before we go in. I could stand having some of my mental cobwebs cleared out by the fresh air. What about you?"

"Yes," she agreed.

They walked past the house, past the gazebo and came finally to the riverbank. The Hudson had the gleam of pewter today.

Such a short time before, Midge thought, the trees on the opposite shore would have made a fit subject for some of the nineteenth-century artists who had lived in this valley and established the famous Hudson River school of painting. One evening she had taken a book about these artists from the shelves of the late Horace Vandervelt's library, and glancing through it had learned that their work focused upon a romantic love of nature, an idealized concept first brought to public awareness through a series of river scenes painted by William Guy Wall. Engravings of these landscapes were later published, in 1828, as *The Hudson River Portfolio*, and Midge had no doubt at

all that somewhere within the Vandervelt archives
was a copy of this valuable work.

Now, though, the distant trees that only a few days
earlier had been a visual feast, blazing with the entire
spectrum of rich autumn tones, had been stripped of
their leaves by the chill winds that presaged November and the oncoming winter. The bare branches lent
a starkness to a time already too grim in so many
ways.

Brian seemed unmoved by the scene before him.
Flashing Midge a smile, he asked, "Want to climb
down the bank?"

"Should you?" she demanded.

He frowned. "Midge, for God's sake, I'm not an
invalid!" he said tersely. "Stop treating me like one,
will you?"

It seemed to her that these days tears were forever
threatening a form of emotionalism she hated. She
bit her lip, flinching from a gaze upon her suddenly
gone very cold, and he asked impatiently, "Well? Or
would you rather go back to the house?"

"No. I'd like to go down to the river edge."

He nodded curtly. "I'll go ahead of you," he told
her. "I know the path, such as it is, like the palm of
my hand. Just take it sideways, step by step, and
hang on to my hand."

She followed instructions, clinging to his hand and
even clutching it occasionally where the going was
rough. She wished she were not so conscious of the
strength so evident in his clasp, and the tantalizing
warmth of his flesh. When finally they reached the
small dark-sanded beach she'd looked down upon so
often from the top of the bank, she said, scuffing at

the sand with her shoe, "I can just imagine you and Becky sneaking down here and going swimming."

He had bent to pick up a stone, which he now skimmed idly out into the river, circles banding and widening as it splashed the water. But he repeated, "Swimming?" and she knew that he had caught at least part of what she had said. "You must be talking about Becky and me," he guessed, his smile wry. "Right?"

"Yes."

"You can't imagine how good it felt to come down here and splash around on a hot summer day," he told her. "I'll admit it probably wasn't the cleanest water in the world, but Becky and I couldn't have cared less about that, nor did it matter to us that the sand was close to black instead of beige!

"It was a good time in many ways," he went on, "being here with Becky. It's such a great river. When I was a kid I used to think that if there were such a thing as reincarnation I'd like to come back as Henry Hudson."

"Brian!"

"True, I did," he insisted. "He was a terrific explorer, a shipmaster of real experience and a mystery man, as well. No one has ever figured out when or where he was born; in fact no one had ever heard of him until he walked into a church in London in 1607, and his name got into the church records. By then he was a married man and had three sons. Incredibly, he died in 1611 up at the bay in Canada that was named for him, so we only really know about four years of his life. During them, though, he surely proved himself to be one of the most daring adventurers of the late Elizabethan era."

"Was he Dutch or English?" Midge asked.

"English," Brian said promptly. "The Dutch used their version of his name—Hendrik—when he went to Holland and signed a contract with the Dutch East India Company. As you probably know, he came to this part of the world to try to find the Northwest Passage. He was a friend of the famous Captain John Smith, who founded the Virginia Colony, and Smith had told him there might be an inlet along the coast that would lead across an isthmus into the Pacific.

"When he came upon the Hudson River, he actually thought he'd reached his goal. This was in early September, in 1609, and Hudson and his crew cruised up the river for about three weeks in the *Half Moon*. His mate, a man named Robert Juet, kept the ship's log, and he was quite a good writer: his observations make fascinating reading. They were all of them struck by the tremendous beauty of the river and the richness of the whole area, the huge walnut, oak and chestnut trees, and the abundance of fish and fur-bearing animals, like deer and beaver and otter. Juet wrote that they saw enough corn and beans growing at one Indian town along the river to load three ships.

"Hudson may have been disappointed for a while when the river grew shallower the farther upstream he went, but he knew that he had come upon a very valuable find, even though it wasn't the fabled Northwest Passage, and he didn't miss a trick. He even had the idea that the Palisades and the cliffs in other sections might prove to be sources of valuable metals. He said he saw a cliff on what's now Manhattan Island that was a 'white green' color, and he thought it must be pure copper or pure silver.

"Hudson's employers actually named the river The River of the Prince Mauritius, after a member of the Dutch royal family. Later it was called the North River, to distinguish it from the Delaware, which was known to the early explorers as the South River. Still later it was named after Hudson, and that's the name that has stuck.

"You know," Brian continued, "the river actually begins as a little trout stream that flows out of a small lake on the side of Mount Marcy, which is the highest of the Adirondack Mountains. The lake's called Tear-of-the-Clouds. I've always loved that name."

"Tear-of-the-Clouds," Midge mused. "It's lovely."

"So are you," Brian said abruptly. She looked up to find him gazing at her intently, and she saw a spark of desire flicker in his eyes, which had never seemed grayer. She felt a response come to life within her so quickly it was as if they both shared an emotional tinderbox, and she knew that in another moment she would be in his arms...and that this could not continue to happen without passion once more completely overtaking them.

But she was wrong. A raindrop came to splash his cheek, and Brian said, "Damn! Let's get up the bank before it really starts to pour. It can become very slippery."

They made it to the top none too soon, and by the time they raced across the lawn the rain was pelting down upon them. It was a cold autumn rain, yet they held hands as they dashed through it laughing like children.

For a moment Midge thought he might seek shelter in the gazebo, but he didn't, and she felt a sharp stab of disappointment. At the back of the house he said, "Let's go around to the kitchen door," and she nodded, so that soon they burst in upon Clara, who was cutting up vegetables at the kitchen sink.

"Land," she exclaimed when she saw them, "it's a good thing I haven't taken the towels I washed this morning upstairs yet!"

She disappeared in the direction of the laundry room to return with thick bath towels, which she thrust into their hands. "Go put on some dry clothes soon as you stop dripping," she commanded, and they grinned at each other.

For the moment, as Brian smiled into her eyes, Midge felt young and carefree and very much in love. She only wished it were a moment that might last... and knew that it could not.

CHAPTER EIGHTEEN

MAUDE SEEMED VERY FRAIL to Midge that evening.
Again Clara brought them their dinner on trays, and
they watched television as they ate, but Midge noticed that the old lady had as little appetite as she
herself had.

On the other hand, Maude seemed to be in a relaxed and pleasant mood, and Midge felt certain she
wasn't really aware of the insidious situation revolv-
ing around her late husband's will. No, Brian had
managed to keep the knowledge of danger from his
aunt even as he had from his twin sister. He had
borne the burden of the inheritance entirely alone,
just as he had carried the burden of his deafness on
his own strong shoulders, allowing no one to get
close to him for any length of time.

Midge stayed with Maude until they'd viewed the
last of the favored television programs. Then she said
good-night, kissing the old lady on the cheek and giving her a brief affectionate hug, to which Maude
responded with touching enthusiasm. As she left the
sitting room, the house stretching on all sides of her
seemed vast. She felt as if she had been set adrift in it,
and now that she did not have Maude to think about
all of her attention turned to Brian.

Jerry had called for him and they had gone off to
the Valley Men's Club dinner without even pausing

to have a drink first. Jerry had been solemn, and Brian had matched his mood. The laughing young man who had raced with her earlier through the driving rain seemed to have disappeared.

Now, glancing at her watch, she saw that it was nearly ten-thirty; they should have been back by now. Worry clutched at her, then she told herself they probably had stopped somewhere for a drink. Yet immediately on the heels of that thought came the sure knowledge that Jerry wouldn't favor that idea, not tonight.

Finally she wandered into the big entrance foyer and was standing by a window draped in antique olive green brocade, staring out at the driveway, when she saw car headlights. She flung open the massive front door, and Brian came across to her quickly, looking down at her as if he were seeing a vision.

"You waited up for me?" he asked huskily.

"Yes," she nodded.

Jerry was right behind him, and Brian led the way directly to the dining room and the liquor cabinet, foraging for a bottle of Horace Vandervelt's vintage Scotch. "Let's go light a fire in the library and sample some of this," he suggested, holding it aloft.

Jerry said, "I suppose I'm technically on duty," but he didn't protest further.

As they pulled comfortable chairs into a semicircle in front of the fireplace with its ornate mahogany mantel, Jerry sighed, "I'm glad that's over! Strathmore was very good, incidentally. Even I understood what he was talking about, and I'm not much for economics ordinarily."

Brian said slowly, "He's a fine person, and he has

a lot on his mind. I appreciated his coming tonight. People asked so many questions," he added, turning to Midge, "that the meeting ran later than it ordinarily does."

"I wondered," she admitted.

"They're a good group," Jerry commented, and Brian nodded.

"Stuffy sometimes," he said, "but basically sound. Once you get your degree, I want you to come into the club. Andrew Summers isn't getting any younger; we're going to be needing another lawyer in our midst."

"Law?" Midge questioned.

"Yes," Jerry told her. "I've been studying nights. It's meant cracking the books a lot when I'm home, besides going to classes when Lucille and I could have been doing things together. It's been rough for her—one of these years I hope I can make it all up to her."

Brian leaned forward to put another log on the fire, and Midge caught her breath as she gazed at him. The firelight spilled tones of bronze over his skin and hair, and he had never looked more handsome. But there was a wistfulness to his expression that struck at her.

He said, "Lucille will come through all that, Jerry, just as she'll get over her jealousy. What's important is that she loves you. You're very lucky. . . ."

His words trailed off, and shortly afterward Jerry left them, with the reminder that either he or another trooper would be checking the house during the night. As she and Brian walked back to the library, having bid goodbye to Jerry at the door, Midge observed, "He's ambitious."

"Yes, and I'm sure he'll make a good lawyer,' Brian agreed.

"Does he come from an old Coxsackie family?"

"Not really, but Jerry was born here, of course, as was his father. Dr. Mueller, too, for that matter."

"You've told me a lot about Coxsackie's history," she said, "but you've never gone into too much detail about your own family. Well, I take that back—you did mention that they came here about the same time as the Broncks and those other early settlers."

"Yes," he responded, again pausing to tend to the fire. "The Vandervelts, like the Broncks and some others, were here by the mid 1600s. I did mention to you that they've always had fingers in the various local industries, and Uncle Horace kept up the tradition. Also, he was a person who liked to pull strings. Although he never gave up his controlling interest in a number of enterprises, in time the *Valley Voice* became the real focal point of his life. He knew that by controlling a newspaper that circulated throughout this entire area he could become and remain a major civic force, whereas politicians come and go with the elections. Uncle Horace influenced the people in power; he played with men as if they were chess pieces. More recently he was involved with interests that were pressing for yet another nuclear power plant to be built. Some of his property farther up the river would have made an ideal site."

"Was he for it or against it?"

"He hadn't committed himself publicly," Brian said, "but you may be sure he would have been for it if the price were right."

"And you?"

He slanted a quick glance at her. "I'm definitely

opposed," he said. "I can see both sides of the issue and I'm certainly not against progress, but my feeling is that there's already too much radioactive waste in the world, and I'm not about to add to it. Had my uncle lived, this would have been just another area of disagreement between us."

He had stood as he spoke and fixed another drink for them without asking her whether or not she wanted one, and now he handed her a glass. "Take it, Midge. You need it tonight."

Thoughts were whirling through her mind, but she focused on one of them. "Don't you have a headache?" she asked him.

"A headache? No," he said. "Should I have one?"

"You usually do after an evening at the Valley Men's Club," she pointed out.

"True," he agreed, "and I can thank you, mother hen, for the fact that I don't tonight. That trick of yours of trying to latch onto words alone—especially last words—instead of the whole thing works surprisingly well. I found I was amazingly relaxed, for me, and I even caught quite a bit of what Wilson said."

"Why is Mr. Strathmore so beset with problems, Brian?" she ventured to ask. "I saw him one day when he was coming out of your office after you had sent for me...."

"Yes, I remember." Brian absently stirred an ice cube with one finger, then explained, "He found out that day that Moira, his wife, is a very sick woman. She's going to have to have major surgery in a few weeks, and her chances are not too good. It's especially rough because they have no children, and they're a devoted couple."

"Oh," Midge said, and there was sympathy in the one small word. She was remembering Moira Strathmore and Maude enthusiastically discussing that ikebana class, and Wilson Strathmore's own old-fashioned courtliness.

"At least," Brian went on, "they've been happy together for a number of years. Few people are that fortunate. Also, I would say that Moira has that all-important will to live, and I'm betting that she'll make it."

He looked away from her as he spoke about shared love, his face taut, then he stretched his long legs out in front of the fire and rested his head against the chair back so that his face was in shadow. In quite a real sense he had put himself beyond her reach and out of communication. Then, in a stillness that was intense except for the sound of the crackling logs, she heard the clang of the knocker on the front door, and at the same time the bell pealed.

"Brian!" she cried, so sharply that her voice reached him.

He looked up quickly. "What is it?"

"Someone's at the door," she said, and felt a flutter of panic.

The bell pealed again, and he laughed shortly. "Even I can hear that! We can't accuse our nocturnal visitor of being stealthy."

"Perhaps you shouldn't answer," she cautioned. "Perhaps you should call Jerry." But he only flung a scathing glance in her direction.

With Midge at his heels, Brian strode out of the library and across the foyer to the front door, flinging it open wide to stare in disbelief at the woman on the threshold.

"Becky!" he exclaimed as his sister stepped forward, threw her arms around him and burst into tears.

THEY REKINDLED THE FIRE, and Brian turned on several of the lamps in the library. Midge knew he had a motive for this: he needed good light to help him lip-read, and she prayed he would get away with it for the moment. There would be time enough later for Becky to find out about his hearing.

He held her tightly while she cried, and finally she stood back and said disbelievingly, "You're alive! Dear God, you're alive!"

"Of course I'm alive, Bec!" he soothed her.

He had given her a handkerchief. Now she wiped her eyes and looked across at Midge. "How could you *do* such a terrible thing?" she demanded.

"What are you talking about, Becky?"

"How could you call and tell me Brian was dying?"

Midge, sickened, said, "Becky, I can't believe what you're saying!"

Becky raised red-rimmed eyes. "I heard you myself," she stated flatly. "After all, I spoke to you."

"But I didn't call you," Midge protested dully.

Miserable, Becky insisted, "I wish I could believe that. I can't tell you how much I wish it!"

"Bec," Brian interrupted cautiously, "it's easy to make a mistake about someone's voice."

"Not when you know someone as well as I know Midge," Becky said decisively. "Her voice has something different about it, a kind of lilt. You must have noticed, Brian."

Glancing swiftly at him, Midge saw the stricken expression that flickered across his face, and her heart ached for him. But he said only, "Bec, no matter what you may think, Midge didn't make any phone call to you. I'll guarantee that."

"Thanks," Midge said bleakly.

"Oh, please," Becky sighed. "*Please!* You two should know that the last thing in the world I want to do is to accuse Midge of anything. But when your best friend calls you and tells you that your brother is dying and you'd better get the first plane East...."

The words came out in a rush, a babble, and Midge realized that most of them had been lost on Brian. Looking across at her, he raised his eyebrows in a kind of question mark, and she got the meaning: he wanted to know if he was supposed to answer Becky, and she shook her head slightly.

"Becky," Midge said slowly, "I can understand how confusing this must be to you, but I think we can explain it. Two days ago Brian got a call from a long-distance operator who supposedly was trying to place a call from you. That call never came through."

Becky stared at both of them, her pretty tear-streaked face bewildered. "Why?" she asked.

Brian said simply, "Because someone wanted to detain me. They also wanted you here before the weekend. It's a long story, Bec, but if you'll sit down and be patient I'll try to make sense out of it for you."

There was an intimacy in his tone, an obviously deep affection, that gave Midge an odd kind of twinge. She looked from one to the other of them, feeling very much an intruder, knowing that she was an outsider looking in. They belonged, Brian and Becky. They were both Vandervelts.

She said, "I'll leave you two alone."

"No," Brian told her abruptly, then added, softening, "Please, Midge. This involves you, too."

She wanted to say, *it doesn't involve me at all! It's simply that you don't want to be alone with Becky, and I can bridge the gap for you....*

She turned to him. "Sooner or later—"

Brian shook his head. "Not just yet," he insisted. "Please."

She sat down, feeling as bedraggled as Becky looked, and Brian put another log on the fire, then set about making his sister a drink. As he poured he began slowly, "Bec, when Uncle Horace died you called and said you were coming East for the funeral, even though you'd just had Brenda. I told you not to, remember?"

"Yes."

"There was a reason," Brian told her. "There's been a reason all this time why I've been trying to keep you away from Coxsackie."

At Becky's bewildered look he went on, "You know the terms of the will. You know about the two-year probationary period, and you do understand, don't you, that if I don't pass it I'm to be cut off with a dollar?"

"Yes."

"Then," he continued, "you must also know that if I were to die before you do you'd get my share of the estate, but the four department heads would inherit the newspaper."

"Yes."

"Conversely, if you were to die before I did, I would get everything including the newspaper, if I survived my probation."

"Yes."

"Well," Brian said, "there *is* something more. If both of us die before November first of this year, the department heads, or whichever of *them* survive, stand to inherit. Did you know that?"

"Not really," Becky confessed. "Tim and I both read the will, but to tell you the truth the whole thing was so appalling I've tried to put it out of my mind as much as possible. I was worried about you, Brian, that's all, so I guess I didn't pay as much attention to the contingencies as I should have."

Becky was wiping her eyes again and half mumbling into her handkerchief, and Brian sent Midge a desperate look. She cut in quickly, "It's understandable that you wouldn't pay attention to all the extra details, Becky."

Brian smiled wryly, flashing her a look of gratitude. "True," he responded. "And I suppose you could say I primarily was worried about *you*. It occurred to me way back that this could be especially dangerous for you. If I failed the probation period I would have been kicked out, but you stood to inherit no matter what I did.

"Now," he went on, "we're very close to the deadline. So in a sense you and I are both clay pigeons, and I can't deny that it's a bad situation. An attempt was made on my life very recently."

"What?"

"You'll remember Mike Stabler, Becky," Brian explained. "He was killed last week—an accident. The phone call Midge mentioned that was supposedly from you came just as I was about to leave for his funeral. The other department heads went on without me, so I used my own car and the brakes went out as I rounded a curve. They'd been tampered with."

Becky was ashen. "Oh, dear God!" she moaned. She attempted a wan smile. "So despite your efforts to keep me away I've come at the worst possible time. Or, I guess you'd say, I was lured here."

"Yes."

Becky hesitated. "Bri," she said then, after a thoughtful moment, "I believe everything you've told me, but I think there's even more."

"What do you mean?"

"I know you too well. Something was wrong before Uncle Horace died. There has been something wrong ever since your accident. I've thought all this time that it must have been connected with the accident; obviously it wasn't."

Midge could hear the fire crackling in the silence that followed, and she realized she was holding her breath. Brian was very still; she could only imagine the wrench this must be causing him. She wished she could do something, anything, to delay what was surely an awful moment of truth for him, but then he sighed and said reluctantly, "It *was* the accident, Bec."

"How could it have been?" Becky demanded.

The words came slowly. "The explosion caused me to lose my hearing, or the better part of it," he told her.

"*What?*"

His smile was twisted. "That's *my* word," he said softly, but his allusion was lost on Becky.

She stared at him disbelievingly, then she asked, her voice trembling, "Are you trying to tell me you're. . .deaf?"

Deaf. The word thudded between them like a

heavy stone, and in its echo Midge found that she'd got to her feet without even realizing it, and clenched her hands.

"Becky," she said, her voice tight with suppressed emotion, "don't you dare start crying again! Yes, technically Brian is deaf, but it doesn't matter. It doesn't really matter at all!"

She could feel the level gray eyes sweeping her face, and time stopped. Then he said, an odd catch in his voice, "Doesn't it?"

"No." She was fighting back her own tears now. "No, it doesn't...."

FINALLY THEY WENT UPSTAIRS, Midge insisting that Becky share the huge master bedroom with her at least for tonight. In the interim they had caught up on things to a point, both Brian and Midge explaining why Midge was now living in the house, and also bringing Becky up-to-date on Maude, long since fast asleep.

Brian left them at the foot of the stairs. He kissed his sister lightly on the forehead, but his eyes lingered on Midge. There was a soberness to his gaze, despite the slight smile that curved his mouth as he said, "Don't worry, mother hen; I'll bolt the doors. And Jerry and his colleagues will be keeping an eye on us, as well."

Now Becky asked, "Who was Brian talking about? Not Jerry Mueller by any chance, was it?"

"Yes," Midge said. "He's a state trooper."

Becky laughed. "I can't believe it. He was a devil when he was a kid. Handsome, though."

"He still is. He's married," Midge told her. "His wife's name is Lucille."

"That must be Lucille LeClair," Becky said, "if she's from around here. Brunette and very pretty?"

"Yes. You and Jerry were teenage sweethearts, weren't you, Becky?"

"Not really." Becky dismissed this as if it were ancient history. "We got a bit intense one summer, then we both went in different directions. Midge...."

"Yes?"

"What happened with Brian and Grace? They were engaged."

"She broke it off when she found out about his hearing. Now she's married to somebody else."

"I see." Becky's eyes darkened with anger. "And what about John?"

"John?"

"John Pemberton. You cannot have forgotten him!"

Astonishingly, she had. She answered, "I told you in San Francisco that it was over. We spoke on the phone once, after I got back to New York. It really *is* over, totally over, on my part at least, and I'm sure he'll recover."

"Brian might not," Becky said thoughtfully.

"I think he will. I'm sure he was deeply hurt, but Brian has too much character to be crushed forever by anyone."

"I wasn't speaking about his former fiancée," Becky reproved her.

"Oh?"

"Midge, come on! He's so much in love with you he can hardly keep his eyes off you."

Midge shook her head. "That isn't love, Becky. He has that rather intent way of looking at a person because he depends quite a bit upon lip-reading.''

"I can't believe it," Becky said sadly. "Isn't there any hope he'll get his hearing back?"

"Not until medicine comes up with some new discoveries," Midge said flatly. "But he's learned to cope; he gets better at it all the time. I admire him tremendously."

"Only admiration, Midge?"

Midge shook her head. "Becky, you've always been a great one for getting things out of me, but this time I'm standing mute."

Becky smiled with obvious satisfaction. Then she said, "Midge. . .just as long as it isn't pity. It's easy to confuse pity and love, and Brian would never want pity."

Midge's smile was tinged with bitterness. "I know that only too well."

She was standing at the window as she spoke, and she saw the state police cruiser drive in. "That's probably Jerry now," she said.

Becky came to her side. "I've got to see him in uniform," she chuckled.

The cruiser stopped in front of the house, and Jerry got out. Impulsively Midge raised the window.

"Jerry," she called.

He looked up. "Midge—you're all right?"

"Yes."

Now Becky came to stand beside her. "Hi, Jerry," she called.

He hesitated, peering through the darkness. "It isn't. . .Becky?"

But it was not welcome Midge detected in his voice; rather, it was worry.

CLARA, ON THE OTHER HAND, was ecstatic when Midge and Becky walked into the kitchen the next morning. She at once suggested that Becky take a breakfast tray in to her aunt.

"It's early for her, but that don't matter," Clara insisted. "Mind now, you're going to see quite a difference in her. She's failing, but she's never been so happy. Think about the happy part."

Midge said, "I'll probably be gone before you come back out, Becky. This is a workday for me."

"No, it isn't."

Brian was standing in the kitchen doorway, and when she started to protest he said firmly, "There's no need for you to go in on a Friday."

"I cut out early yesterday," she reminded him. "I'd really like to clear up my desk, Brian."

"I'd rather you stayed here with Becky," he told her.

"But you shouldn't be going in there at all," she protested, fear surfacing again. "Today of all days!"

"Today of all days I should be there," he declared. "Let me take the Volvo, though, will you? They're still working on the Jag."

He was wearing a light gray suit that emphasized his eyes, and there was a fresh bandage strip on his forehead. "Clara, no eggs and stuff this morning, okay?" he requested. "Just toast and coffee, like Midge and Becky."

"All right," the housekeeper agreed reluctantly.

Brian turned to his sister. "Sleep well?"

"Remarkably, considering the fact that I was sharing Uncle Horace's room and it is absolutely monstrous," Becky responded. "How do you stand it, Midge?"

She smiled. "At first I didn't think I could, but I'm getting used to it."

"Heaven forbid!" exclaimed Becky, and left with Maude's tray.

Brian, sitting down at the kitchen table, remarked, "It's wonderful to see her. If it weren't *now* . . . ."

"I know."

"As for you," he went on, "please remember that we may be dealing with someone who isn't entirely rational. You and Becky both stay in the house till I get back, will you? Play backgammon or something."

"Do you?"

"Yes, and I'm damned good at it."

"Challenge?"

He laughed. "It's a date!"

Following him to the kitchen door, she tugged his sleeve slightly, and he looked down at her. "Be careful yourself, will you?" she told him, all her worry in her eyes, and in a blinding moment she could read only love for her on his face, and she wanted to stop time until she could be sure, *sure*, that what she was seeing was real and not merely wishful imagination. Then he cupped her chin in his hands and bent to kiss her, and at once her arms went around him and she was clinging to him as their mouths fused.

He released her gently, and she was still in a process of recovery when she heard a car door close and the Volvo engine start.

Clara behind her said, "Well, now!" She was smiling, and Midge knew that she actually was blushing.

Becky came back, saying, "Clara, Aunt Maude looks *awful*. What does Dr. Mueller say?"

"Not too much," the housekeeper answered. "Her heart's bad, but he says to let her be."

"I suppose that's all we *can* do," Becky admitted. "She's going out to lunch with Mrs. Strathmore. Is it all right for her to go out?"

"It's all right for her to do anything she wants to do," Clara said stoutly.

At the proper time Tom brought the Rolls-Royce around to the front door, and Maude sallied forth dressed in autumn gold. Watching from the window of the front parlor, Becky commented, "Priceless!" She turned to Midge. "Clara is right: I've never seen Maude so happy. No matter what, it's worth it. . ."

Through the course of the morning they caught up on conversation, discussing family and old friends. They had lunch at the kitchen table, this over Clara's protests, but then, with the afternoon, silence descended, draping them like swaths of gray velvet cut from an endless bolt. Worry, Midge found, could be a tangible thing.

Maude came back from her luncheon date and went to her room for a nap before dinner. Midge kept waiting to hear the sound of a car on the driveway outside, but when toward four-thirty she finally did, it was not Brian but Jerry who strode into the room, in full uniform.

She went limp with fear. Then she saw his eyes light as he spied Becky, and Becky ran forward and they hugged exuberantly, muttering all sorts of nonsense. So she knew that the visit—thank God—had nothing to do with Brian.

Jerry told them, "I'm on patrol again, so I thought I'd make this my first call of the day. You've filled Becky in?"

"Yes, but I'm not sure she's a total believer."

"Believe," Jerry affirmed tersely. His eyes lingered on Midge. "Are you all right?"

"Yes."

He turned back to Becky then, and as the two of them chatted Midge saw to her relief that Lucille had little to worry about. Jerry and Becky were good friends, nothing more.

Brian came in shortly after Jerry left, and Midge looked him over so thoroughly from head to foot that he laughed and asked, "Do I pass inspection?"

"Yes. How did the day go?"

"Routinely," he said, "for the most part." And she knew he was not about to elaborate on that.

At six when they joined Maude in her sitting room the old lady was resplendent in her plum satin. Clara brought the tray with the sherry decanter and four glasses.

Brian made a face. "Bourbon for me, please," he requested, but he did stay with them, went in to dinner with them, lingered over dessert and coffee and even went back with them to the library, where television was dispensed with tonight in favor of conversation.

Maude was delighted to have such company; she literally sparkled as she recalled incidents of the twins' childhood, relating them with great relish. Shortly after ten she brought the evening to a close, announcing that she'd had quite a day, one of the best ones in her life, and now was going to get into bed with a new novel. Then she kissed each of them, embracing Midge just as fondly as she did Brian and Becky.

It was the last time they were to see her. Before going back to the quarters she shared with Tom over the garage, Clara, for a reason she never herself could explain, went in later to be sure that Maude was all right. She found the old lady still dressed in her plum satin, sitting in her favorite armchair... but this time the sleep into which she had fallen was the sleep of eternity.

CHAPTER NINETEEN

JERRY CAME FIRST, and then Dr. Mueller, and then a succession of other people, and the things that had to be done were done. Shortly after midnight Becky, Brian and Midge were sitting around the kitchen table while Clara, still sniffing, her eyes red from weeping, insisted upon making coffee for them.

Becky said, "We shouldn't be so gloomy; she wouldn't want it. But I can't help feeling I'm to blame. This morning she was so startled when I barged in on her that she couldn't get her breath for a minute. Without any makeup, her lips were blue...."

She looked at Brian appealingly—she was seeking reassurance, Midge knew—and he said, "Bec, I'm sorry. I wasn't paying attention. Could you go through it again?"

Midge found herself saying, "She's blaming herself for Maude's death, Brian," and she caught a strange little expression in Becky's eyes.

"You had nothing to do with it, Bec," Brian consoled his sister. "I spoke to Dr. Mueller: he said he examined Aunt Maude for the first time shortly after Uncle Horace died, and he wouldn't have believed it possible she could live this long. I'm only glad she got the chance to see you one more time."

"That's right," Clara agreed. "She told me this afternoon it was the best thing that ever happened.

Three young people in the house, she said. She loved all of you.''

They ate in silence, a little surprised to find that they could eat at all. Then Becky said, ''I want to call Tim.''

''Go ahead,'' Brian told her. ''Use the phone in the library, why don't you?''

''I think I will.'' And she followed his suggestion.

Clara said, ''I'll go on over to Tom, if it's all right with you two. He's kind of shaken up.''

Midge nodded and found herself saying sympathetically, ''Of course, Clara,'' as if she had the right to voice her opinion here in the Vandervelt household at all.

Brian refilled their coffee cups and glanced toward the rain-streaked kitchen window, commenting, ''It's been raining off and on all day.'' Midge realized she hadn't even noticed the weather. ''It's been a rotten Halloween for the kids—not much good for the trick-or-treaters.''

She had also forgotten that the day just past had been Halloween, but now memory of Halloweens past swept over her: the witch's costume her mother had made her; the time she had dragged her orange paper trick-or-treat bag through damp grass so that when she got home the bottom had come out and there was nothing left, apples and candy bars all lost in the darkness, strewn across suburban lawns.

She asked, ''Did you and Becky trick-or-treat?''

''Before we came here,'' he said. ''Later. . .no. No one else came out here to trick-or-treat, either. I think half the town has always thought the place is haunted, and you can hardly blame them.''

''That's what I was going to do for Maude,'' Midge told him. ''And now it's too late.''

"What were you going to do for her?"

"I was going to work with her on a project to redecorate this house. First we were going to paint the outside white, then change the interior colors to make it livable. That's why she liked ikebana so much—because it's so simple."

Brian was watching her steadily. "For someone as young as you are," he said, "you seem to have an unusual capacity for understanding the needs and feelings of other people."

Midge laughed a little shakily. "You make yourself sound so ancient. Yet you're the same age as Becky, which means you're twenty-six, and so am I."

Staring at her, he murmured reflectively, "Twenty-six. Sometimes I feel a hundred and twenty-six. Then other times, when I'm with you. . . ."

Her pulse began to hammer, and when he didn't continue she asked, "Yes?" But he shook his head.

"This isn't the time to talk about it," he said firmly. "Look, you must be exhausted. Why don't you go on to bed? There's no need for you to stay up."

There was a curtness to his tone that stung, but she was determined to ignore it. She asked instead, "Are you trying to get rid of me?"

"Get rid of you?" He frowned at her; he seemed honestly puzzled. "No," he said then, "that wasn't my intention. Trying to spare you, yes. I would say your association with the Vandervelts has put you through far too much as it is."

"Life is meant to have some. . .some sharing in it," she told him. "There will be a lot to do in the morning. Arrangements. . . ."

She shrank from the subject, but Brian said swiftly, "I've talked to Andrew Summers, Midge, and he told me what Maude's wishes were. She wanted to be cremated, so that's what will be done. She asked that those of us who care for her gather for a brief memorial service, and I thought we'd do that Sunday."

So, Midge thought dully, she couldn't be of help to him even in sharing some of the burden connected with Maude's death.

Someone knocked at the kitchen door, and she stiffened, but Brian said, "A knock, wasn't it? That will be Jerry. He planned to come back after he got off duty, and he said he'd try to persuade Lucille to come with him."

Lucille had agreed. Sleepy eyed but very lovely, she went directly to Brian and kissed him. "I'm sorry," she said, and Brian gave her a brief wordless hug.

Becky came back from making her phone call, and her response to her introduction to Lucille was an instinctive one. "Jerry's always been like another brother to me," she declared, "which means that finally I have a sister!"

Brian asked, "Midge, would you mind digging out some of Uncle Horace's brandy for us?"

She didn't mind at all. She wanted to tell him that she'd gladly go to the moon for him, that she would in fact go anywhere or do anything for him.... Fighting back a rising tide of emotion that could only lead to frustration, she got the brandy and five long-stemmed glasses.

As they clustered around the wooden table, a rising wind was howling through the trees outside, and raindrops spattered hard against the windows. They talked as they sipped brandy, but Brian seemed so remote from them that at one point Midge actually wondered if he had turned off his hearing aids. Twice when Jerry spoke to him he said, "I'm sorry. What was it?"

Now, on the third such occasion, Jerry asked with some asperity, "What's bugging you?"

Brian swirled the brandy in his glass. "I'm not sure," he answered slowly.

"Well," Jerry persisted, "you do admit you haven't been with us for the past half hour or so?"

"Yes," Brian nodded.

"Look—" Jerry was striving for patience "—is it something you'd like to talk about, or is it purely a Vandervelt matter? In other words, something that shouldn't concern the peasants?"

Brian's eyebrows rose. "Ouch," he said. "Touchy, aren't you?"

"Not without reason," Jerry replied. He glanced at his watch. "Eleven hours to go," he observed soberly.

"I know that. It brings something else to mind, as a matter of fact. Andrew Summers called me at the paper this afternoon—yesterday afternoon, I should say—and he insists that you come to the meeting in my office, Becky, which is what Jerry is referring to. It's scheduled for noon today."

"The final revelation?" Becky spoke with a bitterness that was very unlike her.

"Yes, the final revelation. But I think to be there would be to place you in needless danger. I'd like you to stay here in the house with Midge. In other words, I don't want you there."

"Thanks a lot!" Becky scowled at him.

"Whew!" Brian looked around at them. "What a sensitive bunch of people! For God's sake, Becky, you can guess why I don't want you there, can't you? Unless, that is, everything blows up sooner."

His last words drifted off, and after a moment Jerry said, "We're losing you again. I know that look when I see it."

"No," Brian insisted. "Believe me, I'm still with you."

"Then what is it?"

"Something someone said," he told them slowly.

"Something you heard?"

"No," Brian said. "Something I saw."

Jerry shook his head. "I think I need another drink," he decided. "You're telling me that what's bothering you is something you *saw* people say?"

Brian nodded. "That's right. I was in my office, looking out of the window, admittedly woolgathering. There are side draperies on the windows, and sheer curtains over the glass that have a kind of sheen. From the outside you can't see in too easily. Anyway, there were two people in the parking lot, not too far from my window. One was turned toward me, and so I lip-read."

"I'll be damned!" breathed Jerry.

"I'm not the world's best at it," Brian conceded, "and even when someone is very good it's easy to make a mistake. Certain sounds are formed the same way as certain other sounds; there are all sorts of complications. Even so, I'm relatively sure of what was said. What worries me is the interpretation of it. I could be wrong—so for the moment I'm not going to identify the people involved."

Jerry swore softly. "How *dense* can a person be? For God's sake, Brian, what kind of a game do you think this is? These stakes are for keeps, remember?"

"Yes. Still. . .this particular incident could have an entirely different connotation. If it doesn't, we don't have to worry until noon."

"What do you mean by that?"

"Whatever is going to happen will happen at the meeting itself," Brian told them.

"You mean catastrophe will strike when all of you are assembled at the board table?" Jerry asked acidly.

"Something like that," Brian agreed.

"Come off it!"

"No, I'm serious. Especially since I think I stumbled upon the whole plan just a few minutes ago."

Jerry sighed. "Maybe it's the brandy," he said plaintively, "or maybe I really *am* losing my mind."

Brian ignored this. "Look," he said, "a few minutes ago I told Becky I didn't want her at the meeting unless everything blows up sooner. Remember?"

Jerry stared at him. Then he said, very slowly, "Do you mean what I think you mean?"

Becky cut in, "Couldn't you two be a little less cryptic? Maybe Midge knows what you're talking about, but I certainly don't."

Midge began, "You really think—"

"Yes," Brian said.

And Becky cried irritably, "You're all *impossible*!"

"You think," Midge persisted, disregarding Becky for the moment, "that it really could be a bomb?"

"What better way of getting rid of everyone who stands in one's way all at once?" he asked her.

"What about Andrew Summers? He's the one who wants Becky there tomorrow. Would he profit?"

"He's scheduled for a hundred-thousand-dollar bequest anyway. He'd have no motive." Brian sighed with ultimate weariness. "I keep wondering which one of the others is hungry enough for money to kill for it. I've known Strathmore and Weissman and Handel since I was a kid, and I certainly can't picture Trent Clayton as an assassin, either. It's unreal to think that any one of them would try to blow up all the rest of us. Yet. . . it almost has to be the answer.''

''It makes sense,'' Jerry admitted. ''The bomb idea, that is. It's not worth taking a chance on, anyway. We should close off the whole building right now.''

''No,'' Brian disagreed. ''Then nothing might happen, true, but we still wouldn't *know*. Also, spite and vengeance can make just as good motives as profit and power.''

Becky asked, ''What happens if we all survive past noon, Bri?''

''Well,'' explained Brian, ''my own will goes into effect when the clock reaches 12:01 P.M. Then, according to Summers, I inherit the *Hudson River Valley Voice* and this property, now that Aunt Maude is gone, and you and I share in the rest. Clara, Tom, Summers and the department heads will all receive fairly substantial bequests, but the chance for the real pot of gold will be gone.''

Jerry said, ''Damn it, you're both going to be alive at 12:01 tomorrow, and after that you can be filthy rich and turn your noses up at the poor people like Lucille and Midge and me, okay?''

Midge could feel those clear gray eyes focusing on her, and she looked away hastily, because it was true. He *would* be filthy rich. Until now she hadn't thought too much about the implications of Brian's becoming a very, very wealthy man. Now she remembered what he had said the other day about knowing that he could buy such things as a wife if he inherited Horace's estate. True, he had also said he didn't want it that way. But would he ever have enough faith in a woman to believe she didn't care about his money?

Jerry's voice cut into her thoughts. "We've got to decide when to close off that building, Brian. The risk would be too great otherwise."

Brian nodded. "I agree. I'd like to set a trap, that's all."

"Look," Jerry went on, "I'm no hero, and I don't like bombs. We have guys who are experts in that field, and the sensible thing is to call them in now. Let them find the damned thing, if there is one, and get rid of it."

"I'm no hero, either," Brian told him. "That's why I don't want to have to keep on wondering what's going to come at me, when or from where. I don't think the bomb's in the building yet, anyway. Figure it out for yourself. Think what you'd do if you wanted to plant a bomb at the *Valley Voice*. You'd wait till sometime between darkness and dawn, closer to dawn probably. Perhaps you'd park somewhere and go down to the railroad tracks at the back of the plant—"

"Okay," Jerry said. "Okay, let's take it that way. Our guys can be right there waiting for him—"

"And risk having the damned thing go off? Or of having him detonate it when he knows the contest is over, and maybe getting out of there still unidentified? No way!"

"Well," Jerry responded with exaggerated politeness, "what would *you* suggest?"

"I suggest that you let your guys go in well after daylight, probably around 9 A.M."

"That would give them from three hours to eternity to find whatever may be there." Jerry shook his head. "That's slicing it thin."

"It isn't slicing it *that* thin," said Brian. "We're to

meet in my office: that's the scene of action. The bomb shouldn't be too far away.''

Jerry suggested, ''It would be better to stake out the plant for the rest of the night. We could also stake out the homes of your four department heads.''

''That would be too much of a tip-off,'' Brian pointed out. ''No, we'll have to wait it out.'' He stirred restlessly. ''Bec, how about making another pot of coffee?''

Midge offered to do it, but Becky said, ''No, that's okay.''

''Another thing, Jerry,'' Brian went on. ''You can't let your men go in there looking like cops, with all the apparatus those demolition crews carry.''

''Then how do you expect them to find your bomb? Do you think they can sniff it out?''

''No. Camouflage them, that's all.''

''Any suggestions?''

''I have one,'' Midge said unexpectedly. ''Dress them up as painters. It would be logical to paint on a Saturday morning when not many people are working, and the front lobby needs a coat of paint anyway. So do most of the offices, for that matter. You could hide all sorts of equipment in empty paint pails and buckets and ladders. . . .''

Painters.

CHAPTER TWENTY

"I WILL NOT STAY HERE. I simply will not!" Midge was adamant.

Brian, tight-lipped, said, "There is absolutely no reason for you to come to this meeting."

"So," she retorted, stung, "it's none of my business, is that it?"

"I didn't say that, Midge." He was plainly impatient with her. "Do I have to spell the whole thing out all over again? You know what we're dealing with. Anything I could say to you would be pure repetition."

"Would it?" she asked, her eyes glinting dangerously. "Brian, how can you possibly think I could sit here all by myself while you and Becky are at the *Valley Voice*—"

"Clara and Tom will be here," he interrupted.

"Damn you!" she snapped vehemently.

She turned away from him, going to the window that faced the driveway to stare out at a sullen Saturday that matched her own charcoal mood. She had lain awake into the early hours of the morning, grieving for Maude and brooding about Brian, terribly conscious that he was alone above her in his solitary tower.

Once she had actually slipped out of bed and reached the door of the room before, berating herself for being a fool, she had turned back, moving quietly so as not to awaken a miraculously sleeping Becky. Brian, she suspected, must want her tonight as much as she wanted him—and she nearly moaned aloud as she thought of just how much she wanted him! But the steel control that he seemed able to summon at will would come to the fore, she knew, before he let his emotions rage unbridled. And, she thought sadly, perhaps he would be right at that. This was not the moment to indulge all those surging feelings that had been like a mounting tide between them.

No, this was not the moment. Yet it seemed to her that in almost everything that came to a reckoning point between them the timing was sadly wrong. And now Brian was already in effect putting her on the shelf. He was setting her aside in a moment of crisis, as if she had no stake at all in what was to happen before the morning was over.

Already, too, it had been proved that the bomb theory was no fantasy. At precisely nine o'clock, according to reports relayed by Jerry, a truck belonging to a local painting firm had pulled up in front of the newspaper building. Painters had unloaded ladders and pails, brushes and buckets, then had gone into the building and set about their work. As Brian had surmised, it had not taken them too long. The bomb had been planted on a shelf in a closet just back of Brian's desk.

"Strictly an amateur job, but there was enough force in it to blow the whole damned room up," the officer in charge of the demolition squad had told Jerry with devastating simplicity.

The bomb had been set to go off at twelve o'clock. High noon precisely.

Midge shuddered, then heard Becky's light step on the stairs behind her. "Ready, Brian?" his sister asked.

"Yes," he answered.

Becky paused at the front door, looking back. "Aren't you coming with us, Midge?" That was invitation enough.

"Yes, I am," Midge declared, her chin high, her lovely face defiant as she glanced toward Brian.

His face was expressionless, the mask set firmly in place, but she saw the fury in his eyes. He said stiffly, "I don't think I asked you if you mind if we use the Volvo. I didn't want Tom to bother with the Rolls."

She said, equally stiff, "There's no need for you to ask me. It's your car anyway."

The mask slipped, and he shot her a thoroughly irate glance that was at least human. Becky, missing this byplay, suggested, "You get in front, Midge," but she shook her head.

"No. You do," she said. She slipped into the back seat of the car, staring at the two blond heads in front of her, and suddenly she felt very much out of place. This was their world, as Jerry had indicated succinctly in his banter about becoming filthy rich. Despite the episode in the tower room she had really been only on the fringes of it all along, and she warned herself this was something she had better remember.

They were silent on the drive to the paper, and it was only as they were turning into the parking lot that Becky looked at her watch and said, her voice very small, "It's a quarter to twelve."

Brian, Midge felt sure, hadn't heard this; in any event, he pulled up by the walk leading to the front entrance, instructing, "You two get out here."

Becky turned to him, instantly apprehensive. "What about you?" she demanded.

"No need to push the panic button," he said. "I'll park and join you shortly."

There was really no way of protesting, yet Midge felt a nagging sense of discomfort. She could not refrain from glancing back as she and Becky went into the lobby, but the doors swung closed and the Volvo, and Brian, immediately were lost from sight.

She frowned as she saw men at work, scaffolds still in place. The bomb had been found, after all. Did this mean that Brian had taken her remarks about the rooms needing painting all that seriously? Even as she asked herself this, it came to her who the men were and why they were here. Demolition experts, no. Police officers, yes.

A conference table had been set up in Brian's office, and Wilson Strathmore and Fritz Handel already were seated at it. Both men seemed delighted to see Becky; even Handel was less taciturn than usual and went so far as to make a joke about her having become a bit plumper since the last time he'd seen her.

Andrew Summers came in almost immediately, and Wilson Strathmore introduced him to Midge. He was a small bald-headed man with an air of quiet confidence and an unexpectedly charming smile.

As she sat down with the others at the table, Midge found herself swallowing nervously and watching the clock on the wall, which was now pointing at five to twelve. Then they heard footsteps and Abe Weissman appeared in the doorway, mopping his round face with a soggy handkerchief.

"You wouldn't believe it!" he told them.

"They've got some kind of a parade going on up in West Coxsackie. I thought they'd never let me through."

"That's all right, Abe," Strathmore said. "Two of us are still absent, anyway—Clayton and Brian." He turned to Becky. "Didn't Brian drive you two girls over here?" he asked.

"Yes," Becky said, and glanced anxiously at Midge, because Brian certainly had had more than enough time to park by now.

Jerry Mueller appeared in the doorway to say, "Clayton's on the way. He couldn't get his car started, so we've sent a cruiser over to pick him up." He surveyed the table, then demanded, "Where's Brian?"

"Outside," Becky told him. "At least, he was going to park the car...."

Outside in the lobby a clock began to chime, and Midge, tensing, counted each tolling stroke. One... two... three... four... five... six... seven... eight... nine... ten... eleven... twelve.... As the last note sounded, leaving a mournful echo in its wake, she shuddered.

Jerry Mueller, she noted, had disappeared. Now it was Trent Clayton who appeared in the doorway, but this was a different Trent than she had ever seen before. His face was haggard as he came to take his place with the rest, his eyes sweeping the table only to linger on the empty chair at its head.

"Where's Vandervelt?" he asked hollowly, but before anyone could answer him there was an entirely new diversion.

Midge stared disbelievingly at the slender figure of a girl standing on the threshold, a girl who, incredibly, was pointing a large, very black, very ominous-looking gun in *her* direction.

"It's over," Ellen Brent said, her voice wavering but her hand astonishingly steady. "But if I can't have everything that money could have bought me, you're certainly not going to have Trent!"

It took a second for Midge to realize that the girl actually was speaking to her, and she started to her feet only to have Ellen cry out hastily, "Stay where you are! One move, just one move, and I'll shoot. I'm not fooling. I'm as good with guns as I am with cars."

It didn't make sense. It didn't make sense at all! Midge felt as if she had been frozen into a tableau in which she had no real part. Then she saw Brian appearing in the doorway, coming to stand directly behind Ellen; it was incredible, how silently he could move, considering his size. She wondered almost irrationally if this was something he had learned at Annapolis.

Probably. Probably.

Brian could move swiftly, too. His arm shot around Ellen in an encircling movement that twisted the girl in his direction, and simultaneously her finger, already flexed, pulled the trigger.

Midge heard a shot that seemed to reverberate throughout the old newspaper building, echoing and echoing and echoing....

Then blackness took over, and the dark never had been so welcome.

BRIAN SAID, "Lucille told me way back that we ought to have a couch in the ladies' room, and she was right."

"You shouldn't even be in the ladies' room," his sister reminded him. "Look, Midge is all right."

Gray eyes, amazingly clear gray eyes, looked down at her. "*Are* you all right, Midge?" he asked softly.

"I don't know," she answered feebly. She struggled to a sitting position, her head still reeling. "Yes," she said somewhat weakly. "Yes, of course I'm all right."

"Brian," Becky interrupted, "they're all waiting, there in your office. You have to say something to them."

He nodded. "Of course. Will you stay here with Midge?"

"No," Midge said, "we'll come with you."

She wanted to tell him that she wished she never had to leave him again. She was torn between fury, because certainly there had been deception in his saying that he was going to park after leaving them at the door, and a blinding admiration for the way he had handled Ellen Brent.

Ellen.

It was still unbelievable.

She stood shakily, and now they made a rather strange trio, she and Brian and Becky, as they went back to his office to join the others.

Surveying the conference table, Brian began, "I'm glad you got out the brandy, Wilson. How about pouring three more glasses?"

Strathmore smiled and complied, and Midge let the fiery hot liquor run down her throat, watching Wilson Strathmore and Abe Weissman and Fritz Handel and . . . yes, Trent Clayton.

They had all been touched by horror, and yet the tension seemed to have evaporated. Even Trent appeared calmer—though he also looked unutterably weary.

He started to say, "Brian," but Brian waved this aside.

"Later," he said. "Later. Just now I want to tell all of you how much I appreciate your sticking through this very long probation period with me. Naturally I know you haven't enjoyed it any more than I have, but you stayed, and I'll never forget that. I knew, you knew, we all knew, that there was something very wrong within this newspaper family of ours. But I want to add that I personally could never bring myself to suspect any one of you, and now my faith, my confidence, has been vindicated."

He paused and picked up his glass. "I hope that today will mark a new beginning for the *Valley Voice* and everything else it touches upon, for me and for all of you. I think as a team we have places to go. Here's to us!"

He lifted the glass in a toast, and briefly Midge's eyes were blinded by tears, because she was so proud of him... because she loved him so much.

Finally Andrew Summers left, with Wilson Strathmore following closely after him. Then Abe Weissman and Fritz Handel went out together, and Midge suspected that shortly they'd be up the street having a beer. Jerry left, and the police officers, and the few members of the staff working today were told to go home.

Now, in Brian's office, he, Becky, Midge and Trent made an oddly assorted quartet. Brian said abruptly, "I'm not blaming you, Clayton. It wasn't your fault that she fell in love with you."

"I don't know about that," Trent answered slowly. "I encouraged her, at least before Midge came here. Remember, Midge, Thursday I wanted you to have a drink with me? I told you I wanted to tell you something?"

"Yes," she conceded.

"I wanted to talk about Ellen," he said. "She'd been saying some strange things; I couldn't figure them out. I was afraid her jealousy of you might lead her to try something foolish."

"I think she already had," Midge told him. "At least I think it must have been Ellen who left a hideous note in my motel room when I first came here, warning me to leave."

"I'm sure it was," Brian agreed soberly. "After I saw her talking to you yesterday, Trent, I did some heavy thinking."

"When was that?"

"You were outside my window. Ellen was facing me, and I managed to lip-read a certain amount of what she was saying. It seemed to me that she was urging you to go off with her somewhere today."

"Yes, she was," Trent admitted. "She wanted me to go down to New York with her; she tried to convince me it was a matter of life-and-death importance. But," he finished wryly, "I thought it was her life she was talking about, not mine! Naturally I told her this was a meeting I couldn't possibly miss under any circumstances...."

"Right," Brian nodded. "So on her way to plant the bomb here she managed to stop by your place and fix up your car so it wouldn't start."

"Ellen must be a regular mechanical genius," Trent remarked wryly.

"She is," Brian agreed. "After my accident I

realized that whoever was involved in all of this had to be pretty knowledgeable about cars—a mechanic at least. I knew you used to race cars too, and Handel's a mechanical wizard himself. So I thought any one of you wouldn't have had too much trouble getting to my car and tampering with it.

"I never thought of Ellen. But after I eavesdropped on your conversation yesterday I got out her personnel file. She has several brothers, all of whom have been into motorcycles, stock racing, things like that, and she's gone right along with them. She got a prize in chemistry when she was in high school. She's very good with her hands—witness her ability as an artist. When we realized there was a bomb involved, everything tied together. She had the motivation: she was doing it for you, Trent."

Trent stared at him, horror-struck. "How do you figure that?"

"If she'd blown the place up, only you would have inherited," Brian pointed out coolly, "and I'm sure she felt you'd be eternally grateful to her for making you an instant millionaire!"

"My God!" Trent's face was gray.

"She must have gone through hell when the explosion didn't happen on schedule," Brian went on. "Then she saw you come in here, and she realized that the bomb must have been found and her dream had died. But she still had one more trick to play. She could wound you—both of us—by going for Midge."

"You realized that?"

"Yes," Brian said heavily, "though I didn't know she'd have a gun. If any of us had known that...."

Trent said slowly, "You must have had some very special training in the navy."

"Yes, I did. Look," Brian added, "don't be too harsh on Ellen. She'll have expert psychiatric care; there may still be hope for her." He paused. "I think we could all use a drink. Will you come back to the house with us?"

Trent shook his head. "Thanks, but no," he answered somewhat unsteadily. "I think I need to be alone for a while."

CLARA HAD MADE SANDWICHES, and they munched on them around the fireplace in the library, surprised that they could be even slightly hungry.

Becky said, "I vaguely remember Ellen. She was such a little mouse, though. Now I'd say that in addition to her other talents she's quite an actress. It must have been she who called me." She turned to Midge. "She had your voice down perfectly."

"I can't help but feel sorry for her," Midge sighed.

Brian cut in, "Must you always champion the underdog?"

"I wasn't aware that I did," she responded defensively, and Becky glanced curiously from one to the other of them.

"Lucille wants the three of us to come for brunch tomorrow, after the memorial service for Aunt Maude," she told them.

"Thanks," Brian said, "but I think I'll pass. You two can go."

"Thanks very much," Midge said stiffly, "but I had something else in mind. I think you should go, though, Becky. I know Lucille would like a chance to get to know you better.''

Becky frowned. "What is it with you two?" she demanded. "If it weren't for the way we all feel about Aunt Maude we should be out celebrating. It's all over! Don't you realize that, Brian?''

"I realize it only too well," he answered tersely, rising from his chair. Then he said, "Excuse me, will you, please," and didn't wait for an answer before stalking out of the room.

Becky, puzzled, observed, "I've never seen him like this. Maybe it's the letdown after months of tension.''

"Maybe," Midge conceded.

"Maybe it's you," Becky continued.

"Becky, get that off your mind!" Midge said sharply.

Becky protested, "You don't have to snap at me. Look, darling, why don't you come back to San Francisco with me? I've booked a flight for late tomorrow afternoon; maybe we can wangle another ticket on it.''

Midge shook her head. "No," she said, "I took a three-month contract with the *Valley Voice*, and I intend to honor it. The time won't be up until the end of December, so I'll stay till then, unless Brian actually asks me to leave. Meantime I'll move back to Prescotts'—that's the motel where I was staying when I first came here. As a matter of fact, I must call Mrs. Prescott soon, though I'm sure she'll have a place for me.''

"I can chaperon you until I leave," Becky offered somewhat facetiously. Then as she saw the expression on Midge's face she added, "Well, you do seem

terrified to be alone with him, and I'd say he's reacting the same way about you.''

"I don't know how he's reacting about anything,"
Midge said crossly, and this surely was true enough.
Brian Vandervelt, the crisis over, seemed more of an
enigma to her than ever before.

GRACE DE WITT called in the middle of the afternoon. Brian was working in the library, and it was
Midge who happened to answer the phone as she and
Becky sat reminiscing, not too successfully, about
old times in the small family parlor. There was
nothing for it but to go to the library and give Brian
the message, and he looked up with a pleasant
enough but cool thank-you before lifting the receiver. Midge backed away hastily, not wanting to
hear the warmth in his tone as he spoke to his ex-
fiancée.

A bit later he came to the parlor to tell them he'd
be out for dinner. "Grace," he said in answer to
Becky's unspoken question.

"Grace De Witt?" Becky echoed disbelievingly.
"Are you seeing her again?"

"She wanted to ask my advice about something,"
he explained, adding, "You both look comfortable,"
as he surveyed Midge and his sister.

"We are," Becky told him. "Won't you join us?"

"Thanks, no," he said. "I've quite a bit of
paperwork to get through before I go out. I have
to meet with Summers on Monday; there will be a
lot to attend to before everything is straightened
out."

"I can imagine," Becky said dryly. "I'm glad I
won't be around to suffer through it. Incidentally,

can you drive me to the airport tomorrow afternoon?''

"Sure," he responded, with a smile that seemed more than slightly forced. "Maybe I can prevail upon Tom to try me with the Rolls," he said. "Then I won't have to borrow the Volvo, Midge."

"As I've already said—" she began, but he held up his hand.

"Let's not argue. Anyway, I won't have to ask you for it tonight. Grace is going to pick me up here."

It was the crowning barb. The day drew on, to be followed by an equally trying evening, since Midge found it impossible to get out of her mind the fact that someplace, somewhere, Brian was with the tall beautiful blond who surely still seemed to be very much attracted to him.

People called to offer condolences about Maude, and Becky knew most of them. Much of the time she chattered on the phone while Midge stared aimlessly into the fire they'd made in the library after dinner, trying to read one of the Hudson River valley history books she'd taken down from the shelves.

She slept restlessly, waking to find that November was still pure gray. The memorial service was short but poignant. Somehow along with everything else he'd had to do Brian had managed to give the minister a selection of readings dealing with subjects Maude had loved. Members of the ikebana class had made an arrangement that was singularly beautiful in its simplicity; it was the only floral decoration in the small chapel where the service was held.

At the last minute Midge decided to go to the Muellers' for brunch with Becky after all, as there seemed no reason to return to the house. She wasn't even sure that Brian would be there.

They lingered at the Muellers', so the interval before Becky's departure became slightly frantic. Finally she pronounced herself ready to leave, and when Midge made no move to get a coat for herself she asked in surprise, "Aren't you coming to the airport?"

"No, darling," Midge told her. "I think you and Brian should have some time together. You must have private things to talk about."

"We've got to get going, or I'd argue that," Becky said, frowning. "Look, you don't have to stay in the East; you know that."

"I know. I may cut the time short at that and head to San Francisco for Christmas."

"That's the spirit!" Becky hugged her friend exuberantly. Then as she was about to climb into the car she added, her blue eyes sparkling, "Be sure to bring my brother with you!" And before Midge could answer she closed the car door, smiling widely as she waved through the window.

Clara and Tom were standing in the doorway. Her face crumpling, Clara sighed, "I hate to see her go."

"She'll be back for visits from now on," Midge promised. "I'm sure of it."

And, she thought as she slowly climbed the front stairs a few minutes later, Becky certainly would be coming back for visits, and she and Tim and the children would make the old house resound with laughter. By then maybe Grace would have got her divorce, and she and Brian. . . .

It seemed darker and drearier than ever in the upstairs parlor, and again Midge wished there had been more time for her to bring light into both Maude Vandervelt's life and her house.

As she thought about Maude she was glad the old lady had been so blissfully unaware of the many things going on around her; in the end everything had come out right for Brian, and that was what would have mattered most to her. For Brian had been Maude's joy, reminiscent always of his father, her own lover.

Weary, drained by both the weekend and her own emotions, Midge sat down on the late Horace Vandervelt's brown velvet couch and began to cry softly, both for Maude and for herself.

CHAPTER TWENTY-ONE

MIDGE HEARD THE SOUND OF TIRES on the gravel driveway and the slam of a car door. Moving to the window, she saw Brian getting out of the Volvo, but he did not come toward the house. Rather, he started around the side of it, and it seemed to her that there was a sag to his shoulders as he walked, staring down at the withered grass. Then he passed from her view, as if he had been swallowed by the deepening haze of twilight.

She had called Mrs. Prescott; her room at the motel was ready for her. She had packed her suitcases, and the only thing that remained was to ask Tom to help her take them downstairs, and then to say goodbye to him and to Clara.

This, she knew, would be a wrench. She had become very fond of the old couple, and it was a feeling she knew they returned. Yet, although she intended to stay in Coxsackie until the end of the year, she had no intention of coming back to this house again after today. To do so would be much, much too painful.

She would have to return the Volvo, she reminded herself, and could imagine how angry Brian would be when she did. Nevertheless, she had no intention of keeping it.

Tomorrow at lunchtime she would see about renting a car. In the interim, of course, she would have to face going into the office in the morning, and that would not be easy. She anticipated no trouble from Trent: Ellen's terrible act had subdued him, and she felt it would be a long time before he'd get over the shock of it. Far more daunting was the knowledge that while she stayed on at the paper she could hardly hope to avoid seeing Brian now and again. She would have to handle it coolly, that was all. There was such a thing as pride.

Pride. He had hurt her pride this weekend, there was no doubt about it, and she could not really understand why. Also, he had avoided being alone with her for even a minute.

Now she couldn't help remembering their conversation about what money could and could not buy, and it seemed to her that with his inheritance finally established, money had come to loom like an almost physical barrier between them. Brian was now a very rich young man, and rich people, she knew, were often suspicious of other people's motives, sometimes not without cause. Had Brian become suspicious of her motives?

The thought was unbearable.

The phone rang, a shattering intruder. She stared at it, surprised, then lifted the receiver almost timidly. "Midge—is it you?" Becky's voice came across the wire. "Listen, they're about to call my plane; I haven't much time, but for God's sake speak to him, will you, darling?"

"Becky, what are you talking about?" Midge demanded.

"Brian," Becky told her. "He doesn't think he's good enough for you. Try to work some sense into his thick Dutch head, will you? Darling, I've got to run!"

The receiver at the other end of the line clicked, and Midge stared down at the mouthpiece in her hand, thunderstruck.

He doesn't think he's good enough for you.

Brian?

Unbelievable, she told herself. *He's the most arrogant, independent person I've ever met!*

Then she remembered something else, something Dr. Mueller had said.

Brian thinks he's a burden to people.

A burden.

The dusk was deepening, she saw as she glanced out the window. But there was still light enough to see; even light enough to lip-read! She slipped on a warm quilted coat and left the house by the front door. Although the kitchen way would have been a bit closer, she didn't want to run into Clara just now.

She walked across the lawn toward the gazebo, and since the ground sloped, she was nearing it before she saw him sitting on the steps facing the river. She moved close to him, then said softly but distinctly, "Brian!"

For a moment she thought he hadn't heard her. Then he looked up, his gray eyes mirroring the cloudy skies.

She swallowed hard. "I'm leaving," she told him. "I just wanted to say goodbye to you."

She saw him clench his hands, yet his face remained impassive. "So soon?" he asked.

"Yes."

He moved over and patted the space beside him. "Sit down," he invited. "You're not in that much of a hurry, are you?"

She didn't answer this, but she did sit down beside

him, feeling as if she were about to tread on fantastically thin ice.

Brian turned sideways, leaning his head back against a post so that he could look directly at her face. He said, gravely formal, "Do you mind my asking where you're going? Or shall I make a guess? I'd say that you're heading back to New York."

"No," she answered.

"California?"

"No."

"Where then, Midge?"

"Prescotts'," she said, and he couldn't suppress a flash of astonishment.

"Do you mean to tell me you intend to stay in Coxsackie?" he demanded.

"I have a three-month contract with your paper," she reminded him.

"A verbal promise," he pointed out. "Do you mean to say you are seriously considering working at the *Valley Voice* until the three months are up?"

"Do you have any objection to my doing so?"

"Objection?" he echoed. "No." He stared at her. "But I can't imagine why you'd want to keep on at the paper," he said frankly.

"I believe in keeping my word," she told him levelly. "What about you, incidentally?"

"What about me?"

"Well, I more or less wondered what you plan to do. This is such a big house for one person."

His lips quirked. "Are you suggesting I ask someone to share it with me?"

"No," she said quickly. "I'm not about to suggest anything."

He raised those telltale eyebrows, but he said only,

"I haven't made a final decision yet about what I'm going to do, Midge; obviously there hasn't been time. I have given some thought to turning this place over as a combined educational and recreational center for deaf children. It could be a wonderful place for kids if it were painted white, as you suggested, with everything else redone accordingly."

Touched, she exclaimed, "That's a marvelous idea! But. . . where would you go if you did that?"

"I don't know," he replied. "I suppose I could keep on living in the tower. Also, there's other Vandervelt property with a river view, which is the one thing I've always loved about this place. I could build a house. I suppose the principal thing is that I've decided to stay here in Coxsackie and try to do something constructive with the *Valley Voice* and some of Uncle Horace's other enterprises."

"Won't Grace have something to say about that?" Midge ventured to ask. "About where you're going to live, I mean?"

"Should she have?"

"Shouldn't she?" Midge persisted.

"Grace has decided to try for a reconciliation with her husband, as I've been urging her to do," Brian said. "That's why I had dinner with her last night. They got off to a bad start, largely because he thought she was still in love with me. Something of the Jerry-Lucille situation in reverse. At least *that* has been solved, especially now that Lucille and Becky have become friends. It's nice occasionally to see a happy ending."

There was a rough edge to his voice, and she didn't dare look at him. Then he asked, "What are *you* going to do—after December?"

"I haven't thought that far ahead," she admitted.

"You're not considering a permanent advertising career with the *Valley Voice* are you?" he asked tantalizingly.

"No," she said abruptly. "I think you know I couldn't stand being around you every day for very long...."

The sudden silence was stark, and as she looked up to see that he couldn't hide the pain in his eyes, she realized he had entirely misunderstood her.

"Brian," she began, but he waved her away.

"That's okay," he assured her, with an effort at steadiness. "I'm glad you've finally come out and said it. It's a relief, actually."

Midge shook her head despairingly. "You do jump to conclusions, don't you," she told him. "It wouldn't occur to you, would it, that the reason I couldn't bear seeing you every day is that I...I love you so much it would be more than I could handle."

Again there was silence, and she found herself holding her breath. Then he said, "Would you repeat that?"

"No." Her voice was choking. "I think you heard me the first time."

"I did hear you the first time," he told her. "I'd like to hear it again, that's all." He actually smiled. "It's going to take a while for it to sink in."

"Never mind," she retorted, clenching her fists as her emotions whirled toward chaos. "I know only too well the way you feel about me! You think I'm a...a fortune hunter!"

"*What?*" he thundered, and she knew that the word this time had nothing to do with his hearing.

"You told me once you supposed you could buy a wife," she reminded him.

"For God's sake, Midge!" he exploded, horrified.

"Oh, don't brush it aside," she said, worked up to a pitch now from which there was no turning back. "You *are* extremely rich, you know, wealthy, young and handsome in the bargain. You surely must be aware of the fact that you're quite a catch, Brian Vandervelt. In fact, the only thing anyone could say against you is that you have a ridiculous hang-up about your hearing."

He glared at her, outraged. "Stop it, Midge!"

"No," she persisted, "I'm going to say it all. You've got this crazy idea of being a millstone around people's necks, and it's made you downright paranoid. You think the only thing any girl could be after you for is your money!"

He said between clenched teeth, "I didn't know you could be so absolutely—absurd! One more such sentence out of you and, so help me, I'll put you over my knee and whack some sense into you!"

"After I've finished," she said, "I don't care whether you put me over your knee and whack me or not. You see, in addition to the money problem, there's the matter of pity. You've always expressed such a horror about anyone feeling pity for you that I looked the word up in the dictionary, and do you know what I found? It says pity is sorrow for another's suffering or misfortune. Is there anything so wrong about that? Is there anything *wrong* about my being sorry you have a problem with your hearing?"

Her voice trailed off, and now the stillness that came between them seemed to have a disturbing life of its own. Night was only a breath away, and in the last deep purple of twilight's veil Midge strained to see the river, trying to fix the view from here in her mind for all time.

She said finally, "I suppose I'd really better go."

"Do you think so?" he asked coolly.

She knew her cheeks were stinging, and she tried to control her voice. "Yes, I think so." Feeling as if her arms and legs had suddenly turned into brittle untrustworthy sticks, she started to her feet, only to find that in an amazingly swift instant he was standing beside her, and a strong familiar arm shot out to restrain her.

"I think I know another way of injecting some sense into you," he warned, his voice dangerously calm. Then all at once she was within the circle of his embrace and he was kissing her with an urgency that left no doubt at all about his motives. Pressing her close to him, he said, "You beloved little idiot, did you really think I was such a fool I'd ever let you go—at least if it were only myself I was thinking of?"

His sigh was ragged. "Yesterday when I saw Ellen pointing that gun at you I knew how totally my life would be over if anything were to happen to you. But at the same time I wondered if I could ever find the courage to say—all the things I've wanted so desperately to say to you. Can you understand that?"

She paused to get control of her breath, and to suggest unsteadily, "You could at least have told me you wanted me."

"Wanted you! My God," he said, "I've *wanted* you from the first minute you walked into my office, even before I knew who you really were! You looked at me with those enormous brown eyes and I yearned to drown in them, just as I've wanted to drown in your sweetness ever since.

"I was so damned jealous of Trent," he admitted, "to say nothing of the other men in your past—and don't look at me like that, darling! I know that in both cases my jealousy was unfounded. I know that you were as finished with your past as I was with mine. My caution, if you want to call it that, was because of *me*, not you.

"Once, though, I did forget about caution, about everything, as you very well know. But I also realized to the fullest what kind of person you are, and what kind of commitment you made to me that day; and afterward I came close to hating myself. It seemed to me that I had no right at all...."

He paused, his voice broken. "You see," he confessed, "you're right about quite a few of the things you just said, though not about the money. Dear God, not about the money! How could you ever think I might consider you a fortune hunter? The one thing I *have* been sure about is that your feelings toward me would be unchanged whether or not I had a cent!"

She nestled close against him. "That's very true," she murmured, and felt his hands clench.

He said wryly, "That's a case in point. I think I know what you said, but to be sure I'd have to ask, 'What?' I suppose I can't help thinking the day may come when you'll get very tired of hearing me say, 'What?' And then...."

She shook her head, tilting her face back so that he could see her features in the deepening dusk. "Never," she told him firmly. "I'd rather listen to you say 'What?' twenty-four hours a day than be without you for a single instant!"

He commented on this with yet another kiss, this one so intense that a fire akin to molten lava coursed through Midge, and she kissed him back with a fervor that left no doubt about her own desire.

He laughed. "Did you say you were going to Prescotts' tonight?"

"Yes."

"We'd better phone and cancel," he suggested. "For tonight I think we can let Tom and Clara do the chaperoning... provided they guarantee to stay in their own quarters, far away from the house."

"Aren't you afraid that you may draw down Rip Van Winkle's thunder?" she asked him.

"Rip," he assured her blandly, "was almost certainly an ancestor of mine, so how could he possibly do anything but approve of my actions?"

And even had his lips not been closing upon hers again, Midge knew, blissfully that she could find no answer to refute this.

No answer at all.